waking hour and scream through every single one of his drunken nights. Written with a wonderful touch for the politics of the post-Good Friday agreement, it is as fresh and subtle as you could wish for. Awesomely powerful, fabulously written, and with a hero who is also a villain that you cannot help sympathizing with, this novel is simply unmissable."—*Daily Mail* (UK)

"[*The Ghosts of Belfast*] is a revenge tragedy in the Elizabethan mode, scripted by Quentin Tarantino and produced by the makers of *The Bourne Identity*. . . . But it possesses a profound and wider significance. . . . [It] is an important part of [Northern Ireland's] purging."—*Irish Times* (UK)

"Stuart Neville's blistering debut thriller is a walk on the wild side of post-conflict Northern Ireland that brilliantly exposes the suffering still lurking beneath the surface of reconciliation and the hypocrisies that sustain the peace." —*Metro* (UK)

"Neville's debut is as unrelenting as Fegan's ghosts, pulling no punches as it describes the brutality of Ireland's 'troubles' and the crime that has followed, as violent men find new outlets for their skills. Sharp prose places readers in this pitiless place and holds them there. Harsh and unrelenting crime fiction, masterfully done."—*Kirkus Reviews*, Starred Review

"[A] stunning debut. . . . This is not only an action-packed, visceral thriller but also an insightful insider's glimpse into the complex political machinations and networks that maintain the uneasy truce in Northern Ireland."
—*Publishers Weekly*, Starred Review

"In this well-crafted and intriguing series debut, Neville evokes the terrors of living in Belfast during "the Troubles" and manages to makes Fegan, a murderer many times over, a sympathetic character . . . The buzz around this novel is well deserved and readers will be anticipating the next book in the series."
—*Library Journal*, Starred Review

"Neville's debut novel is tragic, violent, exciting, plausible, and compelling. . . . *The Ghosts of Belfast* is dark, powerful, insightful, and hard to put down."—*Booklist*

"Stuart Neville will go far as a writer. . . . It's a wonderful novel, brave and fierce and true to its place and time. I sincerely hope it sells a million copies."
—Declan Burke, *Crimespree*

"Both a fine novel and a gripping thriller: truly this is a magnificent debut."
—Ruth Dudley Edwards, author of *Ten Lords-A-Leaping*

"Neville's debut thriller grabs hold and doesn't let go . . . [a] frighteningly assured first novel." —George Easter, *Deadly Pleasures*

THE GHOSTS OF BELFAST

THE GHOSTS OF BELFAST

Stuart Neville

Published in Great Britain in 2009 by
Harvill Secker Random House as *The Twelve*.

Published in the United States in 2009 by
Soho Press, Inc.
853 Broadway
New York, NY 10003

Library of Congress Cataloging-in-Publication Data

Neville, Stuart, 1972–
The ghosts of Belfast / Stuart Neville.
p. cm.
ISBN 978-1-56947-600-0
1. Assassins—Fiction. 2. Northern Ireland—Fiction. I. Title.
PR6114.E943G47 2009
823'.92—dc22
2009011312

Paperback ISBN 978-1-56947-857-8

10 9 8 7 6 5 4 3 2 1

For Ellen Emerald Neville

"The place that lacks its ghosts is a barren place."
—John Hewitt

THE GHOSTS OF BELFAST

TWELVE

I

Maybe if he had one more drink they'd leave him alone. Gerry Fegan told himself that lie before every swallow. He chased the whiskey's burn with a cool black mouthful of Guinness and placed the glass back on the table. *Look up and they'll be gone*, he thought.

No. They were still there, still staring. Twelve of them if he counted the baby in its mother's arms.

He was good and drunk now. When his stomach couldn't hold any more he would let Tom the barman show him to the door, and the twelve would follow Fegan through the streets of Belfast, into his house, up his stairs, and into his bedroom. If he was lucky, and drunk enough, he might pass out before their screaming got too loud to bear. That was the only time they made a sound, when he was alone and on the edge of sleep. When the baby started crying, that was the worst of it.

Fegan raised the empty glass to get Tom's attention.

"Haven't you had enough, Gerry?" Tom asked. "Is it not home time yet? Everyone's gone."

"One more," Fegan said, trying not to slur. He knew Tom would not refuse. Fegan was still a respected man in West Belfast, despite the drink.

Sure enough, Tom sighed and raised a glass to the optic. He brought the whiskey over and counted change from the stained table-top. The gummy film of old beer and grime sucked at his shoes as he walked away.

Fegan held the glass up and made a toast to his twelve companions. One of the five soldiers among them smiled and nodded in return. The rest just stared.

"Fuck you," Fegan said. "Fuck the lot of you."

None of the twelve reacted, but Tom looked back over his shoulder. He shook his head and continued walking to the bar.

Fegan looked at each of his companions in turn. Of the five soldiers three were Brits and two were Ulster Defence Regiment. Another of the followers was a cop, his Royal Ulster Constabulary uniform neat and stiff, and two more were Loyalists, both Ulster Freedom Fighters. The remaining four were civilians who had been in the wrong place at the wrong time. He remembered doing all of them, but it was the civilians whose memories screamed the loudest.

There was the butcher with his round face and bloody apron. Fegan had dropped the package in his shop and held the door for the woman and her baby as she wheeled the pram in. They'd smiled at each other. He'd felt the heat of the blast as he jumped into the already moving car, the blast that should have come five minutes after they'd cleared the place.

The other was the boy. Fegan still remembered the look in his eyes when he saw the pistol. Now the boy sat across the table, those same eyes boring into him.

Fegan couldn't hold his gaze, so he turned his eyes downward. Tears pooled on the tabletop. He brought his fingers to the hollows of his face and realised he'd been weeping.

"Jesus," he said.

He wiped the table with his sleeve and sniffed back the tears. The pub's stale air clung to the back of his throat, as thick as the dun-colored paint on the walls. He scolded himself. He neither needed nor deserved pity, least of all his own. Weaker men than him could live with what they'd done. He could do the same.

A hand on his shoulder startled him.

"Time you were going, Gerry," Michael McKenna said.

Tom slipped into the storeroom behind the bar. McKenna paid him to be discreet, to see and hear nothing.

Fegan knew the politician would come looking for him. He was smartly dressed in a jacket and trousers, and his fine-framed designer glasses gave him the appearance of an educated man. A far cry from the teenager Fegan had run the streets with thirty years ago. Wealth looked good on him.

"I'm just finishing," Fegan said.

"Well, drink up and I'll run you home." McKenna smiled down at him, his teeth white and even. He'd had them fixed so he could look presentable for the cameras. The party leadership had insisted on it before they gave him the nomination for his seat in the Assembly. At one time, not so long past, it had been against party policy to take a seat at Stormont. But times change, even if people don't.

"I'll walk," Fegan said. "It's only a couple of minutes."

"It's no trouble," McKenna said. "Besides, I wanted a word."

Fegan nodded and took another mouthful of stout. He held it on his tongue when he noticed the boy had risen from his place on the other side of the table. It took a moment to find him, shirtless and skinny as the day he died, creeping up behind McKenna.

The boy pointed at the politician's head. He mimed firing, his hand thrown upwards by the recoil. His mouth made a plosive movement, but no sound came.

Fegan swallowed the Guinness and stared at the boy. Something stirred in his mind, one memory trying to find another. The chill at his center pulsed with his heartbeat.

"Do you remember that kid?" he asked.

"Don't, Gerry." McKenna's voice carried a warning.

"I met his mother today. I was in the graveyard and she came up to me."

"I know you did," McKenna said, taking the glass from Fegan's fingers.

"She said she knew who I was. What I'd done. She said—"

"Gerry, I don't want to know what she said. I'm more curious about what you said to her. That's what we need to talk about. But not here." McKenna squeezed Fegan's shoulder. "Come on, now."

"He hadn't done anything. Not really. He didn't tell the cops anything they didn't know already. He didn't deserve that. Jesus, he was seventeen. We didn't have to—"

One hard hand gripped Fegan's face, the other his thinning hair, and the animal inside McKenna showed itself. "Shut your fucking mouth," he hissed. "Remember who you're talking to."

Fegan remembered only too well. As he looked into those fierce blue eyes he remembered every detail. This was the face he knew, not the one on television, but the face that burned with white-hot pleasure as McKenna set about the boy with a claw hammer, the face that was dotted with red when he handed Fegan the .22 pistol to finish it.

Fegan gripped McKenna's wrists and prised his hands away. He stamped on his own anger, quashed it.

The smile returned to McKenna's lips as he pulled his hands away from Fegan's, but went no further. "Come on," he said. "My car's outside. I'll run you home."

The twelve followed them out to the street, the boy sticking close to McKenna. McKenna had climbed high in the party hierarchy, but not so high he needed an escort to guard him. Even so, Fegan knew the Mercedes gleaming in the orange street lights was armored, both bullet- and bomb-proof. McKenna probably felt safe as he lowered himself into the driver's seat.

"Big day today," McKenna said as he pulled the car away from the curb, leaving the followers staring after them. "Sorting the offices up at Stormont, my own desk and everything. Who'd have thought it, eh? The likes of us up on the hill. I wangled a secretary's job for the wife. The Brits are throwing so much money at this I almost feel bad taking it off them. Almost."

McKenna flashed Fegan a smile. He didn't return it.

Fegan tried to avoid seeing or reading the news as much as he could, but the last two months had been a hurricane of change. Just five months ago, as one year turned to the next, they'd said it was hopeless; the political process was beyond repair. Then mountains moved, deals were struck, another election came and went, while the shadows gathered closer to Fegan. And more often than before, those shadows turned to faces and bodies and arms and legs. Now they were a constant, and he couldn't remember when he last slept without first drowning them in whiskey.

They'd been with him since his last weeks in the Maze prison, a little over seven years ago. He'd just been given his release date, printed on a sheet of paper in a sealed envelope, and his mouth was dry when he opened it. The politicians on the outside had bartered for his freedom, along with hundreds more men and women. They called people like him political prisoners. Not murderers or thieves, not extortionists or blackmailers. Not criminals of any kind, just victims of circumstance. The followers were there when Fegan looked up from the letter, watching.

He told one of the prison psychologists about it. Dr. Brady said it was guilt. A manifestation, he called it. Fegan wondered why people seldom called things by their real names.

McKenna pulled the Mercedes into the curb outside Fegan's small terraced house on Calcutta Street. It stood shoulder to shoulder with two dozen identical red-brick boxes, drab and neat. The followers waited on the pavement.

"Can I come in for a second?" McKenna's smile sparkled in the car's interior lighting, and kind lines arced out from around his eyes. "Better to talk inside, eh?"

Fegan shrugged and climbed out.

The twelve parted to let him approach his door. He unlocked it and went inside, McKenna following, the twelve slipping in between. Fegan headed straight for the sideboard where a bottle of Jameson's and a jug of water awaited him. He showed McKenna the bottle.

"No, thanks," McKenna said. "Maybe you shouldn't, either."

Fegan ignored him, pouring two fingers of whiskey into a glass and the same of water. He took a deep swallow and extended his hand towards a chair.

"No, I'm all right," McKenna said. His hair was well barbered, his skin tanned and smooth, a scar beneath his left eye the only remainder of his old self.

The twelve milled around the sparsely furnished room, merging with and diverging from the shadows, studying each man intently. The boy lingered by McKenna's side as the politician went to the unstrung guitar propped in the corner. He picked it up and turned it in the light.

"Since when did you play guitar?" McKenna asked.

"I don't," Fegan said. "Put it down."

McKenna read the label inside the sound hole. "Martin. Looks old. What's it doing here?"

"It belonged to a friend of mine. I'm restoring it," Fegan said. "Put it down."

"What friend?"

"Just someone I knew inside. Please. Put it down."

McKenna set it back in the corner. "It's good to have friends, Gerry. You should value them. Listen to them."

"What'd you want to talk about?" Fegan lowered himself into a chair.

McKenna nodded at the drink in Fegan's hand. "About that, for one thing. It's got to stop, Gerry."

Fegan held the politician's eyes as he drained the glass.

"People round here look up to you. You're a Republican hero. The young fellas need a role model, someone they can respect."

"Respect? What are you talking about?" Fegan put the glass on the coffee table. The chill of condensation clung to his palm and he let his hands slide together, working the moisture over his knuckles and between his fingers. "There's no respecting what I've done."

McKenna's face flushed with anger. "You did your time. You were a political prisoner for twelve years. A dozen years of your life given up for the cause. Any Republican should respect that." His expression softened. "But you're pissing it away, Gerry. People are starting to notice. Every night you're at the bar, drunk off your face, talking to yourself."

"I'm not talking to myself." Fegan went to point at the followers, but thought better of it.

"Then who *are* you talking to?" McKenna's voice wavered with an exasperated laugh.

"The people I killed. The people *we* killed."

"Watch your mouth, Gerry. I never killed anybody."

Fegan met McKenna's blue eyes. "No, the likes of you and McGinty were always too smart to do it yourselves. You used mugs like me instead."

McKenna folded his arms across his barrel chest. "Nobody's hands are clean."

"What else?" Fegan asked. "You said 'for one thing'. What else do you want?"

McKenna circled the room, the boy following, and Fegan had to twist in his chair to keep him in sight. "I need to know what you told that woman," McKenna said.

"Nothing," Fegan said. "I'm not much of a talker. You know that."

"No, you're not. But a reliable source tells me the cops are going to start digging up the bogs near Dungannon in the next few days. Round about where we buried that boy. His mother told them where to look." McKenna moved to the center of the room and loomed over Fegan. "Now, how did she know that, Gerry?"

"Does it matter?" Fegan asked. "Jesus, there'll be nothing left of him. It's been more than twenty years."

"It matters," McKenna said. "If you open your mouth, you're a tout. And you know what happens to touts."

Fegan tightened his fingers on the chair's armrests.

McKenna leaned down, his hands on his thighs. "Why, Gerry? Why'd you tell her? What good did you think it'd do?"

Fegan searched for a lie, anything, but found nothing. "I thought maybe he'd leave me alone," he said.

"What?" McKenna straightened.

"I thought he'd go," Fegan said. He looked at the boy aiming his fingers at McKenna's head. "I thought he'd leave me alone. Give me some peace."

McKenna took a step back. "Who? The boy?"

"But that wasn't what he wanted."

"Christ, Gerry." McKenna shook his head. "What's happened to you? Maybe you should see a doctor, you know, get straight. Go away for a while."

Fegan looked down at his hands. "Maybe."

"Listen." McKenna put a hand on Fegan's shoulder. "My source talks only to me, nobody else. You've been a good friend to me over the years, and that's the only reason I haven't gone to McGinty with this. If he knew you opened your mouth to that auld doll, it's your body the cops would be looking for."

Fegan wanted to jerk his shoulder away from McKenna's hand. He sat still.

"Of course, I might need you to return the favor. There's work I could put your way. I've a few deals going on, stuff McGinty isn't in on. If you can stay off the drink, get yourself right, you could be a big help to me. And McGinty doesn't need to know what you said to that boy's mother."

Fegan watched the boy's face contort as the other shadows gathered around him.

"Do you understand what I'm saying to you, Gerry?"

"Yes," Fegan said.

"Good man." McKenna smiled.

Fegan stood. "I need a piss."

McKenna stepped back and said, "Don't be long."

Fegan made his way up the stairs and into the bathroom. He closed and bolted the door but, as always, the followers found their way in. Except the boy. Fegan paid it little mind, instead concentrating on keeping upright while he emptied his bladder. He had long since gotten used to the twelve witnessing his most undignified moments.

He flushed, rinsed his hands under the tap, and opened the door. The boy was there, on the landing, waiting for him. He stared into the darkness of Fegan's bedroom.

Fegan stood for a moment, confused, as his temples buzzed and the chill pulsed at his center.

The boy pointed into the room.

"What?" Fegan asked.

The boy bared his teeth, and his skinny arm jerked towards the door.

"All right," Fegan said. He walked to his bedroom, glancing back over his shoulder.

The boy followed him into the darkness and kneeled at the foot of the bed. He pointed underneath.

Fegan got to his hands and knees and peered under the bedstead.

Thin light leaking in from the landing showed the old shoebox hidden there.

He raised his head, questioning. The boy nodded.

Fegan could just reach it if he stretched. He pulled it towards himself. Something heavy shifted inside as it moved, and Fegan's heart quickened. He removed the lid and was met by the greasy smell of money. Rolls of banknotes were bundled in here, twenties, fifties, hundreds. Fegan didn't know how much. He'd never counted it.

But there was something else, something cold and black lying half-concealed in the paper. Something Fegan didn't want in his hand. In the semi-darkness his eyes found the boy's.

"No," Fegan said.

The boy stabbed at the object with his finger.

"No." The word felt watery on Fegan's tongue.

The boy's mouth gaped, his hands grabbing clumps of hair. Before the scream could come, Fegan reached in and lifted the Walther P99 from its nest.

A grin blossomed on the boy's face, his teeth glinting. He mimed the act of pulling back the slide assembly to chamber the first round.

Fegan looked from the boy to the pistol and back again. The boy nodded. Fegan drew back the slide, released it, hearing the snick-snick of oiled parts moving together. The gun was solid in his grasp, like the shake of an old friend's hand.

The boy smiled, stood, and walked towards the landing.

Fegan stared down at the Walther. He had bought it a few weeks after leaving the Maze, just for protection, and it only came out of the box for cleaning. His fingertip found the trigger curled inside the guard.

The boy waited in the doorway.

Fegan got to his feet and followed him to the stairs. The boy descended, the lean grace of his body seemingly untouched by the light below.

Fegan began the slow climb downward. An adrenal surge stirred dark memories, voices long silenced, faces like bloodstains. The others came behind, sharing glances with one another. As he reached the bottom, he saw McKenna's back. The politician studied the old photograph of Fegan's mother, the one that showed her young and pretty in a doorway.

The boy crossed the room and again played out the execution of the man who had taken him apart with a claw hammer more than twenty years ago.

Fegan's heart thundered, his lungs heaved. Surely McKenna would hear.

The boy looked to Fegan and smiled.

Fegan asked, "If I do it, will you leave me alone?"

The boy nodded.

"What?" McKenna put the framed picture down. He turned to the voice and froze when he saw the gun aimed at his forehead.

"I can't do it here."

The boy's smile faltered.

"Not in my house. Somewhere else."

The smile returned.

"Jesus, Gerry." McKenna gave a short, nervous laugh as he held his hands up. "What're you at?"

"I'm sorry, Michael. I have to."

McKenna's smile fell away. "I don't get it, Gerry. We're friends."

"We're going to get into your car." The clarity crackled in Fegan's head. For the first time in months his hand did not shake.

McKenna's mouth twisted. "Like fuck we are."

"We're going to get into your car," Fegan repeated. "You in the front, me in the back."

"Gerry, your head's away. Put the gun down before you do something you'll regret."

Fegan stepped closer. "The car."

McKenna reached out. "Now, come on, Gerry. Let's just calm down a second, here, all right? Why don't you give that to me, and I'll put it away. Then we'll have a drink."

"I won't say it again."

"No messing, Gerry, let me have it."

McKenna went to grab the gun, but Fegan pulled his hand away.

He brought it back to aim at the center of McKenna's forehead.

"You always were a mad cunt." McKenna kept his eyes on him as he went to the door. He opened it and stepped out onto the street. He looked left and right, right and left, searching for a witness. When his shoulders slumped, Fegan knew there was no one. This was not the kind of street where curtains twitched.

The Merc's locking system sensed the key was in range, whirring and clunking as McKenna approached.

"Open the back door," Fegan said.

McKenna did as he was told.

"Now get in the front and leave the door open till I'm inside." Fegan kept the Walther trained on McKenna's head until he was seated at the steering wheel.

Fegan slid into the back, careful not to touch the leather upholstery with his bare hands. He used a handkerchief to pull the door closed. Tom had seen him leave with the politician, so his prints around the front passenger seat didn't matter. McKenna sat quite still with his hands on the wheel.

"Now close the door and go."

The Merc's big engine rumbled into life, and McKenna pulled away. Fegan took one glance from the back window and saw the twelve watching from the pavement. The boy stepped out onto the road and waved.

Fegan lay down flat in the cloaking shadows. He pressed the gun's muzzle against the back of the driver's seat, exactly where McKenna's heart would be, if he'd ever had one.

Fegan knew the streets around the docks would be deserted. The Merc's engine ticked as it cooled, punctuating the occasional rumble of traffic from the elevated motorway behind, where the M3 became the M2. In front of them, the River Lagan flowed into Belfast Lough. The lights of the Odyssey complex shimmered across the water. The nightclubs inside it would be thronging with the young and affluent; young enough to have no memory of men like Fegan, affluent enough not to care.

Beyond the Odyssey stood Samson and Goliath, the massive gantry cranes towering over the old shipyard. On the other side of Queen's Island, a small airplane circled the City Airport, now renamed after the great George Best, the footballer who destroyed himself with alcohol. The plane's engine whined and buzzed. McKenna's shoulders rose and fell with each breath.

Fegan raised himself up to sit behind the politician, the gun still at the center of the seat-back. The sweat-damped fabric of his shirt slid across his shoulder blades. He looked around the patch of waste ground they were parked on. No CCTV, no people. Only the rats to witness it.

And the followers.

They moved between the pools of darkness, watching, waiting. All except the boy. He leaned against the driver's door, cupping his hands around his eyes, staring at McKenna though the glass.

"Look at that," McKenna said, indicating the stretch of land around the cranes. "They're calling it the Titanic Quarter now. Can you believe that?"

Fegan didn't answer.

"There's a fortune being made out of that land. It's good times,

Gerry. The contracts, the grants, all that property they're building, and everybody's got their hand out. But, Jesus, they're naming it after a fucking boat that sank first time it hit the water. Isn't that a laugh? This city gave the world the biggest disaster ever to sail the sea, and we're proud of it. Only in Belfast, eh?"

McKenna fell silent for a few seconds before he asked, "What do you want, Gerry?"

"Make a phone call," Fegan said.

"Who to?"

"Tom. Tell him to close up. Tell him you dropped me off and you went to see someone at the docks. If he asks who, tell him it's about a deal you're doing."

McKenna's laugh betrayed his fear. "Why would I do that? Why would I phone anyone?"

"Because I'll kill you if you don't."

"I think you'll kill me anyway."

Fegan looked up to the rear-view mirror. He could just make out McKenna's eyes in the darkness, his glasses reflecting the light from across the water. "There's dying and there's dying, Michael. Two very different things. You know that."

"Jesus." McKenna's shoulders shook as he exhaled. "Oh, Jesus, Gerry. I can't."

Fegan raised the Walther's muzzle to the base of McKenna's skull. "Do it."

McKenna bowed his head and sighed. His mobile phone's screen washed the car's interior with a blue-green glow. The phone beeped and burbled in his trembling hand before he brought it to his ear.

"Yeah . . . Tom, listen, just lock up and take the cash home with you . . . He's all right. I put him to bed. I'm over at the docks . . . To meet a fella . . . Just business. Listen, gotta go. I'll pick up the cash tomorrow . . . Yeah, all right . . . See you then."

The phone beeped once, and its soft light died.

McKenna turned his head. "Do you remember when we were kids, Gerry?"

Fegan smelled sweat and fear, McKenna's and his own. Enough memories were stirring without this.

McKenna continued. "Do you remember that time the Brits got us for bricking them? What were we, sixteen, seventeen? Remember, I threw the first one and went running. Wee Patsy Toner was too scared to do it, so he came running after me."

He craned his neck, trying to see Fegan. Fegan jabbed the gun's muzzle against the back of his head until he looked straight ahead. Ahead to where the followers waited. Except the boy. He still stared through the driver's window.

McKenna laughed. "Not you, though. You were never scared. Not of anybody. You stood your ground. You waited till you saw the whites of their eyes before you chucked yours. Remember, you hit one of them in the face. Their heads were poking out the top of the Land Rover and the brick hit him right in the nose. Blood pissing everywhere."

"Enough," Fegan said. Memory cursed him.

"And then they chased us up the Falls. Jesus, do you remember? You and me laughing, and wee Patsy screaming for his ma."

Fegan pressed the gun harder against McKenna's skull. "I said *enough.*"

"And they got us in Brighton Street. Christ, they kicked the fuck out of us, didn't they? Oh, that was a beating. And do you remember . . ." McKenna's shoulders shook with laughter. "Do you remember they got hold of wee Patsy, and he pissed himself all over one of them?"

A smile found Fegan's lips and he wiped it off with his free hand. "They broke his arm for that."

"That's right," McKenna said, the laughter dying in his throat. "And we joined up the next day. Broke your ma's heart, that, didn't it?"

"That's enough." Fegan's eyes burned.

McKenna's voice turned to a snarl. "It was me got you in, Gerry. Me. I got you in with McGinty and the rest. They'd have never taken you without me. Don't you forget that. You'd have been nothing without me, just another Catholic boy on the dole."

"That's right," Fegan said. "I'd have been nothing. I'd have *done* nothing. And those people would be alive. That boy would be alive. He'd have a wife, children, a home, all of that. We took that away from him. You and me."

McKenna's voice boomed inside the car. "He was a fucking tout. He squealed to the cops. He was dead the second he opened his mouth."

A stillness settled in Fegan. "That's enough," he said.

"Gerry, think about what you're doing. The boys won't let it go, ceasefire or not. Stormont or not. They'll come after you."

A tear traced a warm line down Fegan's cheek and he tasted salt. "Jesus, I promised myself I'd never do this again."

"Then don't, Gerry. Listen, it's not too late. You're drunk and you're depressed, I know. You're not at yourself. There won't be any trouble if you stop now."

Fegan shook his head. "I'm sorry."

"Thirty years, Gerry. We've known each other thirty—"

The Walther barked once, throwing red and grey against the windscreen. McKenna slumped forward onto the steering wheel, and the Merc's horn screamed at the night. Fegan reached forward, pulled him back against the seat, and silence swallowed them.

He climbed out of the car and used his handkerchief to open the driver's door. In the scant light from across the water he saw McKenna's dull eyes staring up at him, his designer glasses cracked and hanging off one ear. Fegan put another bullet in his heart, just to be sure. The pistol's hoarse shout rippled across the Lagan towards the glittering buildings.

Fegan wiped the wet heat from his eyes and looked around him. The followers emerged from the dark places and jostled for position around the open door, glancing from Fegan to the body, from the body to Fegan. He studied each of them in turn, his eyes moving from one to the next. He counted them as they retreated to the shadows.

The boy wasn't among them.

One down.

Eleven to go.

ELEVEN

"That's him," McSorley said, pointing to a blurred image on a stained sheet of paper. It showed an elderly man unlocking the door of a post office.

Davy Campbell turned the page on the tabletop to get a better look. *Soft target*, he thought. *Typical.*

McSorley slurped at his beer and wiped his mouth clean. His denims were at least fifteen years too young for him. Hughes and Comiskey lounged on the other side of the booth. The drink had already reddened their eyes, and it was only lunchtime.

McSorley addressed them. "You two hold on to his wife, and me and Davy will take care of him."

Campbell looked out the window to the sun-baked car park, the two rusted vehicles sitting there, and the mountains beyond. No traffic moved along the road on the outskirts of Dundalk. The diversions for the new motorway's construction had whittled down business at the Player's Inn to the extent that Eugene McSorley could talk aloud about his plans without fear of eavesdroppers. In a few months four lanes would carry traffic from the heart of Dublin all the way to Newry, just across the border in the North, and then on to Belfast. The port town of Dundalk would be bypassed altogether, along with the Player's Inn.

The Gaelic football memorabilia on the walls used to impress the tourists who landed by the busload on their way through to Dublin. They didn't know how bad the food was until it arrived on chipped plates, wallowing in grease. The football shirts and trophies displayed around the bar looked a little sad now the only customers were this shower of shit.

The landlord's father, Joe Gribben Senior, had been on the 1957

Louth team that won the Sam Maguire Cup, and Joe Gribben Junior would never let it be forgotten. Born and raised in Glasgow, Campbell had no interest in Gaelic football. And Joe Gribben Junior wisely had no interest in this discussion, so he stayed at the far end of the bar, out of earshot.

Comiskey leaned forward and waved a finger at Campbell. "How come he gets to go? Why've I got to stay with the auld doll?"

Campbell reached out and seized the finger. "Get that out of my face before I break it off."

"Quit it," McSorley scolded as he separated their hands. "Davy's going with me 'cause he knows what he's doing. All you know how to do is sit around and scratch your arse, so shut your trap and do what you're told."

"Away and shite," Comiskey said. He sat back and folded his arms.

Campbell returned his stare until the other backed down. Were these really the best men McSorley could gather up? Taking a post office might raise enough cash to get some decent weapons, but what was the point of putting them in the hands of people like Comiskey? He'd probably shoot his own toe off.

Not for the first time, Campbell wondered what the fuck he was doing with this lot. They called themselves Republicans, truer to the cause than those sell-outs north of the border, but they could barely organise a round of beers. One insane act nine years before had almost wiped the dissidents out. The disastrous bombing of Omagh killed twenty-nine civilians and two unborn twins on a summer afternoon in 1998, just months after the signing of the Good Friday Agreement. What little support the breakaway Republican groups had evaporated overnight. The changes in the North were swelling their numbers, however, as more and more foot soldiers drifted to the dissidents; they feared becoming nobodies again now the movement had no further use for them. The peace process had left many idle hands, and the devil was busy doling out work.

Some of the boys had objected to Campbell's presence, seeing as he wasn't even Irish, but his reputation had travelled ahead of him from Belfast. When he crossed the border to Dundalk, McSorley sought the

Scotsman out and made him his right-hand man. The dissidents were made up of gangs like McSorley's, some larger, some smaller, all loosely affiliated under a common cause. Soon, maybe this year, maybe next, they would pull together and be a real threat once more. Until then, they would continue bickering amongst themselves while knocking over country post offices.

A job's a job, Campbell reminded himself. He sighed inwardly and let his eyes wander while McSorley recited the plan for the tenth time.

His eyes stopped at the silent television over the bar. A photograph of a familiar face was replaced by footage of men in white paper overalls and surgical masks examining a Mercedes.

"Look," Campbell said.

McSorley was too wrapped up in his own plan to notice, so Campbell slapped his shoulder.

"What?"

"Look." Campbell jerked his head at the television. "Hey, Joe! Turn that up, will you?"

The landlord obliged and the refined tones of an RTÉ reporter said, "A police spokesperson has refused to speculate on who might have been behind the killing of Michael McKenna, but security analysts have indicated that Loyalists or dissident Republicans are primary suspects."

"Well, fuck, it wasn't me," McSorley said.

Comiskey and Hughes laughed. Campbell did not. A tingle of excitement sparkled in his stomach. He swallowed and pushed it down.

The reporter went on. "Although there had been rumors of a rift between Mr. McKenna and the party leadership, an internal feud has been ruled out by all observers. Security analysts have, however, speculated on the further political ramifications of Michael McKenna's murder. As a senior Republican, and a member of Northern Ireland's Executive at Stormont, his killing has the potential to destabilize the hard-won settlement in the North just as the newly formed government finds its feet."

"Fuck me," McSorley said. "Someone finally got Michael McKenna.

Thank Christ for that. I won't have to look at that slimy bastard's face on the telly any more."

The television switched to archive footage of McKenna being interviewed in front of his office on Belfast's Springfield Road. Hughes and Comiskey jeered when the camera zoomed in on the party's logo. As the report wrapped up, the northern correspondent said, "Police forensics officers remain at the scene."

"They'll find fuck all," Campbell said. "Their forensics are shite. I'm surprised they found the bloody car." His hand went to his pocket, feeling for his mobile phone. He wondered if he'd missed a call.

McSorley snorted. "Whoever it was, I'll buy him a pint. Here, Davy, you knew McKenna, didn't you?"

"Pretty well," Campbell said. "He didn't take it too kindly when I left to come down here. Said he'd break my knees if I showed my face in Belfast again."

"Looks like someone did you a favor, then."

Campbell gave it a moment's thought. "Maybe. There'll be trouble, though. The boys in Belfast won't let that go. Somebody's going to pay. I'll tell you that for nothing."

McSorley chuckled, his red-lined cheeks glowing.

"You look pretty chuffed about it," Campbell said.

"Chuffed?" McSorley grinned and swept back his greying hair. "I'm as happy as a dog with two cocks and two lamp-posts to piss on. As the old saying goes, Davy, *tiocfaidh ár lá*. Our day will come."

He draped his arm around Campbell's shoulder and leaned in close. His breath stirred the coarse hairs of Campbell's beard. "Those bastards in Belfast have had it their way too long. They cashed in and left us swinging. Tell you what, I'll get a round in and we'll drink a toast to whatever cunt killed Michael McKenna."

Campbell stood to let McSorley slide out of the booth, relieved to be free of his embrace. McSorley stopped halfway to the bar and came back to Campbell. He reached out his hand. Campbell gripped it in his.

"We need boys like you, Davy," McSorley said, squeezing Campbell's fingers. "I'm glad you're with us."

McSorley released Campbell's hand and turned away. Campbell wiped it on his jeans. He slipped back into the booth and noticed Hughes and Comiskey's attention.

"What?" he said.

Comiskey gave him a lopsided smile. "You might fool him, Davy, but you don't fool me. Just remember, I'll be watching you."

"Is that right?" Campbell raised his eyebrows and returned the smile.

"That's right. You put a foot wrong and I'll have you, boy." Comiskey placed his elbows on the table, formed a pistol with his fingers, and mimed cocking it. "Click-click, Davy."

"Ready when you are, pal," Campbell said. He held Comiskey's gaze just long enough to make his point before turning his eyes to the mountains beyond the window. He thought of Michael McKenna's corpse lying in a car in Belfast, and his gut twisted with a mix of sweet anticipation and cold unease.

4

Two officers sat across the table from Fegan, and Patsy Toner at his right hand. The interview room in Lisburn Road Police Station had the bland clinical feel of a hospital.

"And Mr. McKenna just let himself out after he put you to bed?" the older officer asked.

"Mr. Fegan has already answered that question," Toner said. His rumpled navy suit looked like it had been slipped over his bony frame in a hurry.

"Well, I'd like him to answer it again. Just for confirmation." The officer smiled.

"As far as I know, yeah, he let himself out," Fegan said. "I was drunk. I passed out as soon as I hit the pillow."

The truth was he'd slept very little the previous night. It took him an hour and a half to work his way through the streets, avoiding CCTV cameras on his route home. He climbed a wall into the back yard of one of the derelict houses two streets away from his place and hid the gun under some wood in a crumbling shed. He slipped quietly into his home and went straight upstairs. For the first time in two months he lay down in peace, but the ringing in his ears and the memory of the boy's savage grin kept him staring at his ceiling. Sleep evaded him until light crept through the crack in the curtains.

"Fair enough," the officer said. "That'll do us for now."

As they walked to Toner's car, Fegan asked, "How did you know to be waiting there for me?"

Toner smiled and said, "We've got a friend inside. Have done for years. He rang me as soon as he heard the Major Investigation Team were going to question you. He doesn't see much action these days, but he's still useful to have."

Toner had a good career as a solicitor. Small and thin, he still looked like the boy Fegan had run with all those years ago, despite the thick moustache. He claimed to be a human-rights lawyer when he talked to the press, though Fegan knew exactly whose rights he fought for. And his Jaguar proved they paid well.

Toner cleared his throat as he started the engine. "I've to take you to see someone before I bring you home," he said.

"Who?" Fegan asked. He let his hand rest near the door handle, ready to pull it and run.

"An old friend." Toner gave him a reassuring smile as he pulled away.

Fegan moved his fingers away from the door handle and steeled himself. He was grateful for Toner's silence as the Jaguar made its way north along the Lisburn Road, stopping every few dozen yards for pedestrian crossings. Designer boutiques, restaurants and wine bars passed on either side. Students and young professionals crossed at the lights.

They think the city belongs to them now, Fegan thought. If the peace process meant they could buy overpriced coffee without fear, then perhaps they were right. A young woman in a business suit crossed in front of the Jaguar's bonnet, a mobile phone pressed to her ear. Fegan wondered if she was even born when they scraped the body parts off the streets with shovels.

He turned his mind away from that image, angered at his own bitterness. The quiet after weeks of clamor unsettled him. Now that the followers had left him alone, now the chill at his center and twists in his stomach had abated, he found the clarity disorienting. But seven years of shadows and glimpses would not end for the passing of Michael McKenna. The eleven were there somewhere, just beyond his vision, waiting. Fegan was sure of that.

Eventually, Toner turned left onto Tate's Avenue, heading west across the city. Back to where they belonged.

The exterior of the old Celtic Supporters Club had seen better days. Tricolors and footballs decorated the sign above the entrance, but the paint flaked away to expose rotting wood. Behind metal grilles, the grubby painted-over windows made the building appear blinded.

Toner led Fegan inside. The sole afternoon drinker kept his eyes on his newspaper as they entered. A smell of stale beer and cigarettes laced the dimness; the smoking ban would never be enforced in places like this.

They went to the rear of the club and entered a dank and narrow corridor with doors to the toilets at either side, and another marked PRIVATE at the end. As Toner went to open the door to the back room, a flash of pain burst in Fegan's head, a lightning arc between his temples. He stopped and leaned against the wall. A chill crept inward from his limbs, crawling to his core like icy spider webs.

Toner looked back over his shoulder and said, "Jesus, Gerry, what's wrong?"

Fegan breathed deep. "Nothing," he said. "I'm tired, that's all."

Eleven shadows moved along the corridor, past Toner, and became one with the darkness beyond. Toner came back to Fegan and put a small hand on his shoulder.

"He only wants a word," Toner said. "Don't worry."

Fegan brushed Toner's hand away. "I'm not worried; I'm hungover. Come on."

He pushed past Toner, went to the door, and opened it. His heart lurched at the sight of the man who waited there.

Vincie Caffola's bald head reflected light from the bare bulb above. Boxes and barrels had been moved to the outside of the room, and a single wooden chair placed at its center. Plastic sheeting covered the floor, and Caffola wore new overalls that struggled to contain his bulky shoulders.

"Gerry, how're ya?" Caffola's smile made Fegan's stomach turn.

"All right."

"I'll wait in the car." Toner patted Fegan's back and disappeared the way they had come.

"Take a seat," Caffola said.

Fegan sat down, placing his hands on his knees, fighting the urge to cover himself. The light bulb above swung lazily in the draught from Toner closing the door. It made Caffola's shadow sweep across the wall. Other shadows followed it, crossing one another, solidifying. Fegan swallowed and blinked against the ache settling behind his eyes.

"Bad news about Michael, eh?" Caffola wore a grim expression.

Two forms stepped out of the dark corners, young men long dead. Blood and black earth streaked their uniforms. Fegan focused on Caffola even as they raised their hands to form pistols with their fingers.

"Yeah," he said. "I thought it was all over."

"It'll never be over." Caffola paced the floor. The two Ulster Defence Regiment men moved with him. "Not till the Brits get out. I made my position clear to McGinty and the rest of them. I don't like what's going on. Supporting the peelers, sitting at Stormont, all that. But I go with the party, no matter what."

"You were always loyal," Fegan said.

"Yeah, loyal." Caffola seemed to like the word. He clapped his hands once. Back to business. "So, I need to find out what happened to Michael. He left you home last night. What time?"

"About quarter past, half twelve. Something like that."

"Did he say where he was going?"

"No, we didn't talk much. I was pissed." There had been a time when Caffola took orders from Fegan. The admission of his weakness shamed him.

"Did he say anything about these boys he was doing business with?"

Fegan looked up at the big man. "What boys?"

"A bunch of fucking Liths." Caffola's mouth twisted as if the word had a foul taste. "Dirty bastards. I swear to God, this place is getting so full of foreigners it won't be worth getting the Brits out. Fucking Lithuanians, Polish, niggers, pakis, chinks. You walk through town any day you hardly hear an Irish accent. All foreigners. And Dublin's worse. Have you been there lately?"

"No," Fegan said.

"Fucking foreigners everywhere, dirty fuckers serving you food. I can't eat out any more 'cause some black bastard's got his hands all over it." Caffola shuddered.

Fegan's mind chased memories as he watched the two UDR men

aim at Caffola's shaved head, executing him just as the boy had McKenna. His breath caught in his chest when the memory snapped into place. It was in a room like this, in Lurgan, twenty miles south-west of the city.

The old Ulster Defence Regiment was once made up of part-time soldiers recruited from the local population. Like the police, they were almost entirely Protestant. Some were also Loyalists abusing the job to target Catholics while they patrolled country lanes and smaller towns. A unit of six had been ambushed in a landmine attack near Magheralin. Two died instantly, two lay broken but still alive at the roadside, and two fled across the fields. A gang of local boys who were there to pick off the survivors caught them within ten minutes and brought them to a shebeen on a housing estate on the edge of Lurgan. Caffola and Fegan reached the drinking club within the hour.

Vincie Caffola was better at getting information than anyone in the movement. He was a big man, but slow. He knew how to inflict pain, he was an artist in that way, but he was no good in a fight. Fegan came along just in case.

The two UDR men were bleeding hard, both crying with pain and terror. Their mouths gaped, dripping red from shredded gums as their teeth lay scattered on the floor. They'd given up the little they knew an hour before, but Caffola kept going. He was kneeling on the floor, pulling out a toenail with his pliers when, suddenly, the foot he was working on kicked out, throwing him off balance. Caffola landed on his back, and the UDR man was on his feet, his bonds falling away. Caffola just lay there, staring up at the screaming soldier, unable to move. Fegan put a hole through the soldier's head before he took his second step. The other, still fixed to the chair, squealed as his friend's body hit the floor. Fegan silenced him with a shot to the temple. He looked down at Caffola, still sprawled in the blood and teeth, and told him to clean this fucking mess up.

Now Fegan considered his possibilities. If Caffola's questioning became physical, Fegan was confident he could handle the big man. But there'd be no escaping. The boys would be after him. He decided to be still.

"I don't know any foreigners," he said.

"So you don't know this cunt, then?" Caffola went to a cupboard door and opened it. A tall thin man was curled up inside, bound hand and foot, gagged. He stared out at them, shaking. Red blotches stained his grey suit.

The two UDR men moved back into the dark corners. Fegan lost them among the shadows, and the pain behind his eyes faded to a murmur.

"No," he said. "I've never seen him before."

Caffola reached down and pulled the gag away from the man's mouth. He pointed to Fegan. "Do you know him?"

The man looked to Fegan, then back to Caffola. He shook his head. "You sure?"

The man lifted his bound hands and began to plead in some Slavic language. Caffola placed a hand on either side of the door frame to brace himself and swung his boot into the cupboard, punctuating his words with the sound of leather on flesh. "Speak . . . fucking . . . English . . . you . . . dirty . . . bastard . . . or . . . I'll . . . kick . . . your . . . face . . . in."

"Stop!" the man wailed. "Please, sir, stop!"

"Out you come," Caffola said as he grabbed a handful of blond hair. He heaved and the man came screaming after. "I need the chair, Gerry."

Fegan stood up and went to the edge of the room.

Caffola hoisted the man up onto the chair and indicated Fegan. "Do you know him?"

The man shook his head.

"He doesn't know me and I don't know him," Fegan said.

Caffola held a hand up to silence his old comrade. "All right, I just wanted to be sure. Now let's see what he does know."

The man's terrified eyes darted between Fegan and Caffola. His breath came in shallow rasps. A bitter, stale smell filled the room.

"Who is he?" Fegan asked.

"This is Petras Adamkus," Caffola said. "Say hello, Petras."

Petras looked from one man to the other.

Caffola gave him one hard slap across the cheek. "I told you to say hello."

"Hello," Petras said in a small, high voice.

"Better," Caffola said. "Now, let's get down to it. Why did you kill Michael McKenna?"

Petras gaped up at him.

Caffola slapped him again, harder. "Why did you kill Michael McKenna?"

Petras held his bound hands up. "No, no. Michael my friend. We make business. Good deal. Good girls. Young girls. No hurt him."

Caffola drew back his heavy fist and launched it at the Lithuanian's chin. It connected with a wet smacking sound, and Petras's head rocked back, tipping the chair. He landed hard on the floor, blood dripping from his already swelling lip.

Caffola smiled at Fegan. "Brings it all back, doesn't it?"

When he took a pair of pliers from his pocket, Fegan asked, "Can I go?"

"No stomach for it any more?"

"No."

"All right," Caffola said. "You say you had nothing to do with it, that's good enough for me."

Fegan opened the door to the corridor. A spark flared in his temple, and he looked back over his shoulder. The two UDR men raised their fingers to Caffola's bald head.

"Another time," Fegan said.

"Yeah," Caffola said as he lifted the Lithuanian back onto the chair. "See you again, Gerry."

Fegan turned his back on them and walked through the corridor and the bar beyond, out onto the street where Patsy Toner waited in his Jaguar.

The Minister of State for Northern Ireland, Edward Hargreaves MP, teed off in afternoon sunlight. He shaded his eyes as the ball soared up and away into the sky above the Old Course at St Andrews. It drifted, veering to the left, and began a slow descent. It bounced three times and disappeared into a patch of gorse.

"Bastard," he said, and handed the club to the caddy without looking at him.

"Bad luck, Minister," the third man present said as he placed his tee. A gun bulged at the small of Compton's back as he bent over.

Hargreaves was glad his new Personal Protection Officer was reasonably affable, unlike the sour fellow he'd had before, but did they have to give him someone so good at golf? Compton's perfect swing sent the ball off to land precisely between two bunkers, an easy chip away from the green.

Today had been rotten so far, and would likely worsen. The phone at Hargreaves's hotel bedside had woken him at eight, bearing bad news. Hargreaves had found Michael McKenna to be entirely objectionable on the few occasions they'd met, so he felt no grief, but the trouble his killing would stir could derail years of hard work.

The hard work of Hargreaves and the Secretary of State's predecessors, admittedly, but still.

God help him, he might even have to visit the forsaken place again this month. He'd just returned from a solid week there, and surely that was enough? Had it been up to Hargreaves he would have cut the hellish waste of land adrift years ago. But there were those in government, and in royalty, who felt some misguided sense of duty to the six counties across the sea, so it was his burden to carry.

Now Northern Ireland's factions had finally agreed to share

governance amongst themselves, Hargreaves's role was largely a matter of passing papers on to the Secretary for signing, so it wasn't altogether a disaster. Just as long as the natives behaved, that was.

The phone in his pocket vibrated. The call he dreaded. He answered it with a heavy heart.

A woman's voice said, "The Chief Constable is ready to speak with you now, Minister. It's a secure line. Go ahead."

"Good afternoon, Geoff," Hargreaves said. "What have you got?"

"Not a great deal," Pilkington said.

Hargreaves didn't like the Chief Constable, but he respected him. Geoff Pilkington was a hard man who had worked the streets of Manchester before climbing the ranks. He was one of the few Chief Constables who had done any real police work in his career, rather than using a public school and Oxbridge education to grease his way into the position. He took grief from no one, but had a keen political savvy that belied his rough exterior. He knew when to shout, and when to whisper. If Pilkington had aimed for Parliament instead of the senior ranks of the force, Hargreaves was sure he'd have been in the Cabinet by now. He had taken the top job in the Police Service of Northern Ireland as it completed its transition from the Royal Ulster Constabulary, and it had been a testing time. But he had weathered it, achieving the impossible by earning the respect of the whole of Northern Ireland society, albeit begrudgingly from some quarters.

"Who was it?" Hargreaves asked. "Loyalists? Dissidents?"

"Neither, we think. It was done at close range, no sign of a struggle. We're pretty sure it was someone he knew."

"His own people?" Hargreaves walked after his ball, Compton and the caddy following.

"Unlikely," Pilkington said. "There's been no indication of a split. Even if there was, they wouldn't want to rock the boat. Not now they've got their feet under the table at Stormont."

"Then who? I have to tell the Secretary something."

"We know he was doing business with some Lithuanians, bringing illegals up over the border from Dublin. Girls, mostly, for the sex trade."

"I didn't think McKenna's lot were into all that. More the Loyalists' forte."

"The official line from the party is no criminal activity at all, but they don't control what individuals choose to do. Leaves people like McKenna with a little more freedom to operate. If there's money in it, they'll do it. And whatever the party says, the money still flows uphill."

It never ceased to amaze Hargreaves that people would vote for criminals in full knowledge of their nature. He doubted there was a more cynical electorate in the world. The average Northern Irish pleb could read between the lines of a speech better than any professional political analyst, disbelieving every treacherous word. Yet still they voted as predictably, election after election. He wondered why they didn't just have a sectarian headcount every four years and be done with it.

He'd desperately hoped for a Cabinet spot, anything, in the last reshuffle. As it turned out, he didn't even get Secretary of State for Northern Ireland, the job no one wanted. No, he was the fucking *assistant* to the job no one wanted. He ground his teeth as he walked.

"So, do you have anything to link them?" Hargreaves asked.

"Not directly. We've very little solid information to go on at the minute."

"What *do* you have?" Hargreaves stopped to allow Compton and the caddy to catch up. He would bring Compton jogging in the morning, get him match fit.

"We've got his last movements. He owned a bar on the Springfield Road. His brother's name's on the licence, but it was his. He gave a drunk a lift home from there, then the barman received a call from him thirty to forty-five minutes later. He said he'd left the drunk home, then gone to the docks to meet someone on a matter of business. We're still checking CCTV footage from the route, but what we've got so far shows him driving alone. The last camera caught him on York Street, turning under the M3 flyover and into the docks. We reckon whoever did it met him there. Forensics are still going over the car, but I doubt they'll get much. It was a clean job. Professional."

Hargreaves felt a small trickle of relief. "So, we don't think it was political, then? I don't need to tell you how troublesome it would be otherwise."

"No, Minister, you don't. Early indications are a business deal gone sour. We've already questioned the drunk, but he didn't know much, despite who he is."

The trickle of relief halted, and Hargreaves set off towards his ball again. "What do you mean? Who is he?"

"Gerald Fegan. He's suspected of as many as twelve murders, two while he was on compassionate leave from prison for his mother's funeral. He was convicted of the butcher's shop bombing on the Shankill in 1988. Three died in that, including a mother and her baby. He was a foot soldier, and one of their best, or worst, depending on your point of view. A killer, plain and simple."

"And he isn't a suspect?"

"Not at the moment. He's been quiet as a mouse since he got early release in . . ."

Hargreaves heard the shuffling of paper.

"At the start of 2000. From what I understand, he'd been suffering some psychological problems before his release, and he's taken to drink in recent times."

The trickle of relief started again. "I see," Hargreaves said as he neared the gorse patch that had devoured his ball. "So, it's not political. Let's try and keep it that way, shall we?"

"Of course, Minister. The politicians on all sides are gearing up to make the most of it, but that's only to be expected. Don't worry, we'll keep a lid on it."

"Good man," Hargreaves said. He hung up and returned the phone to his pocket as he kicked at the gorse. "Now, where's that bastard ball?"

6

The whetstone glided along the guitar's neck, skimming the frets. Fegan loved the sensation it sent through his hand, his wrist, on into his forearm and up to his shoulder: the feeling of oiled stone sliding on metal. As the boat-shaped block swept from one end of the finger-board to the other, it ground away years of wear. Too much pressure would destroy the frets. Not enough would leave the finish uneven, and the guitar unplayable. It was a question of balance and patience.

Ronnie Lennox had taught him that.

Fegan had spent hours in the Maze Prison's workshop, watching the old man at his craft. Ronnie hated being penned up with the rest of the Loyalists, so the guards let him pass the time in his own corner of the woodwork room. The Republican prisoners tolerated his presence when they had the use of the place, thinking him harmless, and even let him teach them a thing or two. Fegan always paid close attention. Ronnie's delicate hands bore a myriad of scars, decades of cuts and abrasions earned at the shipyard. He'd been a ship's carpenter before he did the awful thing that sent him to prison. Like so many men who worked there, he had been left with the wheezy rattle of asbestosis in his chest.

Fegan remembered Ronnie's hands most of all, and he knew why. They were like his father's. When he could get the work, Fegan's father had also been a chippie. Except, since he was Catholic, the shipyard never had any use for him.

Mixed in with the bad times, when he came home drunk and stinking, there were good times. Like the day, when Fegan was very small, that his father borrowed a car and took him and his mother to Portaferry on the shore of Strangford Lough. They went across the Lough and back three times just for the pleasure of riding the ferry.

Then his father went to the pub while Fegan and his weeping mother got the bus back to Belfast. He didn't come home for three days.

Of details from those good times, few as they were, it was his father's hands Fegan remembered best. He recalled the coarse and bony feel of them, the hardness and the warmth, long fingers stained orange by nicotine.

Fegan was nine years old when he last held them. It was in his parents' small bedroom on a cold morning. The wallpaper bubbled and peeled with damp. He remembered how the mildew smell mixed with his mother's floral scent when she entered. She sat down on the bed, picked up a hairbrush, and scraped it across his scalp.

A few minutes passed before she asked, "Who were you talking to when I came in, love?"

"No one," he said.

The boar hairs scratched like nails. His collar felt like fingers wrapped around his neck, making a tickly sickness at the base of his throat. He watched her in the mirror over her good mahogany dressing table. He stood with his hands on the cool wood. Her eyes were red and wet.

"You were talking to someone. Was it your friends? The ones you fib about?"

"No," he said.

She swiped the hairbrush across his backside and the sting forced him up on his tiptoes, his buttocks clenched.

She resumed brushing. "Don't be telling lies today of all days, Gerald Fegan. Who were you talking to?"

He sniffed once and stared hard at her reflection. "Daddy," he said.

The brush stopped at his crown. The bristles gnawed at his scalp. She blinked once and a crystal bead escaped her left eye. "Don't," she said.

"It was Daddy."

"Your Daddy's going in the ground today." She placed the brush on the bed beside her and gripped his shoulders hard. Her breath burned his skin. "They'll screw the lid down soon, but it's still open. I didn't make you look at him because I knew you didn't want to. But

I'll make you look at him now if you tell me fibs like that. Do I have to make you look at him?"

Fegan wanted to shake his head to please her, but his desire for her to know was greater. "He was holding my hand," he said.

She spun him around to face her. Brilliant light flashed in his head as her palm slammed against his cheek. He staggered, but she held firm to his shoulders.

"You listen to me, Gerry." Her face became pointed like a bird's, pale and fierce. "No more of this . . . this . . . devilment. No more. Do you hear me?"

He opened his mouth to argue, and another lightning bolt struck his cheek.

"Not one more word. You don't see anyone. You don't talk to anyone. You turn away from them. Do you want people to think you're mad? Do you want to end up in the hospital with all the soft-headed old men living in their own filth?" She shook him hard. "Do you? Is that what you want?"

Blinded by tears, Fegan shook his head. He wanted to wail but the cry stayed trapped in his chest. It swelled between his ears until at last air came tearing into his lungs. It burst out again in hacking sobs. He collapsed into his mother's bosom and let her arms circle him.

"Oh, wee pet, I'm sorry. Shush, shush, shush. Quiet, now. If you're quiet they'll leave you alone. Always be quiet."

She took his wet face in her hands and smiled. "Turn away from them and be quiet. The devil can't go where he's not wanted. Do you understand?"

He nodded and sniffed.

"Good boy," she said. "Now go and polish your shoes."

Thirty-six years ago. Fegan didn't like to think of time, and how he could never hold on to it. But sometimes it couldn't be avoided. He was twenty-six when he went inside and thirty-eight when he got out. The seven years since had drifted past almost unnoticed. Nearly half a lifetime wasted. Fegan shook the thought away and turned his mind back to his task.

He sat at the table beneath his window, his shirtsleeves rolled up.

In the daytime it gave him light to work. At night, a desk lamp arched over the tools placed neatly about him. For this job he had masking tape, files, wire wool and olive oil. He set the stone on some newspaper and used a soft cloth to wipe away the swarf, the tiny specks of metal left by the abrasion on the masked-off pieces of fingerboard.

The radio on the sideboard murmured soft blues music. Fegan didn't understand it, the droning chords and the mournful voices, but he had a notion of learning to play the C.F. Martin guitar when it was finished. Ronnie had said it was a collector's piece, but guitars weren't for collecting. They were for playing, he said. So Fegan listened to the radio while he worked, hoping some of its music might seep into him.

When the music stopped and the presenter said the news was coming up, Fegan reached across and turned it off. Everyone was talking about McKenna. Politicians, cops, security analysts – the reporters had even started interviewing one another in their rush to squeeze every last drop of blood out of the story.

Fegan picked up the whetstone and ran it along the fingerboard again, back and forth, the rhythm soothing him. Nine o'clock. He hadn't had a drink tonight. Like every other night, he promised himself he wouldn't. Somewhere beneath his heart he knew he would break that promise. He knew they would come again tonight, even though he had given McKenna to the boy. They wanted more.

They wanted Caffola.

Fegan swept the stone back and forth, smooth movements flowing from his arm. *Be quiet*, he thought. *Turn away from them and be quiet.*

Balance and patience.

A tingling gathered in his temples the way electricity hangs in the air before a storm. He closed his eyes and let the stone's rhythm fall in step with his heart.

Balance and patience.

Sparks flashed behind his eyes.

Fegan put the stone down and lowered the guitar to the felt sheet that protected its lacquered finish. He stood, went to the sideboard, and poured two fingers of Jameson's and the same of water. The whiskey warmed his center as the shadows crept along the walls.

Balance and patience.

7

"So, who do you think got McKenna?" McSorley asked as he hauled the steering wheel to the left.

Campbell looked back over his shoulder to where the old man lay on the van's cold floor, whimpering inside the pillowcase that had been placed over his head.

"Don't worry about him," McSorley said.

Campbell returned his attention to the winding country road, involuntarily pressing his foot against the worn carpeting, trying to brake for McSorley. He'd waited for his mobile to ring all day. He had to force himself not to check for missed calls every ten minutes. The anticipation gnawed at him.

"Well?" McSorley prompted. "Who do you reckon?"

"Whoever it was has got to be fucking crazy," Campbell said. "Or stupid. They won't get away with it. The boys won't let it go. They'll break the ceasefire if they have to."

The van hit a pothole and Campbell had to brace himself against the dashboard. The old man cried out as he bounced between the van's inside wall and its floor. Comiskey and Hughes were back at his tiny cottage, holding his wife until Campbell and McSorley returned with the contents of the post office safe. It was only a short journey into the village.

"I suppose you'd have been one of the boys going after him, eh?"

Campbell tried to read McSorley's face, but darkness obscured all but the watery sheen of his eyes. "Might've been."

"No need to be shy with me, Davy. We're mates, eh? You don't talk much about what you got up to in Belfast."

"Not much to talk about."

McSorley gave a chesty laugh. "Oh, aye. I bet there's not."

His face took on a sickly glow as they cruised into the village, its street lights washing them in orange. "I heard a story about you and some boy who tried to set up Paul McGinty. I heard you beat the life out of him."

"Yeah?"

"That's what I heard."

"Well, people talk. You can believe whatever you want."

The van's headlights picked out the green *An Post* sign and its brakes whined. The engine juddered as it died. McSorley gave the old man one quick glance and turned back to Campbell.

"Some of the lads don't trust you," he said, his eyes narrow.

"You mean Comiskey?"

"Him and some of the others. They think it's a bit funny, you just upping sticks and coming down here to us. Seeing as you were so close to McGinty and all. Some of the lads are worried about you."

Campbell let his hand wander to his thigh. His jeans stretched tight over the Gerber knife in his pocket. "Are *you* worried?"

McSorley's tongue pressed against the inside of his cheek, making his stubble bristle. "I don't know. It could be McGinty sent you down here to keep an eye on us, see what we're up to. Or it could be like you say: you just wanted to see some action."

Campbell kept his eyes locked on McSorley's. "Like I said, you can believe whatever you want."

A sly grin spread on McSorley's face as he nodded. "I think you're all right, Davy, but I'll tell you this." He raised a finger at Campbell. "You ever prove me wrong, you better run like fuck, 'cause I'll skin you alive."

McSorley splayed the bills out between his fingers. The balaclava didn't mask his fury. "Three hundred and twenty fucking euro?"

Campbell felt a guffaw climb up from his belly, but he trapped it in his mouth. The woollen mask made his beard itch.

The old man cowered on his knees in front of the open safe. McSorley grabbed his pyjama collar with his free hand.

"Three hundred and twenty? I didn't do all this for fucking three hundred and twenty, you miserable auld shite. Where's the rest?"

The old man raised his shaking hands. "That's all there is, I swear to God, that's all."

McSorley shook him back and forth. "Quit talking shite and tell me where it is."

"I swear to God, that's all. We only open half days. There's some change in the till. You can have that if you want."

"Christ!" McSorley released the old man's collar and shoved the notes into his pocket. He pointed to the counter at the front of the shop. "Davy, go and empty the till. And fill the bag up with fags. That's all we're going to get. Fuck!"

Campbell went to the till. The next morning's meagre float lay in its open drawer. He scooped up bills and coins, guessing them to total no more than forty or fifty euro, and dropped them into the sports bag. The shelves behind the counter were stacked with cigarettes and he swept them into the bag, on top of the money, feeling like a petty thief.

Feeling like it?

No, that's exactly what I am, he thought as cigarette packets fell at his feet. *Like a fucking druggie stealing fags to feed his habit.*

He cursed under his breath.

"Come on," McSorley shouted. He dragged the old man by the wrist, not even bothering to bind and gag him again.

"I'm coming," Campbell said, shoving the cigarettes down into the bag.

McSorley stopped at the door. "I said come on, for Christ's sake!"

"All right!" Campbell pulled the zipper shut and hoisted the bag over his shoulder. He followed McSorley and the old man out to the street.

McSorley dragged his whimpering captive to the back of the van and opened the doors. Something across the street grabbed the old man's attention: a light at a window.

"Help." The cry was weak, but he tried again. "Help!"

McSorley went to cover his mouth, but the old man found the strength to push his hand away. "Help me! Help!"

Campbell walked towards them.

"Shut up or I'll fucking do you one," McSorley hissed as the old man writhed in his grip.

The bag slipped from Campbell's hand, and he peeled the balaclava back from his face.

"Help me! Somebody! Help!"

The rage was white-hot and glorious as Campbell let it rain down on the old man's head, and the force of it sent McSorley reeling. Blow after blow, the anger burned brighter, until the old man was a limp shape dangling from the van's lip.

"Davy!"

Campbell drove his fist into the old man's gut.

"Jesus, Davy, stop!"

He kicked at the old man's knee.

McSorley grabbed Campbell's waist and pulled him back. "That's enough, Davy. Come on."

Campbell tore McSorley's arms away and spun to face him. "What do you think I am?"

McSorley stepped back, his hands up.

"Eh? What do you think I am? A fucking shoplifter?"

"Davy, calm down a minute." He pulled the balaclava from his head.

"A thieving junkie? You think I came all the way down here to steal fucking cigarettes from old men?"

McSorley's mouth worked silently, his eyes white circles around black points.

"Fucking amateurs!" Campbell turned on his heels and grabbed the bag from the ground. He threw it into the back of the van and bundled the old man's legs in after it. "Come on to fuck," he growled.

Without asking, he climbed into the driver's seat and sparked the engine. McSorley didn't take his eyes off Campbell as he hoisted himself into the passenger seat.

They drove in silence, McSorley giving the Scot sideways glances, while Campbell thought of the hole in Michael McKenna's head, and the killer whose own life was surely forfeit.

8

Michael McKenna's big house in the suburbs didn't sit well with the party's socialist manifesto, so Fegan wasn't surprised his wake was held elsewhere. Instead, people paid their respects to McKenna at his mother's terraced house on Fallswater Parade, a small red-brick two-up-two-down. It stood in a row of identical houses just off the lower end of the Falls Road, the jugular vein of the Republican movement in Belfast. Back in the bad times, people had compared this part of the city to Beirut. Fegan had always thought of it as the road home, leading as it did to the apex between the Springfield Road and the Falls, where his mother's old house stood.

As Fegan approached he tried to count the men crowding the tiny walled garden. They spilled onto the street, smoking, laughing and swapping stories. He gave up when the number passed twenty. He edged through them, returning the respectful nods and mumbled greetings. He knew most of these men, hard lads all, and liked none of them. They came from all over Belfast: Andersonstown, Poleglass, Turf Lodge, and some from the Republican enclaves in the north of the city and the Lower Ormeau. Fegan recognised a few faces from outside Belfast, places like Derry and South Armagh. A few wore shirts and ties to mark the solemnity of the occasion, more wore leather blazers, and the remainder dressed as casually as they did on any afternoon.

Fegan caught a young man glaring at him from the living-room window of the house next door. He probably owned the Volvo estate whose bonnet some of the boys rested on. Not that he would complain. He realised he'd been noticed and dropped the curtain in front of the window. Fegan imagined many of the street's newer residents would eye this gathering with apprehension. The property boom had driven the young middle classes into parts of the city they'd never contemplated before. Pensioners who'd never seen money in their lives suddenly found themselves with hundred-grand nest eggs to cushion their dotage.

Fegan went inside. The narrow hallway was shoulder-to-shoulder with mourners, and he had to fight a sense of drowning as he dived deeper into the house.

"Gerry!" A small, elderly lady waved from a dense forest of black leather and green-striped Celtic shirts.

Fegan squeezed through the mass of bodies until he reached her. "Mrs. McKenna, I'm sorry for your trouble."

She stretched up to embrace him. "Och, my boy's gone, Gerry. Some bastard went and shot him. Here's him fighting for peace and they shot him." Her eyes were damp and angry as she looked up at him. "May God forgive them, for I won't."

"Where is he?" Fegan asked.

"Up the stairs, in his old bedroom. Sure, you know where it is, love. You spent plenty of time up there when you were kids. It's a closed coffin." Her voice cracked and her lip trembled. "I couldn't look at him like that, not my handsome boy."

"I'll go up and see him," Fegan said before giving McKenna's mother one more hug.

He fought his way to the foot of the stairs and slowly made his way up, one step at a time. The smell of body odor rose with the heat and thickened as he climbed.

McKenna's old room was at the front of the house, overlooking the street. A respectful quiet lay between the four walls, and Fegan was grateful for the relative peace. The few mourners in here whispered amongst themselves, and Fegan's sweat cooled on him. He could think of worse places to be than in a room with Michael McKenna's coffin.

Fegan made the Sign of the Cross as he approached the casket. This was a modest box, far beneath what a man of McKenna's wealth might expect to rot in, but the humility of its grain, molding and fittings was not an accident. Tomorrow it would lead a procession along the Falls

Road draped in an Irish Tricolor and Fegan would walk behind it, possibly even carry it some of the way. He was not a man of words, but he knew what hypocrisy meant. Still, hypocrisy was not rare among his old comrades, or in the party. He could live with it.

He first met Michael McKenna on a hard bench outside the principal's office in the Christian Brothers School. They both awaited a caning on a warm June afternoon, just a week or so from the end of term. Fegan couldn't remember what his caning was for, but McKenna's was for fighting. McKenna was a year older than Fegan, and as stocky as Fegan was skinny. He had blood on his knuckles. They sat in silence until Brother Doran called them in.

Fegan took his strokes without making a sound. The corners of his eyes twitched as the WHAP! of bamboo on palm ricocheted off the office walls. He focused on the picture of the Virgin that hung above Brother Doran's desk and set the pain aside. *Turn away and be quiet*, he thought. Brother Doran's face grew more florid with each swipe. After five, he rested the cane on the joint between Fegan's thumb and the heel of his hand.

"You're a stubborn little bastard, aren't you, Fegan?" he said.

The cane swished as it cut the air. It caught the joint hard. Fegan's hand dropped away and he shifted his feet to center his balance. A small sun burned in his hand, but again, he set the pain aside. He raised it for more as a blood blister formed beneath the skin.

Brother Doran stared into his eyes as his jowls trembled. "Stand in the corner, you impudent little shite."

Tears lined Michael McKenna's cheeks by his third stroke. The fourth was half-hearted as Brother Doran seemed to tire. He dismissed the two boys with an angry flourish.

As Fegan walked along the corridor outside, McKenna called, "You tell anyone I cried and I'll beat your head in."

Fegan stopped and turned. "Go fuck yourself," he said.

McKenna blustered up to him, wiping his nose on his sleeve. "What did you say?"

"Fuck off," Fegan said. He turned and resumed walking.

Two balled fists slammed into his back, and he staggered forward.

He regained his balance and spun to face McKenna, his right hand ready.

McKenna took a step back and jabbed at him with a grubby finger. "Just you watch yourself, right?" He turned and ran in the opposite direction.

The next day, McKenna stopped Fegan in the playground and demanded to see his hand. Fegan showed him the purple and brown blood-blossoms on his palm.

"Fuck me," McKenna said. "Is it sore?"

"What do you think?" Fegan said.

"Looks it. Do you want to meet up later?"

"What for?" Fegan asked.

Lines appeared on McKenna's forehead as he shuffled his feet. "Just, you know, for a laugh and stuff."

Fegan thought about it for a few seconds. He didn't do that kind of thing. No harm in trying, though. "All right," he said.

He made many friends that summer. His mother didn't approve. She reminded Fegan that Michael McKenna's older brother was doing time in Long Kesh for having a gun. Fegan didn't care. It felt good to have friends.

Most of those friends were now in McKenna's mother's house, swapping stories of the old days, and Fegan dreaded listening to them. He stepped back from the coffin and crossed himself once more.

The quiet in the room faded to utter silence. Fegan became aware of his own breathing and a presence behind him. He turned and saw a woman, ash-blonde and pale, tall and willowy, in the doorway. She was dressed simply and elegantly in a black trouser suit and white blouse. Fegan stepped aside as she approached.

She extended her hand to the coffin, stopping when her fingertips were within millimeters of its glossy sheen. Her grey-blue eyes fixed on something Fegan couldn't see, something far away. A small ache entered his heart as he wondered if she would weep at some memory of the man inside the box. She inhaled as she came back to herself. She blinked once and mouthed four words. Fegan's ache turned to something darker when he traced the shapes her lips made.

You had it coming.

As she turned from the coffin, her eyes caught his and she froze, locked in Fegan's knowledge of her words.

You're right, he wanted to say. *He got what he deserved.* Instead, he gave her the smallest of nods.

Her cheeks flushed and she headed for the door. One of McKenna's three sisters stood by it, watching the blonde woman. When Fegan saw the hate in Bernie McKenna's eyes he knew who the woman was.

Marie McKenna, daughter of Patrick and Bridget McKenna, niece of the late Michael McKenna. Seven years ago, at around the same time Fegan was first getting to know his followers, Marie McKenna had scandalised her family by taking up with an officer of the hated Royal Ulster Constabulary. Even worse, he was a Catholic cop at a time when joining the police was still an act of treachery. She was already in poor favor amongst many Republicans as she wrote for one of the Unionist rags, the *Telegraph* or the *Newsletter*, Fegan couldn't remember which. A romance with a peeler cut her off from all but her mother.

Gossip, shunning, even death threats against each of the couple were not enough to separate them. But pregnancy was. When Marie's belly began to swell two years into their relationship, the cop made his excuses and left. For the sake of Bridget McKenna, Marie was begrudgingly allowed back into the family. Had she accepted an offer, made in kindness, to sort out the absent father, then perhaps the community would have opened its arms a little wider to her. As it stood, she was a pariah.

Fegan could see the loneliness, the isolation, on her skin, just as he felt it on his own. The ache in his heart returned, heavier than before.

Marie kept her eyes focused down and forward as she left the room. Her aunt scowled as she passed, and Fegan heard the word "Bitch!" hissed after her. Heads turned to follow her progress through the bodies packed on the landing, and whispers cut the thick warm air.

Fegan felt an inexplicable, irresistible urge to go after her. He fought it for a moment, but its strength dragged him to the door and out onto the landing, cutting the same path through the gathered people as she did. He was a tall man, but still he struggled to see over the mourners. There, between two shaved heads, he caught a glimpse of blonde hair, turning at the top of the stairs. He made it to the banister and watched Marie struggle down the steps for a second before he resumed his attempt to follow her. By the time Fegan reached the top step, she was at the bottom. He began picking his way down, watching her as she embraced McKenna's mother, then seeing the mother's mouth curl as Marie headed for the door.

He lost her in the sunlight as he neared the bottom, and was making for the street when a hand caught his upper arm. Startled, Fegan turned, his weight on both feet, ready to fight. A bolt of bright pain flashed in his temple.

"Jesus, Gerry," laughed Vincie Caffola. "I thought you were going to split me then."

Eleven shadows moved between the mourners, taking shape, dissolving again. Two came alongside Caffola, the vague forms of their arms lifted to aim at his head. *Turn away and be quiet*, Fegan thought.

He focused on the bald-headed thug's eyes. "What do you want?"

Caffola smiled and put a hand on his shoulder. "Me and some of the boys are going to the pub after. You fancy it?"

The two UDR men made guns with their fingers. Fegan tried hard not to see them.

"All right," he said. "Look, I'll see you later. It's too crowded here for me."

"You should hang around a bit," Caffola said. "McGinty's coming over soon. He was saying he hadn't seen you in ages."

"No, I'll go on." Fegan pulled away from Caffola. "Sure I'll see him tomorrow. At the funeral."

"Suit yourself." Caffola slapped his back as he left. "I'll see you later."

Fegan gulped cool air when he got outside, relieved to be free from the crushing stomachs and shoulders. Men were still gathered in front of the house, smoking and swapping stories. Again, he returned respectful nods and mumbled greetings until he was clear of them. He gripped the lapels of his jacket, flapping them to cool his body. He wiped a slick layer of sweat away from his brow and began his walk home.

The eleven followed.

"Don't you lot get tired?" he asked. He turned to look at them. Eleven dead people, big as life, trooping along the pavement and looking right back at him. A laugh escaped his belly, and a giddy wave passed across his forehead. None answered his question, so he asked another.

"What was that about in there? What was I doing going after her? What was I going to say to her if I got her?"

The woman, her baby supported in one arm, stepped ahead of Fegan and turned to face him. She brought a finger to her lips. Shush. With the same finger she pointed over his shoulder. Fegan heard a car draw up, then slow down beside him. He looked towards it. A Renault Clio, a new one. The passenger window lowered with an electric whirr and Fegan stopped walking.

"Can I give you a lift?" Marie McKenna asked, her blonde head dipping to see him from below the car's roofline.

Fegan looked back towards the house, then in the direction he'd been walking. He looked at his followers. The woman with the baby gave him a single nod.

"All right," he said.

Fegan kept his hands in his lap and his mouth shut for the duration of the short journey. His knees pressed against the Clio's dashboard, but the heavy silence caused him more discomfort. He almost wished the followers were in here with them. Marie had been on the verge of saying something from the moment he lowered himself into the car, but she seemed unable to let it out. Now, parked outside his house on Calcutta Street, off the Springfield Road, she struggled visibly with whatever she needed to say.

He was just about to thank her and go when she said, "I didn't mean it."

"Mean what?" he asked, even though he knew.

"What I said back there, by the coffin." Marie stared straight ahead.

"I didn't hear you say anything."

"Yes, you did. I didn't say it out loud, but you know what I said."

"I suppose so," he said, unable to put his heart into a lie.

"Well, I didn't mean it. Please don't tell anyone I said it." She turned to face him. Fegan expected to see pleading in her eyes. Instead, they were cool like slate. Only their tiny movements betrayed her.

"Why would I tell anyone?" he asked.

"I know who you are. I know you were his friend. It must've really offended you. I'm sorry. Please don't tell anyone."

Marie's voice cracked and her eyes softened. Fegan wondered if she feared him, and he hated the idea. Once he might have taken pleasure in it, but now it clawed at him.

"I won't tell anyone," he said. "I'm not . . . with them any more. I don't . . ."

She waited while he struggled. "Belong?" she asked.

Fegan reached for the door handle, uncertain whether to stay or flee. "That's right," he said.

"I know the feeling." A tentative smile flickered on Marie's lips. "You can't choose where you belong, and where you don't. But what if the place you don't belong is the only place you have left?"

Did she expect an answer? She had enquiring eyes, like the psychologists in prison. Fegan considered it. "Then you get on with it, or get out," he said.

"Okay." Her smile bloomed to fullness, and she reddened. "Listen to me, questions, always questions. Well, thank you for understanding. And I'm sorry. I really didn't mean it."

"Yes, you did," Fegan said. The words fell from his mouth before he was conscious of the thought.

Her face paled, the red sinking beneath her skin. Her smile disappeared. "What?"

"You meant it," he said, opening the passenger door. "And you were right."

Fegan climbed out and stepped onto the pavement. He bent down and looked back into the car at her. "He deserved it," he said before swinging the door closed.

Marie stared back at him through the glass for endless seconds before swinging into the traffic, tyres squealing, forcing a black taxi to brake. Its horn blared as the Clio disappeared down the street.

Fegan turned in a circle, looking for shadows. "What's happening to me?" he asked.

Blankets of gloom filled the bar, layer on layer, concealing those men who wished to drink unseen. Fegan moved among them, avoiding their eyes and words. He sipped Guinness, not whiskey, to keep a clear head for his work.

He had always thought of killing as work. Just a job to be done, with no care or feeling behind it. He hadn't considered himself a craftsman, more a skilled laborer. Not like those assassins who made it art. It only took a certain hardness of the soul, a casual brutality, a willingness to do what other men wouldn't. He supposed he had a talent for it, just as Caffola had a talent for inflicting pain. And that talent had earned him respect.

But where did the line between respect and fear lie? All those knowing nods he'd received over the years – were they made out of reverence or the worry he might turn on those giving them, break them, like he had so many before? The twelve, now eleven, who had shadowed Fegan for seven years marked the lives he had wiped out. But he had scarred many more.

Although he hadn't meant to, he'd killed three in the butcher's-shop bombing. He knew there were also men and women who had lost arms, legs and eyes because of the same bloody act, damning them to lives of anguish. The struggle to grasp the weight, the shape, the *realness* of it had kept him from sleep for many years. He didn't need the shadows of the dead for that.

As Fegan moved through the drinkers he tried to keep his mind from the past but it had a way of finding a route there without his help. He thought of the woman at the graveyard, the twelfth follower's mother.

"You're Gerry Fegan," she'd said. She was small and grey. Her anger burned him. "You're Gerry Fegan and you killed my wee boy."

Fegan rose from the miserable bunch of daffodils he had placed on his own mother's grave. He searched for something to say, anything, but could only think of the awful thing that had happened to her son.

"Where did you put him?" she asked. "I come here every Sunday. I walk around the gravestones and I read the names. Sometimes I forget myself, and I look for his name. I know I won't find it, but I look anyway. Sometimes I have to think for a minute because his name won't come to me. It's like he never lived at all."

She took a step towards Fegan, her shaking hand reaching out to him. "Tell me where you put him. Please. That's all. Just tell me where he is."

He remembered the boy's blood as McKenna worked on him.

He remembered how red it was.

"Gerry, how're ya?"

Fegan blinked the memory away and turned to see who had slapped his shoulder.

Patsy Toner grinned up at him from behind his moustache. "McGinty was asking for you today," he said. "At the house. You should have stayed."

"What's he want with me?" Fegan took a sip of Guinness.

"He doesn't like to see a good man go to waste. You do all right out of that Community Development job he set up for you. With his connections he can keep that job funded for years and you don't have to lift a finger for it. Just cash your checks, and nobody cares." Toner sighed and placed a hand on Fegan's shoulder. "You did your time so the party looks after you, but you need to give something back. Nothing much, just a wee job now and then. You'll get paid, like."

"I'm not interested," Fegan said, turning to go.

Toner gripped his elbow. "It's not as simple as that, Gerry. I'm sure you've heard the rumors. Things haven't been so smooth between Paul and the leadership, if you know what I mean. He needs to know who his friends are. Just listen to what he has to say, and do whatever he tells you."

Fegan jerked his elbow away. "What are you, his messenger boy?"

"I'm just saying." Toner held his hands up and smiled. "That's all, Gerry. Just letting you know the situation. Sure, McGinty'll see you tomorrow."

"Yeah," Fegan said, leaving Toner standing with his palms up and out, like a man surrendering.

Fegan made his way to the back of the bar, to the darkest corner, behind a computer quiz game no one ever played. It gave him a good view of the room and the drunks moving between its shadows.

Just a wee job now and then, Toner said. Fegan knew what sort of wee job he was talking about. There were many errands a man like McGinty needed doing. Even now the politicians had taken over the movement, even though they were shifting away from the rackets, the extortion, the thieving, people still needed to be kept in line. Competition for the bars and taxi firms needed quashing. Drug dealers needed discouraging from selling in certain areas – unless they paid their dues, of course. Come election time, reluctant voters needed gathering up and escorting to the polling stations where they would be reminded whose name to mark. And then there were the many hundreds of people who only existed on election days.

The last election, just two months ago, had been the watershed. For the first time the country's voters went to the polls knowing they would elect a real government, that at last it was over. *Over for who?* Fegan thought. The headaches started around then. The shadows darkened, the faces grew clearer. He had tried to turn away, to be quiet, but still they came.

Then the screaming.

By the time Toner shoved a bundle of polling cards into Fegan's hand, he hadn't slept for a week. He only voted once – some nobody campaigning about fuel tax got his mark – and threw the rest of the cards in a bin. The boys ran a sweepstake on who would cast the most votes. Eddie Coyle had won, having voted twenty-eight times between eleven different polling stations. He got nearly five hundred quid which his wife promptly took from him. McGinty gave him an extra five hundred on top, and Coyle wisely kept the reward secret. Five hundred was a small price for McGinty to ensure he kept his seat. The talk on the streets was the leadership wanted to pass McGinty over. He was tainted by the old ways, no matter how hard he tried to play the politician. But if he kept his vote solid, the leadership couldn't discard him like they had so many others on the climb to government.

A familiar spark flared in Fegan's temple. Icy webs crawled towards his center. A commotion at the bar's front door announced Caffola's arrival. Fegan had expected him to be here when he came an hour before, otherwise he would have spared himself the ordeal of being among these people. He decided to remain in his shadowy corner for now. It was early yet. Plenty of time.

As the ache behind his eyes deepened, Fegan watched.

Caffola's cranium and gold earring reflected the dim lighting. His thick neck melded with his broad shoulders to give the impression of power and strength. He was strong, all right, Fegan knew that much, and vicious. It would be hard, but Fegan could take him.

When and where? Tonight, if he could. Somewhere away from here, possibly in Caffola's own home. The thug was already drunk; his staggering gave him away. He might leave early. Fegan could follow him. Or he might be invited to someone's home to drink the night through. If Fegan knew where, then he could go there, enter through some open window, and finish Caffola in his stupor.

Balance and patience, he thought as the shadows gathered. *Balance and patience.*

Caffola cornered Fegan in the toilets, backing him against the cold tiles. As red-faced drunks blinked at the urinals, pissing down their own legs, Caffola's spittle made cold pinpoints on Fegan's face. The alcohol on Caffola's breath mixed with the reek of urine. Fegan swallowed bile.

"I think the world of you, Gerry," Caffola slurred. His eyelids looked like they weighed a tonne. "Swear to God. You and me. Mates. Right?"

"Right," Fegan said. The pressure behind his eyes pulsed.

"I'm only telling you 'cause I respect you, right?" Caffola placed his left hand on Fegan's chest. His right hand pressed against the tiles above Fegan's shoulder.

Fegan kept his eyes on Caffola's. "Right."

"McGinty's worried about you. You used to be the boy. I mean, everyone knows you were the boy, right?"

"Right." Fegan ignored the chill at his center.

"But now you're staying away, you're drinking, acting all mad and stuff. It's no good, Gerry." Caffola rested his palm on Fegan's cheek. "I'll tell you that for nothing. I'll tell you that for sweet fuck all. McGinty wants to talk to you. Get things straight, like. He's worried, but I told him. I says, Paul, don't you worry about Gerry Fegan 'cause Gerry Fegan's fucking sound, right?"

"Right."

"He's the boy, right?"

"Right."

"Then McGinty says to me about Michael, that you was the last one seen him." Caffola's eyes darkened. "And that Lithuanian cunt. I gave him a proper going-over, like. And all the time he says he knows nothing. Even when I was showing him his own teeth, he says he knows nothing."

Fegan tried to step away from the wall, to slip by Caffola. The big man pushed him back against the tiles.

"You see my problem, Gerry?"

Fegan looked over Caffola's shoulder. The bathroom was empty now, except for the eleven shadows taking form around them. Two separated from the others, hands raised. Could he do it here? No, there'd be no way out.

"You say you'd nothing to do with it, I believe you. That's what I told McGinty. I stood up for you, Gerry, so don't make a cunt of me. Right? You talk to McGinty tomorrow." Caffola's finger stabbed at Fegan's chest. "You talk to him and do what he wants, right?"

"Right," Fegan said, remembering a time when Caffola was afraid of him. Yes, he could do it here, do it now. He could get out before anyone knew what had happened. Get out and run. Leave everything and run. Caffola's throat looked so tender, his Adam's apple bobbing over the collar of his shirt.

The door burst open, tearing Fegan's attention away from the other man's neck. "There's trouble brewing," Patsy Toner said, his little face shining with glee. "There's peelers all over the place and kids making a barricade. There's going to be a row. A proper kicking match."

Caffola looked from Toner to Fegan, beaming. "Fucking class," he said.

"How the fuck did this start?" Caffola asked, incredulous. He indicated a burning mound of mattresses, wooden pallets and rubbish in the middle of the Springfield Road, just a few feet from the corner where McKenna's bar stood. A mob of thirty or so youths, children mostly, surrounded it, chanting.

Half a dozen PSNI Land Rovers idled thirty yards down the street. They looked less intimidating these days, painted white with colorful stripes instead of the battleship grey of the past. The peelers milling about weren't in riot gear yet, but it was only a matter of time before suitably dressed reinforcements would arrive.

Fegan felt a strange stirring inside, a quickening of the spirit, as he watched them. The followers had left him; their shadows receded. He stayed on the footpath, close to the wall, as Caffola and Toner paced.

"Kids," Toner said. "There's more patrols about because of the funeral tomorrow. Some of the kids took exception to it and started chucking stuff. The peelers lifted a couple of them, so some more started throwing stuff, then a couple more got lifted and so on and so on."

A grin cracked Caffola's face. "Jesus, we haven't had a proper ruck in ages. I wonder if we can get some petrol bombs rustled up quick."

"There's hardly time," Toner said. "We might get a few, like, but not a proper stock. Nobody's prepared for it these days."

Caffola sighed. "Aye, I suppose that's a good thing, really."

"Aye," Toner said. "We can still get the bigger kids to fill some wheelie bins with bricks and stuff. Tom's got a big bin full of bottles in the alley behind the bar. Some of the kids could steal that, maybe."

"Sounds like a plan," Caffola said. The adrenalin seemed to have sobered him. "Somebody better let McGinty know. Do you want to ring him?"

"All right," Toner said, fishing a mobile from his jacket pocket.

Caffola turned to Fegan, rubbing his hands together, a smile lighting up his face in the growing darkness. "What about it, Gerry?" he asked. "You up for it?"

"I'll hang about," Fegan said. "See what happens."

"Good man." Caffola patted his shoulder.

Young men and older boys swelled the mob. Fegan knew the cops would hold back, hoping the drama would fizzle out. Most times it would, leaving nothing more than a blackened mess for the road sweepers to clean up in the morning. Not tonight, though. Fegan could feel it like thunder in the air. The atmosphere crackled with it.

He looked up at the sky. Things had developed too quickly to get a helicopter in the air. In the old days, the Brits would have scrambled two or three of them from their bases in Holywood or Lisburn, and would've had the area covered in minutes. They'd be out for the funeral tomorrow, hovering high above the crowds, but the sky stayed clear this evening.

A boy, red-haired and wiry, twelve at most, pulled a lump of burning wood from the mound. He half ran, half hopped six paces and hurled the blackened timber with every bit of his strength. It clattered to the ground, throwing up red sparks, midway between the smoldering mound and the waiting policemen. The other boys gave a triumphant cheer.

"For fuck's sake," Caffola said. "Hey!"

He waited a moment then shouted again. "Hey! You!"

The red-haired boy turned.

"Yeah, you," Caffola called. "C'mere!"

The boy approached slowly.

"What are you at?" Caffola asked. "Are you stupid?"

"No," the boy said.

"Well, for fuck's sake quit acting like it. Cover your face with something so the cameras don't get you."

"Okay," the boy said. He pulled a wrinkled handkerchief from his pocket and returned to his comrades at the burning mound, tying the square of soiled material into a mask over his nose and mouth.

"Kids know nothing these days." Caffola shook his head. "When we were kids we'd have had this place wrecked by now. Petrol bombs, concrete slabs, catapults with ball-bearings." He grinned and pointed down the street to the Land Rovers. "And them cunts, they'd have been firing plastic bullets at us. Changed times, Gerry."

"Yeah," Fegan said. "Changed times."

These streets had seen more riots than just about anywhere in the world. From the civil rights protests of the late Sixties, when Fegan was too small to know what it meant, to the groundswell of anger at internment in the early Seventies, when young men were imprisoned without trial. Journalists gave kids five-pound notes to throw stones and bottles at the Brits, hoping to set off another battle for the cameras. Then the anguish of the hunger strikes in the early Eighties when ten men starved themselves to death in the Maze, fanning the embers on the streets. No payment was needed then; rage seethed in the city, and anything could ignite the flames. Mob violence, children as weapons: those were the tactics of the time. A photograph of a bleeding child, no matter how they got injured, packed more power than a dozen bombs. Political animals like Paul McGinty learned that early on and acted accordingly. Fegan had seen it so many times before, this wasteful anger bubbling over into violence. It tired and excited him all at once.

More men wandered out of the bar and onto the street. Some remained inside, preferring to drink in peace rather than get involved.

Patsy Toner snapped his phone closed.

"Well?" Caffola asked.

"He says go ahead," Toner said. "Just don't let it get out of hand. Don't touch any property. Don't fight anyone but the peelers. There's lots of press about for the funeral so they'll all come over here once it gets going. McGinty's going to turn up in an hour or so. Make sure everyone knows to settle down then so the press sees he calmed the situation."

"He always was the smart one," Caffola said. He slapped his palms together and smiled. "Right, let's go."

A riot is like a fire. It has a life of its own, and does as it will. But it can be fanned or quelled. Fegan knew that as well as anybody. The police and the kids were the kindling, paper and dry wood. Men like Caffola were the naked flame, ready to set them alight. Others, like Father Coulter, were water to douse the burning. But Father Coulter wasn't here this evening, so Caffola sparked and blazed unabated. Morbidly fascinated, Fegan watched him work.

Caffola moved between groups of boys and young men, slapping backs and issuing commands. They obeyed without question.

Within minutes older boys were off fetching ammunition. They returned quickly, wheeling it in plastic bins. Their missiles were gathered from the nearby derelict houses and patches of waste ground. Bricks, bottles, concrete fragments, scrap metal. Everything they needed. Two boys in their mid-teens appeared at the corner pushing the bar's bottle bin, its innards clanging and clattering as the wheels juddered across the tarmac. They stopped out of view of the cops.

The peelers huddled and passed orders back and forth. Their stance changed. They knew this one wasn't blowing over. Some strapped body armor across their torsos and donned helmets.

Within ten minutes Caffola got a phone call telling him there were six containers of petrol in a back alley two streets away. He instructed the boys to wheel the bottle bin over there. "And grab whatever you can off washing lines for rags," he said. He pulled a ten-pound note from his pocket and pressed it into one of the boys' hands. "And here, get some sugar. Remember to mix it in the petrol so it'll stick, right? And get some crates off Tom for carrying the bottles back."

"Right," the boy said. He and his friend wheeled the jangling bin back around the corner.

Soon masonry began to fly. Sporadically at first, but the bombardment gathered pace. The peelers stayed behind their Land Rovers for now, content to let things simmer until they had enough officers to deal with the situation.

The first news crew pulled up in a van behind the police line. Word had started to spread. The mob around the growing pile of burning debris swelled. Caffola stood with his hands on his hips, watching it all unfold, his nose tilted up as if he were sniffing violence on the air.

Fegan's nostrils flared too, the old scent waking memories in him. "How bad?" he asked.

"Not too bad," Caffola said. "Just a bit of a scrap. Nobody'll get killed."

Fegan looked to Caffola's throat. "You sure?"

"Aye. It's not the Eighties any more. Fuck, it's not even the Nineties. A few stitches, that'll be the height of it." Caffola's belly jerked with a sudden laugh. He pointed towards the row of Land Rovers. "You see her?"

Fegan followed the line of Caffola's finger. He saw a young policewoman hunkered down, her back to them, as she talked to her colleagues. Blonde hair crept out from under her cap, and the image of Marie McKenna flashed in Fegan's mind. He shook it away.

Caffola nudged him. "At the back of the Land Rover. You see her?"

Fegan almost said yes, he saw her, but he caught himself, hoping Caffola would pick another target if he kept quiet. No such luck.

"Watch." Caffola lifted an empty bottle from the bar's windowsill. He ran a few steps, the bottle suspended over his right shoulder. He threw his body forward and released the missile.

It rose in a slow arc, then descended towards the policewoman. Fegan willed it to miss, to splash impotently at her feet. *Miss, miss, miss,* he thought. He closed his eyes until he heard it crash on the tarmac.

He opened them to see the cops scatter, taking shelter behind the Land Rovers.

"Fuck," Caffola said. He winked at Fegan. "Close, though."

Fegan breathed deep. He knew this was Vincent Francis Caffola's last night on earth.

With that thought, his temples sparked and a cold wave rippled through him. The setting sun cast long shadows. Shapes emerged from them, solidified, and drew near. The two UDR men flanked Caffola, their arms raised, their fingers aiming. The rest circled Fegan. The woman, her baby restless in her arms, smiled at him.

Engines roared and brakes squealed at the police line. Men in full riot gear streamed out of six more Land Rovers. They wore helmets with clear visors, fireproof balaclavas masking their faces, and thick body armor. Their gloved hands held riot shields and batons.

They were ready. The mob was ready. Fegan was ready.

Caffola turned to him once more, grinning. "Fucking class," he said.

At first, the police maintained their line. As lumps of masonry came in waves they simply raised their shields to deflect each missile. A senior officer, distinguishable only by his gait, paced behind their ranks, barking orders. Fegan couldn't hear them from this distance, but he knew what they were just the same.

Steady. Hold your line.

Things changed when the first petrol bombs arrived. One of the kids came half running, half staggering, struggling with a crate loaded with petrol-filled bottles. He remained out of sight of the police line, signalling Caffola from the side street, his back against the wall. They had selected the larger bottles, filled them with a mixture of fuel and sugar, and plugged the tops with petrol-soaked rags.

Fegan clenched and unclenched his fists, fighting the adrenalin already coursing through him. The followers circled, watching.

At Caffola's signal, boys ran to the corner to fetch the deadly bottles. Smoke from the burning pile of mattresses and wood obscured the details of their actions from the police, but there could be no surprise in what was to come. The petrol bomb had always been the weapon of choice on these streets.

Fegan didn't see who threw the first one. He saw only its fiery ascent, smoke following its fall. There was the sound of shattering glass, then the WHUMP! of the liquid igniting ten feet from the peelers. Those nearest took a step back and their commander scolded them as the mob cheered.

The next was thrown by the same skinny red-haired boy Caffola had instructed to disguise himself only a short while before. He gave the throw everything he could, but it landed twenty feet from the line, its fuel scattering everywhere and failing to catch light. The boy kicked at the ground in frustration.

The third was the charm. An older boy, perhaps sixteen or seventeen, lit the rag on his bottle and made his way out from behind the burning barricade. Air rippled around the flame as the boy held the bottle over his shoulder. He ran five steps and launched it. He froze and watched the petrol bomb arc upwards. The now hundred-strong crowd held its breath as the bottle reached its zenith, then fell, twisting and turning, leaving a smoky trail. Policemen scrambled backwards as the accuracy of the shot became apparent. It splashed at their feet, throwing flames around them, and the roar of the mob was deafening. As Caffola laughed and slapped his shoulder, Fegan watched the four cops touched by the fire drop and roll, their colleagues swatting at the flames with their gloved hands.

More petrol bombs flew, and more found their targets, some crashing against the Land Rovers, some making little hells at the feet of the police. Every successful hit brought another chorus of triumph from the boys and men surrounding Fegan. The eleven followers gathered around him, rapt in the spectacle.

"They'll charge soon," Fegan said, his temples throbbing, his heart racing. "They'll run at us, drive the Land Rovers at us, try to break us up. They'll want to scatter everyone into the side streets."

"Yeah, I know," Caffola said. He winked. "I've done this before, remember?"

"I remember," Fegan said. He remembered everything. The charge, and the scattering, would be the key; his chance to get Caffola away and on his own.

Any minute now, he thought. He looked back to the police line. The Land Rovers maneuvered into position. They would come first, the cops following. The mob quieted, the boys and men bracing themselves. Caffola gave a girlish giggle as the police commander's voice drifted on the breeze. The Land Rovers' engines revved and the cops raised their batons.

"Here they come," Fegan said.

II

The youngest boys ran first, fleeing just as the charge started. They screamed and laughed as they streamed past Fegan. The older boys held their ground longer, jeering, launching bricks and bottles even as the Land Rovers reached the barricade. Fire licked the armored vehicles as they broke through the mound. Burning debris flew in all directions. The cops came behind, roaring as they waved their batons.

"C'mon," Caffola said, grabbing Fegan's sleeve.

They ran to the side street, arms and legs churning, and ducked into an alley. They dodged old bicycles and plastic bins as dogs barked from inside the walled yards. Caffola's laughter echoed in the narrow space.

They emerged onto a patch of waste ground and kept running, aiming for the streets opposite. When they reached the other side Caffola headed for one of them, but Fegan pulled him towards an alley. "No, this way," he gasped.

Caffola followed him, and they ran until they reached a dead end. As they slowed to a halt, Caffola bent double, letting out a long moan.

"Jesus," he said between desperate heaves of air, "I'm not fit for this any more."

"Me neither," Fegan said as his ribs screamed. He leaned against the wall, his head swimming. The pain behind his eyes swelled until he was sure his skull would not contain it. He pressed his palms to his temples and sucked air through his teeth.

Caffola grabbed his stomach with one hand and a bin with the other. "Aw, Christ," he said. His mouth opened wide, and Fegan heard a splashing sound. The sour stink of vomit reached him and he covered his nose and mouth.

Fegan screwed his eyes shut. The pain came in hammer blows,

smashing against his forehead. Even with his eyes closed, he felt them, the eleven, pushing at his consciousness. Without knowing why, he breathed deep and opened himself to them. A last bright bolt flared in his head, and the pain evaporated. He kept his eyes closed for a moment, letting the sudden cool giddiness wash over him. He opened his eyes, unsure of what he'd see.

The followers gathered in the alley's dimness. They kept their distance, watching. The two UDR men stepped forward. Their faces burned with hate and savage pleasure.

Fegan turned his eyes to Caffola. The cold beginnings of rain dotted his face and forehead as he watched the other man retch. He looked back to the UDR men. Their eyes glinted in the gloom of the alley while the other darkened forms moved behind them. Their lips parted in toothless grins, loose red flesh revealed within.

Fegan closed his eyes again and wished for another way. As foolish as it was, he wished for another life away from this. He wished for peaceful sleep and bloodless hands.

He wished.

Fegan sighed, opened his eyes, and reached into his pocket. He took out a pair of surgical gloves. As he slipped them on he asked, "Do you remember those two UDR men in Lurgan?"

"What?" Caffola straightened, wiping his mouth with the back of his hand.

"In Lurgan," Fegan said. "It would've been about '87 or '88. Do you remember? You tortured them till one of them fought back. You fell on your arse and I had to finish them for you."

"Yeah, I remember," Caffola said, a smile coming to him as he fought for breath. He coughed and spat. "They screamed the fucking place down." Caffola's brow creased as he looked down at Fegan's hands. "What're those for?"

As the rain began in earnest, the two UDR men drew closer. The downpour didn't touch them.

"They want you," Fegan said.

"What are you talking about, Gerry?" Caffola leaned back against the wall, his chest still heaving.

"The UDR men." Fegan crouched down, searching the wet ground as the evening grew darker. "They want you."

"What's going on?" Caffola stepped away from the wall.

Fegan found what he needed and stood upright. "I'm sorry," he said. He couldn't be sure if he was apologising to the UDR men or to Caffola. Maybe both. He walked towards the other man.

Caffola backed away, his hands up. "What are you doing, Gerry?"

"What someone should have done years ago."

Backed into the deepest corner of the alley, Caffola could go no further. "It *was* you, wasn't it? You did McKenna."

"That's right," Fegan said as he raised the brick over his head. In what remained of the evening light, he saw the other man's eyes flash in realisation. Before he could bring the brick down, Caffola launched himself forward, his shoulder ramming into Fegan's chest.

They hit the ground hard, and Caffola's weight crushed the air out of Fegan's lungs. The brick rattled against the wall. Their legs tangled as Caffola scrambled to his feet and he fell again, this time at Fegan's side. Fegan pulled at the other's jacket, trying to get a firm grip, and he heard the tearing of cloth. Caffola swung his elbow back, catching Fegan's cheek. For a moment he was free and managed to find his feet before Fegan grabbed his ankles, bringing him down again.

There was a loud, sickly crunch as Caffola tried to break his fall, instead breaking his wrist. His scream echoed through the alley. Fegan straddled his back, reached for the brick, and raised it above his head once more. Caffola craned his neck around and gave one last cry before Fegan drove the brick into his temple.

Fegan felt Caffola go limp beneath him, and he threw the brick towards the followers. They stepped aside as it bounced into the darkness. The two UDR men approached and hunkered down so they were at eye level with Fegan. They aimed at Caffola's broken head. Blood coursed from the wound on the bald man's temple, and his glassy eyes fluttered as he moaned.

"All right," Fegan said. He leaned down and pinched Caffola's nose between his gloved fingers, covering his mouth with his palm. He let his weight settle on the other man's back and, as the body began to jerk, Fegan squeezed tighter. A slick wet heat covered his gloved hand as Caffola began to vomit again, and Fegan applied yet more pressure. At last, he felt Caffola's life slip away beneath him.

Fegan closed his eyes and searched his heart, looking for some sense of what he'd just done. He found nothing but the cold hollowness of his wishes.

He took his hand away from Caffola's face, letting the vomit spill onto the ground. The rank odor and the warmth on his palm reached down to his stomach. *Turn away and be quiet*, he thought. He looked up at the followers. The woman stepped forward, carrying her baby, her floral dress pretty in the gloaming. She nodded and gave Fegan her small, sad smile.

The two UDR men were gone. Nine followers remained.

"Who's next?" Fegan asked.

NINE

Campbell stared at the ceiling, his heart thundering, wondering what had woken him. He was a light sleeper – he needed to be – and the slightest stirring could rouse him. His mobile rang again, and he knew what had pulled him to waking. He reached over to the bedside locker and grabbed the phone. He squinted at its little display. Number withheld, it said. His heart rammed against his breastbone.

He thumbed the green button and brought the phone to his ear. "Yeah?"

"Come in," an English-accented voice said.

"Now?" he asked, keeping the hope from his voice. "I've just got my way in here."

"Change of plan," the voice said. "This is urgent. Number one priority. That's from the top."

"Where?" he asked.

"Armagh. There's a car park by a chapel, opposite the council buildings. Do you know it?"

"Yeah, I know it." Campbell swung his legs out of bed. He rubbed his face, his beard prickling his palm. "There's cameras all over that place."

"They'll be looking the other way."

"Fucking better be. When?"

"An hour."

"I'm in Dundalk. I've got to get packed up, get out of here, get my car, and there's roadworks—"

"An hour." The phone died.

"Fuck," Campbell said.

His clothes lay on the floor where he'd thrown them the night before. He dressed quickly and quietly. A wardrobe leaned against the wall, its doors hanging at odd angles. He took a holdall from inside and stuffed it with the few garments he owned. His mobile and a set of keys were the only personal items remaining. Pocketing them, he stepped out onto the landing.

Gurgling snores came from the adjoining room. He pushed the door open and looked inside. Eugene McSorley lay sprawled on the bed, fully clothed, a beer can still in his hand.

Campbell wondered if he'd ever come back and finish what he'd started here. It had taken months to bring this about, to work his way into the gang. So far it had come to nothing. But still, McSorley might make a nuisance of himself if someone didn't keep tabs on him.

An idea flashed in Campbell's mind. He could cross the room and silently dispose of McSorley. It would be so easy just to kneel on his chest and put the correct pressure on his throat. He gave it a few seconds' thought.

"Fuck it," he said, and moved away from the door. He descended the stairs and let himself out. The sun was only beginning to creep above the houses opposite as he climbed into the old Ford Fiesta. Its tired, wheezy engine coughed into life and he pulled away, heading for the port where his own car, his real car, was safely locked away.

Fifty-two minutes after his phone woke him, Campbell steered his BMW Z4 Coupé into the car park by the chapel. Its engine burbled as he pulled alongside the anonymous Ford Mondeo. Like his own car, the Mondeo's windows were tinted, obscuring its occupants from casual glances. He could just make out the shapes of two men in the front seats. His shadow stretched long in the early sunlight as he climbed out of the BMW. Armagh's cathedrals loomed over the small town, reminding him it was actually a city. The man in the Mondeo's driver's seat reached across and opened its rear door.

Campbell lowered himself in and said, "Let me guess. McKenna, right?"

The two men exchanged glances. The one in the driver's seat, the handler, passed Campbell a palmtop computer displaying a photograph of two men. It was poorly lit, but he could make them out, standing on a street corner.

"You know them?" the handler asked.

"Yeah," Campbell said. He swallowed his confusion and focused. "Gerry Fegan and Vincie Caffola."

"Tell us about them."

Campbell thought about it for a moment. "Gerry Fegan's from before my time, but he's a legend. Everybody talked about him in Belfast. A vicious bastard. He did twelve years. Last I heard, he was hitting the bottle pretty hard. Sits and talks to himself while he gets pissed, apparently."

The handler looked back over his shoulder. "And Caffola?"

"He's an animal. Thick as pig shit, but dangerous."

"Not any more, he's not. He's dead," the handler said. "His body was found in an alley last night. He had a broken wrist and a gash on his temple, but not enough to kill him. Early reports say he most likely passed out, then choked on his own vomit. There'll be a post-mortem this morning."

"Fuck me," Campbell said. He felt his calm mask slip. He caught it and wetted his upper lip.

"You've heard about Michael McKenna's demise, obviously."

Campbell smiled. "Couldn't have happened to a nicer fella."

The man in the passenger seat spoke for the first time. "It's no laughing matter," he said. "This is going to cause some major problems for us."

Public school, Campbell thought. The handler was Army, maybe even ex-SAS, going by his haircut and the scars on his face. He'd seen action. But this other was government. Northern Ireland Office, probably, one of the bureaucrats who'd run this place when it was too busy fighting to run itself. Chinless office clerks at the helm of a country drowning in its own blood. *Not for much longer*, Campbell thought.

"I don't need to tell you how delicate the situation is," Public School continued. "The political process is on the right track, at last, but it's as fragile as ever. We can't afford any upsets, not with the money and time that's been invested. Relations between McGinty's faction and the party leadership have been strained enough as it is. We can't have it turning into a feud. Have you seen any news this morning?"

"No," Campbell said. He hadn't even turned on the car radio for the journey across the border.

"Well, it's not pretty. As soon as word got out Caffola was dead, what should have been a minor skirmish turned into a major riot. It only settled down in the last few hours. The leadership want to play it down, but our friend inside tells us McGinty is going to say the police did it, even if it's proven to be an accident. He'll make a song and dance about it at McKenna's funeral today. He'll make out Caffola was beaten by the police, then left to choke to death in an alley. We're told he'll threaten to withdraw support for the PSNI, even though the party hasn't approved it. He wants to stir up some headlines for himself, show the party leadership he's not going to be sidelined. Problem is, talk like that will rattle the Unionists. If they think the party wants to back out of policing, they might walk away from Stormont, and the Assembly will collapse. Again."

"And you're sure the cops didn't do it?" Campbell thought it was a reasonable question.

"We're not sure of anything," Public School said.

"So, where does Gerry Fegan fit into this?" Campbell asked, thinking of the tall, thin man he'd met only once. It was on an industrial estate north-west of Belfast, and it had been bloody. He thought about it as seldom as possible.

"That's what we need you to find out," the handler said. "Fegan was the last person to see McKenna alive. It seems he was also the last to see Caffola. A bit of a coincidence, don't you think?"

"Why don't you nab him, then?"

"He was questioned last night," the handler said. "Said he and Caffola got split up when they were running from the police."

Campbell snorted. "And you think he's above telling lies?"

"Our friend inside says McGinty believes him. Fegan's been keeping his head down for years. There's no reason he would turn on his friends now. Besides, there's nothing to actually tie him to McKenna's killing. All evidence says he was at home at the time, piss-drunk."

"Then who did kill McKenna?" Campbell leaned forward, following the blood-scent.

"McKenna was dealing with a Lithuanian, Petras Adamkus, on some people trafficking. A very shady character. The leadership had got wind of it and were putting pressure on McGinty to nix it. The last contact anyone had with McKenna was when he phoned a barman and told him he was meeting someone on business at the docks. Next thing we know, McKenna's brains are all over his windscreen, and Mr. Adamkus is nowhere to be found."

"But you're not satisfied with that," Campbell said.

"No, we're not," the handler said. "On the surface it looks like the party cleaned up their own mess over McKenna and Adamkus, and it suits them to blame the police for Caffola's death. We know Caffola wasn't happy with the political end of things, particularly the party supporting law and order. The party won't tolerate dissent in the ranks. They've done it in the past, taking out one of their own and blaming the security forces or the Loyalists, so it would be par for the course. Still, something doesn't add up."

"And you want me to find the missing pieces." Campbell sat back, burying a peal of excitement deep inside himself.

Public School shot the handler a condescending smile. "You said he was bright," he said, his voice oily. He peered around the headrest at Campbell. "We need you to go back to Belfast, tell them you're not happy with the dissidents, that you want to come back into the fold. See what you can find out about Fegan. If he's behind it, deal with him. Or tip the party off and let them do the honors."

"They'll tell me to fuck off," Campbell said. "They know I was running with McSorley's lot in Dundalk. McGinty won't like it. Have you no other mug to do it?"

He knew the answer.

"We've never had an agent as close to McGinty as you," Public School said. "Our friend inside will smooth things over for you. Besides, if I'm correctly informed, Mr. McGinty owes you a pretty big favor. You'll be welcomed with open arms. Trust me."

"Not for a second," Campbell said.

Public School gave him a hard look. "There'll be a generous bonus, of course. Fifteen thousand for going in. Another fifteen if you're able to resolve matters to everyone's satisfaction."

Campbell looked from Public School to the handler and back again. "Twenty-five first, twenty-five after. And I want what I'm owed for Dundalk. It wasn't my decision to leave."

"You're a mercenary bastard, aren't you?" Public School said, smiling. "All right. I'm sure you'll give us our money's worth."

"Every penny," Campbell said. He tried not to picture Gerry Fegan's blood-spattered face or the bodies at his feet.

13

Fegan stood among the gravestones, sweat drawing cool lines down his back. It had been the warmest spring he could remember. Black Mountain loomed over the graveyard, its craggy slopes bright and hard in the May sunlight. Father Coulter droned on by the graveside amid polite coughs and gentle weeping.

Fegan looked around the cemetery. It was a decent turnout, a few hundred, but not as many as he'd expected. Some had chosen to stay away. Fegan had heard grumblings, loud whispers, as the mourners gathered. Some called it an insult, a slap in the face. Certain men, certain politicians, should have been here to bear the coffin, to stand solemn-faced by the graveside. Their absence glared like a sore.

As Fegan scanned the crowds he watched for a flash of ash-blonde hair, a long and slender frame. She was here somewhere, but she was keeping her distance. And why did he care?

"God knows," he whispered to himself.

He took a handkerchief from his pocket and mopped his forehead and the back of his neck. His eyes were dry and heavy, and his skull was full of sand. The cops had kept him until nine this morning and he'd had barely two hours' sleep before he'd had to get up for the funeral. He savored the peace, but it didn't last long enough.

A haze of pain hovered around his temples, and shadows moved at the edge of his vision. He pushed them away. In this place, among these people, the shadows were sure to gather and pick out the living. Fegan was certain of it, and wondered how long he could hold them back.

Luck had been with him so far. But then, he'd always been lucky when it came to killing. He had a knack for it. Last night's riot had provided the perfect cover. If his luck held, it would even look like an accident. He had stashed the brick deep inside a bin five streets away, and then found the makeshift petrol-bomb factory. He took one of the bottles and used the fuel it contained to burn the gloves.

He had returned to the Springfield Road, wanting to be seen there, away from Caffola's body. McGinty was already negotiating with a senior police officer in view of the cameras, the man of peace restoring order to the troubled streets once more. Not for long, though. As soon as cops searching for petrol bombs discovered Caffola's body, all hell broke loose.

Fegan spent the rest of the night in the company of the police. Their questioning had been half-hearted and perfunctory. They did not grieve over the loss of Vincie Caffola, and Fegan doubted they would expend much effort on the investigation. He left the station unafraid of being charged with Caffola's killing.

Now, in the windswept graveyard, he covered his mouth to yawn. The pressure increased in his head and he shuffled his feet for balance. Chills washed through him, and he wrapped his arms tight around his midsection.

Father Coulter's service over, it was time for politics. A platform stood by the grave, and two men took up position holding a banner that read *Building for Peace, Building for the Future.* Another man joined them, holding a portable amplifier with a microphone. Fegan's stomach churned, knowing who would follow.

Paul McGinty, fifty-five years old, tall and handsome, stepped up to the podium. Low whispers crept through the crowd; it should have been one of the party leaders up there, eulogising the departed. Instead, McGinty faced the mourners, his countenance grim. The breeze tousled his hair as he waved for the applause to stop. The assistant raised the microphone to McGinty's mouth.

He greeted the assembly in forced Irish, as was the custom. Some embraced Ireland's native tongue, others did not. Fegan didn't care for words, English or Irish, so it meant little to him.

The formality over, McGinty began his speech.

"Comrades," he said in his carefully maintained West Belfast accent. "Today would have been a sad day without the news that came to us last night. But it is sadder still for the passing of Vincent Caffola, a tireless community worker and party official. And I have much to say about his passing, but ladies and gentlemen, I must first pay respect to the man who was buried here today.

"Michael McKenna was a great man." McGinty paused, his blue eyes taking in the cemetery as applause and isolated cheers rippled through it. "Michael McKenna was a great man because he believed in the fight for justice and equality on this island, and he fought for justice and equality every single day of his life. It is a tragedy for all who knew him that that goal was just within his reach when his life was taken."

Pain, bright and fiery, burst in Fegan's skull. "Christ," he hissed.

A few heads turned in his direction. He ignored them.

The shadows moved in from the edges of his vision. The pain flared again, brighter than before.

"Christ. Not now."

One of the funeral-goers, a stocky man in his mid-twenties, turned to scowl at him. Fegan stared back until the scowler turned away.

He closed his eyes and breathed deep, willing the pain and shadows to recede. A cry almost escaped him when he opened them and caught a glint of ash-blonde. He turned his head towards it, searching. There, another flash, between the black-clad bodies. He watched as she emerged from them, her face glowing in the spring sunlight. Her hair fluttered in the breeze, and she calmed it with her delicate hand. She caught him staring and froze.

Fegan's heart lurched in his chest as his eyes locked with Marie McKenna's. He wanted to raise his hand to wave, but it hung useless at his side. Time became an abstract notion, a meaningless measurement. Then her eyes slipped away from his, and time moved on. She retreated back to the throng, losing herself among them, sparing him only one glance over her shoulder.

Only when he'd lost her did Fegan realise the nine followers surrounded him. The pain dissolved, leaving a feathery lightness behind his eyes. The woman rocked her baby and smiled at him.

"What's happening to me?" he asked her.

The scowler turned to face him again. "Shut up and listen to the speech."

Scowler's friend tugged on his elbow and whispered in his ear, "That's Gerry Fegan."

Scowler's face greyed. "Sorry," he said, and turned back to the platform.

Fegan watched the followers move among the living, studying the mourners as if they were creatures in a zoo, sometimes touching them. The woman stayed close to Fegan. Her skin caught none of the sunlight beating down on the cemetery, and the breeze did not disturb her black hair. She smiled up at him again, her fine features showing none of the hate she must have felt.

Turn away and be quiet, Fegan thought. He ignored her and concentrated on McGinty's speech.

'Vincent Caffola's murder," he blustered, "And it can only be described as murder, throws us back to the bad old days. The days when the young people of our community lived in fear of the RUC. The bad old days when sectarianism was the law. When bigotry was the law. When instilling terror into the Nationalist and Republican people was the law."

A rumble of agreement rolled through the faithful. McGinty paused, letting it subside.

The woman turned her black eyes to the politician as the baby writhed in her arms.

"But I say no more," McGinty continued. "No more will our community stand by and allow such brutality to go unchallenged. Last night a good man, a tireless worker for his people, was viciously assaulted by the forces of so-called law and order. He was beaten until he passed out, his head split open, his wrist shattered, and left to choke to death on his own vomit. And still they say we should support an institution steeped in the traditions of oppression and fascism."

The crowd rumbled again, louder now. McGinty let it pass, his eyes marking the beat.

"But I say no more. I will not rest, my party will not rest, my community will not rest until those responsible are brought to justice. And that will be the test, comrades. When those witnesses I spoke to this morning, those witnesses who saw Vincent Caffola dragged into an alley by the forces of so-called law and order, when they go to the Police Ombudsman and tell what they saw, will justice be served?"

The crowd inhaled in expectation, and McGinty held his chin high. The audacity of the lie shouldn't have surprised Fegan so.

"And if it isn't . . ." McGinty's chest swelled as he sucked in air. "I WILL SAY NO MORE!"

An angry roar tore through the men and women; fists stabbed the air.

"I will say no more. The test will have been failed, and I will not hesitate to recommend the party withdraw its endorsement of the PSNI. We know the implications of that action, and believe me comrades, the decision will not be taken lightly. But that is the choice faced by the British Government, by the Ombudsman and by the police service that claims to represent all sections of our society."

Fegan wondered at McGinty's conceit, at his temerity in making such threats. The leadership would never have approved it, Fegan was positive. But then, he had no stomach for politics. Not any more. The cause he once killed for was long gone, swallowed up by the avarice of men like McGinty.

Sometimes he wondered if he had ever believed in any of it. As a boy, he'd seen the scars left on his community. He remembered the raids, the cops and the Brits breaking down doors. They pulled young men out of their beds to imprison them without trial at Long Kesh, the old RAF base that would later become the Maze, or on the prison ship at Belfast Docks. He remembered the anger, the hate, the poverty and the unemployment. The only way to have anything, to be anything, was to fight. Get the Brits out, seize power from the Unionists, take freedom at gunpoint. That's what they said, and he believed them.

But there was more than that. Fegan had been a solitary boy, quick with his fists but slow with words. When McKenna befriended him thirty years ago, it seemed to be a path to a bigger world. A world where he mattered. McKenna fought for Fegan to be brought along on the camping trips across the border, to the forests and lakes around Castleblaney, where he and the other boys played soldiers and shot air rifles at paper targets.

McKenna called it a youth club. Fegan's mother called it indoctrination.

Paul McGinty drove them on the first trip, picking them up in an old Volkswagen Camper. McGinty was not yet in his late twenties, but everyone knew his name. He had been interned at Long Kesh a few years before. He went in a snot-nosed thug, and came out six months later quoting Karl Marx and Che Guevara. He sat at the camp fire reading aloud from *Das Kapital* while the boys ate beans and passed cigarettes around.

Now McGinty stood dressed in a designer suit, about as far from the young revolutionary of Fegan's memory as a man could be.

Somewhere between Fegan's sentencing for the murder of three innocents in a Shankill butcher's shop and his release twelve years later, the world had changed. South of the border, in the Republic of Ireland, the old parochial ways vanished, washed away by money and the country's new vision of itself. The North had become the poor relation, the bastard child no one had the heart to send away. The struggle for the North's reunification with the rest of Ireland was rendered pointless.

The rest of Ireland didn't want them any more.

So the longing for freedom, whatever that was, had given way to the lust for money and power. The paramilitaries, Republican and Loyalist alike, maintained the façade of their political ideals, but Fegan knew the truth. Sometimes he wondered if, deep inside, he'd always known the true desires of men like Michael McKenna and Paul McGinty.

Fegan looked again to the nine followers wandering around him, the three Brits, the two Loyalists, the cop, the butcher, the woman and her baby. What was it for? To line McGinty's pockets?

The woman stared at McGinty, as did the butcher who died with her. Slowly they raised their hands, forming them into pistols. The woman turned to look at Fegan, her soft smiling lips like a knife wound.

She nodded.

Fegan shook his head, his mouth open.

She nodded again. Fegan wanted to turn and run. He closed his eyes and tried to force the followers back to the edge of his consciousness. Lightning arcs flashed between his temples. He gritted his teeth and pushed, but the shadows resisted. Air escaped his lungs in a slow hiss of defeat. He opened his eyes, resigned to the followers' presence.

But they had more to tell him.

Father Coulter approached.

The three Brits watched him move among the crowd, shaking hands with the mourners. The priest was a squat barrel of a man, with thick grey-black hair. From Sligo originally, Fegan thought. The Brits' arms stretched and aimed at Father Coulter. But why would they possibly want him?

Then, one memory finding another, Fegan knew. As the sun seared the back of his neck, he closed his eyes and remembered.

The family, three girls and their parents, squealed in unison when the blast rattled their windows. They were safely tied to one another upstairs, well away from any glass that might shatter. Fegan and Coyle had made sure of that. As the rumble faded, rolling off across the rooftops, a silence fell. Then moaning came from the street outside. Moaning grew to crying, and crying grew to screaming.

Fegan peered out through the crack in the door. He looked at Coyle. "You didn't get them all."

"Fuck," Coyle said. "What do we do?"

"You tell me. You planted it, you triggered it."

"Do we go and finish them?" Coyle's voice edged on panic.

Fegan took the pistol from his pocket and held it out butt first.

"Fuck, no!" Coyle said. "I can't do that. You do it."

"Christ," Fegan said. "You're grand when you're fifty feet away, but you don't like getting close."

"I did my bit."

"Not too well." Fegan nodded to the door. "Listen to them."

"They must've split up. How am I supposed to know they'd split up?"

"They do three-and-threes all the time. You should've waited till the first three was past and the other was coming up. You would've got all of them."

"Christ, what do we do?" Coyle pleaded again.

Fegan sighed and pulled the balaclava down over his face, leaving just his eyes and mouth exposed. Coyle did the same and followed Fegan to the street. They walked quickly towards the drifting smoke at the corner. There the remains of a litter bin were scattered across the road and the window of the shop it belonged to was blown inward. Street lights reflected off the glittering fragments of glass and sweet wrappers.

Fegan didn't pay any attention to them. Instead he looked at the six bodies on the ground. Three of the British soldiers were dead, but three still jerked and shivered. Two of them had even escaped with their limbs intact. They might have been called lucky, had it not been for Fegan. The other survivor had lost most of his right arm – he was the screamer – and shock had now reduced him to quivering silence. It was a small bomb, designed for maximum casualties within a localised area, with minimal wider damage to the surrounding property.

A woman scampered out of the house next to the shop, pointing to her living-room window. "Look what you did! I'll be hoovering up glass for a month." She noticed the men on the ground and crossed herself. "Oh, Jesus, them poor boys. God love them."

Fegan aimed the pistol at her forehead. "Go back inside," he said.

The woman did as she was told without another word. Fegan readied himself to finish the job, but he and Coyle both spun on their heels when they heard the rapid slap-slap of shoe leather from behind them.

"Oh, no," Father Coulter said as he slowed to a stop, breathless. "Oh, no, no, no. Oh, God."

"We're not finished here, Father," Fegan said. He moved from body to body, kicking the soldiers' weapons away.

"Let me give them their Last Rites, for God's sake," the priest said.

"When we're finished."

Father Coulter stepped closer to the nearest three, his eyes widening as he looked from soldier to soldier. "These men are alive," he said.

"You'd better go, now, Father," Fegan said. "Come back in a few minutes."

"No," Father Coulter said. "These men can be saved. I can't let them die, no matter who they are."

"Come on, Father," Coyle said, 'you hate the Brits as much as anyone. All those times you took the boys in, hid them, gave them alibis."

Father Coulter's mouth opened and closed for a few seconds. "No," he said, 'that's not true."

Fegan shot Coyle a warning look. He turned back to the priest. "All right, Father, they haven't seen our faces. We'll let them live if that's what you want. But you'll have to explain why you stopped it when you're asked."

Fegan stepped in close to Father Coulter and whispered, "You'll have to tell McGinty when he comes calling, and believe me, he *will* call. You're a brave man, Father Coulter, but are you that brave?"

"I . . . I . . . I . . ." Father Coulter stammered. Something forced his stare to the ground. "Oh, Christ."

"Please," one of the Brits hissed, tugging at the priest's trouser leg, blood trickling from his ears, his helmet gone. "Help me," he whispered through blackened lips.

Father Coulter jerked his leg away and took a step back. Fegan chambered a round and pressed the pistol to the back of the soldier's skull. "Your choice, Father."

"Jesus, Gerry, quit it," Coyle said.

"Shut your fucking mouth," Fegan said. "If he wants to judge me he better be ready to go all the way."

He turned back to the priest. "You hear that, Father? You stand there in chapel every Saturday night, every Sunday morning, telling us to turn from sin. All the time you're taking handouts from McGinty to keep your mouth shut, to see nothing, to hear nothing, to turn away and be quiet. And the next Saturday, the next Sunday, you're telling us to take the other way. There's always another way, right? Now's your chance to prove it. Tell me to take the other way and I'll do it. But you better be ready to stand over it. You better be ready to answer to the boys who run these streets."

Father Coulter blinked at him. "Please, this isn't . . . it's not . . ."

Fegan pressed his pistol's muzzle harder against the back of the soldier's head. "What's it to be, Father? Have you the guts to practise what you preach? Or will you shut your eyes and say nothing like you always do?"

As the Brit held out his hands, as he whimpered on the ground, the priest's face went slack. He looked to Fegan once, and then looked to the ground. He turned and started walking.

"No!" The soldier tried to crawl after him. "No! No, no, please! Help!"

Father Coulter's stride was broken only slightly by the booming discharge as it resonated through the street.

Fegan kept his eyes closed until McGinty's speech was finished. When he opened them, she was there, facing him.

"Hello," Marie McKenna said.

Fegan blinked, unable to respond. The followers lost themselves amongst the thinning crowd.

"Sorry, I didn't mean to scare you," she said.

"It's okay." He scrambled for something else to say but could find nothing.

"Are you going to the house?" she asked.

"Yes," he said. "Just for a while."

"Do you need a lift?"

"No, I'm all right," he lied.

"Oh. Well, I'll maybe see you there." Marie smiled and left him among the gravestones.

Fegan stood in the May heat, waiting for the crowd to dissolve. When he was sure she had left, he began walking to the cemetery gates.

In his younger days Fegan had been glad of women, and the ease with which he could work his way into their beds. Some of the lads, like McKenna, had the words to charm them. But Fegan had never needed that; his reputation was enough. He knew they relished the danger of it, and he was happy to use them. Since leaving the Maze he'd had only a few encounters, moments here and there to scratch the itch, but that was all.

Marie McKenna troubled him. She was clearly not to be toyed with, but he didn't know how else to deal with women.

"What's happening to me?" Fegan asked himself. The isolation of his voice sounded strange among the gravestones. He swallowed his questions, put his head down, and kept walking. He stopped at the gates. A long silver car waited there, its engine running.

The tinted rear window rolled down and Paul McGinty, smooth-skinned and handsome, smiled out at him. "Hop in, Gerry," he said.

14

When the Northern Ireland Office and the security forces worked in unison, they could be impressively efficient. *A pity they don't do it more often*, Campbell thought as he tossed the holdall on the bed. They'd organised a flat in the Holylands, the warren of streets called so in honor of their names – Palestine Street, Jerusalem Street, Damascus Street – not their inhabitants. It was a smart move, putting him here. The area was almost entirely populated by students attending Queen's University, the sprawling complex of Victorian and modern buildings at the bottom of the Malone Road. The students came and went at all hours of the day and night. They were noisy and careless of their environment. Campbell could slip in and out without drawing attention.

He went to the window of the small living room. He was on the top floor of a house on University Street, just off Botanic Avenue, over-looking a church. Students, shoppers and workers slipped past one another on the pavement below. His rusted Ford Focus sat at the curb across the way. He'd picked it up in a retail park just south of the city. An extra mobile phone and a Glock 23 were waiting for him in the glove box, the phone never to leave the flat and only to be used to dial one number.

It had almost broken his heart to swap his BMW for the Focus. The journey from Dundalk to Armagh, then up the motorway, was the first time he'd driven the Z4 in a month. He had to remind himself it was this work that paid for the car. But then, why do it if he never got to enjoy the spoils?

That was a good question, one he asked himself constantly. He was thirty-eight years old and had been an impostor for the last fifteen. He could admit a perverse pleasure in living a lie. The permanent risk of discovery had a strange sweetness. There was certainly a dark thrill in watching those around him accept a counterfeit, but surely there was more to it than that?

He had spent many nights staring at one ceiling or another, turning it over in his mind, but every time he came close to the answer he looked away. One day he might have the strength to see that part of himself.

When he joined the Black Watch Royal Highland Regiment at the age of twenty, David Campbell had no concept of where his life would lead him. He was following the path of many boys from Glasgow, and knew full well he'd end up in Belfast, patrolling the streets, dodging bricks and bottles. The first time a woman spat on his boots, he had stopped in his tracks, staring at her in shock.

"Fuck away off home," she'd said.

"Ignore her, lad," the sergeant called from behind.

Belfast was a different place now. When Campbell approached the city just an hour before, he was impressed by the number of cranes dotting the skyline. These metallic signals of prosperity towered over every corner of Belfast; in the west where the Republicans' power was strongest; in the east where the Loyalists held sway; in the south where the city's wealthy had always lived; in the north where Protestant and Catholic fought over every inch of ground.

The city's invisible borders remained the same as when Campbell first walked its streets holding a rifle eighteen years ago. The same lowlifes still fed off the misery they created, deepening the divisions wherever they could. The same hatreds still bubbled under the surface. But the city had grown fat, learning to mask its scars when necessary and show them when advantageous.

He turned from the window, went back to the sole bedroom, and dumped the holdall's contents into a drawer. A flash of color caught his eye. There, among the worn clothes, pistol and loose rounds, lay his old Red Hackle. He lifted it, feeling the plume between his fingers. He hadn't been able to wear the Black Watch's traditional insignia for long.

Campbell was just five days past his twenty-third birthday, with less than three years of service, when he had been called to see the Commanding Officer. Lieutenant Colonel Hanson was a gruff man with a deeply lined face, who instilled fear into all under his command. Campbell's chest fluttered as he knocked on the door.

"Enter," a voice barked from inside, the Scots accent thick and hard.

Campbell opened the door, stepped inside, closed the door without showing the colonel his back, marched five paces, snapped his heels together and saluted. The colonel casually returned the gesture from behind his desk. Campbell kept his eyes straight ahead, ignoring the third man present.

"You may sit." The colonel indicated the empty chair facing him. Campbell did so.

"Congratulations on your promotion, Corporal," Colonel Hanson said.

"Thank you, sir."

"I'll get straight to the point. Have you heard of Fourteen Intelligence Company?"

"I've heard rumors, sir," Campbell said. His nervousness intensified. Fourteen Intelligence Company was undercover, annexed to the SAS. It didn't officially exist, but it was no secret. Fourteen Int did the dirty work, the stuff no one owned up to, the kind of things ordinary people go to prison for.

"Then you'll know Fourteen Int is charged with intelligence gathering, and plays a vital role in our operations in Northern Ireland. It works closely with, but independently of, the Royal Ulster Constabulary, Special Branch, MI5, Force Research Unit and regular Army. It handles agents and informants in all the paramilitary groups in the Province and has saved countless lives." Major Hanson indicated the third man, seated to his right. "This is Major Ross."

"Good morning, Corporal," Major Ross said. He wore no uniform but was instead casually dressed. His accent was Birmingham, or maybe Dudley.

"Good morning, sir," Campbell said. Sweat trickled down his ribs. Major Ross lifted a file from the desk and opened it. "David Patrick

Campbell. Born in 1969 to a mixed-religion marriage, rare in Glasgow, and raised Catholic. Do you practise?"

"Sir?"

"Your religion. Do you go to Mass?"

"Not since I was at school, sir." Campbell kept his back stiff, his hands on his knees.

"You left school at sixteen, no real qualifications, despite having above-average intelligence. Various menial jobs, a few stretches on the dole, before you joined the Black Watch. Why did you sign up?"

Campbell shifted in his seat. "There was nothing else to do, sir. No job. No future."

Major Ross smiled. "I see. And what did your parents make of it?"

Campbell stared at Major Ross while he searched for a lie.

"Answer the major," Colonel Hanson said.

A lie wouldn't come, so Campbell was left only the truth. "I wasn't speaking with them at the time, sir."

"And why was that?" Major Ross asked.

"We'd had a falling-out a couple of years before, sir."

"Over what?"

"I'd rather not say, sir."

Colonel Hanson's face reddened. "You'll answer the question, corporal."

"I had some trouble with the law, sir. My parents didn't take it very well." Campbell looked down at his hands.

"Some trouble with the law," Major Ross echoed with a sly smile. "That's one way to put it. You kicked the shit out of a nightclub doorman is another way."

Campbell looked the major in the eye. "The charges were withdrawn, sir."

"Yes – very conveniently for you, several witnesses changed their stories. You wouldn't have had anything to do with that, would you, Corporal?"

"No, sir."

Major Ross looked back to the file. "Your record since joining the Black Watch has been good, but not exceptional. With your brains you should have been corporal a year ago. You're a quick thinker, you're tough, but you lack discipline. I'm told you're good in a scrap. In fact, I'm told you've got a serious mean streak. You came close to a court martial last year after assaulting a protester at a Loyalist parade. Care to comment?"

"It was self-defence, sir. The charges were dropped."

"Conveniently for you, yet again." Major Ross smiled and placed the file back on the desk. "You've no family that you're in contact with, and no friends outside this barracks, correct?"

"Yes, sir." Campbell watched the two officers share a glance. "Can I ask what this is about, sir?"

Colonel Hanson went to shout some admonishment, but Major Ross raised a hand to silence him. "I want you to come and work for me," he said.

So in the following months Campbell began to spend days at a time in England, at RAF Cosford and the Commando Training Center in Lympstone, being brutalised for the good of the country. When he flew back to Belfast he frequented some of the bars he and his colleagues had been warned to avoid. He wore a Glasgow Celtic shirt to pubs where matches were being screened, cheering loudest when they scored against Glasgow Rangers. An insider in Fourteen Int's pay introduced him to some men, vouching for him. He answered questions about his Black Watch regiment, about the patrols he walked in. When they got more specific, when they asked about times and dates, he played coy. When he was discharged from the Black Watch a few months later for a contrived disciplinary breach, he grew less shy with the details. He worked his way into the enemy's ranks, a little deeper every day, while once a week he met a handler in a car park or a country lane and reported on what he'd learned. Occasionally he would check a savings account, opened under another name, to see he had been well paid.

The first time he had to kill to protect his cover was difficult. They'd warned him it would happen eventually, but even so, the image of executing his old sergeant still woke him in the night, even fifteen years later. It was the wild hope in Sergeant Hendry's eyes that burned in Campbell's memory. Not the begging, not the weeping, but the moment Hendry recognised him, believing he was saved. Hendry's hope died an instant before he did, when he watched Campbell's finger tighten on the trigger.

Campbell shivered, suddenly cold despite the sun breaking through the bedroom window. The church bell signalled two o'clock. It was time to go. Time he went to McKenna's bar to meet his contact.

15

McGinty's imported Lincoln Town Car floated along the lower Falls Road like a magic carpet. The boys had swapped rumors about how much it cost to bring over from America. They said the leadership considered it distasteful, a vulgar display unbefitting the current climate. A glass screen separated Fegan and McGinty from Declan Quigley, the politician's driver.

"You never got a driving licence, did you, Gerry?" McGinty asked.

"No," Fegan said.

"Me neither. I can't afford to take a chance on driving without one these days, so . . ." McGinty waved a manicured hand at the car's black leather interior. "As needs must," he said.

Fegan felt as if he was in a steel cocoon. The tinted windows appeared black from outside, and he imagined the car could withstand any attack from bullet or bomb.

"You wanted to see me," he said.

"We'll get to that," McGinty said. Fegan could see his rictus smile from the corner of his eye. "I was hoping we could catch up a wee bit first."

"All right," Fegan said.

McGinty patted Fegan's knee. "So, what's the story? What's been going on?"

"Nothing much."

"How's the Community Development job going?"

"I cash the checks."

"You're entitled to it, Gerry. You gave us twelve years. We won't forget it. That job will keep paying as long as you want it, no questions asked."

Fegan spared McGinty a sideways glance. "Thanks," he said.

"Shame about Michael, eh?" McGinty said.

"Yeah," Fegan said.

"And Vincie Caffola now, too."

Fegan kept his eyes on the glass divider and the road beyond. They passed the right turn into Fallswater Parade, moving further away from McKenna's mother's house. The gable walls were painted over with murals, propaganda messages written as art. "You really think the peelers did it?" Fegan asked.

"Maybe," McGinty said. "That's my public position, anyway."

"You said you had witnesses."

"Of course I do, Gerry." McGinty gave a short laugh. "Of course I do."

He placed his hand on Fegan's knee and kept it there. "The thing is . . . look at me, Gerry."

Fegan closed his eyes for a moment, then opened them, turning to face McGinty.

"The thing is," McGinty continued, 'somebody might have done me a favor, all things considered."

"How?" Fegan asked.

McGinty smiled. "Well, Michael, God rest him, was getting mixed up in things he shouldn't have. See, times have changed. Some of us – not all, but enough of us – want Stormont to succeed. On all sides. Us, the Brits, even the Unionists. This is a different world. The bombs won't work any more. The dissidents put an end to that in Omagh. The people won't tolerate violence like they used to. Then 9/11 came along. The Americans don't look at armed struggle the same way. Used to be we could sell them the romance of it, call ourselves freedom fighters, and they loved it. The money just rolled in, all those Irish-Americans digging in their pockets for the old country. They don't buy it any more. We've got peace now, whether we like it or not."

Fegan watched the murals drift past, images and slogans, portraits of Republican heroes next to expressions of solidarity with Palestine and Cuba. Another mural declared Catalonia was not part of Spain. Fegan couldn't say if it was or it wasn't, but he sometimes wondered what it had to do with anyone on the Falls. Then there was an image of George Bush sucking oil from a skull-strewn Iraqi battlefield, declaring it *America's Greatest Failure.*

McGinty continued, "We're walking a tightrope, and we can't go upsetting the balance. Sure, the Brits allow us a certain leeway these days – you know, turn a blind eye to keep things stable – but we're pulling away from all the shady stuff. We have to. We can still embark on our little enterprises, turn a few pound, so long as we're careful. So long as we keep it quiet. But I'm in a difficult position now. I've put the years and the work in, along with everybody else. I put my neck out just like the rest of them, and I want my share of the rewards. But if I want my place at Stormont, then I have to be clean. Spotless, you understand."

McGinty's smile dissolved. "But Michael had become a problem. I told him to keep out of trouble, that any shit he got into would stick to me, but he didn't listen. People smuggling, for Christ's sake. The Liths were bringing in girls from the South, and Michael was dipping his toe in the water. Fair enough, there was good money there, but Jesus, kids? I mean fifteen-, sixteen-year-olds. Even the Brits wouldn't let that go. He should've left all that to the Loyalists; they're too stupid to know any better. If he'd been caught he could have done me a lot of damage. The leadership was concerned about him. They went to the old man about it."

Fegan's thigh tensed and he ground his shoe against the Lincoln's carpeting as McGinty squeezed his knee.

"And then there's Vincie. Now, don't get me wrong, Vincie was a good volunteer. Best interrogator we ever had in Belfast. But he was mouthing off, how he didn't like us sitting at Stormont, how he didn't like us supporting the peelers, how we were selling out. And you know how the old man is, Gerry. Bull O'Kane doesn't like dissent in the ranks. It unsettles people. I was called down to the farm just last weekend, and he told me to sort things out. Clean house, you know? Get everyone in line or I'd be out."

Fegan knew the farm he meant, a few acres of land and a modest house that straddled the border between Northern Ireland and the Republic, where County Armagh became County Monaghan.

O'Kane ran his empire from that remote bolt-hole, and Fegan some-times heard whispers of how much cash the old man turned over. Millions, some said, maybe hundreds of millions. He buried it in property investment all over the world – England, Spain, Portugal and America – and kept layers of paperwork between him and the money.

These days, most of that money came from the endless demand for cheap fuel. The Bull ran dozens of laundering plants on farms along the border, each churning out millions of gallons of chemically stripped agricultural diesel – government-subsidised fuel intended for cash-strapped farmers. This diesel was processed, cleaned of its dye, and resold to petrol stations, motorists, hauliers and anyone else who wanted to get their hands on cheap fuel. Bull O'Kane now fought for Ireland by poisoning its countryside with chemical waste.

"How is the Bull these days?" Fegan asked.

"Oh, you know Bull," McGinty said. "He's kicking the arse of seventy, and he could still take any man came near him. Still as smart as a fox. You only met him a few times, didn't you?"

"Twice," Fegan said, his mouth drying at the memory. He swallowed. "It was a long time ago."

"Anyway," McGinty said, 'the point is if someone had a personal thing, some score to settle with Michael McKenna and Vincie Caffola, they just might have done me a favor in the process. They might have done my cleaning-up for me, so to speak. Do you understand, Gerry?"

Fegan remained silent as McGinty's hand patted his knee again.

"The fact is Michael McKenna and Vincie Caffola were becoming liabilities. The party's no poorer without them. Now I've got an excuse to see off some foreigners who were eating into my business, and a new stick to beat the peelers with. Who knows, if I can convince the media the cops killed Vincie, we might be able to squeeze the Brits with it."

"I see," Fegan said. He could see both their reflections in the glass facing them. His own face appeared skeletal next to the other man's.

"You were always smarter than you let on, Gerry," McGinty said. "You could have done well for yourself if you'd wanted to. Anyway, my point is this: if someone unknown to us, a man working alone, had some bone to pick with Michael McKenna or Vincie Caffola, I might be prepared to overlook his transgression. Just this once. As it happens, he's done me a good turn, so we can let it go."

McGinty took his hand away from Fegan's knee and draped it around his shoulder. "But that's all. So far, no harm done. But no more, or I might have to take action. One thing, though." McGinty leaned in close, his breath warm on Fegan's ear. "He better not take me for an arsehole. Ever."

Fegan cleared his throat. "I'm sure he won't."

"Not if he's half the man you are," McGinty said as he took his arm from around Fegan's shoulder. "Now, to business. I'd like to see more of you around, Gerry. You always were a good fella to have about. There's always work for a man like you. I need to know who my friends are in these trying times. Who I can trust, you know?"

"I try to keep myself to myself these days," Fegan said.

"Fair enough, but you can't become a hermit on us. It'd do you good to be active, you know, shake away the cobwebs."

"I suppose."

"And the drink, Gerry. You've got to knock that on the head. I've been hearing stories about you lately. About you sitting in McKenna's bar, getting hammered. I hear you're talking to yourself."

"I've been cutting back these last few days," Fegan said, truthfully.

"Glad to hear it. The drink killed my father. Yours too, if I remember right."

Fegan turned his head away, looking to the street outside. Kids rode bicycles in the sunshine. The Lincoln turned right, then right again, doubling back towards Fallswater Parade. "Yeah," he said.

"So, anyway, I've a wee job for you."

Fegan turned back to the politician.

"Don't worry," McGinty said, smiling. "It's nothing heavy. Thank God, very little is nowadays. Just a message I need you to deliver."

Fegan thought about it for a moment and said, "All right."

"Marie McKenna, Michael's niece."

Fegan's fingernails bit his palm. "Yeah."

"Seems you're on friendly terms with her. She gave you a lift yesterday."

"I don't know her." Fegan said. "Not really. I never talked to her before."

"Well, she offended a lot of people, shacking up with a cop like that." McGinty watched the houses, the murals and the flags sweep past his window. "Having a kid to him and all. There's a lot of people would like to make their displeasure known to her. But Michael made sure she was left alone for her mother's sake. Now Michael's gone, it might not be so easy to keep them away."

"They split up years ago," Fegan said. "Why would anyone care now?"

"People have long memories, Gerry. Especially when it's somebody else's sin. We remember Bloody Sunday. We talk about it like it was yesterday. But we forget about the people who died in the days before and the days after. It's human nature."

I remember my sins, thought Fegan. *They follow me everywhere.* He wondered if McGinty remembered his.

"I'd like you to have a wee word with her," the politician said. "No threats. Subtle, like. Advise her she might be wise to move on. Across the water, maybe."

"You want me to tell her at the house?" Fegan asked.

"Oh, no, not at Michael's mother's. She has a flat off the Lisburn Road, on Eglantine Avenue. Call by there later and have a chat with her. Like I said, keep it friendly. All right?"

Fegan couldn't return McGinty's smile. "All right," he said.

16

The house on Fallswater Parade brimmed with black-garbed friends and family, but not as densely packed as the day before. Today, Fegan was able to breathe. He tried not to stay in one spot too long, lest some old acquaintance should corner him and grind him down with stories of past days. He filched a can of beer from the table in the living room and slipped out to the hall.

McGinty and Father Coulter were in the house somewhere, eating sausage rolls and slapping the faithful's shoulders, but Fegan avoided them for fear of seeing shadows.

A moment of indecision gripped him. He had to stay a respectable amount of time, just for appearances, but where could he drink his beer in peace? Upstairs, in one of the bedrooms? No, that would be intrusive. The yard would be full of smokers. Where, then?

He remembered the alcove under the stairs. There was a telephone table with a seat in there. He could slip in, sit down in the semi-darkness, and if anyone questioned him he could say he was just resting his feet.

Fegan squeezed past a group of men and ducked into the small alcove. When he realised Marie McKenna had the same idea, and was already perched on the seat, he could only stare at her, his back bent, his head pressed against the underside of the stairs.

"Hello," she said. He couldn't tell if her eyes glittered with bemusement or fright. Maybe both.

"Hello," he said. "I was just . . . ah . . ."

"Finding a place to hide," she said, small lines forming around her grey-blue eyes as she smiled. "Me too."

She held a glass of white wine. Lipstick smudged its rim. Fegan wondered what it tasted like.

"I'll find somewhere else," he said, backing out.

"No, there's room," she said. She shifted further along the seat, leaving space for Fegan's wiry body. He hesitated for just a second, then slowly lowered himself to rest beside her.

"I wanted to talk to you, anyway," Marie said. "To apologise."

"What for?" He opened the can of Harp lager and took a sip. The fizz burned his tongue.

"For being all . . . well, weird, yesterday. I said some things I shouldn't have." The wine rippled in her glass as her hand shook.

"It doesn't matter," he said. "Everyone does things they wish they hadn't."

"True," she said. He caught the residue of a smile as he turned to look at her.

"Why did you come here?" Fegan asked. The question was out of his mouth before he could catch it. He looked back to the beer can in his hand.

Marie stiffened beside him. "What?"

Nothing. That's what he would have said if he wasn't losing the remnants of his mind. Instead, he said, "They don't want you, but you came here anyway. And yesterday. Why did you do that?"

She breathed in and out through her nose three times before saying, "Because it's my family. For better or worse, it's where I came from. I won't be driven away, no matter how hard they try."

"That doesn't make sense," he said. "If they don't want you, why bother?"

"Do you read much?" she asked.

He turned back to her. "No. Why?"

"There's a little book called *Yosl Rakover Talks to God*. It turned out to be a hoax, but it appeared to be written by a Jewish man hiding from the Nazis in the Warsaw Ghetto. The most awful things have happened to him, but in the end, he stands up to God. He says, 'God, you can do what you want to me, you can degrade me, you can kill my friends, you can kill my family, but you won't make me hate you, no matter what.' "

Marie gave a long sigh. "Hate's a terrible thing. It's a wasteful, stupid emotion. You can hate someone with all your heart, but it'll never do them a bit of harm. The only person it hurts is you. You can spend your days hating, letting it eat away at you, and the person you hate will go on living just the same. So, what's the point? They may hate me, but I won't hate them back. They're my family, and I won't let their hate push me away."

Fegan studied her skin's tiny diamond patterns stretching across the back of her hands, the fine ridges of the bones, the faint blue lines of her veins. "I'd like to read that book," he said.

"Well, you can go to the library. I don't have it any more. When I was seventeen, my father showed my copy to Uncle Michael. Uncle Michael made me tear it up. He said it was Jewish propaganda. He told me to remember what the Jews were doing to the Palestinians. I remember thinking it strange at the time. He didn't say the Israelis; he said the Jews. I don't think he'd ever met a Jewish person in his life, but still he hated them. I just didn't understand it. Funny, I hadn't thought about that book in years, but I've been thinking about it ever since Uncle Michael died."

A minute of quiet passed, both of them sipping their drinks, before Marie said, "Seeing as we're asking difficult questions, why did you come in here to hide?"

"Too many people here I used to know," Fegan said. "I can't listen to them."

"You're a respected man around here," she said.

"They don't respect me. They're afraid of me."

"I'm not afraid of you."

Fegan plucked at the beer can's ring-pull. "You know what I did?"

"I've heard things," she said. Her shoulder brushed against his and he shivered. "Listen, I've known men like you all my life. My uncles, my father, my brothers. I know the other side, too, the cops and the Loyalists. I've talked to them all in my job. Everyone has their piece of guilt to carry. You're not that special."

The last words were softened with kindness.

"No, I'm not," he said. Somehow, he liked that idea.

"Anyway, I don't think you're like that now," she said. "People can change. They have to, or there's no hope for this place. Are you sorry for what you did?"

"Yeah."

"It shows. On your face. In your eyes. You can't hide it."

Fegan wanted to look at her, but he couldn't. He ran his finger around the can's opening, feeling it bite at his fingertip. Words danced just beyond his grasp.

"I should go," he said, raising himself off the seat. He stepped out of the cubby-hole and turned, ducking down to see her. "Can I come and see you later?"

Marie's mouth opened slightly as she considered it. "I don't know," she said. "I was going to take my wee girl out for a walk after tea, if the weather stays clear."

"I could come with you."

She closed her eyes and inhaled. After an eternity, she opened them again and said, "Okay. You can come with us. I live on Eglantine Avenue."

She told Fegan the house number. He smiled once and left her in the alcove.

17

The Minister of State for Northern Ireland had been sitting in the back of the car for more than twenty minutes, and they had travelled less than two hundred yards. Compton and the driver sat up front, staring at the back of a bus. The constant blaring of horns and rumble of London traffic did nothing to ease Edward Hargreaves's headache. The vibration of his phone only soured his mood further.

The voice told him the Chief Constable was on the line.

"Geoff," Hargreaves said.

"Good afternoon, Minister," Pilkington said.

"Please tell me we're making progress on the Belfast situation."

"Some. Our colleagues have sent a man in to see what's going on."

"And?" Hargreaves asked, impatient. The car advanced another five feet closer to Downing Street. "I'm meeting the Secretary and the PM shortly, and I need something to tell them. Was it this Fegan character?"

"We simply don't know, Minister. Circumstances point to him, but McGinty says otherwise. He says the Lithuanians got McKenna, and my men got Caffola."

"*Did* your men get him?" Hargreaves asked. He knew the answer, but found amusement in irking the Chief Constable.

"Certainly not, Minister. He's using it for propaganda, trying to better his position in the party by grabbing headlines. He gave a speech a couple of hours ago saying he'll recommend the party withdraws its support for the PSNI if some of my men don't swing for it. The brass neck, as if it was up to him."

Hargreaves couldn't help but smile at Pilkington's predicament. "Yes, I've got a transcript in front of me now. He's a clever bastard, that McGinty. And the Unionists are already making noises about walking away from Stormont. This needs to be nipped in the bud, Chief Constable. If our man can't get to the bottom of it, you'll have to be prepared for sacrifices."

A second or two of silence passed before Pilkington said, "Are you suggesting I allow my men to be charged with Caffola's killing when I know they're innocent? Minister, let me make it clear: I will not throw good police officers to the wolves for the sake of political expediency. If you think—"

"How noble of you," Hargreaves interrupted. "Political expediency is our stock in trade, Geoff; you should know that better than anyone. How many little transgressions have you let slide to keep the wheels turning, hmm? How many robberies have gone unsolved on your watch for want of a little effort? How many punishment beatings have been ignored for the sake of a quiet life?"

"Minister, I really don't—"

"Don't lecture me about expediency, Geoff." Hargreaves felt his smile stretch his dry lips. "How many of your men would be standing trial if not for expediency?"

Pilkington sniffed. "I won't dignify that with an answer, Minister."

"Sacrifices," Hargreaves said. "Everyone must make sacrifices for the greater good. Keep me informed."

He hung up without waiting for a response.

18

Davy Campbell stood at the bar, alone, conscious of being the only man here not wearing a black suit. The sideways glances had started as soon as he entered McKenna's, murmurs passing from person to person, heads nodding in his direction. They recognised him; they knew he was the one who had drifted to the dissidents in Dundalk. He waited for a challenge, some demand to know what he was doing back in Belfast. None came, perhaps out of respect for the departed. Had he been a stranger, he would have been tackled within seconds of entering. This wasn't the sort of pub you just dropped into for a quick drink as you passed by. Peace only went so far.

The late Michael McKenna's bar might have been a dive, a place for lowlifes to swill, but there was no denying they served a decent pint. Campbell raised the pint of dark Smithwick's ale to his mouth, and its cool smoothness slicked the back of his throat.

"You've some fucking nerve, boy."

Campbell didn't turn his head. Eddie Coyle's reflection stared back at him from the grubby mirror behind the bar. He stood a full six inches shorter than Campbell, his thinning blond hair standing in tufts above his round face. Campbell wiped foam from his beard.

"What are you doing here?" Coyle asked. "You get fed up playing toy soldiers with them cunts in Dundalk?"

"Something like that," Campbell said.

Coyle stepped closer. "What, you think now Michael's gone you can just waltz back in?"

"I'm just having a pint, Eddie, all right?" Campbell turned to face Coyle. "You want to have one with me, dead on. If not, then fuck off out of my face."

Coyle's eyes narrowed. "You what?"

"You heard me." Campbell placed his glass on the bar.

A smile crept along Coyle's lips, wrinkling his blotchy cheeks. "Did you just tell me to fuck off?"

"I think that was the gist of it, Eddie, yes." Campbell smiled. "If you don't want to take a drink with me, then fuck off. Clear enough?"

He was aware of the punch coming even before the man who threw it. Campbell had learned many years ago that to best a man in a physical struggle, all one need do is keep one's balance while throwing the other's. Coyle made the simple error of sacrificing balance for power, and all Campbell had to do was raise his left forearm, guiding that power past him, and Coyle's weight would follow. Like so.

Coyle sprawled into a line of bar stools and landed on his back, cursing. He found his feet and came again. Once more, Campbell diverted the blow, sending Coyle to mash his chest against the bar. Coyle turned, ready to swing again, but Campbell was quicker. He got hold of Coyle's blond hair with his left hand and formed a fist with his right. He slammed it into Coyle's upturned face until his knuckles were slick with red. Campbell released his grip on Coyle's hair to let his chin bounce off the bar with a satisfying thump.

The rest came at him then. Campbell didn't know how many, but a wall of black-suited men collapsed on him. He felt one hand grab his hair, another his ear, while a pair gripped the lapels of his denim jacket. The fists raining down on him blocked one another, rendering them all but harmless, as he brought his forearms up to cover himself.

"Hey, hey, hey!" A small body squeezed itself between Campbell and the angry mob. "Leave him! He's with me."

"But look what he did to Eddie," one of them protested.

"Eddie started it," Patsy Toner said. "Now leave him alone. Right?"

"But—"

"Leave it!" Toner pointed a stubby finger at the nearest of them. They backed away, grumbling and cursing. Toner grabbed Campbell's elbow. "Come on, for fuck's sake."

Campbell grinned as Toner dragged him out to the street, his senses buzzing.

"What the fuck are you at?" Toner asked, his watery eyes incredulous, his mouth gaping under his thick moustache.

"He was asking for it," Campbell said.

Toner straightened his black tie. "Jesus Christ, Davy. Eddie Coyle's an arsehole, everyone knows that, but you don't beat the shit out of him in front of his mates. Not if you're looking to make friends around here." He wagged a finger at Campbell. "Just remember I'm taking a big risk for you."

Campbell inclined his head towards the Jaguar at the curb. "That yours?"

"Aye," Toner said, seeming to grow a full inch taller.

Campbell wiped blood from his knuckles with a handkerchief. "Well, quit yapping and take me to McGinty."

McGinty's jacket was slung across the back of a chair, his tie loosened, and his sleeves rolled up. He stood in the bereaved mother's living room as if it were his own house, and he the master of it. The politician's face hardened and slackened as he spoke on a mobile phone. He took a last drag on his cigarette, then threw it into the fireplace.

Campbell and Toner waited in the doorway, watching. Toner leaned close and whispered, "Looks like there's trouble. I think the higher-ups didn't like what he said at the funeral."

McGinty snapped his phone closed before Campbell could reply, and scowled as he waved Toner over. They both glanced back at Campbell as they spoke, but theirs weren't the only eyes on the prodigal Scot. The debris scattered around the room told of many people having been here a short while ago, but now only a few remained. They all eyed Campbell as if he might pocket any unguarded valuables. With a self-important flourish, Toner beckoned.

McGinty extended his hand as Campbell approached. "Good to see you, Davy."

"You too, Mr. McGinty," Campbell said, matching the other's hard grip.

"Did you get bored pissing about with McSorley and that shower of shit he runs with?" McGinty's grin was wide and his eyes were cold.

"They didn't know what they were at," Campbell said. "I shouldn't have gone near them."

McGinty's grip tightened. "That's right, Davy. You shouldn't have. That annoyed a lot of people, especially the dear departed."

Campbell prised his hand away. "See, that was the thing. When I heard about Michael, it got me thinking. I made a mistake. I'm really sorry, Mr. McGinty. If there's anything I can do to make it up to you, I will."

McGinty nodded. "I know what it's like, Davy. You're a man of action. You want to be in the thick of it. I used to be like that once upon a time, so I can sympathise. Things got too quiet for you here, so you went to see what the dissidents were up to. And I bet you were disappointed, eh?"

"Too fucking right," Campbell said, returning McGinty's easy smile. "They just sat around getting pissed and talking about what they were *going* to do."

McGinty lifted his jacket and slipped it on. He placed his arm around Campbell's shoulder and guided him towards the kitchen. "Let's get a bit of air."

A slender blonde woman stepped aside to let them through. Campbell recognised her as McKenna's niece. She did not meet his or McGinty's gaze, even though they both eyed her as they passed. The other women formed a production line, passing plates and glasses back and forth between sink and cupboards. They gave Campbell curious glances as McGinty led him to the back yard.

Two young men stood there, smoking. McGinty jerked his head at the door and the men dropped their cigarettes to grind them with their heels.

"Don't litter Mrs. McKenna's yard," McGinty said. "Show some respect. Pick them up and take them with you."

The two young men obeyed in silence, bending down to pick up the crushed butts. As they passed McGinty on their way to the door, he grabbed the younger man's sleeve.

"When I'm finished talking with my friend, you and your mate can sweep the yard out. Right?"

"Okay," the young man said, keeping his gaze on the ground.

"Good lad. Off you go." McGinty turned back to Campbell and smiled. "So, Davy, you're back in town. I don't remember telling you to come back. I don't remember telling you your work was done in Dundalk." He stepped closer and lowered his voice. "And if I'm not mistaken, there's still money going into that wee savings account I set up for you. So what the fuck are you doing here? It was your idea to get in with McSorley's lot in the first place."

"Like I said, Mr. McGinty, I was wasting my time there. They're no threat to you."

McGinty snorted. "Christ, you didn't need to jump into bed with them to figure that out. Listen, if I send you to do a job, you do it. No questions." His forefinger prodded Campbell's chest. "I don't care if you think it's doing any good. That's for me to decide."

Campbell cast his eyes down, showing the politician the deference he expected.

McGinty sighed. "All right, but remember – this stays between you and me. I don't want anyone thinking I was worried about McSorley. Not the way things are now."

"Of course," Campbell said, raising his head.

"So, what are your plans?"

"Nothing in particular," Campbell said. "I was kind of hoping you might need some jobs doing."

"I might," McGinty said. "You were always a good worker. A bit hot-headed, though. I got a text from Tom over at the bar. Eddie Coyle's off getting stitches."

"He was looking for a fight. He got one."

"Eddie Coyle's a prick, but that doesn't mean he deserves a beating."

Campbell knew when to back down. "Yeah, fair enough. I'm sorry."

McGinty smiled. "You can apologise to him next time you cross each other's paths. He'll be told to let it go. Anyway, I might have a wee job for you. It's kind of a sensitive one."

"Oh?"

"You were always good at sniffing out troublemakers. Our internal security's lost a good volunteer. Vincie Caffola was the best at clearing out touts and such, but I seem to remember you were pretty sharp yourself."

Campbell looked up at the sound of a helicopter. "I had my moments."

McGinty moved close to the yard's back wall, out of sight of the intruder in the sky. "You sniffed out that bastard Delaney when he sold me to the Loyalists." McGinty sneered. "Ulster Freedom Fighters, for Christ's sake. Bunch of fuckwits pretending they're Al Capone, not a brain between them. What was Delaney thinking? They'd never have pulled it off. Still, they could've gotten lucky if you hadn't twigged it. It was you who beat it out of him. I haven't forgotten that, Davy."

Campbell watched McGinty closely. "Delaney was easy. It was Gerry Fegan who got the UFF boys."

"If you hadn't fingered them, Gerry wouldn't have sorted them out, and I wouldn't be standing here. I owe you and him a lot. That's the only reason Gerry Fegan's still alive this afternoon."

"What do you mean?"

McGinty's eyes narrowed. "Who else do you know would have the balls to take out Michael McKenna and Vincie Caffola?"

"I heard it was—"

"Forget what you heard," McGinty said. He beckoned Campbell to come close. "You don't need to know the details. Just believe me when I tell you it was Fegan."

Campbell played it sceptical, stringing McGinty along. "I heard he'd lost it, took to the drink."

"Maybe so." McGinty nodded as a shallow smile spread across his mouth. "But don't you ever underestimate Gerry Fegan. He's strong, but there's stronger. He's smarter than he lets on, but he's no genius. You want to know what makes Gerry Fegan so dangerous?"

Campbell couldn't help but play along. "What?"

McGinty took a packet of cigarettes from his pocket, placed one between his lips, and tucked the packet away again. "He's fearless. Gerry Fegan isn't afraid of any man alive. Not one."

"Fearless means careless," Campbell said.

"Maybe for some. But not Gerry." McGinty lit the cigarette and stuffed the lighter back into his pocket. He took a drag. "I'll tell you a little something about Gerry Fegan. Years ago, late Seventies, him and Michael McKenna were just kids, fifteen, sixteen, something like that. Me and Gusty Devlin, God rest him, used to take some of the young lads down to Carnagh Forest, just over the border, for camping trips. Michael nagged me to take Gerry, but I didn't want to. I didn't like him. He was too quiet, always watching, saying nothing. But Michael talked me into it, and we took them in this old Volkswagen Camper I had."

McGinty smiled and straightened his designer jacket, blue plumes of smoke leaking from his nostrils. "I didn't dress so smart in those days. Fancied myself as a working-class hero, you know? Anyway, we got stopped at a checkpoint just this side of the border. The cops knew all about us, thought we were carrying guns. Some of the boys went to bits when the peelers searched them, had them down to their socks and their underpants on the side of the road. Not Gerry. He looked every one of those fuckers in the eye.

"So we get to the forest, set up camp, and Gusty hikes them round the lakes for a couple of hours. Everybody's knackered, so we turn in. About two or three in the morning, all hell breaks loose. Gerry's up shouting there's people in the trees, watching us. Can you believe that? A kid who'll stare out a peeler who's ready to take his head off, and he's scared of shadows?"

Campbell tried not to flinch as McGinty laughed, blowing smoke in his face. "You said he wasn't scared of anything."

"Not of any man. The dark, maybe, but no man. Anyway, next morning Bull O'Kane arrives with the guns the cops thought we'd be carrying. Nothing much, just a couple of air rifles and an old .303 from the war. So, Gusty sets up paper targets for the lads to practise with and, fuck me, Gerry can't hit anything. Up close, he's fucking deadly, but more than twenty feet? Couldn't hit a cow on the arse with a shovel."

Campbell nodded, smiled, and filed that fact away.

"So one of the other lads, can't remember his name – he was a thick shite, blew himself up with a pipe bomb – he starts slagging Gerry, how he's no use, he's scared of the gun, he's scared of the shadows in the trees, he should get his ma to come for him. So Gerry fucking lit on him. He's battering the shit clean out of him, pasting his nose all over his face, and we're all stood back laughing.

"All of a sudden, Bull says, 'Enough of this,' and grabs a-hold of Gerry, pulls him off the other lad, and he's still kicking and screaming. Bull plonks him down on his feet, and before anyone knows what's happening, Gerry spins around and – POP!"

Campbell blinked as McGinty slammed his fist into his palm.

"Gerry only goes and smacks Bull O'Kane, the scariest fucker I ever met, right in the mouth."

"Jesus," Campbell said. He'd never heard of anyone crossing Bull O'Kane and getting away with it. With genuine curiosity, he asked, "What did the Bull do?"

"Fucking decked him." McGinty grinned. "Bull's got hands like sides of beef. He belted Gerry and he went down like a sack of spuds. Now, I've never seen anyone raise a hand to Bull O'Kane before or since. So, I was thinking, Christ, what now? He'll kill him. I'm thinking we'll have to bury this kid in the forest."

McGinty's smile washed away. "Well, Bull goes and gets one of the air rifles, puts a pellet in the breech, and comes back to Gerry. Gerry just stares up at him, breathing hard. Bull aims the rifle, says, 'You've got some balls, son.' I says, 'Jesus, Bull, he's just a kid, he didn't mean it.' Bull says, 'Just a kid? Takes more than a kid to clout me. You better watch this young fella, he's got great things ahead of him.' "

Campbell realised his mouth was open. "And?" he asked.

"And he shot Gerry in the thigh. Tough wee bastard never made a sound. We drove all the way back to Belfast, him with a pellet in his thigh, and all he did was sweat and bleed till we dropped him at his ma's house."

"Christ," Campbell said. "And now you think he's done McKenna and Caffola?"

McGinty shrugged and dropped the cigarette butt to the ground. "Like I said, who else?"

"So why hasn't he been sorted out?"

"Because I'm getting soft in my old age." McGinty smiled as he slapped Campbell's shoulder. "That's all I'm saying. So, I've given him a wee job, you know, to see if he'll do what he's told. To see if he's under control." McGinty leaned in close. "Now, here's what I need you to do for me . . ."

The little girl sized Fegan up as he stood on the other side of the low garden wall.

"What's your name?" she asked from the doorstep.

"Gerry," he said.

"I've got new shoes." She extended her foot for his inspection. "Mummy got me them."

"They're pretty," Fegan said.

"Ellen, show Gerry the lights," Marie said as she closed the door.

Ellen jumped from the step onto the tiny garden's path. Little red lights danced on her heels. She looked up at Fegan and grinned.

"You're good at jumping," Fegan said.

"Yeah, I can jump really high," she said, lifting her arms above her head to illustrate.

"Show me," he said.

"Okay," Ellen said as she squatted down. She launched herself upward with all her strength and landed square on her feet. "That was really high, wasn't it?"

"Yeah," Fegan said.

"How high can you jump?"

"Not very high," he said.

"Show me."

"No, I'm too tired," Fegan said.

"But I showed you." Ellen's little blue eyes pleaded with him.

"Oh, go on," Marie said. "Fair's fair."

Fegan looked up and down the street. Marie and Ellen joined him on the footpath.

"Don't worry, nobody's watching," Marie said, suppressing a giggle.

Fegan sighed and bent his knees, wondering when he'd last jumped for the sake of jumping. He pushed upward and staggered as he landed, his leather soles slapping on the pavement. Marie and Ellen both applauded as he smoothed his jacket. He still wore his black suit, but the tie was tucked into his pocket.

"I jumped far higher than that," Ellen said.

Fegan couldn't argue. "You win."

She grinned at him and her mother in turn then spun on her heels to walk east along Eglantine Avenue towards the Malone Road. She turned to acknowledge Marie's instruction not to go too far ahead. Fegan and Marie followed.

"It's a beautiful evening," Marie said. Trees lined the avenue and the evening sun made shadow patterns on her skin. "You forget how lovely Belfast can be. All it takes is a little sunshine."

Eglantine Avenue's old houses glowed red. Some were better kept than others. Some, like Marie's, were divided into flats. Others housed students or migrant workers, while others provided office space for dentists or lawyers. The avenue ran between the Lisburn and Malone Roads, and the rumble of traffic at either end seemed muted by the gentle May warmth.

"Ellen looks like you," Fegan said.

"So everyone says. She's taken a shine to you already."

"You think?"

"Oh, yes." Marie smiled. "She's a love-or-hate kind of girl. She loves dogs and she hates cats. She loves peas and she hates carrots. With people, it's one or the other, but I think you've got on her good side. That was a wise move, complimenting her jumping skills. You'll have a friend for life."

"Where's her father now?" Fegan asked.

"Oh, he's around somewhere," Marie said. "Sends her money at Christmas. Other than that, we haven't heard from him in years."

"It must be hard, managing on your own," he said.

Ellen waited at the corner of Eglantine Gardens for the adults to take her across the road. Fegan felt something flutter inside when she took his hand instead of her mother's.

"Sometimes it is," Marie said as they crossed. "But we're better off without him."

Ellen didn't release his hand when they reached the other side. She kept his index and middle fingers gripped in her small fist and he wanted to tell her to let go, she didn't know where his hands had been. She would find flecks of old blood in the tiny creases of her fingers if she held his hand too long. He was sure of it.

"I do all right at the paper," Marie continued, "And I can work from home most days, so I don't have to spend too much on childcare, especially now she's started school. Jack knew what I sacrificed for him, and he betrayed me anyway. Ellen doesn't need a man who'd do something like that. Neither do I."

I've done worse things, Fegan thought. Marie seemed to read it on his face. Her smile faltered and she looked straight ahead.

They walked in silence to the Malone Road, and turned north towards Queen's University. This part of the city was alien to Fegan, a million miles away from the Belfast he knew. Grand residences and private clinics lined the Malone Road, guarded by high walls with electric gates.

"Did you go to Queen's?" Fegan asked.

"No, Jordanstown," Marie said. "I used to come to the Students' Union here, though. That was a long time ago, but it hasn't changed much. Did you go to university?"

She realised it was a foolish question.

Fegan shrugged. "I never quite got around to it," he said.

She nodded. "What about in the Maze? Did you study anything there?"

"Woodwork," Fegan said. "A lot of the boys got degrees. Politics, history, that sort of thing. They got a better education there than they ever did at the Christian Brothers. I was never much for studying. I do better with my hands. My father was a carpenter, so I thought I'd give that a go."

"Are you any good?" Marie asked.

"I'm okay," he said. "I had a good teacher."

Her head tilted. "Tell me about him."

Fegan saw that expression on her face again. The same one she had worn in her car the day before, the same one the prison psychologists like Dr Brady speared him with when they wanted him to spill his guts. Lorries and buses rumbled along the Malone Road. They approached the iron fences of Methodist College. The boarding school's windows burned orange as the sun ebbed. Fegan battled within himself, part of him wanting to stay hidden, part of him needing to show itself.

He surrendered.

"He was called Ronnie Lennox," Fegan said. "He was a Prod, from the Loyalist block. He wasn't a teacher, really, just an auld fella with nothing better to do. It was after my mother died, not long after the Agreement in '98. I didn't want to be around the boys any more. I couldn't listen to them arguing and shouting, so I used to stay behind in the workshop. You could do what you wanted in the Maze, not like a normal prison.

"This one day, there was just me and him and a guard in the workshop. The guard was sleeping in the corner. I was building a cabinet for my cell. I was trying to make the carcass with dovetail joints." Fegan looked at the scar on his left thumb. "I cut myself and Ronnie came over, cleaned it, put a plaster on me. Then he showed me how to use a coping saw properly. We talked a bit. He coughed all the time; he had asbestos poisoning from the shipyard. He shouldn't have been in the workshop with all the dust, but he couldn't stick it in the Loyalist block. He loved to show you stuff. You started him talking about joints and dowels, you'd never get him stopped."

Fegan noticed Marie's amused expression. "What?" he asked.

"Nothing," she said, her face glimmering. "It's the first time I've seen you really smile, that's all."

Fegan coughed. "Guitars were Ronnie's thing. He played beautiful. Not like those guys in the pubs, banging out the same old songs, but really playing it. Like he was talking to you."

He caught himself making shapes in the air with his free hand and dropped it to his side. "A couple of the guards had sons who played.

They used to bring their guitars in for him to work on. He could take a cheap plank and make it play like it cost a grand."

"Where is he now?" Marie asked.

"Dead," Fegan said. "The asbestos finished him. The fluid in his lungs. He would have got out two weeks later."

"Christ," Marie said. "I'm sorry."

Fegan shrugged. "He always told me about this guitar he had at home. A Martin D-28 from the Thirties – a herringbone, he called it. He said he would fix it up when he got out. That's what kept him going.

"About a year and a half ago, this woman knocked on my door. She said she was Ronnie's daughter. She handed me this guitar case, all battered and torn up. She said Ronnie had wanted me to have it, he told her that before he died. It took her all that time to find me. It was the Martin. I'm restoring it now. It's almost done."

They reached the end of the Malone Road, where it met University Road and the top of Stranmillis Road. They stopped at the pedestrian crossing.

Marie asked, "And what are you going to do with it?"

Fegan's cheeks grew hot. "I'm going to learn to play it," he said.

"Good," she said, nodding. "Tell me, what was Ronnie in the Maze for?"

Fegan looked across the road to the Ulster Museum, its austere form blotting the blue sky. "He slit a man's throat," he said. "A Catholic who walked into the wrong bar. Ronnie cried when he told me."

Marie fell silent. They watched the traffic lights above the crossing, waiting to be released.

The great red-bricked castle of Queen's University stood a short distance away, to the right, in the midst of its carpet-smooth lawns. It couldn't have been more unlike the ugly grey block of the Student Union building, facing it directly across University Road.

Students gathered in huddles on the grass on one side, and on the concrete steps on the other. Young, pretty people Fegan would never know. It occurred to him that most of these children had never been torn from sleep by a bomb blast in the night, the force of it hammering their windows like a thousand fists, freezing their hearts in their chests. For a moment he might have resented them for it, but then he felt Ellen's fingers adjust their grip on his, and he was glad for them. He thought of Ellen as a young woman, and how she would never comprehend the awful, constant fear that had smothered this place for more than thirty years.

The lights changed. Ellen kept hold of Fegan's hand while she took her mother's, and they crossed the road towards the Ulster Museum. The three of them were swallowed by tree-shade at the entrance to Botanic Gardens, the park sprawling ahead of them behind the university buildings. Fegan had the urge to run from them, from Marie and her child, but the little girl's hand felt good on his. His skin felt clean where she touched it. *This is what normal people do*, he thought. *This is what normal people feel like.* He had never thought it possible to feel terror and stillness in the same heart, but both beat in his chest as they walked among the green lawns and the budding flowers.

They stopped at the seats facing the Palm House. Fegan and Marie sat down while Ellen went to peer through the glass at the plant life within.

"Thanks for letting me walk with you," Fegan said.

"You're welcome," she said.

"Can I ask you a question?"

"You can ask," Marie said as she swept blonde hair from her face. She settled back in the seat. "Doesn't mean I'll answer."

Fegan leaned forward, his forearms on his knees, his fingers laced together. "Why would you go for a walk with someone like me? Why did you give me a lift yesterday?"

"I'm not sure," she said. She thought for a few seconds. "You saw what I said over Uncle Michael's coffin, but you didn't judge me. I've gotten so used to people judging me. The people I work with know where I come from, who I'm related to, and they judge me. The people I come from can't forget what I've done, as if falling in love with a cop was an act of treason, and you saw how they looked at me today and yesterday. Everywhere I go, people know who I am, where I'm from, what I did, and they judge me for it. I guess that's why. You didn't judge me."

"I'm in no position to judge anybody," Fegan said.

"But you know what it's like to be judged."

"Yeah, I do. You don't deserve it, though. You didn't do anything wrong. Not like me."

"How do you live with it?" she asked.

Fegan watched Ellen move from pane to pane of the giant greenhouse, standing on tiptoe for a better view. A chill crawled over him, despite the evening warmth. Shadows lengthened as the sun sank. "I don't," he said. "Most people wouldn't call it living, anyway."

"Well, you're breathing, aren't you?"

"I suppose." He wanted to tell Marie about the followers, about the screaming and the baby crying in the night. He looked round to her. "I'm going to put things right, though. I'm going to make up for what I did."

She sat forward to meet his gaze. "How?"

"I haven't figured it out yet," he said. It was only half a lie. He knew what he had to do, just not how to go about it. "But I'll find a way. I always find a way."

"You're an interesting man, Gerry Fegan." The strange crescent of Marie's lips made something shift inside him. "I'd like to get to know you, if you'll let me."

He turned his eyes to the ground where cigarette butts and old chewing gum, things people no longer wanted in their mouths, were trampled into the path. "I'm not a good person to know."

"We'll see," she said.

He couldn't see her face from the corner of his eye, but he imagined Marie McKenna was smiling, playfully biting her lower lip. He had to say it now.

"Paul McGinty wanted me to give you a message," Fegan said.

Her weight shifted beside him. "Oh?"

He studied the detritus at his feet. "He wants you to leave. He says now your uncle's gone it isn't safe here for you."

Marie shot to her feet and extended her hand towards her daughter. "Come on, Ellen, it's time to go."

Ellen spun towards the sound of her mother's voice, frowning in protest. "No, Mummy!"

"No arguing," Marie said. "Come on."

"Wait," Fegan said as he stood up.

Marie turned to face him. "Tell McGinty he can go fuck himself. They couldn't scare me away back then, and they won't do it now." The hardness in her face dissolved as her eyes glistened. "How can you do that? How can you hold my daughter's hand one minute, and deliver McGinty's threats the next?"

"You don't understand," he said.

"Don't I? I thought it was pretty clear." She turned to where Ellen lingered by the Palm House. "Ellen, get over here now."

"I don't want you to go," Fegan said. "You've done nothing wrong. I won't let McGinty hurt you. Or Ellen. If he sends anyone I'll take care of them."

Ellen came over, dragging her heels, pouting. Marie took her hand. "We've been managing for five years now," she said. "We don't need your protection."

"Maybe not, but I want to help you anyway."

Marie bared her teeth. "Why? Why do you care? If you're his errand boy, why don't you go and see what other odd jobs need doing? Go and collect some protection money for him, or rob a post office, or hijack some cigarettes. Why waste your time with a traitor to the cause like me?"

A hundred reasons flashed in Fegan's mind; some he dared not speak, more he dared not think. He looked down at the little girl hugging her mother's thigh. "Because Ellen held my hand," he said.

Marie sighed and covered her eyes. "Christ, this place. Sometimes I think there's a future here for me, and for Ellen. Then I remember men like McGinty are still running things. I should've gone years ago when I had the chance."

"I don't want you to go," Fegan said again.

"So you said." She uncovered her eyes and allowed him a hint of a smile.

"If anyone comes around, phone me."

"What's your mobile number?"

"I don't . . . I'll buy one. Tomorrow morning."

She gave an exasperated laugh. "Jesus, who doesn't have a mobile phone?"

"I don't," Fegan said.

"Me neither," Ellen said. "Mummy won't get me one."

Marie looked down at her daughter. "You're five, Ellen. Who are you going to phone?"

Ellen gave it some thought. "Santa," she said.

Marie reached into her bag and produced a pen. She took Fegan's hand, holding it as she wrote on his palm. Her skin was soft and warm. "Call me when you get your phone," she said. "I can't promise I'll answer, but you never know."

"Thank you," Fegan said. He smiled at Ellen. "You practise jumping. Next time I might jump higher than you."

"No, you won't," Ellen said as her mother led her away.

Fegan watched them until they were lost among the trees. The chill that had been creeping along his limbs finally reached his center, and his temples buzzed. He felt them watching, waiting for him.

He turned to see the black-haired woman, the baby in her arms, nodding her head towards two of the followers. The Loyalists, the Ulster Freedom Fighters, were pointing to the trees over at the Botanic Avenue entrance. Their stares flitted between Fegan and the shadows under the branches.

"What?" Fegan asked. He walked over to them and searched for whatever they were looking at. He saw nothing but the students wandering in and out of the park, their plastic bags full of beer and cider ready to start their evening's drinking in the sun and fresh air.

The two UFF boys slowly lowered their tattooed arms. Whatever they wanted Fegan to see was gone.

20

"He didn't see me," Campbell said. He held the phone between his shoulder and his ear while he ate cold beans from a tin. He had slipped out of the park and back to his flat as soon as Fegan started peering in his direction. It was only a few minutes' walk from Botanic Gardens to his flat on University Street, just off Botanic Avenue.

"Have you reported back to McGinty yet?" the handler asked.

"No, I'll do that next."

"What'll you tell him?"

"The truth. I don't think Fegan told her to get out. She argued with him for a minute, but they looked like they parted on friendly terms. Didn't look much like a threat to me."

Campbell put the tin on the windowsill and lifted a glass of milk. He took a cool swallow as he watched the students wander along the street below. Some swigged from beer cans as they walked, probably on their way to one of the student haunts like The Bot or Lavery's. They'd wander back in the early hours of the morning, gangs of them singing and shouting, no concern for the people who needed their sleep.

"And what do you think McGinty will do about it? Will he take Fegan out?" The handler sounded hopeful.

"I doubt it," Campbell said. "Not yet, anyway. He's still playing the angle that the cops got Caffola. He won't want to do anything to distract the media from that."

"What, then?"

"He'll probably send one of his heavies to put the woman out."

"Not her, I don't care about her. What'll he do about Fegan?"

"I'm not sure," Campbell said. "He might let it go for now, but it's only a matter of time. McGinty doesn't let anyone cross him and get away with it. He'll make Fegan pay sooner or later."

"See if you can make it sooner, there's a good lad," the handler said. "We've got the Northern Ireland Office, the Chief Constable and the Minister of State breathing down our necks. They want it over before any more damage is done. If we can prove it was Fegan who did Caffola, not the police, so much the better."

"I'll see what I can do," Campbell said. He hung up and tossed the phone onto the sofa. He pulled the other phone from his pocket and dialled McGinty's private number. The politician answered, and Campbell told him what he'd seen.

"Gerry will have to be dealt with," McGinty said, "But not just yet. We'll leave it until after Vincie's funeral."

"What about the woman?" Campbell asked.

"Let me worry about that," McGinty said.

21

Fegan sat alone in McKenna's, nursing a pint of Guinness while he watched Father Coulter down brandy at the bar. He knew the priest would be here. It was well known that Father Eammon Coulter only drank after weddings, christenings, first communions and funerals, but once he got started he would drink until he fell.

When he'd left Botanic Gardens, Fegan had gone straight to the derelict house on the next street to his, climbed into its back yard, and retrieved his Walther. Now it nestled at the small of his back. He kept it against the wall so no one could see.

The followers circled the room. They hadn't left him all evening. Fegan's temples buzzed with their presence, and a chill sat lodged at his center. The three Brits paid close attention to Father Coulter while the two UFF boys paced, opening and closing their fists.

A cheer rang through the bar as Eddie Coyle entered, escorted by Patsy Toner. The lawyer still wore his black suit from McKenna's funeral. Coyle's left eye was swollen shut and a gauze pad covered a wound on his brow. "Fuck off," he shouted at the drinkers.

"Sit down, I'll get you a drink," Toner said.

Coyle did as he was told, taking a seat two tables away from Fegan. He cursed quietly to himself for a full minute before he raised his head.

"What are you looking at?" he demanded.

"You," Fegan said.

"Well, you can fuck off, too." Coyle couldn't hold Fegan's gaze. He dropped his eyes to the tabletop.

"Jesus, calm down, Eddie," Toner said as he carried two pints back to the table. He rolled his eyes at Fegan and shook his head.

"Calm down?" Coyle pointed to his face. "Look at the cut of me, for Christ's sake. That cunt's going to get it, Patsy. I don't care what McGinty says."

Toner pointed at the door. "Go on, then. Go and get him. Then you can go and tell McGinty what you did and see what he says."

"Go fuck yourself," Coyle said, reaching for his beer.

"Get who?" Fegan asked.

Coyle set his pint back on the table, letting it spill over his fingers. "What's it to you?"

"Jesus, Eddie, settle yourself," Toner said. He turned to answer Fegan. "Davy Campbell's back in town. Him and Eddie had a run-in this afternoon."

The two UFF boys drifted to Toner's table, suddenly showing interest in the little man's words. The hairs on Fegan's forearms bristled beneath his sleeves. "I thought he was with McSorley's lot these days."

"Looks like he had a change of heart," Toner said. "He phoned me up last night, said he wanted to come back to Belfast. He's a good lad, so I squared it with McGinty this morning."

"He's a cunt," Coyle said.

"Aw, give over," Toner said. "You shouldn't pick fights with boys you can't take. Now, quit mouthing about it, will you?"

Coyle muttered something under his breath and got back to drinking his beer. Over at the bar, Father Coulter got ready to go.

"Och, come on, Father, you'll have another wee one," one of the young men who drank with the priest said.

"No, no, no," Father Coulter said, waving away the offered glass. "I've had quite enough. It's way past my bedtime, so God bless you all the same, but I must go."

He shuffled away from the bar, turning in circles as he struggled to find the sleeve of his overcoat. The young man helped him on with it and guided him to the door. Shadows followed.

Fegan looked at the clock above the bar and took a mouthful of Guinness. He would give it five minutes before following the priest. What would he do when he caught up with him? He didn't know.

Fegan studied the wet circles his glass left on the tabletop and ignored the pressure of his gun at the small of his back.

It didn't take long to catch up with the priest. Father Coulter had made slow progress through the streets, and Fegan found him propped against a Lexus within minutes of leaving the bar. Fegan remembered a time when only the most well-to-do owned cars. Now the streets were lined with them, crammed into every space available. The priest had chosen the most comfortable-looking to lean on.

Father Coulter waved as he approached. "Gerry Fegan," he said. "You caught me. I was just having a wee rest. Will you walk with me?"

"Of course I will, Father," Fegan said. He began walking slowly, the priest at his side.

"I haven't seen you at Mass for a long time, Gerry," Father Coulter said.

"I was there today," Fegan said.

"Apart from funerals, I mean. When was the last time you went to Mass?"

Fegan tried to remember. He had been once or twice since he got out of the Maze, but when? "Years ago," he said.

Father Coulter clucked and shook his head. "That won't do, Gerry. Have you no thought for your soul? What would your mother have said?"

"My mother was ashamed of me," Fegan said.

"Nonsense!" Father Coulter placed his hand on Fegan's arm.

"She told me. She was ashamed of what I did."

The priest wagged a finger at him. "You're a hero of the cause, Gerry Fegan, and don't you forget it. You didn't choose a war; it was forced upon you. The good Lord knows why you did what you did. God forgives all soldiers. John Hewitt wrote that. The poet. He wrote—"

Fegan stopped walking. "We're here."

Father Coulter looked round to see his own front door. "Oh, so we are. Will you come in for a wee drop?"

Fegan looked up and down the empty street. "All right," he said.

Father Coulter fished a key from his pocket and turned to insert it in the lock. It scraped against wood as he missed his mark. He tried, and failed, twice more.

"Here," Fegan said, taking the key from the priest's hand. He unlocked the door and let it swing open. "There you go."

"Thank you, Gerry." Father Coulter patted his shoulder and went inside. Fegan followed him, slipping the key into his own pocket.

The small house was clean and sparsely furnished. Father Coulter ushered Fegan through to the living room. A fire in the hearth blasted heat at them. Sweat broke out across Fegan's brow and back, but the chill stayed at his center. Father Coulter flicked the light on and a caged bird, a cockatiel, hissed at them.

Father Coulter went to the cage, clucking. "Now, now, Joe-Joe, it's only me." He threw his coat over the back of a chair and turned to Fegan. "Sit down, Gerry."

The priest took a bottle of brandy from the sideboard and poured two generous glasses. He handed one to Fegan and sat down facing him.

His bleary eyes searched Fegan's face. "Tell me, do you dream much?" he asked.

"No," Fegan said. "I don't sleep too well."

"I dream," Father Coulter said. He took a sip of brandy and coughed. "Terrible dreams. I've seen awful things, Gerry. There's things I could have changed. Things I could have stopped. Things I should never have done. I always told myself I'd no choice, but I was wrong. I always had a choice. You know what I'm talking about."

Fegan moved his glass in slow circles and watched the firelight refracted in the reddish-brown liquid. "Yes, Father."

"So many times I could have said something, told someone. Men like you making your confession, telling me the things you've done, then I give you forgiveness so you can go out and do it again."

Father Coulter watched the fire, his wet eyes reflecting the orange glow. "Maybe in a different place, I could have been a better priest. Maybe I could have done right by God. Or maybe I never really had it in me." He reached across and gripped Fegan's hand. "I dream a lot, Gerry."

"You're drunk, Father."

The priest released Fegan's fingers and smiled. "I know, I know. I'm drunk and I'm tired. I worry about you, Gerry."

Fegan looked up from his brandy. "Why?"

"Because you're carrying so many things around with you. When did you last make your confession?"

"When I was in the Maze." It had been a week after he returned to prison from his mother's funeral, the blood of two Loyalists on his hands.

Father Coulter beckoned. "Come here to me, son."

Fegan stared into his glass. "No."

The priest leaned forward and took Fegan's hand again, gently pulling. "Come on. Do it to ease an old priest's conscience."

"No," Fegan said, resisting but not letting go. He set the glass on the floor.

"For your mother, Gerry."

Fegan slipped off the chair and allowed Father Coulter to guide him to his side, kneeling. He rested his forearms against the chair and clasped his hands together. A minute passed, the ticking of the clock over the fire hammering against Fegan's temples.

Father Coulter turned his head just a little. "Don't you remember what to do?"

"I'm afraid, Father."

The priest turned in his chair and circled Fegan's hands with his. "Don't be. Just—"

"Bless me, Father, for I have sinned." Father Coulter's hands slipped away from Fegan's. "It's been nine years since my last confession."

Father Coulter waited for a few seconds. "Go on."

"I've been quiet for so long. I turned away and I was quiet. But they won't leave me alone."

"Who won't?"

"The people I killed."

The priest nodded. "Guilt is the heaviest of all emotions. It'll eat you alive if you let it. Have you confessed to these sins before?"

"Yes, Father. In the Maze."

"Then you have absolution. But guilt remains, of course it does. You must carry that burden. That is your penance, not any prayer. You must carry it and live on, however painful that might be."

"Father." Fegan hesitated, squeezing his eyes shut. He let the air out of his lungs in a long hiss and opened them again. "Father, I've killed two more men."

The priest shifted in his chair. "When?"

"This week."

"This . . . this week?"

"Yes."

"Oh God, Gerry. Oh, sweet Jesus."

"I didn't want to. I swear to God, I didn't want to."

"Oh, my Lord. Michael McKenna? Vincent Caffola?"

"Yes, Father." Fegan pressed his interlocked hands against his forehead.

"Jesus. Jesus, why?"

Fegan looked up. Father Coulter stared back at him. "Because I had to."

"What do you mean?" The priest shook his head.

"I told the boy's mother where his body was. I thought that would do it, make him leave me alone. Then Michael found out. He came to me, said he'd tell McGinty if I didn't do what he wanted. Then the boy told me what to do, and I did it."

"What boy? What are you talking about? Dear God, Gerry, this is madness."

"Then Vincie, he was coming after me, asking questions. And the UDR men, they wanted him, and I—"

"Stop it."

"I had to give—"

"No."

"—give him to them."

"Enough!" Father Coulter slammed his fists into his thighs. "Enough. No more."

Fegan closed his eyes. "I'm sorry, Father."

A long silence passed. The ticking clock sent jolt after jolt into Fegan's temples. The chill at his center deepened.

After an age, Father Coulter whispered, "The Sacrament of Penance is my curse. The things I've had to carry for men like you. A curse is what it is."

He bowed his head and made the Sign of the Cross. "God the Father of mercies, through the death and resurrection of His Son, has reconciled the world to Himself and sent the Holy Spirit among us for the forgiveness of sins; through the ministry of the Church may God give you pardon and peace, and I absolve you from your sins in the name of the Father, and of the Son, and of the Holy Spirit."

Fegan asked, "My penance, Father?"

"Your penance?" Father Coulter gave a thin, sad smile. "The same as it's always been. The same as it always will be. Your burden, Gerry Fegan. That is your penance."

The priest looked away. "Now get out," he said.

Fegan watched him for a moment before standing. Without looking back, he went to the hallway where the shifting shadows waited. They parted for him, moved around him, as he opened the front door and stepped out onto the street.

The three Brits came to him and stared over his shoulder at the house, hateful longing on their faces.

"No," Fegan said. He crossed the street. An alleyway faced the priest's house. He let its darkness devour him and the nine followers. The bricks cooled his forehead as he rested against the wall.

"Christ," Fegan said. "He doesn't deserve it."

The three Brits pointed to the door.

"Jesus, he didn't do anything."

The priest's upstairs light glared for a moment before blinking out again. The Brits walked out to the street, their arms raised towards the window.

"I didn't give him a choice. Not really."

The Brits went to the door, and one pressed his ear against it. The woman stepped out into the orange glow of the street lights and pointed to the window. The butcher joined her, then the cop and the two UFF boys.

Fegan followed them.

"He was scared," Fegan said. "All right, he could have stopped it, but I threatened him. Look, he knows he did wrong. You heard him."

The woman moved close to him, her eyes blazing. Fegan looked down at the baby in her arms. It stared back up at him, its toothless mouth contorted with hate.

"Christ!" Fegan backed into the alley's dark harbour and covered his eyes. "Leave me alone. I can't do it."

He reached for the small of his back and pulled the Walther from his waistband. He chambered a round and placed the muzzle between his teeth. It was cold and slick. He had a moment to wonder what it would feel like, that explosion in his skull, before another thought appeared in his mind.

He thought about Ellen's small hand, and how his skin felt clean where she held his fingers in her fist. Then he thought about how the sun found the gold flecks in Marie's hair. And then he thought about the promise he'd made, that he would protect them from McGinty's threat.

Slowly, Fegan took the pistol from his mouth. He released the round from the chamber and dropped it into his pocket, alongside the priest's key. The nine followers stared as he emerged from the alley. He tucked the Walther back into his waistband and began the walk home. The Brits overtook him, pointing back to the priest's house.

"No," Fegan said. "Not him."

They were screaming even before he was in his own home. The sound of their agony echoed through the streets, and Fegan wondered how the city could sleep through it. Once inside, without turning on the lights, he went straight for the sideboard and the bottle of Jameson's. He unscrewed the cap and brought the bottle to his mouth. He was on his fifth deep swallow, trying not to retch from the burn, when the baby started crying.

22

Fegan woke late the next morning and immediately ran to the bathroom to throw up. He'd drunk almost a full bottle of whiskey the night before and it had taken its toll. He would have retreated to bed, dug himself in beneath the covers while he waited for the greasy waves of the hangover to ease, but he had a mobile phone to buy.

He walked to the supermarket on watery legs, keeping his gaze from the morning shadows. Every step of the way he felt eyes on his back. Occasionally, he spun on his heels, looking for whoever followed. But part of him knew.

Campbell, probably sent by McGinty.

Once, as he paid for the cheap phone, he looked up and caught a flash of denim disappearing behind a magazine rack. On his way home he considered stopping, doubling back, and confronting Campbell. He dismissed it as foolishness. He kept his head down and kept walking. A quick glance up and down Calcutta Street didn't reveal anything, but once he was inside his own home the feeling left him.

While he waited for the phone to charge, Fegan worked on the guitar to soothe his aching head. He polished the frets with steel wool in the good light from the window. He had shaped them with a rounded fret file and sandpaper, sighted a line down the fingerboard to make sure they were even, and now he worked over them one by one, giving them a mirror finish.

Fegan thought of Ronnie Lennox as he worked. The old man got his release letter around the same time he did. Like Fegan, it had brought on sleepless nights, but for different reasons.

They talked about it often in those last days. While Fegan swept up chippings from the workshop floor and Ronnie rested on a stool, they talked about the changes outside, the Good Friday Agreement that supposedly settled it all, and the referendum that followed. Two years after Ireland, north and south, had voted in favor of the Agreement, the Maze Prison stood almost empty. The last few inmates moved around the place as they wished, captives and guards happy to keep the peace and count the days.

Ronnie looked at Fegan with rheumy eyes and said, "If it sticks, if this peace deal works out, you've got to ask yourself something."

Fegan propped the broom against the workbench and scooped up chippings with a dustpan. "What?"

"If there's peace, if it's really over, then what use are we?"

Fegan had no answer.

Ronnie turned his attention to an acoustic guitar that a guard had left for repair. The guard had said his son was driving him crazy about it, that the boy loved the guitar more than his own mother. Ronnie would get a couple of sets of strings for payment. His face glazed with concentration as he held his ear to the guitar's face. He pressed the wood with his fingertips and squinted.

"Aye," he said. "There's a brace gone."

Ronnie laid the guitar flat on its back atop a felt sheet so the coarse workbench wouldn't scratch it. Hunkering down, he stared across its surface for a moment and said, "See? She's starting to belly."

Fegan bent down at the opposite side of the bench. Ronnie smelled of mint and linseed oil. Yes, there it was: a slight deformation in the guitar's smooth face. "I see it," Fegan said. He ran his fingertips over the satin-finished cedar.

Fegan reached in through the guitar's soundhole and felt the loose brace just inside. "Glue it and clamp it?" he asked.

"That ought to do it," Ronnie said. He coughed and spat into a tissue, his face reddening. "Grab us the aliphatic resin like a good fella."

Fegan went to a storage cupboard and found a bottle of the glue. He brought it to Ronnie, but the older man shook his head and eased himself back onto his stool.

"You have a go," Ronnie said. "Dab a bit of that on a spatula and slap her on."

Fegan hesitated. "You sure?"

Ronnie nodded. Fegan worked while Ronnie watched, the old man softly humming an old jazz tune in his wheezy voice. Fegan recognised this one as "Misty'. Ronnie had played it for him once on his guitar. He said Clint Eastwood made a film about it.

As Fegan tightened a G-clamp to hold the glued brace in position, Ronnie asked, "Are you sleeping any better?"

"No," Fegan said.

"Still those dreams?"

Fegan wiped away the excess glue with a tissue. He did not answer.

"Don't tell me," Ronnie chided. He coughed and smiled. "See if I care."

"It's just . . ." Fegan rolled the tissue in a ball and threw it on the workbench. "It's just I'm not sure they're dreams."

Ronnie scratched his stubbly chin. "Why?"

"Because I'm awake when they come. I know I'm awake. And sometimes . . ."

Ronnie waited. "And sometimes?"

"I've seen them in the daytime." Fegan screwed the lid back on the bottle of glue. He didn't look at the other man.

"What does Dr. Brady say?"

Fegan shrugged. "He says it's guilt. He called it a manifestation."

Ronnie wiped his mouth with his tissue and raised his eyebrows. "Big word. Must be serious. And what do *you* think it is?"

Fegan crossed the room and stowed the glue in the cupboard. He stayed there, his back to Ronnie. "When I was small, before my father died, I used to see things. People. I used to talk to them." He listened for some response, some dismissal. When none came, he said, "I never told anyone that. Not even Dr. Brady."

He waited for a long minute before turning back to Ronnie. The old man sat hunched on the stool, staring at the tissue in his fingers.

Fegan took a step closer. "Ronnie?"

"You're talking about the dead," he said. He hacked and spat, his face going from red to purple. When he was done, he wiped his lips and inhaled a deep, rattling breath. "Don't talk to me about the dead.

This stuff's eating away at me, the asbestos, eating me from inside. You'll be out of here in a few weeks, but I might not make it that far. The quack says some of these nights I'll just drown in my sleep, same as if someone held my head under water. Every night I put my head down I pray I'll lift it again in the morning. And I pray if I don't, He'll take care of me." Ronnie's shoulders hitched and his eyes welled. "You know what I did."

Fegan nodded.

"Aye." Ronnie sniffed and coughed. "Don't talk to me about the dead, Gerry." He raised himself from the stool and shuffled towards the door. "I'll meet them soon enough."

Ronnie stopped in the doorway while the guard checked his pockets. He looked back over his shoulder. "Take care of yourself, Gerry." He winked. "No one else will."

Fegan never saw him again. He wept the day Ronnie's daughter brought the guitar to him.

Sunlight from his window made glistening pools on the Martin D-28's finish. Fegan propped the guitar back in its corner and admired the wood's grain. The lacquer had yellowed with age, making the guitar even more handsome. He had a set of strings, eleven-gauge bronze, for when it was done. He wasn't sure how to tune it, but he would figure it out.

Fegan checked the time. The phone had been charging for its requisite two hours. Despite the shaking of his hands, and the throb behind his eyes, he finally managed to put the little plastic card in place, cover it with the battery, and snap the phone's back cover on. The instructions lay open on the coffee table in front of him, and he traced the small words with his fingertip. He pressed and held the green button. When it vibrated in his hand, he placed it on the coffee table and watched its colorful screen play a series of animations.

He looked at his palm. The string of digits was faint, but still readable. Following the instructions, he dialled Marie McKenna's number. He closed his eyes and listened to the ring tone, remembering she had made no promises about answering. The phone almost slipped from his fingers when she did.

"It's Gerry," he said.

He heard a long exhalation. "I'm glad you called," she said.

"Are you?"

"Yes." Her voice had the slightest of shakes. "I had a visitor this morning."

"Who?"

"Would you believe, Father Coulter?"

Fegan was silent for a moment before asking, "What did he want?"

"He advised me to leave. He said it would be best for me and Ellen. His exact words were 'It'll avoid any unpleasantness.''

Fegan thought about the Walther. He sensed it beneath his bed. It lay in the shoebox amid rolls of banknotes.

Marie continued. "He kept going on about how he'd hate to see anything bad happen to my wee girl, how he'd hate to see her get hurt. He kept telling me to think of Ellen and not be so stubborn. There were people who wanted to hurt us, and there might be no stopping them if I stayed. And all the time he had this look on his face, like the sight of me offended him."

Fegan looked at his palm, imagining the cold weight of the gun there.

"Can you believe it?" Marie asked. "McGinty's getting priests to deliver his threats now. Father Coulter said he was just telling me as a favor."

"What did you say?"

"Nothing, at first; I was too shocked. Then I told him to get out." Fegan listened to her breath against his ear. "They'll be coming for me now, won't they?"

"Yeah," Fegan said. "They'll come after dark. Nothing serious at first. Maybe just break a window. Next time, they'll use a petrol bomb or a shotgun."

"Jesus, what about Ellen? I can't let her go through that. I've no one she can even stay with."

"I'll come over this evening. They won't do anything while I'm there."

"Please," she said. "Please come over."

Fegan made a fist with his free hand. "Don't worry. I'll take care of it."

He said goodbye and hung up. He stood, crossed the hall, and climbed the stairs. Perched on the end of his bed, he reached under and pulled out the shoebox as shadows gathered around him, watching. He removed the lid and was met again by the greasy smell of money. Once more he wondered how much there was. Fegan had never counted it. Thousands, anyway, maybe ten or more. He'd saved it from the salary that McGinty's bogus Community Development job paid out.

The pistol's baleful sheen entranced him for a while. Loose bullets rolled beneath the money like mice in a nest.

"No," he said.

The three Brits came forward, the other six behind them. The woman stepped around them and knelt next to Fegan. She smiled as Fegan took the gun from its nest. It was cool and heavy in his hand.

"No," Fegan said. He put the Walther back among the bills and bullets. "Not Father Coulter."

But they would let him sleep. If he gave them everything they wanted, they would give him peace and let him sleep.

The wonderful thought of closing his eyes, hearing nothing but his own breathing, lingered in his mind. Suddenly, an even sweeter thought came to him, one which had never occurred to him before: the thought of falling asleep with his head on Marie McKenna's breast, letting her warmth soak through him, her heartbeat drowning out all else.

Fegan blinked and wiped the thought away.

"No," he said. He replaced the lid and slid the shoebox back under his bed.

The late Vincie Caffola's girlfriend was red-faced and puffy-eyed when she shook Fegan's hand. Caffola's two sons looked bemused at the attention they were receiving, the older battling tears while the younger wept freely. They both looked like their father, the eldest as tall as Fegan.

He felt a sour turning in his gut when he told them he was sorry for their trouble. The boys couldn't meet his eyes as he spoke, and Fegan was glad of it. Some insane part of him wanted to beg their forgiveness. Caffola might have been a mindless thug, but he had been a father to these boys. The younger was about the age Fegan had been when his own father fell down a flight of stairs, drunk.

Fegan finished his condolences and moved away, desperate to be free of their grief-reddened eyes, but Caffola's girlfriend gripped his wrist.

"Nobody's doing anything," she said. "The party, the cops, none of them."

Fegan tried to ease her hand away, but she gripped hard.

"Nobody cares," she whispered. "So long as he's buried and gone, no one gives a shite who done it. It's not right, Gerry."

He prised her fingers from his wrist and stepped back. "I'm sorry," he said.

"It's not right," she said again as Fegan turned his back on her and walked away.

Caffola's house was not as crammed as McKenna's mother's had been, but air was hard to come by nonetheless. Fegan made his way upstairs to view the corpse. The mourners parted respectfully to let him through. Like McKenna's, Caffola's coffin was modest, but probably for economic reasons rather than appearances. Fegan crossed himself, but didn't kneel to pray. He'd had enough of God for now. Instead, he paced a circle around the box. The undertakers had made a good job of concealing the injury to the deceased's temple.

Fegan thought of Marie and how she had lingered over McKenna's coffin. He whispered to himself, "You had it coming."

A hush settled on the room, and Fegan looked up from the body, knowing who he'd see.

"Hello, Gerry," McGinty said.

Fegan nodded.

McGinty addressed the others in the room. "Can I get a few minutes with my friend?"

The room emptied quickly, leaving only Fegan, McGinty, the pale cadaver and the deepening shadows. Fegan kept his eyes on the politician, the coffin between them.

"We have a wee problem," McGinty said, smiling.

Fegan didn't answer. The chill pulsed at his center. Despite himself, he put a hand on his own heart in case the politician would see its cold glow.

"You didn't do what I asked you," McGinty said. "Why not?"

"She's no threat to you. There's no reason to put her out," Fegan said, fighting to keep the anger from his voice.

McGinty stepped closer and rested his hands on the edge of the box. "If I let her stay I look weak. I can't afford to look weak, Gerry. Not now. I've too much at stake. I've already been more generous than that girl deserved. She would've been in the ground long ago if I hadn't indulged Michael. There's a limit to how generous I can be." He looked down at the corpse. "I've already allowed too many things to slide. I owe you a lot, Gerry, but my patience is wearing thin."

Fegan moved around the coffin, heading for the door. McGinty blocked his path.

"I mean it, Gerry. Don't test me. You don't want to tell her, all right, but don't interfere."

Fegan stepped to the side, but McGinty gripped his arm, and the two looked hard into each other's eyes. The politician's thin lips broke into a soft smile. He cupped Fegan's face in his hands, leaned in, and placed a dry kiss on his cheek.

"We've always been such good friends," McGinty said. "Ever since you were a kid. Don't fuck it up over a woman. Not a whore like Marie McKenna."

Fegan's cheek burned. He pulled away and finally reached the door. The people on the landing made way for him, and he hurried down the stairs. He stopped dead when he reached the bottom.

Davy Campbell nodded. Fegan nodded back, ignoring the crackling in his temples and the shadows moving in from the edge of his vision. Campbell had changed since Fegan saw him last. Thinner. Darker round the eyes. Death clings to men who've wielded it, like the stench of the abattoir. Fegan imagined they could smell it on each other, as a dog knows friend from enemy by scent alone. He opened the front door and left Campbell staring after him.

23

Campbell watched Fegan disappear around the corner. As he went back into the house the mixture of fear, hate and anger in Fegan's eyes lingered with him. He looked like a killer, the purest kind, the kind who killed more out of want than need. Campbell sniffed and wiped his nose with the back of his hand. He made his way upstairs, struggling to squeeze through the mourners who had parted so easily for Fegan. He entered the bedroom where Caffola's body lay. McGinty had his back to the door.

"I want that cunt sorted, Davy," McGinty said without looking round.

"When?" Campbell asked.

"The day after tomorrow. I don't want the press getting distracted from my speech at the funeral, but no later than that."

"Whatever you say." Campbell walked around the coffin to face McGinty. "What about the woman?"

"Eddie Coyle can sort it out," McGinty said. "I made a kind gesture, letting Father Coulter speak to her, and she threw it back in my face. Well, no more. Eddie won't be so polite about it."

"What if he fucks it up? He's not the brightest."

"What's to fuck up? All he's got to do is put a brick through her window. Still, you've got a point. Maybe you should go with him."

"He won't like that," Campbell said.

"I don't care what he likes," McGinty said. "He'll do what he's told. And, Davy, listen to me."

"Yeah?"

"Whatever happens, don't hurt Marie or the wee girl, all right? Frighten them if you have to, but don't hurt them."

Something moved behind McGinty's eyes. Campbell only caught a glimpse of it.

"They won't get hurt. I'll make sure of it." Campbell looked down at Vincie Caffola's peaceful face. "Why'd Fegan do it?"

"Christ knows. He's off his head, so maybe he didn't need a reason. Anyway, if he hadn't done it, I would have, eventually. Caffola had a big mouth. It's no great loss."

"Then why go after Fegan now?" Campbell asked.

"Because if he thinks he can get away with it, where's he going to stop? Besides, the old man has spoken. Bull O'Kane won't have any unauthorised actions, even if they're against pieces of shit like this."

Campbell caught a scent and followed it. "So, the Bull still calls the shots? I thought he'd retired."

"Bull?" McGinty's laugh was laced with a little fear. "Christ, he won't retire until he's in a box himself. And no, he doesn't call the shots. But the boys on the street still look up to him. Us politicians have to indulge him sometimes."

McGinty stepped away from the coffin, then stopped and turned to look down at the corpse. He leaned forward and spat on Caffola's pale face. "You had it coming," he said, and left the room.

Campbell hung his new black suit from the handle on his bedroom door as he held the phone between his shoulder and his ear, listening to the ring tone. The handler answered, breathless.

"McGinty told me to do Fegan," Campbell said.

"When?"

"Day after tomorrow."

"After the funeral. Clever bastard. He wants to milk Caffola's death all he can. Try to move it forward a bit – give the press something else to think about – no point letting McGinty squeeze any more out of this than absolutely necessary."

"I'll see what I can do." Campbell removed the price tags from the suit. It was cheap, but it would do. It was only a thug's funeral, after all. "By the way, he let an interesting scrap slip: Bull O'Kane's still in the picture."

"The Bull was supposed to have retired," the handler said. "Last I heard he was putting his feet up at that farm on the border."

"Well, apparently not. That old bastard still carries some weight. The politicians don't have it all their own way."

"I'll pass it on. Anything else?"

"Just one thing. Once I've taken care of Fegan, what then? Do I stay in Belfast with McGinty or go back to Dundalk?"

"Not so fast," the handler said. "We've been talking at this end. My superiors think it's time you came out for good. I agree. You've been under for a long time."

Campbell gave a hard laugh. "What are you talking about?"

"How old are you now? Thirty-eight? You're not getting any younger. All right, you're still sharp enough, but for how long? All it takes is one slip. Get out while you're still young enough to have a life in the real world, away from all that shit."

Campbell dropped the suit onto the bed. "This *is* my life."

"Life? You call that a life? You've been under too long, Campbell. It's just not healthy. And besides, things are winding down there. You've seen the changes. The soldiers are off the streets, the watchtowers are being pulled down. Think about it: once this mess is cleaned up, what good are you doing there?"

"The dissidents. They're organising. They'll be—"

"They're a bunch of has-beens who can't accept it's over. Plumbers and bricklayers who call themselves soldiers. They're no use to anybody now, just dinosaurs who forgot to lie down and die. They destroyed themselves in Omagh, and they'll never recover. You know that, you spent time with them."

"There's the Loyalists. They're still—"

"They're what? They're pushing drugs and counterfeit handbags between bumping each other off. The police can deal with them." The handler sighed. "Listen, I'm not asking, I'm telling. Once you're done there, you're coming out. At least take some leave, just to get your head straight. And don't worry about money. I'll make sure you're looked after."

"Fuck the money. It's not about the money."

"Take it easy, Campbell. We'll organise some leave for you when you've taken care of Fegan. A holiday. Where would you like to go? The Mediterranean, the Bahamas, Thailand?"

"Fuck you," Campbell said as he hung up.

He threw the phone on top of the suit and paced the small bedroom. Leave? Get out? Why? Go back to what?

Campbell crossed to the dressing table, opened the drawer, and ran his fingers through the soft plume of his Red Hackle.

24

The sun dipped towards the rooftops as Fegan rang Marie McKenna's doorbell. Her flat was on the ground floor of the old red-brick terraced house. The drawn curtains twitched in the bay window by the door. His skin tingled when he heard her footsteps approach from inside.

Marie opened the door and smiled. "Thanks for coming," she said. She stepped back to let him in. Her eyes were puffy from crying.

"Have you eaten?" she asked as they walked along the hallway. A bicycle was propped at the foot of the stairs leading to the flats above.

"Not since this morning," Fegan lied. His stomach had still been reeling from the whiskey and no solid had passed his lips that day.

"You must be starving," Marie said, showing him into the flat. "I'm just about to make something for Ellen and me. You'll have some too."

It was more an instruction than an invitation.

"Hiya!" Ellen chimed as he entered. She lay on the floor, a coloring book and crayons strewn around her. The flat was open-plan, with the living area to the front, a kitchenette to the rear. Two doors opened off this room, leading to the back of the house.

"Hello, Ellen," he said.

Fegan took in the large open space, and the homey objects scattered about it. His own home was drab and spare by comparison, decorated only by the wooden objects he'd made himself. He clutched one of them, wrapped in plastic.

"Lookit," Ellen said, climbing to her feet. She brought the coloring book over for him to see. There was a picture of a pig in a little dress. Ellen had colored it all green.

'Very good," he said.

Marie stroked her daughter's hair. "Ellen, leave Gerry alone a while, okay?"

Ellen pouted. "Okay."

As Marie took his coat, Fegan said, "I brought you something." He handed her the plastic bag as his cheeks grew hot.

"Oh?" She opened it.

Fegan had found the piece of oak on a derelict site near his home. It might once have been a small part of a mantelpiece or a banister. He had worked with the grain over weeks, sanding into its flow, until it became a fluid shape like a river current. He smoothed out the hole where a knot had been, and built up thin layer after thin layer of varnish, buffing between coats until it looked like it burned from within. To finish, he mounted it on a slate base.

"It's beautiful," Marie said.

"It was just gathering dust in my house," Fegan said. "It'll look better here."

"Thank you." She placed it on a table by the window next to an open laptop computer.

"Anything?" Fegan asked.

"Nothing. It's been quiet. I've been working, mostly." She studied the piece in what little light the drawn curtains let through.

"It'll be dark in a couple of hours. They'll come after that."

"And what'll you do?" she asked, turning back to him.

"Talk to them," he said.

"Talk? I doubt they'll listen."

"Well, then I'll try . . . something else."

Marie stared at him for a beat then said, "I'm glad you came."

Dinner was simple – grilled chicken breast with boiled new potatoes and salad – but Fegan devoured it like it was his last meal. When Marie asked if he wanted more, he said yes before she'd finished the question. The time since anyone had made him a home-cooked meal could not be counted in weeks, months or even years. It was almost two decades since he had last sat at a table and eaten with people he knew and liked.

Ellen had meticulously separated the red-leaf salad from the green, and banished it to the side of her plate. Likewise, she had removed dark spots from the potato skins with the care and precision of a surgeon, and deposited them with the unwanted salad. Other than that, she had cleared her plate whilst chatting to Fegan about shoes, drawing and Peppa Pig.

"What's Peppa Pig?" Fegan asked.

Ellen giggled, and said, "Silly."

Fegan didn't inquire further.

When the meal was done, Marie stood and shooed Ellen away to her coloring books lying strewn around the living area.

"So, what happens after tonight?" she asked. She began clearing the table. "Say you see them off. They'll just come back with more tomorrow, won't they?"

"Maybe," Fegan said. "I'll come back and take care of it again, if you want me to."

She brought the dishes to the sink where pots were already soaking. "And what about after that? They'll come back with more and more. I don't want Ellen to see that. And I don't want you to get hurt."

"I won't," he said. He joined Marie at the sink, took a towel, and began drying dishes as she handed them over. "I'm going to take care of it. In a few days, it'll be sorted."

"How?"

"Don't worry about that," he said. "I'm going to take care of it, that's all you need to know. You and Ellen won't have to worry any more."

She held on to a plate as he went to take it from her. "What does that mean?"

He smiled at her. It felt easy and honest on his lips. "You won't have to worry. That's all."

Marie returned his smile, but Fegan glimpsed something hard and jagged in it as she turned away.

Marie told Fegan about Jack Lennon, how the handsome policeman had asked her out as she packed her Dictaphone away. The story had been about Catholics in the police service at a time of reform. Jack had been a good interview, open and eloquent. Charming, even. He blushed when Marie asked if Jack Lennon was really a John.

Within six days, Marie was in love.

She had kept it secret at first. Her family's disapproval of her working for a Unionist newspaper had been made clear. Her father had never spoken about his involvement in the conflict, but she knew her Uncle Michael was up to his neck in it. Everywhere she went, people knew who she was, and who she shared her blood with. Her friends were from that community, too, and all but a few drifted away because of her job. When she could keep Jack Lennon secret no longer, they deserted her as quickly as everyone else she'd grown up with.

At the age of thirty-one, Marie McKenna found herself isolated, cut off from her old life. But she had Jack, and that was enough. Vague threats would surface now and then, Mass cards with bullets in the post, but the couple were strong. They could survive it.

Two years after meeting him, just a few weeks before the day she realised her period was late, Marie smelt perfume on him. By now, Jack was working CID, out of uniform. He said it was a female colleague, one who had shown no interest in him in the past. Seeing him in a solid relationship with another woman changed that. Day after day she had been throwing herself at him, often physically, but he had resisted her. He always had been, and always would be, faithful.

Jack Lennon was a charming and persuasive man. Marie believed every word he said. In retrospect, she imagined she saw him flinch when she told him she might be pregnant. She couldn't be sure of it, but that was immaterial in the long run. All she could be sure of was arriving home on a drizzly evening two months later and finding their flat empty.

Fegan listened to Marie as she sat next to him on her sofa. Her face showed no emotion as she spoke.

"Do you want to know the really sad thing?" she asked. She didn't wait for an answer. "A week after he left me for her, she dumped him." Marie gave a brittle laugh. "She wanted what she couldn't have, and when she could have it, she didn't want it any more. So much damage, just on a whim. Anyway, he phoned me, begging to come back. I told him to shove it."

"Good," Fegan said. "He sounds like an arsehole."

Ellen looked up from her coloring. "You said a bad word."

"Sorry," Fegan said.

Ellen looked to her mother. "Mummy, can I watch a DVD?"

"It's nearly bedtime, sweetheart," Marie said.

"Can I just watch the start of it?" Ellen implored.

Marie sat forward on the couch and gave it her consideration. "All right, but no arguing when I say it's bedtime, right?"

"Right." Ellen grinned and went to a bookcase laden with paperbacks, CDs and DVDs. She picked a brightly colored case, opened it, and carefully removed the disc.

"Watch this," Marie whispered. "She's an expert."

Ellen went to the player underneath the television, pressed a button to open its tray, and placed the disc at its center, adjusting it with her tiny fingertips. She turned on the television, found the right channel, and bounced over to the sofa. There was just enough room between Fegan and Marie for her to wriggle into. Fegan watched as Ellen manipulated the remote control until the film began to play.

"You're very clever," he said.

Ellen looked up at him, brought her finger to her lips – shush – and pointed to the television. Fegan cleared his throat and did as he was told. He caught Marie's smile from the corner of his eye.

Soon, Fegan knew nothing but the movie. It was about an orange and white fish who searched a big blue ocean for his son. Sometimes he felt Ellen's body jerk and rattle with laughter beside him, and he did the same. They felt strange, these spasms, rippling up from his belly to burst in his mouth. The moving images made shadows dance around the room, but they concealed nothing but Marie's scattered possessions.

Ellen's bedtime came and went with no protest from her mother, but as the film ended, Marie patted her knee and said, "Okay, missy, you got away with that one, but now it's really time for bed."

Ellen slumped forward, despondent. "Do I have to?"

"Yep, it's nearly half-nine and you were supposed to be in bed an hour ago. It's . . ." Marie paused as if remembering something she would rather have forgotten. "It's dark outside."

Fegan raised himself from the sofa. He looked to the curtained window, then back to Marie. She stood, lifting Ellen, and placed her upright on the floor.

"Go and get your jammies on," she said. "Then we'll get your teeth brushed."

Ellen trudged to one of the doors beyond the kitchenette at the back of the house. She turned in the doorway, waved, and called, "Night-night, Gerry."

"Night-night," he said, feeling a little pang of sadness to see her go. He looked down to Marie, who stood with her hands in the hip pockets of her jeans.

"So, here we are," she said.

"Yeah," Fegan said. He was unable to hold her gaze and he looked away.

She cleared her throat and sniffed. "Listen, I'm pretty tired, too. I didn't sleep well last night. I'll, uh . . . I'll see to Ellen, then take myself to bed. Will you be all right here?"

"Yeah," Fegan said. "When they come I'll be ready for them."

"Okay," Marie said. She stepped away, paused, and then came back to him. Standing on tiptoe, she placed a kiss on his cheek and smiled. "I'd say you were a good man, but I'm a terrible judge of character."

Fegan watched her leave the room as the warmth of her lips on his cheek gave way to the slightest chill of moisture.

Once the flat was quiet, he circled the room, switching off lights. Blackness owned him until he opened the curtains. The street light outside coated the room in a dim orange. He sat down at the table by the window and waited.

Occasionally cars moved along the street outside, their headlights illuminating the old houses, making their facades seem to turn and watch the travellers go by.

Now and then, people would pass the window, oblivious to Fegan's vigil. Sometimes they were couples, young men and women clinging to each other, moving as one. The sight of them opened paths in his mind, paths he did not want to follow. He would only find regret and self-pity there.

Instead, he thought about the chill of moisture on his cheek. He brought his fingertips to that place, remembering the warmth before the cold.

Almost three hours passed before the chill crept to his center, a tingling began in his temples, and the shadows around him came to life.

25

Eddie Coyle drove in silence. Campbell had greeted him with a friendly hello when he got into the car a few minutes before, but Coyle had not replied. Now they travelled along the Malone Road, approaching the Wellington Park Hotel and the right turn into Eglantine Avenue just beyond.

"So, you're going to do the business, then?" Campbell asked.

Coyle stared ahead. The swelling over his eye had lessened, but the gauze pad on his brow carried an angry red rose.

"I'll just stay in the car and let you get on with it, will I?"

Coyle's mouth twisted. "Shut the fuck up, you cunt," he said. "You've no call to be here. There's plenty of boys could have come with me. Fuck, I'd sooner do it on my own than have to listen to you."

"Don't blame me if McGinty doesn't trust you to do it right," Campbell said.

His body leaned forward as Coyle stood on the brake pedal.

"You what?"

"McGinty thought you might make a balls of it, so he told me to go along," Campbell said. "Believe me, I've got better things to do than put the frighteners on women and wee girls, but I do what I'm told. Now, get moving before the cops come along and wonder why we're sitting in the middle of the Malone Road. The turn's just there."

"I know where the fucking turn is," Coyle said as he gunned the accelerator. He pulled hard on the steering wheel, forcing oncoming traffic to brake. He let the engine drop to a low rumble as they moved slowly along Eglantine Avenue. The Vauxhall Vectra puttered quietly until they reached the woman's place. The flat was in darkness, but her car was parked outside.

Coyle reached behind Campbell's seat, into the foot well, and retrieved two halves of brick. This sort of thing happened all the time in Belfast. The cops called it 'low-level intimidation'. It was just a way for paramilitaries of all shades to keep the locals in line, nothing special, nothing to get excited about. Unless you were on the receiving end, of course. Coyle opened the door, and went to climb out.

"Careful you don't miss," Campbell said.

"Aw, fuck off," Coyle said. He walked around the front of the car, a half-brick in each hand. He cried out, almost dropping them, when Gerry Fegan emerged from the shadows of the small garden to block his path.

"Leave her alone," Fegan said. Campbell could just hear his calm voice above the engine's idling.

"What are you doing here?" Coyle asked.

"I said leave her alone." Fegan took two steps closer to Coyle, the car's headlights glinting in his hard eyes.

Coyle turned to look back at Campbell. Campbell eased himself out of the car.

"Don't look at him, look at me," Fegan said. "Leave her alone. Get out of here and don't come back."

Campbell thought quickly. He had no gun with him; carrying one on an errand like this was too risky. If the cops stopped them, a brick was easier to explain than a loaded weapon. He wondered if Fegan was armed. Probably not, he thought. Fegan knew the risks just as well as he did.

But then again, Fegan was crazy.

"Get out of the way, Gerry," Coyle said. "This has nothing to do with you."

"One last time," Fegan said, his face impassive. "Leave her alone. Go away and don't come back."

Campbell watched with grim fascination. A man like Coyle couldn't hope to take a man like Fegan. Fegan would rip him to pieces. Christ, if Fegan had been in shape, Campbell wasn't sure he could have taken him, either. Even now, it wasn't a certainty. Crazy can make up for a lot. He waited, part of him relishing the idea of seeing Coyle taken apart.

Coyle raised a half-brick above his head. His voice was shrill. "I mean it, Gerry. Fuck off before I do you one."

Campbell saw shapes and movements at some of the windows. The police had probably been called already. The Lisburn Road station was barely half a mile away. They'd be here in minutes. "Fuck," he said, stepping towards Coyle. "Leave it, Eddie."

"You fuck off, too," Coyle said. "I was sent here to do a job, and I'm going to do it."

"Don't, Eddie. He'll break you in two."

Fegan stood silent, his eyes locked on Coyle.

"Eddie, come on."

Coyle brought the piece of brick down in a clumsy arc, and Fegan caught his wrist effortlessly. He kicked Coyle's legs from under him, and took the brick from his hand.

Fegan drew his arm back, the brick held tight in his fist, ready to drive it into Coyle's upturned face. "Get out of here or I'll fucking kill you."

Coyle scrambled backwards, and Fegan turned to Campbell. Campbell's gut chilled when he saw Fegan's eyes. The madman walked towards him and then stopped, lifting his hands up to his temples.

"Not now," he said. "Not here."

"What?" Campbell said.

"No!" Fegan stared at something to Campbell's left. "There'll be another time. I can't do it here. Not with witnesses."

"Jesus Christ," Campbell said, backing towards the car.

"How can I do it here?" Now Fegan's eyes moved to Campbell's right. "If I do it here I'll never be able to finish it."

"Finish what, Gerry?" Campbell took a tentative step forward. "Who are you talking to?"

Fegan's eyes moved from place to place, focused on something at eye level that only he could see. "There'll be another time. I swear."

Before Campbell could scream at him to stop, Coyle swung at Fegan from behind. Fegan ducked, but not quickly enough, and the second piece of brick glanced off his temple. He moved with the lithe speed of a predator, turning to seize Coyle's forearm before the other could react. Fegan swiped his piece of brick across Coyle's face, rocking his head back. He did it again and Campbell heard a sickening crunch. Coyle's legs crumpled beneath him and Fegan swung twice more, sending blood across the pavement.

The roar of an engine pulled Campbell's eyes to the Lisburn Road end of the street. A police Land Rover came barrelling around the corner. He hesitated for just a second, then turned and ran for the Malone Road.

He cut across it, dodging traffic, and ducked into Cloreen Park. He didn't stop running until he was on the Stranmillis Road. He walked purposefully to the warren of streets around Queen's University and wound through them until he reached the church on University Street. He crossed the road, opened the door to his building, trotted up two flights of stairs, and let himself into his flat. In the darkness he collapsed onto the couch, adrenalin sending wave after wave of tremors through his limbs.

"Fuck," he said to the empty room.

26

Fegan's eyes felt dry and heavy as he sat in his cell. It had been a long night. They'd taken him to the City Hospital on the Lisburn Road to have the abrasion on his temple examined, and the doctor had insisted on a scan. He had to sit on a bed in the Accident and Emergency ward, guarded by two police officers, until the results came back. Coyle had been in the hospital somewhere, too, but Fegan imagined he would have a longer stay.

Now Fegan sat on a thin mattress, his belt and shoelaces removed, waiting for them to let him go. Even if Coyle was in any state to be questioned, he would just clam up. Fegan was sure of that. McGinty would want Fegan away from the cops, out in the open, where he could be gotten to. Besides, despite what the party said in public, it would be considered bad form for Coyle to talk to the cops. That would place him only one step above a common tout. And the party dealt harshly with touts.

Shadows moved along the walls, sometimes taking shape, sometimes fading to nothing. Fegan's temples buzzed. The chill pulsed at his center.

"What did you want me to do?" Fegan asked.

The shadows didn't answer.

"If I'd done it last night, the cops would have got me for it. I'd be in here for murder, not for fighting. Then I wouldn't be able to do any of the others."

Still nothing.

Suddenly, one of the shadows solidified, its form revealing itself against the cold white wall. The Royal Ulster Constabulary officer, his uniform stiff and crisp. He stared hard at Fegan for a moment before turning to the door.

The peephole cover opened with a clang. Fegan saw the glint of an eye and the cover was closed again. Keys jangled and locks snapped. The door opened outwards and a tall, heavy-set policeman of around fifty stood in the opening. He looked up and down the corridor outside, and then back to Fegan. He entered, smiling, and locked the door behind him.

"Good morning, Gerry," he said. He wore a short-sleeved shirt and a tie. His utility belt bulged with equipment, but Fegan noticed the weapons had been removed, and so had his name badge. The RUC man put his fingers to the cop's head.

"You'll be glad to know you'll be released in a few hours," said the cop as he crossed the floor, limping slightly. "Your friend Mr. Coyle swears blind he fell and you were helping him up."

"That's right," Fegan said, keeping his focus on the policeman's round face, and away from the shadows that gathered around him.

"Well, that's grand then, isn't it?" the cop said, smiling. The fluorescent lighting reflected off his pink scalp. "But I've got to give you a wee message before you go. Why don't you stand up?"

"A message from who?" Fegan asked.

"Let's just say a mutual friend," the cop said. "Now, stand up, there's a good fella."

Fegan slowly got to his feet. The smile never left the cop's mouth, even when he drove his fist into Fegan's gut. All air deserted the cell, leaving nothing but a painful vacuum, and Fegan wondered how the peeler could breathe. He collapsed back onto the mattress, clutching his belly. A flash of rage burned in him, but he stamped on it, pushed it down. He couldn't fight the cop here. Not if he wanted to live.

The shadows retreated to the walls. The RUC man's hand recoiled with every silent shot.

The cop placed a hand on Fegan's shoulder. "The message is in two parts. One part's verbal, the other's physical. Let's get the verbal out of the way, okay?"

He slapped Fegan's shoulder and sat down beside him. "Now, first things first. This conversation never happened or Marie McKenna has an accident. I want to make myself clear on that point. That's very important. Now, to the rest of it." The cop took a deep breath. "When you get out of here, you go home, you stay there until our mutual friend sends for you, or Marie McKenna has an accident. If you try to run, Marie McKenna has an accident. If you mess our mutual friend about in any way, shape or form, Marie McKenna has an accident. Are you getting the idea, Gerry?"

Fegan didn't answer. He was concentrating too hard on breathing to form words.

The cop swung his lumpy fist down into Fegan's groin. "I asked you a question, Gerry. Do you get the idea?"

Fegan fell to his side, grabbing at his testicles. His abdomen filled with hot lead. He gasped, scrabbling words from tiny mouthfuls of air. "I . . . under . . . stand."

"Good man," the cop said as he stood up. "Now we do the physical part. Are you ready?"

The cop went to work with the dispassionate care of a craftsman. He found all Fegan's tender spots, every part of him that could accommodate a fist or a boot while remaining concealed under his clothing. Fegan blacked out once, only to be roused by sharp slaps across his cheek. As he lay on the floor, the pain verging on unbearable, he realised the woman was kneeling at his side, the baby held close to her breast. She flinched with every blow.

When he was finished, the cop stood back, proudly surveying his work. "There, now," he said, still smiling, but a little breathless. A sheen of sweat glistened on his forehead. "I'm glad we got that sorted out. Have you any questions?"

Fegan coughed, spattering a fine spray of blood on the floor. "Yeah," he said.

The cop hunkered down. "Oh? What's that, now?"

"Who the fuck *are* you?"

The cop laughed. "Don't you know, Gerry?" He leaned in close and whispered, "I'm the rotten apple that spoils the barrel."

Fegan closed his eyes and listened to the opening and closing of the door, the turning of keys, and the cop's laughter receding in the distance. He rolled onto his back, feeling a deep, sickly weight in his midsection. The shadows gathered round, took shape, and he smiled weakly up at them.

"Are you enjoying it so far?" he asked.

The woman rested her cool hand on Fegan's cheek, and the room slipped away from him.

27

Campbell marvelled at Paul McGinty's ability to twist facts to suit his agenda. The speech was an incredible exercise in spin. The politician stood on the improvised platform just steps away from Vincie Caffola's grave, blustering with all the indignation of the righteous. The same police force that left Caffola to choke on his vomit, he said, had beaten Edward Coyle, party activist, to a senseless mess after stopping his car on Eglantine Avenue. The crowd roared when McGinty vowed to see justice done, and it was all Campbell could do not to join in. No wonder the politician's enemies respected and hated him in equal measure.

News cameras followed McGinty from the podium, but his security men blocked their path. The politician approached Campbell alone. "Walk with me," he said.

They moved among the gravestones and memorials, working their way towards the gates where McGinty's Lincoln waited. The sun warmed Campbell's back.

"So, what do you reckon to our friend Gerry?" McGinty asked.

"He's insane," Campbell said. "That makes him dangerous. If I'm going to take him, it better be soon. He could do anything."

"Our friend on the force gave him a message this morning," McGinty said. "He made it very clear."

"Threats won't do it," Campbell said. "You can't reason with crazy."

McGinty kicked gravel along the path and stopped. "Don't worry, I won't be reasoning with him. Not after what Father Coulter told me this morning. I knew it was him, but Christ, to come right out and say it. Even if he thought Father Coulter would keep that from me, he has some brass neck on him. But it's a question of timing. I've got a press conference lined up for the morning. Eddie Coyle's going to tell them how the peelers kicked the shit out of him. I don't want anything to distract the press from that. It's not just local press, either. Jesus, I've got CNN and Fox News coming. They love this sort of thing. See, this is what old Bull O'Kane doesn't understand, what he never learned from us. As long as I've got the press lapping this stuff up, the Brits are on the back foot. I stir up enough shit, they'll give us anything we ask for. They know we can bring Stormont down if we want to, and they'll bend over backwards to stop it. They'll be eating out of my hand, and the party won't dare pass me over. Not when the cameras are on me. I'm telling you, the media's a better weapon than Semtex ever was."

"The media won't be dancing to your tune if Fegan has a crack at someone else. He was ready to take me on last night, only something stopped him."

"What?" McGinty asked.

"I don't know." Campbell shook his head. "Whatever it was, it was in his head. He's snapped, completely gone, schizophrenic or some fucking thing."

One corner of McGinty's mouth curled up. "That's your medical opinion, is it?"

"It's no joke." Campbell fixed the politician with a hard stare. "You better watch your back. I'm telling you, he—"

McGinty's hand lashed out so quickly, Campbell felt the sting on his cheek before he knew it had moved.

McGinty cleared his throat and smoothed his jacket. He took a cautious look around to make sure no cameras had caught the slap. He leaned in close to Campbell.

"Watch your mouth," he said. "You don't tell me anything; I tell you. Got that?"

Campbell fought back rage as he brought his fingers to the heat on his bearded cheek. Blood rushed in his ears and his head seemed to float above his shoulders. "I'm sorry, Mr. McGinty," he said. "But with all due respect, think about this: he hasn't taken too kindly to Marie McKenna being strong-armed. What if he comes after you next?"

McGinty snorted, but his eyes gave him away. "He'd never get to me. There's boys have been trying to get to me since 1972, and nobody's even come close, even Delaney and those two UFF boys you fingered. Why do you think Fegan could do it?"

Campbell locked eyes with McGinty. "Because I think he'd die trying."

McGinty's stare fell away and he cleared his throat. He set off towards the car again. Campbell followed.

"All right, I'll tell you what," McGinty said as they neared the Lincoln. "The cops will let Fegan go in an hour or so. You follow him and make sure he goes home. Get into the house and do him there. Lock the place up good and tight. With a bit of luck nobody'll find him for a day or two. That'll give me time to get what I can out of the press coverage."

"What about the woman?" Campbell asked. "She might twig if she tries to reach him."

McGinty lowered himself into the back of the Lincoln as his driver held the door. "Don't worry about her," he said. "She's already taken care of."

Campbell hunched down in the rusting Ford Focus and watched Fegan clamber out of a taxi and pay the driver. As the cab pulled away, Fegan took delicate steps towards his front door, his hand pressed to his abdomen. Campbell's Focus sat at the far end of Calcutta Street. He sucked air through his teeth when his quarry stooped to spit blood on the pavement. Fegan straightened, wiped his mouth clean, and let himself into his house.

Christ, Campbell thought, *the message must have been loud and clear. He's really hurting.*

A part of Campbell wished Fegan would have a crack at McGinty. His skin still tingled where the politician had slapped him. The world would be no poorer for that bastard's passing, just as it was no worse off without McKenna or Caffola. In fact, Campbell would have been delighted to help Fegan in a cull of the party. But for every politician like McGinty there were ten thugs who would gladly take his place and guide the party away from weapons like newspapers and television cameras, and back to AK47s and mortar bombs. It was sad, but true: Paul McGinty was the lesser of many evils.

The greatest of those evils was the Bull.

Terrance Plunkett O'Kane, a thickset man who stood six foot four, had risen to prominence as the Seventies became the Eighties, that turbulent time when the party's political wing began to branch away from the paramilitary side. Campbell had never met the Bull, but the old man's reputation travelled far and wide. When Campbell was still a corporal in the Black Watch he heard stories of O'Kane's bloody ways. And when he left the barracks for the back streets of Belfast the stories grew more horrific.

As the political process had gathered momentum, it seemed the Bull's time had come and gone. The twenty-first century belonged to men like McGinty and his nose for a headline. Thus, as his sixties edged towards his seventies, the Bull seemed content to retire and let McGinty and his political colleagues take the reins.

Apparently not, Campbell thought.

McGinty and O'Kane were two sides of the same coin. O'Kane still commanded the loyalty of the old foot soldiers, the Eddie Coyles, and McGinty and the party leadership relied on them for their power on the street. At the same time, the party's political influence had allowed the Bull to operate his fuel-laundering plants in relative peace for the last ten years. Each needed the other, and it was a precarious balance between the old ways and the new.

Now Fegan was tipping that balance. Whatever insane vendetta he was bent on had the potential to wrest the wheel from the politicians' control altogether. If Campbell's hunch was right, and Fegan managed to get to McGinty, it could tear the party wide open. The party could fill his position, all right – in fact, rumor had it they had someone lined up to take his place if they could find a way to sideline him – but McGinty's crew wouldn't stand for it. A feud would almost certainly follow. Stormont was fragile enough as it stood; losing McGinty would leave it on a knife-edge.

There was no question: Fegan had to disappear.

And after that?

Campbell thought about the handler's words. He couldn't imagine quitting. When he closed his eyes and pictured leaving this life, it was like walking off a cliff. A long drop into nothing. It made him dizzy just to picture it.

When Campbell first came to Belfast with the Black Watch, everyone said it would never end. The divisions and hatreds were too deep-rooted. The dirty war would roll on and on, bomb upon bomb, body upon body. The politicians were too busy pandering to the bigotry of their constituents to solve the issues, and the paramilitaries were making too much money to consider any other way.

But, in spite of every apparently insurmountable obstacle, it looked like they had finally done it. Campbell still couldn't quite believe it. It didn't seem real. The politicians had been cajoled, blackmailed and bullied by the British and Irish governments into figuring it out. After eighty-odd years, this tiny country finally had a future.

And Campbell did not.

He remembered an ancient Chinese curse as he opened the car door. *May you live in interesting times*, he thought.

Campbell crossed to an alleyway between two houses. It opened to another alleyway that ran parallel to Calcutta Street, acting as a border between it and the rear of Mumbai Street. He crept along the wall, hugging the brickwork, counting gates as he passed enclosed yards. The paint on Fegan's gate was flaked and blistered, and the wood shifted in its frame when Campbell pressed it with his fingertips. A firm kick would set it free, but he was wary of undue noise. He wasn't keen on scaling the wall here, either. Fegan would only have to look out of a window to see him coming.

Instead, Campbell moved back along the alleyway until he was beyond sight of Fegan's rear windows, two houses down, and hoisted himself over the yard wall. His soft-soled trainers made no noise as he lowered himself on the other side. He went to the house's back wall and used a bin to climb over to the adjoining yard. A small dog yapped at him as he landed on a collection of pot plants. He cursed under his breath and kicked the little mutt away. Christ, he might as well have ridden up on an elephant.

Campbell moved fast in case the dog's owner came to investigate. Sticking close to the wall, he peeked into Fegan's yard. It was a simple weed-strewn concrete patch. Campbell threw his leg over the wall and let his body follow, dropping to a crouch on the other side. His back against the brickwork, he looked up at the kitchen window. The small upper pane was open. He would be able to reach in and down to open the lower latch and slip inside.

Like most old terraced homes in Belfast, the house was a two-up-two-down with an extended kitchen at the back and a bathroom built on top. Amid the dog's frantic barks, Campbell heard a cough and splutter from the open bathroom window above. He pictured Fegan folded over the toilet bowl, retching up gobbets of congealed blood. He pushed up with his legs to peer through the kitchen window.

Empty.

Another cough, then a sniff, from above. Campbell grabbed the window frame and lifted himself up onto the sill. He reached under the small open pane and down to the lower latch. With a little fumbling, he was in.

Carefully, he maneuvered over the few dishes in the sink and gently lowered himself to the kitchen floor. His shoes barely made a sound as he moved across the linoleum, breathing through his mouth. The room was sparsely furnished and clean, apart from some hand tools arranged on a cloth. It opened onto a living room with a staircase to the left. A few pieces of shaped and polished wood sat shoulder to shoulder with a cheap radio and an empty whiskey bottle on the sideboard. More crude sculptures stood along the fireplace, and an old-looking guitar was propped in the corner.

Now he was inside, Campbell didn't hesitate. He went to the foot of the stairs, treading lightly. Although his pistol nestled at the small of his back, he reached for the small Gerber knife in his inside pocket. Quiet would be better. He pressed the thumb stud and the blade, razor sharp and gleaming, snapped open. Fegan would die with barely a sound.

Campbell tried not to think of ripping flesh, the soft tearing sound of a blade parting meat and gristle. He ignored the racing of his heart and began his climb.

He placed his left foot at the outer edge of the bottom step and pushed upward, bringing his right foot to the far edge of the next so the boards wouldn't flex under his weight. Not a single creak announced his ascent. He made his way upwards, his feet to the outside of each step, silent as a ghost.

The bathroom door was closed over, a shaft of light emerging from the crack, and Campbell heard miserable coughs and moans from the other side. Now, at the top of the stairs, he was at the mercy of hundred-year-old floorboards. He had to move quickly and decisively. He waited for another spasm of retching and spitting.

When it came he hit the door hard, his knife ready to open the first vein it found. Instead, it found air as it swung in a useless arc over an empty toilet bowl.

A cold hardness pressed against the skin beneath Campbell's ear.

"Don't move," Gerry Fegan said.

28

Fegan listened to Campbell's deep, steady breathing. The Scot stood primed, ready to move, the knife held before him.

"Don't do it," Fegan said. "I know you want to, but don't. You'll be dead before you move a finger."

Campbell's body rippled with coiled energy. Slowly, his shoulders slumped and the energy evaporated.

Fegan reached out and took the knife with his free hand. He folded the blade back into its grip with his thumb. It fitted neatly into his jacket pocket. He patted Campbell's sides and back until he found a Glock 23 tucked into his waistband, underneath his denim jacket. Fegan heard the other man exhale as he removed it.

"Turn around slowly and sit on your hands," Fegan said.

"Can I put the lid down?" Campbell asked.

Fegan increased the Walther's pressure against Campbell's ear. "Just do it," he said.

Campbell reached forward and lowered the toilet lid. He turned and sat down, slipping his hands beneath his thighs.

"Under your arse," Fegan said. "Palms down, thumbs to the back." He watched Campbell shift from side to side until his hands were in position.

Campbell looked up at him. "What now?" he asked.

"We have a talk," Fegan said, dropping the Glock into his pocket to clank against the knife. He kept his Walther trained on Campbell. As chilled as it was, his heart hit his sternum like a battering ram, and his temples pulsed. He blotted out everything else, every shadow at the corner of his vision, and focused on Campbell.

He'd known that someone would follow him from the police station, and he'd had a good idea it would be Campbell. During the taxi ride he saw the same Ford Focus too many times. When he got home, he went straight to his bedroom and retrieved the pistol before going to the bathroom. Fegan hadn't faked the first retches. The water in the bowl was stained deep red, and strange aches turned in his belly. He hadn't really expected Campbell to come into the house after him, but then he'd heard the little dog's panicked barking from the back.

"What do you want to talk about?" Campbell's reddish-brown mop spilled into his eyes and he flicked his head to clear it away.

"McGinty sent you," Fegan said.

"Of course."

"So, he's going to do me."

"That was the idea," Campbell said.

"Why?"

Campbell laughed and shook his head. "Jesus, why do you think?"

"He knows what I did. He didn't come right out and say it at Michael's funeral, but he knows."

Campbell nodded. "That's right. And the priest confirmed it this morning."

The chill at Fegan's center intensified. "What?"

"Father Coulter. That old bastard couldn't hold his own piss. That was a stupid move, telling him."

The shadows pressed against Fegan's consciousness. "I never thought he'd . . ." He pushed them back and swallowed. "I never thought he'd do that."

"Now you know different."

"Yeah, I do." Fegan nodded, letting the betrayal sink to the bottom of his stomach. It settled there, joining the rest of the slithering aches in his gut. "What about Marie?" he asked.

"McGinty said she'd been taken care of," Campbell said.

Fegan stepped closer and lowered the gun to rest on the Scot's forehead. "What does that mean?"

"I don't know," Campbell said.

Fegan snapped the Walther against Campbell's cheek. "What does it mean?"

Campbell slumped sideways to rest against the wall. "Fuck," he said.

"Sit up straight," Fegan said. "Get your hands back under you. What does it mean?"

Campbell did as he was told. "That's all he said. She'd been taken care of, that's all. I don't know what it means."

Fegan raised the pistol again and Campbell screwed his eyes shut. He lowered the muzzle and pressed it against Campbell's temple. He wanted to pull the trigger. He wanted to hear the roar in this small tiled room, then the whistling in his ears, feel the warm, gritty spots on his face, taste the copper on his lips. He wanted all that and for the two UFF boys to be gone. Christ, they wanted it too. He could feel them, watching, waiting, longing for it. Fegan so wanted to do it, to pull the trigger, but there were things he needed to know. He thought of Marie and the fine lines around her eyes, and of Ellen. The image of them in fear and pain tightened his finger on the trigger. He inhaled, the air cold at the back of his nose, clearing his head.

"Did he hurt her?" he asked, taking the Walther away from Campbell's temple.

A little of the calm returned to Campbell's face, along with a shadow of anger. "I told you I don't know. Now, either take my word for it or shoot me, for fuck's sake."

Fegan swung the Walther at Campbell's cheek again and the impact sent a jolt up to his shoulder. The Scot slumped against the wall, his eyes glassy, blood seeping from the growing welt below his left eye. Fegan took a glass tumbler from above the washbasin, filled it with water, and threw its contents at Campbell's face. Two more glassfuls and Campbell was upright again, sitting on his hands.

"Who's the cop?" Fegan asked.

Campbell's mouth curled in a smile. "The one who did you over? I don't know him." He hunched down, his head between his shoulders, when Fegan raised the gun again. "I don't know, for Christ's sake! He's Patsy Toner's contact. He knows him. I only heard of him today."

"I need to know who he is," Fegan said. "I need to know why the RUC man wants him."

"What?" Campbell raised his head from between his shoulders, a knot in his brow.

"If I'm going to finish this, I need to know why him. What did he do to deserve it?"

Campbell shook his head. "What are you talking about, Gerry?"

Fegan sighed and shrugged. "Christ knows." He put the Walther back to Campbell's forehead. "Well, that's that, then."

"Wait!" Campbell said. "For fuck's sake, wait."

"What for?" Fegan said.

"There's a way out of this. A way to stick it to McGinty."

"That's what I'm doing."

"No, no, listen to me. There's a way, I swear."

Fegan sighed and lifted the pistol slightly. "Go on."

Campbell's quick eyes revealed the working of his mind as the words spilled out of him. "McGinty's milking Caffola's killing for everything he can get, saying the cops did it. And Eddie Coyle, too. He's saying the cops beat the shit out of him. If you give yourself up, go to the law, tell them the truth, everyone will know McGinty's a liar. He'll be disgraced. Tell the press, tell the TV people. They're McGinty's lifeblood."

Campbell was smarter than Fegan had thought. "No, that won't be good enough," he said.

"Come on, Gerry, you know you can't get to him." Campbell's voice belied his wide, easy smile. "He'll get you first. This way, at least you'll live. You'll see him destroyed and you'll live."

"No." Fegan shook his head. "I'm not going back inside. I'll die first. Besides, McGinty can get me just as easy in prison as he can outside. Easier."

Campbell leaned forward, his face upturned and pleading. "Just think about it, Gerry, eh? Just take a minute and—"

"Shush." Fegan pressed the Walther's muzzle against Campbell's lips to silence him. "You know I'm crazy, don't you?"

Campbell gave a nervous laugh as Fegan raised the gun slightly, but he didn't answer.

"I'm away in the head; you know that, don't you?"

"Yeah," Campbell said, his voice cracking.

Fegan sat on the edge of the bathtub, giving in to the insistent pains in his midsection. He kept the Walther trained on Campbell's forehead. "Then why try reasoning with me?"

Campbell blinked sweat away from his eyes.

"I wanted to know who the cop was," Fegan said. "I wanted to know why he deserved it. But I know why *you* deserve it."

"Deserve what?" Campbell asked.

"To die," Fegan said.

The shadows tightened around them.

Campbell shook his head. "Gerry, I—"

"Those two UFF boys," Fegan said. Campbell's head became still. "They were nothing more than cheap hoods, a pair of smart-arses selling dope for beer money. They couldn't have got McGinty in a million years. They couldn't even have dreamt of it. They were too busy getting stoned off their own merchandise."

Campbell's shoulders rose and fell. Blood and spittle hung from his lip.

Fegan said, "You know what that lot were like, the fucking UFF, and the rest of the Loyalists. All of them. Nothing more than jumped-up thugs with a bit of organisation. They were great at killing their own. They were even better at taking out civilians who had nothing to do with us or them. The easy target, that's what they were best at. Even the top boys couldn't have gone after McGinty, let alone those two bottom feeders.

"But somehow it turns out Francie Delaney struck a deal with them. Francie Delaney, an even bigger prick than Eddie Coyle, clubs together with two apes from the UFF and hatches a plan to get to McGinty. Funnily enough, the only person Delaney spills his guts to is you. And you beat him to death in the process of finding that out."

"He sold McGinty to the Loyalists," Campbell said. "Everyone knows that."

"Because you said so, and they believed you. You fingered those two boys to complete the picture, didn't you? You set it up for me to do them to cover your own tracks. What were you up to? Why did you need to get rid of Delaney?"

"They were going to get McGinty," Campbell said. "You and me, we saved him."

"Bullshit," Fegan said. "You remember. They weren't killers. Not like you and me. They died like women, crying and begging."

"Shut your fucking mouth," Campbell said.

"What, you hear them too?"

"Shut up."

"When you close your eyes at night, do they scream?"

Fegan felt something vibrate against his chest and heard a high chiming sound. The phone in his pocket. Only one person knew the number. His eyes flicked downward.

Mistake.

Campbell had his wrist, pushing it away and upward. Reflexively, Fegan squeezed the trigger and plaster dust sprinkled down from the ceiling and into his eyes. He was pushed backwards and his head cracked on the tiles over the bath. As spots and dust danced in his eyes he felt himself slide into the tub. He concentrated all his strength on his right hand, the hand Campbell was grappling with, trying to claim the gun. Fegan's feet hung over the edge of the bath and he kicked out, feeling his foot connect with Campbell's groin. He heard the other man grunt, his grip weakening for just a moment and Fegan forced his hand down, pushing against Campbell until the Walther was between them.

The pistol's angry shout boomed against the tiles, and Campbell fell backwards, his face twisted in pain, a scorched strip torn from the side of his shirt. The mirror dropped in pieces from the wall behind him. Fegan strained to drag himself from the bathtub while a hundred knives in his stomach fought to keep him there. He fired at the blurred shape of Campbell making a crouching sprint for the door. The bullet split the wooden frame.

Fegan spilled over the lip of the bath and onto the floor, crying out as pain roiled in his abdomen. He heard Campbell's quick, light footsteps on the stairs. Fegan used the washbasin to pull himself up as he heard his front door wrenched open. Feet pounded along the street outside as he lurched down the stairs.

Sunlight burned Fegan's already stinging eyes when he got outside. Through the glare he saw Campbell running to the row of parked cars. He aimed and fired, putting a spidery hole in a windscreen. He squeezed the trigger again and a wing mirror splintered, leaving plastic shards and wires dangling. Campbell reached his car, his hand clasped to his ribs. Fegan fired once more and Campbell fell against the hood. A dark circle spread on the back of his thigh. He pulled the door open and was inside the old Ford Focus before Fegan could aim again.

Fegan began to run, but the churning inside weighed him down. The car's engine came alive and Campbell pulled away from the curb in reverse, clipping another parked car. The Focus rocked on its suspension as it swung in a tight circle to face the other way, and its engine squealed along with its tires. Fegan fired one last time, putting a hole in the car's rear just as it reached the corner.

He bent over, coughed, and spat blood onto the tarmac. His stomach and groin smoldered with a deep, hot pain.

So, this was it. No more pretending. It was time to run, time to hide, time to find a way to get McGinty and the others. He straightened and turned in a circle, looking for his nine followers.

"This is what you wanted, isn't it?" he asked the empty street.

He took faltering steps to his open front door, his arms across his belly. He didn't have long. Even in this part of Belfast, afternoon gunfire wouldn't go unreported. He stepped into his dim house.

"Gerry?"

He stopped at the sound of a distant, disembodied voice.

"Jesus, Gerry, what's happening? Answer me!"

Fegan reached into his pocket and took out the phone. "Hello, Marie," he said.

29

"You're a lucky man," the doctor said.

Campbell didn't know if he was smiling or not; his eyes were screwed shut against the pain. It wasn't the wound in his thigh, the one the doctor was currently stitching up, that bothered him. No, it was the one at his side, the one that screamed and roared every time he breathed.

"Almost done," the doctor said. He had been summoned to McKenna's bar shortly after Campbell limped in, leaving a trail of blood on the floor. Now Campbell lay on a table in a back room with the retired GP sewing up the neat hole in his leg.

Fegan's second shot had creased his flank, barely taking any flesh with it, but Campbell knew enough of wound ballistics to understand the transfer of energy from the bullet was like a hammer blow to his ribcage. The doctor couldn't be sure if it had cracked a rib, or merely bruised it, without an X-ray. All Campbell could be sure of was it hurt like hell. A gauze pad was taped over the wound, and Campbell breathed in shallow gasps, trying not to spark another burst of pain.

"There, now," the doctor said. Campbell heard instruments being placed in a dish. "No major damage done. The bullet just nicked you, really. Sliced a bit less than an inch at the back of the thigh. Nine-millimeter wounds are always nice and tidy. It's a long time since I treated any of you boys, and believe me, I've seen much worse."

Campbell opened his eyes and saw McGinty standing over him, still wearing his black suit from Caffola's funeral. He hadn't heard him enter. They watched each other as the doctor washed and packed up his equipment.

"Take it easy for a few days," the doctor said. He placed a small bottle of pills on the table. "Stay off your feet if you can, and take three of these a day. Antibiotics, in case of an infection."

"Thanks, Kevin," McGinty said. He handed the doctor a roll of cash. The doctor nodded and left them.

"You fucked up, Davy," McGinty said.

"He got the drop on me," Campbell said, wincing at the effort. "Even crazy, he's better than I thought."

"It won't do," McGinty said. "You've let me down, Davy. I'm very disappointed."

"Christ, what was I supposed to do? He had a gun to my—"

"You were supposed to fucking kill him!" McGinty slammed his fist against the table, and Campbell howled as the impact resonated up into his chest. "You were supposed to do what I sent you to do instead of running away from him."

"He would've killed me."

McGinty leaned down. "You think I won't?"

"I'm sorry, Mr. McGinty, I never—"

"Bad enough you didn't get him, you even had him shooting up the street. The cops were called. He's done a runner and they'll be looking for him. Our friend in Lisburn Road Station let Patsy know. If they get him, and he talks, it'll get out it was him killed Caffola and McKenna, and him beat Eddie Coyle's head in. How am I going to look then, eh? The press will rip the shit out of me. I'll be a fucking laughing stock."

"Did anyone see me?" Campbell asked.

"Someone saw a silver car, that's all they got out of the neighbors." McGinty pointed a finger at Campbell's face. "And you're bloody lucky, 'cause if they'd tagged you you'd have a fucking bullet in your head right now."

Campbell gritted his teeth to quell a scream as he righted himself on the table. His left leg felt heavy and wooden, and a roman candle burned in his side. "Any ideas where he went? To the woman, maybe?"

"No." McGinty handed Campbell his shirt. "Get dressed. Patsy

Toner's parked outside her place now, keeping an eye on her. He's going to make sure she goes to the airport and takes that flight I booked for her."

"Why not just do her?" Campbell asked as he struggled to get into his shirt. It had a ragged hole in the fabric, underneath the left sleeve.

McGinty's eyes flickered. "That's my business."

Campbell sensed that pressing the politician would be unwise. He lowered himself from the table, feeling a deep throb in his thigh. "Fair enough, but you could use her to draw Fegan out."

McGinty thought about it briefly. "No, too risky. Not with the press conference in the morning. If anything went wrong I'd be fucked."

"What, then? Just wait for Fegan to make a move?"

"I don't think we have much choice," McGinty said.

"I was right about one thing. He's going to come after you. And me, for that matter. He talked about that cop, too."

"The cop can look after himself."

"Maybe," Campbell said. "Can you?"

An hour later, Campbell lay on the threadbare couch in his flat on University Street with a bag of ice resting on his side and the phone to his ear.

"Well, this is a fucking mess, isn't it?" the handler said.

"Oh, don't start," Campbell said, wincing at the sparks in his side. "I've been shot twice, been pistol-whipped, been roared at by Paul McGinty. I don't need any shit from you."

"Need it or not," the handler said, 'you're going to get it."

Before the handler could continue Campbell hung up and dropped the phone to the floor. One of McGinty's thugs had driven him back to the flat in his Focus, leaving Campbell to struggle up the two flights of stairs. Tom the bartender had given him a large bag of ice for his troubles, most of which was now in the small freezer that hummed in the flat's tiny kitchen.

The phone buzzed on the floor and Campbell groaned. He picked it up. "What?"

"Hang up on me again and I'll blow your cover. I'll leave you stranded there without a friend in the world. Understood?"

Campbell sighed. "Understood."

"Okay. Now, what's happening?"

"Nothing much," Campbell said. "We've just got to wait until Fegan shows his face again."

"Well, wherever and whenever that is, you better be ready to take him out."

"Christ, I'm in no fit state to—"

"I don't give a flying fuck," the handler said. "You've got a job to do, so bloody do it. You better pray Fegan doesn't do any more damage before you get him. This is a bad situation for everyone. Maybe we shouldn't have sent you in there in the first place. You've been under too long. For Christ's sake, don't let it get any worse."

The phone went dead, and Campbell threw it across the room. He covered his eyes, frustration burning as brightly as his injuries. Today he had come as close to dying as he had in fifteen years of service, and he'd had some scrapes. He'd let Fegan, a crazy man, almost get the better of him.

Almost?

No, there was no almost. Fegan would have killed him if not for the phone going off. Blind luck was all that had saved Campbell. He shuddered at the thought.

And there was a bigger question, a more troubling idea. How had Fegan known? He was dead right: there had never been a threat from the UFF boys. The Ulster Freedom Fighters were the militant wing of the Ulster Defence Association, the working-class Protestant movement that claimed to defend its people from Republicans. In reality, they were common thugs, the kind the Loyalists bred in abundance. The kind who could walk into a pub and open fire on anything that moved, or call a taxi, wait for it to arrive, and then shoot its driver. But a real hit on a dangerous target? Never. They just didn't have it in them.

It was Delaney. Campbell remembered the night the slimy bastard had cornered him, saying he knew he was a plant. Even now,

Campbell could smell Delaney's breath and cheap aftershave.

"Get me fifty grand," Delaney had said, grinning as his oily black hair spilled into his eyes. "Just fifty grand and I'll forget the whole thing."

Campbell had searched the bar with his eyes, looking for eaves-droppers.

"Even if you weren't talking shite, where do you think I'd get fifty grand?" he asked.

"From your handlers. They'll pay it to keep your cover." Delaney smoothed back his hair.

"You're talking out your arse. Go fuck yourself," Campbell said, pushing the stocky man aside.

"I'll give you a day or two to think about it," Delaney called after him.

Campbell phoned his handler that night, and the plan was in place within twenty-four hours. He would take care of Delaney, and a plant in the UFF would serve up a couple of stooges to complete the story.

When Campbell went to McGinty with the fictitious plot on his life, the politician was furious. Why hadn't Campbell kept Delaney alive? The UFF boys were to pay a heavy price. They would receive a special death, an agonising death. It just so happened that Gerry Fegan was out of the Maze for three days to attend his mother's funeral. The honor system between inmates and their captors, the next man's furlough depending on the previous man's return, meant Fegan could move around freely while he was outside. There was no better man for inflicting a painful end, seeing as Vincie Caffola was on remand for assault. McGinty would take care of the arrangements.

So, seventy-two hours after Delaney took Campbell aside in McKenna's bar, thirty-six after Campbell beat Delaney to a lifeless pulp, he and Gerry Fegan stood over two weeping Loyalists, one of whom had wet himself.

A sour smell filled the room; the stenches of sweat, piss and blood combined to make Campbell's stomach turn on itself. They were in an empty unit on an industrial estate just north-west of the city. Hard fluorescent lighting washed the high-ceilinged room in whites and greys, and the UFF boys' sobs reverberated against the block walls. Blood already pooled on the concrete floor.

Fegan had said little on the journey here. Someone else had lifted the two UFF boys and left them bound to chairs, ready for Fegan and Campbell to interrogate. Campbell watched the other man circle the two Loyalists. Fegan's face was carved from stone, and something deeper than hate or anger burned behind his eyes.

Fegan used a pickaxe handle. It took an hour, and neither of the Loyalists talked. Not because they were brave or strong, but because they never knew of any plot to hit McGinty. All the while, Fegan's face remained blank, his eyes far away. Apart from one moment, that was. When one of the Loyalists wept for his mother, Fegan might have come to himself. Campbell thought he saw a wave of revulsion or pity – he couldn't be sure which – on the other man's face. It was gone before he could be certain.

When the screaming was over, and there was no more blood to spill, Fegan dropped the pickaxe handle to the floor. He finished them with a .22 pistol. Its sharp report boomed in the empty concrete room.

Fegan stood silent for several minutes. Campbell noticed the tear tracks glittering on his face.

"They didn't know anything," Fegan said.

Campbell leaned against the wall, fighting his own churning gut. "Delaney said it was them. He named them."

"He lied," Fegan said.

"Doesn't matter," Campbell said. "McGinty wanted them dead. That's all there is to it."

Fegan wiped his face with the back of his hand, leaving a red smear. "I put my mother in the ground yesterday," he said.

Campbell said nothing.

Fegan's eyes turned glassy, staring at something miles away. "She hadn't spoken to me for sixteen years. She told me she was ashamed of what I did. That was the last thing she ever said to me. They let me out to go and see her in the hospital. She wouldn't let me into the room. She died hating me."

"Why are you telling me this?" Campbell asked.

Fegan snapped back to himself and looked at Campbell, his face creased with confusion. "I don't know," he said. "Can we go now?"

Campbell followed him out into the darkness. As he drove them back to the city, he kept one eye on the road and one eye on Fegan, his heart thundering in his chest.

That had been nine years ago. And now Fegan knew of Campbell's deceit. Did he know he was a plant? Campbell had to assume as much.

The handler wanted Fegan dead. McGinty wanted Fegan dead. Campbell *needed* Fegan dead, because if McGinty learned the truth . . . well, the politician wouldn't let Campbell die easy.

30

Fegan waited in the darkness. From downstairs he heard the patient ticking of the clock over the priest's fireplace, marking time as the last of the day's light faded to black, chiming on the hour. Just past ten, now. Marie's flight for London Gatwick would be in the air, somewhere over the Irish Sea. An associate of McGinty's was to meet her at the other side when it landed at eleven, and escort her to whatever accommodation had been arranged for her and Ellen. That didn't leave much time, but it shouldn't be long until Father Coulter staggered home. Caffola would have been in the ground and the last speeches made by early afternoon. Father Coulter would have drunk his fill by now.

Fegan sat on a hard wooden chair in a corner of the priest's bedroom, behind the open door. The followers wandered between the shadows. Sometimes it was hard to tell where the shadows ended and the followers began. If he concentrated he could focus on them, draw them out of the dark, and separate them from the blankets of gloom. He tried pushing them from his vision, and then drawing them in. But they were always there, watching.

Always watching.

There was no danger Fegan would fall asleep, even as tired as he was. Every time his eyes grew too heavy to bear, their screaming snapped him awake. When tonight was done, when the work was over, maybe they would let him have some silence. There were long hours ahead, but he could steal some sleep on the road, and the promise of a soft hotel bed somewhere miles from here made the task easier to imagine. He would make it quick for Father Coulter. He was a man of God, after all.

Fegan shifted in the seat, trying to dislodge the pain that clambered across his gut. He had stopped spitting up blood hours ago, but the aches still picked through his organs whether he was moving or still. And it was warm. Sweat beaded on his forehead. Father Coulter kept his house well heated, even during what was for Belfast an unusually clement spring. The heavy overcoat Fegan had found in the priest's wardrobe didn't help, but he needed something to keep the blood off his clothes. There shouldn't be much if he did it right, but he had to be careful.

But it was more than heat making Fegan sweat. He remembered the symptoms from watching his father fight the drink. Nearly forty-eight hours had passed since he'd swallowed that last mouthful of whiskey. The shakes were mild yet, just the slightest of tremors, but bouts of clammy nausea came and went. Dryness dusted his tongue, and he gathered saliva to roll around his mouth. He remembered his father's screaming nightmares, the horrors that would send him back to the bottle. Fegan wondered if the followers would let him dream.

Shafts of light moved across the ceiling, squeezing through the gap above the drawn curtains, and the clattering of a diesel engine came from outside. The creak of the taxi's handbrake, a door opening and closing, a hearty voice wishing someone goodnight. A grumble as the taxi moved off, then the scratching of a key trying to find its home.

The shadows stirred and drifted to the darkest corners.

Fegan felt a cool draught around his ankles as the front door opened below. Light switches clicked on and off. There was a flutter and a high screech as the cockatiel in the living room was angered by the priest disturbing its sleep.

Fegan heard Father Coulter slur, "It's all right, Joe-Joe. Sure, it's only me. Go back to sleep, now."

Another light switch clicked off and Fegan heard the priest begin to climb the stairs, huffing as he went, the steps creaking beneath his weight. Fegan heard the bathroom light's pull-cord, then a fly unzipping. Father Coulter hummed to himself as he thundered into the toilet bowl for what seemed like hours. There was a softer running of water, then the rustling of a towel. All the while, the priest hummed some tuneless song.

Fegan tensed as the lumbering footsteps came closer. He kept his own breath quiet and even, while Father Coulter's came in heavy rasps. He heard the priest pause in the doorway and then the click of the light switch.

"Aw, shite," Father Coulter said when the darkness remained. The light bulb lay near Fegan's shoeless feet.

Father Coulter sighed and entered the bedroom. Fegan and the shifting shadows watched his dark form as he kicked off his shoes and climbed onto the bed. He turned onto his back and pulled the white collar from his black shirt. A few seconds of fumbling and his top buttons were undone. He let his arms fall to his sides, and he sprawled on top of the blankets. Within a few minutes his guttural snoring filled the room.

The three Brits emerged from the darkest corners to stand alongside the bed, miming the priest's execution. The woman followed them, her baby's tiny hands clutching at her dress as she rocked it in her arms. She smiled at Fegan. He nodded and stood up. Campbell's knife was light but the grip felt solid in his hand as he crossed the room. He felt for the thumb stud, cold through the thin membrane of the surgical gloves. The blade opened with a small snap.

The snoring stopped. Fegan could just make out Father Coulter's round face and blinking eyes.

The shadows receded.

The priest's voice was a small whisper. "Who's there?"

"It's all right, Father," Fegan said. "You're just dreaming. Go back to sleep."

"Dreaming? I . . . I . . ."

"Shush." Fegan raised the knife.

"Gerry? Gerry Fegan? Is that you?"

Fegan froze. "Yes, Father."

"What do you want, Gerry? What are you doing here?"

"Remember you told me about the dreams, Father?"

The priest tried to raise himself up on his elbows. "What's that you've got there?"

Fegan reached down and smoothed Father Coulter's hair. "Remember? Those Brits. You could have stopped it, but you didn't."

Father Coulter slowly shook his head. "That was so long ago, Gerry. I was scared."

"Aren't you scared now?"

The priest nodded.

"You won't have to dream about them any more," Fegan said.

"Please, Gerry, you're frightening me. What do you want from me?"

"Nothing at all," Fegan said. "You know, I would have let you live."

Father Coulter stiffened on the bed. "What?"

"I was ready to do it the other night, but I lost my nerve. I could have lived with the three Brits, maybe. I thought you didn't deserve it."

"Whatever you're thinking of doing, Gerry, please don't. Let's just talk about it, eh?" The priest tried to sit up and Fegan gently pushed him back down.

"Then you brought that message to Marie. You threatened her for McGinty."

"No, I—"

"And you told McGinty what I said. My confession."

"No, that's not true. I swear, I never—"

"Quiet, Father."

"Oh, Christ, please—"

Fegan closed his left hand over the priest's mouth to stifle his cries. He brought the knife down once, hard, before Father Coulter could raise his arms in defence. It was a good knife, with a strong, sharp steel blade. There was little resistance, even from the breastbone, as the knife pierced his heart. Fegan withdrew it easily, and brought it down twice more.

Father Coulter gripped Fegan's shoulder, his body twisting. In the darkness, Fegan saw gleaming eyes stare up at him. The priest's breath was warm as he screamed into Fegan's palm.

"It's all right, Father," Fegan said. "It won't take long. You'll go into shock soon. It won't hurt at all."

Fegan took his hand away, and Father Coulter grabbed shallow gasps of air. The priest's mouth worked silently, opening and closing. He brought his hands to his chest. There was little blood.

"May God forgive you," he hissed.

Fegan wiped the blade clean on the blankets. "It's not His forgiveness I need, Father. I know that now."

The bubbling of blood filling the priest's chest cavity, the rustling of blankets, and the soft whimpering faded as Fegan watched him die. It took less than two minutes from the first stab to the last hiss of air as the life left Father Coulter's body. Fegan removed the overcoat he'd taken from the wardrobe and covered the corpse.

He folded the knife and put it back in his pocket. His shoes were next to the chair and he slipped them on in silence. A sports bag holding a few clothes, British and Irish passports, two pistols, fifty-seven rounds of ammunition and thousands of pounds in rolled-up bills lay on the floor. Fegan slung it over his shoulder and made his way downstairs. He went through the kitchen to the backyard, closing the door softly behind him. The gate was secured from the inside by a padlock, so he climbed over the yard wall to the alleyway beyond and started walking. It was a long trek from here to the Europa Hotel in town, and the bus station behind it. He'd have to be quick to make the last airport shuttle.

Fegan kept his head down as he walked. Six shadows followed closely.

SIX

31

Marie McKenna lay naked beside him. It was his bed, but it wasn't. It was his house, but it wasn't. Fegan was naked, too, and it shamed him. He went to cover himself.

"Don't," she said, moving his hand away.

"I'm not clean," he said.

She hushed him, and moved in close. Her body was warm against his. She kissed him. Her mouth was soft, like summer air.

When he was free of her lips, he said, "It's been so long. I don't know what it feels like."

"It feels like this," she said, taking his hand and placing it on her breast.

Her skin was soft, her breast round and supple, with a hardness against his palm. *Yes, that's what it feels like. Smooth, warm . . . slick?*

He looked down. His hand had smeared red on her body. She looked down, too, and he saw her mouth twist in disgust. He tried to wipe it away, but only made it worse, great crimson hand-prints across her breasts and stomach. She pulled away, kicking.

"No," he said, grabbing her forearms. The blood made them slippery, and he couldn't hold her. "Please, let me clean it."

He tried again to wipe it away, leaving red tracks along her hips and thighs. "I'll make it better," he said. "Please let me make it better."

She screamed then, writhing, scratching, kicking to get away. "Leave me alone. Get away from me. Help! Help! HELP!"

He didn't know who she was screaming for, who could help her, or who she needed saving from. Surely not him? No, not him. Couldn't be. It was only a little blood. If she would only stay still he could wipe it away. But she wouldn't stay still. She kept kicking, screaming, crying, and he only wanted to make it better, but the hand on his shoulder wouldn't let him. It kept shaking him, holding him back from her, that hand squeezing and shaking him, and now its owner was saying something, talking, but he needed to make Marie clean, make it better, but that hand wouldn't stop, it wouldn't leave him—

"You can sleep on the plane, mate."

Fegan slapped the hand away, his eyes snapping open, and he reached for his pocket where the knife nestled, cold and still.

The bus driver stood back, blinking down at him. "Jesus, take it easy, mate. I'm just telling you we're here."

Fegan looked around, confused. The bus was dimly lit, and outside a few late-night travellers walked to and from the terminal. His heart rattled like an overworked engine and his forehead was cold with sweat. "Sorry," he said. "Thanks."

He gathered up the sports bag and walked along the aisle, the driver's suspicious stare fixed on his back. He stepped down to the pavement, and the door hissed closed. The bus pulled away, leaving Fegan watching the terminal from the other side of a pedestrian crossing. Two Airport Police officers stood chatting between the entrance and exit, their MP5 sub-machine guns slung across bullet-proof vests.

Fegan knew he would be searched if he went near the terminal. Security was tighter now than it ever had been at the height of the Troubles. A war in a desert thousands of miles away frightened them more than a war on their doorstep. Fegan took the phone from his pocket and dialled Marie's mobile number. He pressed the phone to his ear and closed his eyes. When she answered, he felt some small warm thing burst and spill inside.

"I'm here," he said.

"You should've gone," Fegan said.

"No chance," Marie said. Her Renault Clio roared hoarsely as she sped through the roundabouts that led away from the airport, heading north. Ellen dozed in her child seat in the back, having barely woken as her mother carried her and a suitcase out to where Fegan waited.

"It would've been safer," he said.

"Maybe," she said, grinding gears in anger. "But I'd have to live with the knowledge that I let some fucking jumped-up gangster with political pretensions dictate where I could bring up my daughter. No, thank you. I'd sooner live in fear in my own home than live in shame in someone else's."

"No, you wouldn't," Fegan said, glancing back at Ellen.

"Balls," Marie said, with a finality that told Fegan to leave it. "Jesus, the rigmarole in that airport. I could see Patsy Toner following me all the way there in that Jag of his, then walking behind me into the terminal. Jesus, I hope McGinty never relies on him to be discreet. Anyway, I checked in, got my boarding pass, went through security, then just when they called us for boarding I said I wasn't going. God, you should've seen them. Such a fuss! There was this girl, a stewardess, looked like she'd been licking piss off a nettle."

Marie glowed with anger. Fegan stayed quiet.

"Christ, she was spitting bullets 'cause they had to unload my suitcase from the hold. That took nearly forty minutes, and then they had to wait for some security men to come and escort me out. I was only just back out of Departures a few minutes before you called."

She was high on adrenalin and indignation. Fegan asked, "No sign of Patsy?"

"No," she said. "He was gone. I imagine he slinked off as soon as he saw me check in."

"So, where are we going?"

"Portcarrick," she said. "Up on the coast, past Ballymena. My parents took us there a few times when we were little. We always stayed on the caravan park, but there's a hotel on the bay. It's a quiet place, hardly anyone ever stays there. Hopkirk's, it's called. I hope it's still open."

"Me too," Fegan said.

Dreams came and went, some ugly, some beautiful. Fegan had kept his eyes open as far as the outskirts of Antrim, but the endless dual carriageways stretching into the distance lulled him into a fitful sleep, punctuated by jolts and swerves. As he drifted between waking and sleeping, he was aware of the rise and fall of the road, and the darkness they travelled deeper into.

After a time, Fegan woke to see nothing but black around them. The pressure in his ears told him they were up high somewhere.

"We're nearly there," Marie said. "We're in the Glens now. You missed the delights of Ballymena."

She took a left turn, and Fegan felt the car begin a shallow descent. Beyond the window he could pick out coarse grass that rolled away beyond his vision. It felt like a wilderness, miles of nothing.

"It's beautiful country when you see it in the daylight," Marie said. "Peaceful, like the rest of the world doesn't exist. I used to love coming here. I always wanted to buy a home on the bay. I guess that'll never happen now."

Fegan's breath caught in his throat when, for just a few seconds, the moon slid out from behind the clouds. It illuminated the landscape and he could see for miles in every direction, grassy hills climbing up to touch the sky. And up ahead, in the near distance, he saw the silver shimmer in the bay below, the North Atlantic meeting the Irish Sea to make a looking-glass for the moon. Then it was gone, the brilliant disc hiding, and the road cut downward between the slopes.

"I never . . ."

"Never what?" Marie asked.

"I never thought things could look like that," he said. "Not really."

She reached across and squeezed his arm. Fegan didn't know whether to pull away or meet her hand with his own. He did neither.

A strange anticipation bubbled in him when he thought of the six followers. As much as he longed for a peaceful night, part of him wanted them to see this place too. He thought of the woman and her baby, always pretty, always showing him her soft, sad smile. She deserved to see somewhere other than the inside of McKenna's bar or Fegan's sparsely furnished house.

After a last steep drop, the road settled back into a soft undulation and a series of sweeping bends. They arrived at a gathering of low whitewashed houses, and followed the narrow road as it curved around them. And there it was, just as Marie had described it. To the left, a bridge over a small estuary, an ancient church on the other side of it, and a long beach curving north into the darkness beyond. On this side, its dim basalt reflecting little of the car's lights, stood a memorial to a lost fishing crew.

The memorial passed on their left, between them and the river mouth, and a pretty two-storey cottage was just on the far side of the hotel on their right. Fegan could barely make out the mass of cliffs reaching out to sea, but he could feel them looming over the dwelling. Marie pulled the car into the space between the two old buildings. Lights peered through the slats in the cottage's shuttered windows. Shadows moved against the walls, but Fegan couldn't be sure if they were six echoes of the dead, or just the sweep of the car's headlights. He shivered when he realised he didn't know which he most desired.

"Here we are," Marie said. "Hopkirk's."

"Oh, no," Hopkirk said. "No, no, no."

He was a tall, thin man of senior years, a plume of white hair swept back from his forehead. He wore a pointed goatee and thick glasses, and raised his nose and closed his eyes as he spoke, as if his words had a pleasing odor.

"Quite out of the question," he said from behind the bar. One customer sat on a stool, watching the goings-on, a whiskey and a jug of water to hand. Fegan eyed the glass and swallowed.

"Please, we've nowhere else to go," Marie said as she rocked Ellen in her arms. The little girl rubbed her eyes and mewled.

"The rooms aren't aired out and the beds aren't made up," Hopkirk said. "I haven't let rooms in years."

"If you have sheets I'll make the bed up myself," she said. "If not, the mattress will do. It's very late and my wee girl needs somewhere to stay for the night."

It was indeed late, almost two in the morning. The bar's opening hours seemed to be a loose arrangement between landlord and drinker. The customer was a stout man, around sixty, well dressed, with a deep, refined voice. "Come on, Hopkirk," he said, with a crooked smile. "Have you no mercy?"

Hopkirk scolded the customer with a look. "I've no food in for breakfasts," he said. "Really, there's nothing I can do for you."

Fegan put his bag on the floor, unzipped it, and fished inside until he found what he wanted. The bar was coated in generations-thick paint. Fegan placed a roll of notes on the muddy green gloss. Hopkirk and the drinker looked from it to each other and back again.

Hopkirk separated the notes with a fingertip.

"How long can we stay for that?" Fegan asked.

"A while," Hopkirk said without taking his eyes from the money. "I'll make no promises about the service. You'll have to sort your own meals out and you won't have any hot water."

"It doesn't matter," Marie said.

"Wait here." Hopkirk came out from behind the bar and disappeared into a dark doorway.

The bar, with its painted panelling and floral wallpaper, looked as if it hadn't been refurbished in decades. The floor was covered in a loose-laid carpet, trodden thin, that didn't quite reach the walls. A vast fireplace dominated one end of the room, the embers crackling and sighing as they settled down for the night. Fegan's eyes scanned the bottles behind the bar and he swallowed. Some of them looked as old as him.

The sole customer watched Fegan and Marie from his stool. "So, Portcarrick seemed like the place to be at two in the morning?" he asked. His half-smile was kind, in spite of the jibe.

"We just took a notion," Marie said. Ellen was awake now, blinking and rubbing her nose. Marie walked to the bar and set her on the painted surface.

"Where are we?" the little girl asked.

"We're on our holidays," Marie said, "At the seaside."

Ellen accepted the answer without question. "I'm hungry," she said.

"We'll get you some crisps," Marie said.

"I live in the cottage next door," the customer said. "If Hopkirk can't manage anything decent in the morning, give us a shout. I'm sure me and the missus can rustle up a fry."

Marie smiled. "That's very kind."

"Not at all," the man said. He looked at Fegan. "You look like you could do with a good feed."

Fegan nodded and felt the odd sensation of his mouth curling in a smile. He was not used to kindness.

"Albert Taylor," the drinker said as he extended his hand. "Good to meet you. Been in the wars?"

Fegan shook his hand. "George Ferris," he said. His left hand went to the abrasion on his temple and smoothed his hair over it. "I had a fall."

Marie stared at Fegan for a beat, then said, "Mary Ferris." She indicated her daughter. "Ellen," she said. That lie would be too hard to maintain.

Taylor shook Marie's hand. "Just knock the window in the morning," he said. "Don't worry, we'll get you fed even if Hopkirk's not up to it." He leaned forward on his stool, winked, and whispered, "Besides, I'm a better cook."

Beyond the shuttered window the sea whispered and moaned. In the near-blackness, Fegan could hardly see the six shadows. But he could hear them. When his eyes fell shut, his head nodding forward, the screaming began. And the baby crying. Somewhere across the room, Marie and Ellen lay together, clinging to each other in this new place. Now and then, Fegan heard the little girl whimper. Sleep seemed to come no easier to her than to him. The chair he rested on was well upholstered, and with his feet propped on Marie's suitcase he was comfortable enough, even with the rippling pains in his gut.

Sweat chilled his forehead and his hand trembled as he wiped it away. The dry want at the back of his throat deepened as he thought of the bar downstairs, the bottles lined up like whores in a brothel. He imagined the warmth of whiskey on his tongue and the coolness of stout on his lips.

Marie's steady breathing formed a counterpoint to the waves rolling on the beach outside. Fegan's own breath fell into step with hers as his mind wandered. His thoughts drifted from memory to memory – places and people, some bright and summery, others grey and haggard. He thought of the days before the bad times, before he knew not all fathers acted like that. About his mother and the warmth of her arms. About a goal drawn in chalk on a gable wall, and five boys kicking a ball at it, laughing, running, pushing, bare-backed on an August evening. About a girl called Julie who lived not far away but might as well have been from a different country. She shared a bag of toffees with Fegan, and her father beat her senseless for running with the likes of him. As his head rolled forward, he remembered her words and the purple swelling on her lip. *You're the other sort,* she said. *Daddy says I can't be friends with you.*

He was falling head first into the dark when the cop started screaming, pulling him back. The others emerged from the black and joined in, dragging Fegan into wakefulness. Ellen stirred on the old bed, tiny cries escaping her. Fegan's head felt so heavy, like sodden clay. He'd given them the priest. Couldn't they leave him be?

No. The RUC man wanted his price paid. Fegan saw him, closest of the six, walking the floor.

"All right," Fegan whispered to the dark. "Tomorrow night. Please, I'll do it tomorrow night. Just give me a little quiet. Just a couple of hours."

The RUC man hovered for a moment, then lost himself in the shadows. Ellen gave a cry so small Fegan might only have imagined it.

"But I don't want to dream," he said. "Don't let me dream."

He searched the blackness for them, for some assurance they would protect him from the horrors that waited in his mind. The woman stepped out of the dark and brought her forefinger to her lips.

"Thank you," Fegan whispered.

He closed his eyes.

32

Edward Hargreaves was breathless when he answered his phone. The treadmill whirred under his feet. Two miles in less than twenty minutes – not bad. His good mood evaporated when the woman's voice told him it was the Chief Constable on the line.

"Go ahead," she chirped.

"Good morning, Minister," Pilkington said.

"Christ, what now?" Hargreaves asked. He felt no inclination to feign conviviality. It was too perfect a morning to be spoiled by this oik. His top-floor Belgravia apartment afforded him a delightful view of the small private park surrounded by Cadogan Place. The single perk of this job was a top-notch London pad. So far he'd been able to prevent his wife seeing the inside of it. The desiccated old shrew would never cross its threshold if he had anything to say about it. Steam drifted in from the en-suite bathroom, where his new acquaintance was washing the sweat from her sculpted back. No, his wife would never visit this apartment and ruin the only good thing about his rotten job.

"Another killing," Pilkington said.

Hargreaves stepped off the treadmill. "Who?"

"A priest. Father Eammon Coulter. His housekeeper found him ninety minutes ago when she arrived to make his breakfast. Details are sketchy, but he appears to have been stabbed."

"And why are we concerned about a priest?" Hargreaves asked. A reasonable question, he thought.

"A few reasons," Pilkington said. "He's the priest who buried McKenna and Caffola. He was Bull O'Kane's cousin, and not the finest example of the clergy from what I've heard. There was some sort of scandal in Sligo in the late Seventies, all swept under the carpet, and he was moved out of the parish in a hurry. Rumor has it O'Kane himself fixed it for him to be installed in Belfast. He wanted a priest he could control in the area."

"So Fegan did it?"

"We must assume so."

"I see," Hargreaves said. "And why hasn't he been taken care of yet?"

"Our man tried to take care of him yesterday, but he botched it. Our other insider, the one who got our man back in, says McGinty's not best pleased. The leadership are ready to cut him off completely, feud or not. And now Fegan's missing. My men were called to Calcutta Street after gunfire was heard, but there was no sign of him." Pilkington cleared his throat. "And there's another complication."

"Dear God, what now?" Hargreaves's shoulders sagged.

"There's a woman, Marie McKenna, niece of the recently departed Michael McKenna. She fell foul of McGinty years ago, but he left her alone because of her uncle. Now the uncle's gone, he's been trying to intimidate her into leaving the country. Our insider gave her plane tickets for her and her daughter, followed her to the airport, and watched her check in. She never arrived on the other side. Now she's missing, too."

"I don't understand," Hargreaves said. "What's she got to do with anything?"

"Well, she and Fegan were apparently getting close; he was at her flat when he was arrested the night before last. We believe they're together, wherever they are. It means if he's found it'll be harder to do anything about it."

Hargreaves felt a warm hand stroke the back of his neck. He turned to see the girl, her tanned skin bare and glistening. She spoke very little English, not that it mattered. "So, what happens now?" he asked.

"We wait," Pilkington said. "Fegan will turn up somewhere. We'll just have to be ready to deal with him. There is one good thing to come out of this, though."

Hargreaves gave a dry laugh. "Really? Do tell."

"McGinty was due to hold a press conference this morning. He was going to trot out one of his thugs who got a beating off Fegan and claim my men did it. Then he was going to repeat his claims about my men having been responsible for Caffola's demise. He'll most likely cancel it now. Our friend in the party says the priest's murder has stolen McGinty's thunder."

"Lucky for you," Hargreaves said. "Certain sacrifices might not have to be made after all."

"My concern is the rule of law, sir, not politics." Pilkington's voice was hard against Hargreaves's ear. "I'd have resigned before I let any of my men take the fall for Fegan's actions."

"No, you wouldn't," Hargreaves said. He hung up and tossed the phone onto the bed. The girl smiled sweetly as she toyed with the silver hairs on his chest.

33

In less than a minute, Paul McGinty transformed Patsy Toner's office from a drab, efficient workspace into something resembling a landfill. Campbell watched the eruption from a chair in the corner. He had to fight the urge to laugh when McGinty upended Toner's desk, leaving the solicitor sitting in the middle of the room with books, folders and sheets of paper scattered all around him. Campbell was relieved when the urge passed, sparing him the unbearable pain it would have ignited in his side.

When McGinty's rage subsided he stood panting among the destruction. "Jesus," he said. "Look what you made me do."

"I'm sorry," Toner said.

"Sorry?" McGinty slapped Toner hard across the ear. "Sorry? All you had to do was make sure she got on the plane, for fuck's sake."

Toner brought his hands up to shield himself. "She'd checked in and everything. I couldn't go through the security gates to see what she did. Honest to God, I thought she was away."

McGinty paced the room, his hands on his hips. "Well, now you know different, eh?" He pointed at Campbell. "And you, you're no better. I had to phone the Bull to tell him his cousin was dead. You're bloody lucky he didn't tell me to do you."

Campbell went to speak, but his damaged rib protested as he inhaled.

McGinty continued to pace. "I should've been talking to the press right now, showing off Eddie Coyle's face. All that's fucked. Father Coulter, a priest for Christ's sake. What's wrong with Fegan?"

Campbell took a shallow breath. "I told you, he's crazy."

"Not so crazy that he couldn't get the better of you."

"Or maybe that's *why* he got the better of me," Campbell said, returning McGinty's stare. "Don't worry, he'll show up soon enough. He's still got you to come after."

McGinty stopped pacing and glared at Campbell. "Get out, Patsy."

Toner raised his eyes from his lap. "What? This is my office. You can't—"

McGinty spun and kicked Toner squarely on the shin. "Get the fuck out or I'll rip your fucking head off!"

Toner limped to the door, scowling.

When McGinty was alone with Campbell, he said, "Watch your mouth, Davy. I don't want any talk of that. Not when there's other people around."

"All right," Campbell said. "But you better be watching your back. Fegan could come at you any time, anywhere."

McGinty sat down on Toner's chair. "Maybe, if he's got the balls."

"Balls? Balls has nothing to do with it. How many times do I have to spell it out for you? He's insane. He was a vicious bastard before; now he's a *crazy* vicious bastard. All I'm telling you is watch out."

"All right," McGinty said, standing. "Now let me tell you something. If he shows up and you haven't sorted him within thirty seconds, you're the one who'd better watch out."

Campbell held the politician's gaze for as long as he dared before letting his eyes slip away. "So, what's the plan?"

"The news."

Campbell looked back to McGinty. "What do you mean?"

"Maybe you didn't hear it. It's mostly about Father Coulter, of course, how shocked the community is and all that. I did a couple of soundbites first thing this morning. But we got another wee story sneaked into the newsrooms, something about Marie McKenna and her daughter going missing. If some concerned citizen spots them they're to call Lisburn Road Police Station where our friend will be waiting to answer the phone."

"It's risky," Campbell said. "The cops might get to them first."

"I promised our friend a nice bonus if he gets the call and passes it on to me. He loves his money. Mark my word, he won't leave that phone all day. Besides, I don't see what else we can do." McGinty leaned forward and pointed at Campbell. "But listen hard, Davy. Don't fuck it up again. If this flushes Fegan out, I want him done. You sort him or I sort you. Understood?"

Campbell got to his feet, his thigh complaining and his side shrieking. "Understood. If he surfaces, I'll get him."

34

"You're very kind," Marie said.

Mrs. Taylor smiled and set a plate of toast on the table.

The warm smell of fried breakfast filled the cottage and Fegan's stomach rumbled in anticipation, despite the rippling aches still lurking in his midsection. Steam leaked from a big pot of tea at the center of the table. There was milk, sugar, butter and jam.

The lady of the house had a round, glowing face, and clear blue eyes. Like her husband, she was well-spoken but had a good line in swear words. Fegan, Marie and Ellen had been in the house less than thirty minutes, and Mrs. Taylor had already apologised three times for cursing within earshot of the child.

"Get the fu— I mean, get away, Stella," she said to the dog who sat staring expectantly at the table. Fegan knew she was a Boxer – his grandfather had owned one – and Stella had the same kind of face. One that looked permanently guilty, as if some form of mischief was in the recent past, the near future, or both. Stella ignored Mrs. Taylor's instruction, instead licking her chops as Mr. Taylor brought in a plate loaded with bacon and sausages.

Fegan's dry-eyed gaze wandered the room. Paintings covered the walls – oils and watercolors – and small sculptures sat on every level surface.

Another wave of nausea came with the cold prickling of sweat on his forehead and back. He swallowed and wiped his brow before lacing his fingers together on the table, each hand keeping the other still. A headache threatened to blot out the sunshine from outside, where Fegan could see across the mouth of the river, over to where the long beach stretched into the distance. The sky was a hard blue and two boats dotted the horizon. A mass of land was just visible in the haze where the sea met the sky.

Mr. Taylor sat down. "The Mull of Kintyre," he said. He leaned over to Ellen. "See out there? That's Scotland."

Ellen gaped out of the window. "Look, Mummy, that's Scotland!"

Marie smiled and stroked her daughter's hair. "We'll take a walk on the beach later so you can see it better, okay? Now, eat up your nice breakfast."

While Ellen carefully constructed a toast and bacon sandwich, Fegan thought about the Mull of Kintyre. It was 1994, and he was in the Maze when news came of a Chinook helicopter crash on the Mull. Twenty-five MI5, British Army and RUC intelligence personnel, plus four crew members, died when the aircraft ploughed into the hillside in heavy fog. There were celebrations in Republican and Loyalist blocks alike that night. While the other prisoners laughed and cheered outside his cell, Fegan lay on his bed and studied the cracks in the ceiling.

Mrs. Taylor came back with a pot and a wooden spoon. "Who's for scrambled eggs?" she asked. Ellen and Fegan refused. The little girl smiled at him when he wrinkled his nose.

"So, how's old Hopkirk treating you?" Mr. Taylor asked.

"Fine," Marie said. "We're used to roughing it, anyway." She looked at Fegan with a sly smile. "Aren't we, George?"

It took Fegan a moment to remember the lie. "Yeah, we've stayed in worse."

Ellen looked back and forth between them, a crease in her brow. Marie winked at him, and Fegan smiled back.

Mrs. Taylor finally settled at the table, her fussing done, and joined them in eating. The silence was only interrupted by the hostess slapping her husband's arm when he fed the dog a piece of sausage.

"So, what brings you to Portcarrick?" she asked.

"We just wanted a bit of a break," Marie said. "It was all very last-minute."

"Well, yes, landing in Hopkirk's in the middle of the night does seem a bit impulsive."

"We meant to get away earlier, but George got held up at work."

Mrs. Taylor turned to Fegan. "And what kind of work do you do, George?"

Fegan chewed and swallowed his food before answering. "I'm a Community Development Officer," he said.

"In Belfast?" she asked.

"Yes," he said.

"Whereabouts? We're both from Belfast, originally."

Fegan scrambled for a lie, but came up empty. "Different places," he said.

Mrs. Taylor seemed satisfied. "Did you hear the news this morning?"

"No, not yet," Marie said.

"Oh, it's terrible. A priest was killed in Belfast last night. Somebody broke into his house and stabbed him to death. Isn't that awful?"

Marie set her knife and fork on her plate. "Dreadful," she said, looking hard at Mrs. Taylor.

"And the funny thing is," Mrs. Taylor continued, 'he was the same priest who conducted the funerals for those two men who were killed this week. Isn't that strange?"

"Did they say what time it happened?" Marie asked.

"Sometime last night is all they said. His housekeeper found him this morning. What's the matter, love, aren't you hungry?"

Marie stared across the table at Fegan. "I've had enough, thank you. Can I use your bathroom?"

"Of course you can, love. Just through the kitchen, first on your left."

Marie stood and left the room, keeping her eyes on Fegan until she was out of view.

Fegan lost the will to eat.

"What did you do?" Marie asked.

"Nothing," Fegan said. The sun warmed his skin, but a cool breeze came in from the sea. Clean, clear water rolled up to them. The white sand reflected harsh sunlight, stoking the throb behind Fegan's eyes.

"I don't believe you," Marie said. They had left Ellen playing with

Stella in the garden. She was under the watchful eye of Mrs. Taylor as she tended her plants.

"It's the truth," Fegan said. The lie tasted bitter on his tongue, but he didn't know what else to say. She could never understand.

Marie stopped walking and shielded her eyes with her hand. "You said you had something to do before you came for me last night. It was Father Coulter, wasn't it?"

Fegan struggled with the urge to look away. "No. I had to get money."

"Then why is McGinty after you? Why did someone try to hurt you yesterday?"

"Because I stood up to them when they came to put you out."

"No, it's more than that." She started walking along the beach again. "They wouldn't do that just because you helped me. There's got to be more to it."

"There's not." Anger at his own deceit flared in Fegan's chest.

"And what about Vincie Caffola? Jesus, Uncle Michael?"

Fegan hated himself for lying. "Your uncle was getting mixed up in things he shouldn't, and Vincie Caffola was mouthing off about the direction the party was taking. McGinty told me himself. There were plenty of people who wanted them dead."

"You've killed before," she said. "I know you can do it. Whatever part of you that's missing, you've never got it back."

"I've changed." He took her elbow, turning her to face him. "You said so yourself. You said you could see it in me."

Marie studied his face, her eyes red and angry. "Do you swear?"

"Yes," he said.

She put her hand on his chest, over his heart. "Do you swear on your mother's soul?"

Fegan didn't hesitate. "Yes," he said.

Marie kept her hand on his heart and stepped in close, her voice a desperate whisper. "Do you swear on Ellen's life? Do you swear on my daughter's soul?"

"Don't ask me to do that," he said.

Marie gripped Fegan's shirt in her fist. "Do you swear?"

Her eyes flared with hope, but something else burned beneath. Something Fegan didn't want to see.

"Swear and I'll believe you," she whispered.

"I swear," he said.

Marie nodded slowly and turned to look out to sea.

They walked without words along the beach, across the bridge, and into the cottage garden. Neither Ellen nor the dog showed any signs of wearing each other out as they ran in circles around the shrubbery. Mrs. Taylor was on her knees, her bottom in the air, as she tugged grass from beneath a flowering bush.

She looked around at the sound of the gate. "You weren't long," she said. "Too fresh for you?"

"We're a bit tired," Fegan said.

"I'll help you with that," Marie said.

"Oh, no, sure I'm fine," the bright-faced woman protested.

"Please, I'd like to."

"Well, all right." Mrs. Taylor looked up to Fegan. "Why don't you go on inside? You can keep Albert company while he watches his films."

Fegan questioned Marie with his eyes. She pressed on his arm, telling him to go. He went inside to find Mr. Taylor with his feet up on the coffee table, watching a John Wayne movie.

"Ah, George," said Mr. Taylor. "Grab yourself a seat. It's just started."

"What is it?" Fegan asked.

"*The Searchers.* Have you seen it? It's a classic. The Duke's best."

"No, I haven't seen it," Fegan said. "I'll hang my jacket up."

He walked back to the coat hook in the small porch. Voices drifted in from the garden through the slightly opened door. Soft voices, women's voices, punctuated by a child's laughter and a dog's excited yips.

"Don't tell me if you don't want to," Mrs. Taylor said.

"There's nothing to tell," Marie said.

"All right. It's just what it said on the news, a woman about your age, blonde hair, and her daughter."

"No, it's not me. Must be someone else."

"That's okay, love. Just remember, if there's anything you want to tell me, anything you're worried about, I'm here. You're a smart woman, I can tell, but even smart women do silly things when they're afraid."

Fegan listened to five heartbeats of quiet. Only the dog's panting rose above the waves.

"That's the thing," Marie said. "I'm not afraid of him."

Marie didn't look at Fegan as they ate lunch. Ellen's appetite had been inflamed by almost three hours of chasing Stella around the garden. She attacked a stack of sandwiches with fervour. Stella lapped up a bowlful of water and collapsed in a contented heap on the thick rug at Mr. Taylor's feet.

Fegan felt Mrs. Taylor's eyes on him. Not accusing or fearful, but cautious, as a mother regards her daughter's first suitor. He smiled at her once or twice, and she returned the gesture, but her gaze remained firm.

When lunch was finished, Mrs. Taylor allowed Ellen to take a nap upstairs in one of the comfortable bedrooms. The child had complained of noises disturbing her sleep the night before and seemed glad to climb onto the bed and bury her little head in a soft pillow. Stella hopped up and joined her, circling Ellen's feet before curling into a dozing ball.

Marie insisted that Fegan and she should do the dishes while Mrs. Taylor put her feet up. They were alone at the sink, passing soapy plates back and forth.

"I've been thinking about it," Marie said. "I'm going to trust you because I've no choice. You're the only person I know who's prepared to stand up to McGinty."

"I won't let him hurt you," Fegan said.

"So you keep telling me. But what does that mean? When will it be safe to go home? How long do we stay in Portcarrick? These people are so kind, but we can't impose on them for ever."

Fegan added a plate to the dried stack on the worktop. "I'll go to Belfast today. I'll sort it out."

"How?" Marie turned to face him. There were no more dishes. "How are you going to sort it out?"

"There's people I have to see," Fegan said. "In a couple of days you won't have to worry."

Her stare would not leave him. "What are you going to do?"

"I'll sort it out," he said.

"No. I need to know what you're going to do. Tell me."

Fegan threw the towel on the drainer. He gripped Marie's shoulders with his wiry hands. "I'm going to do whatever it takes to make sure you and Ellen are safe. That's all."

Her eyes danced with his. "All right. Whatever it takes, and that's all. Nothing more."

Fegan nodded, and lifted the towel from the drainer. He felt her hand on his forearm.

"And nothing less," she said.

He turned to look into her hard eyes. "I'll need your car," he said.

Campbell moved through Fegan's house, his steps light, even though there was no one to hear. The back window was still open after yesterday's encounter, and despite the pain it caused him he had been able to climb through. The kitchen was clean and neat. The cooker was gleaming white, the linoleum flooring spotless. The only hint of untidiness was the row of hand tools still lying on a cloth. Campbell inspected them. The cloth was actually leather, soft to the touch, and the tools were held in place by loops. They lay on the flat portion of a foldaway table. He ran his fingers over them. There were small saws of different types, chisels and files. All well used, not the playthings of a casual hobbyist.

He stepped through to the living room. A sofa and two armchairs, not new but not threadbare either. A coffee table sat at the center of the room. It looked handmade, competently but not artfully put together, coated with thick varnish. Another home-made piece supported a small television. A mirror hung over the fireplace. Campbell went to it and studied the deepening lines of his face. His beard needed trimming, as did his hair.

A guitar case stood propped in the corner. Campbell opened the clasps and looked inside. He took the unstrung guitar out and peered inside the fist-sized hole in its belly. He turned it upside down and shook it. Nothing. After inspecting a small compartment inside the case, he put the guitar back in its coffin and sealed it.

He went to the table under the window. A felt sheet covered its surface, and a few small files and a ball of steel wool were scattered around it. There was good light here. Campbell imagined Fegan working under the window, his killer's hands creating, not destroying.

The only other piece in the room was a sideboard. It was made of the same wood as the coffee table – pine, Campbell thought – with simple drawers and hinges. A framed photograph stood on top of it. Campbell lifted it. It looked like it had been taken in the late Fifties, early Sixties. A woman smiled at the camera, her hand held over her eyes like a salute, casting them in shadow. She was tall and slender, with blonde hair. Pretty in a clean, simple, girlish way. She stood on a street just like this one, one foot resting on a doorstep.

Campbell caught a warm smile spreading on his lips and coughed. He winced as his ribcage flared, and he put the photograph back.

A stack of unopened mail sat next to an empty Jameson's bottle. He leafed through the envelopes, hoping for some clue as to where Fegan might have gone. If Campbell could find him first, take care of him, all would be well. If McGinty got him – well, he'd cross that bridge when he came to it.

But what if Fegan found McGinty? That was an entirely different problem, and one that could not come to pass. If McGinty was killed, his old crew would scatter, perhaps turn on the leadership. A drift back to violence could destroy the movement, whether it was directed inward or outward. It had been McGinty's feat to form a bridge between the street thugs and the more politically minded. Now McGinty had served his purpose, the leadership were starting to freeze him out, pull away from him and others like Bull O'Kane. But they were doing it slowly, carefully. The old ways were dead and gone, but still their ghosts might come to haunt the political process. The politicos might be smarter, but smart never stopped a bullet.

Nothing but bills. Campbell set them back on the sideboard. He hunkered down, mindful of his wounds, and opened the doors. Empty. One drawer contained a phone book and a Yellow Pages, both still wrapped in the plastic they were delivered in, but that was all. He stood and looked around the room and over to the stairs. No phone. Who the fuck didn't have a phone?

Campbell crossed the room. There were deep reddish-brown spots on the carpet between the foot of the stairs and the front door. His own blood. He followed the trail up the staircase and paused at the top. The bathroom and two bedrooms. He knew he'd find nothing, but he entered the bathroom anyway. Mirror pieces crunched under his feet. There was a small hole in the wall at eye level, and another in the ceiling. The cops had probably missed them when they'd searched yesterday. Campbell pictured tired and jaded officers giving the home of a convicted terrorist a cursory sweep. No spray of blood commemorated Campbell's injured ribcage.

He looked to the windowsill. A glass stood empty, the kind of glass a toothbrush and toothpaste might stand in. All the other accouterments of male grooming remained, apart from a razor. Fegan had left in a hurry, but not so quickly that he hadn't taken the essentials.

The back bedroom contained nothing, not even a bed. It was clean, but completely bare save for cheap, neatly fitted carpeting. Campbell considered tearing the carpet up for just a moment, but it looked like it hadn't been disturbed since it was laid. His aching side would never forgive him.

Back on the landing, an airing cupboard revealed only sheets and towels, all neatly folded and stacked. Campbell dug through them, already certain it was a pointless task.

Just the master bedroom left now. He pushed the door open and it gave a hard creak. Just like Campbell, Fegan didn't oil his hinges. The bed was stiffly made, apart from the slightest impression at its foot where someone had sat some time ago. He knelt down and peered underneath the bedstead. A shoebox was just within reach. Campbell pulled it out and opened it. It was empty, but had the greasy smell of gun oil and money. A single nine-millimeter round rolled from corner to corner.

"Fuck," he said, and tossed the box to the floor. There would be nothing under the mattress or tucked into the pillowcases, so there was little point in pulling the bedding apart. He did it anyway.

"Where the fuck are you?" Campbell asked the pile of sheets and stripped pillows. The mattress leaned against the wall, revealing the bare slats of the bedstead. There was only one place left to look. He opened the wardrobe door and, as he expected, found only a few shirts and a worn pair of jeans. He quickly proved there was nothing in the pockets.

Campbell went to close the wardrobe door, but something caught his eye. Something small and oblong, pushed into the farthest corner. He reached down and lifted it out. It was a long flat wooden box coated in black vinyl. The sort of box loose jewellery might be stored in. He sat on the edge of the bed and opened it.

Letters, all unopened, all postmarked HM PRISON MAZE, all emblazoned with *Return to sender*. Campbell flipped through them, twelve in total. The most recent was at the top. He hesitated for just a second, then tore it open.

It was one page of small, neat handwriting. The words and letters were impossibly uniform in size and spacing, as if the writer were afraid of revealing anything of himself. It was dated the fourteenth of December 1997. A little over nine and a half years ago. Campbell held his breath as he read.

> *Dear Mother,*
>
> *Father Coulter was here today doing his visits. He told me you are very sick. He said you have cancer. I asked my new psychologist Dr. Brady and he said they would probably let me out to see you if I ask them.*
>
> *Please let me see you. I am sorry for what I did. I am sorry I let you down. I know you are ashamed of me. I don't blame you. I am ashamed of myself.*
>
> *Please let me come and visit you. If I could take back what I did I would. I know you have mercy in your heart. I had no mercy in my heart when I did those things but I have now.*
>
> *Please have mercy. Please let me see you before you get any sicker.*
> *Your son,*
> *Gerald.*

Campbell closed his eyes for a few seconds, feeling the paper's texture between his fingers, listening to his own heartbeat. He opened them again and folded the letter before slipping it back into its envelope. Using his fingertip, he smoothed the tear over as best he could and returned the letter to the box. It fitted neatly into the back corner of the wardrobe, in the dark where he couldn't see it.

"Fuck!" he said, startled at the vibration of his phone. He pulled it from his pocket and looked at the screen. Number withheld. It could be anybody. He thumbed the answer button and brought it to his ear. "What?"

"We've found them," Patsy Toner said.

36

"There you go," the young man said, dropping the sponge into the bucket. "Not the tidiest ever, but you wanted it quick."

Fegan pressed two twenty-pound notes into the acne-faced kid's hand. "Thanks."

"You all right, mate?"

Fegan pushed his shaking hands down into his pockets. "I'm grand," he said, and turned to the car.

Viper Stripes, they were called. A pair of ridiculous white bands that drew a line from the green Renault Clio's nose, over the hood, along the roof, and back down the tailgate. They were supposed to look sporty, but Fegan thought they looked stupid, though no more so than the other little cars parked in front of Antrim Motor Kit. They all had spoilers, bulbous wheel arches and lowered suspensions, and they were all driven by spotty youths in baseball caps.

Fegan had stopped at a beauty spot along the coast and removed the number plates from another green Clio. They were now stuck over Marie's plates using permanent tape he had bought in a hardware shop in Ballymena. It would take a most attentive police officer to recognise the car as belonging to a missing woman.

Ten or fifteen years ago it would have been impossible to drive from the coast, through two large towns, and on to Belfast without meeting a roadblock. An army or police checkpoint would have been a certainty along Fegan's route, but not today. Many times he'd been pulled from a car by Brits or UDR, and searched at the side of the road while uniformed men ripped out the vehicle's innards. The young men in their modified cars would be outraged if that ever happened to them, though their fathers, Protestant and Catholic alike, had endured it every day for decades.

The weather had turned. The warm sunshine of the previous weeks had begun to wane, and clouds hung low overhead. The world was turning grey, and Fegan felt a heaviness inside as he opened the driver's door.

He lowered himself into the car, started the engine, and moved off. The Clio jerked at his clumsy gear changes; it had been a long time since he'd driven. He joined the system of roundabouts that led to the M2 motorway. In less than an hour he'd be in Belfast.

37

"Jesus, you're a fucking mess," Campbell said.

"Fuck you," Eddie Coyle said, forcing the words through the narrow opening of his mouth. Fegan had knocked out two teeth and dislocated his jaw. He looked like someone had molded his face from purple and yellow plasticine and sewn the pieces together.

"Shut up," McGinty said from behind his desk. He pointed to the chair next to Coyle. "Sit down."

McGinty had furnished his moderately sized constituency office with functional items, as befitted the party's socialist dogma. Images of Republican heroes like James Connolly and Patrick Pearse decorated the walls. A map of Ireland divided into the four provinces hung above an Irish Tricolor.

"Our friend inside Lisburn Road station headed off a call from a hotel owner this morning," McGinty said. "We were due a stroke of luck after the balls you two made of things."

Campbell pointed to the ceiling, then his ear.

McGinty shook his head. "We're clean. The place was swept for bugs this morning. As I was saying, our friend did well. He'll get a nice bonus for his troubles and – despite my better judgment – you two get the chance to put things right. Do you think you can manage not to completely fuck it up this time?"

Campbell and Coyle did not answer.

"If I didn't need to keep as few people in the know as possible, I'd have given this to someone else. But, as it's a delicate matter, it's up to you two."

"Where are they?" Campbell asked.

"Portcarrick. It's a little village up on the Antrim coast. Very pretty. There's an old hotel on the bay called Hopkirk's. They arrived there late last night, apparently. Gerry Fegan, Marie McKenna and the wee girl."

Campbell knew the answer, but asked the question anyway. "What do you want us to do?"

McGinty gave him a hard stare. "Take a wild guess."

"And what about the woman?"

McGinty's eyes flickered for just an instant. "If she gets in the way, do whatever you have to."

Coyle mopped drool from his chin with a stained handkerchief. He leaned forward in his seat. "And the wee girl?"

McGinty swivelled in his chair to look out the window at the greying sky. He wiped his mouth and looked at his hand, as if expecting to see blood there. "I said do whatever you have to."

"No way I'm doing a wee girl."

Squeezed between tight lips, Coyle's words were hard to hear over the van's rattling engine. It had been bought from a scrap dealer that morning. Red paint and rust had flaked at the touch of Campbell's finger. He drove.

"It probably won't come to that," he said.

"But it might." Coyle dabbed at his mouth.

"We'll see. Do you know how to get to this place?"

"Sort of. Head for the M2. Keep going till you hit Antrim, then Ballymena. After that, we'll have to go by the road signs."

Campbell headed east across the city, onto the Falls Road and past the imposing Divis Tower, once a focal point of violence in the city. The top two floors of the twenty-storey block of flats had been commandeered by the British Army in the early Seventies for its views over the city. Because it stood at the heart of militant Republicanism, they could only access it by helicopter. Campbell had often wondered what it was like for the residents in the floors below, hearing their enemy's footsteps above their homes, and the thunderous clatter of the helicopters bringing soldiers in and out, day and night. The army had abandoned it two years ago. Campbell imagined they were as glad to leave the tower as the residents were to see them go.

The van joined the Westlink, which in turn would lead them to the M2 and north towards the rugged Glens of Antrim. He winced now and then as the van's jostling sparked painful flares in his side. The heavy clutch pedal did little for his injured thigh. The stop-and-start of traffic, backed up by roadworks to the south where the M1 joined the Westlink, only made it worse. What use was progress if all it caused was traffic jams? Peace had cost the people of Northern Ireland dear, but Campbell wouldn't have been surprised if road congestion irked them more than anything else.

He looked across to Coyle in the passenger seat. "Tell me something. What is it with McGinty and that woman? There's got to be more to it than her shacking up with a cop. What's the story?"

"That's none of your business," Coyle said.

"Aw, come on." Campbell shot him a grin. "Just a bit of gossip for the road, eh?"

Coyle sighed and shook his head.

"Jesus, come on, you miserable bastard. Why not tell me?"

"Three reasons." Coyle counted them on his fingers. "One, you're a cunt. Two, asking questions about Paul McGinty's personal life is a fucking good way to get your legs broke. Three, talking hurts like fuck. Now shut your fucking mouth and drive."

38

The air was heavy with coming rain as Fegan watched Patsy Toner's office from the bus stop opposite. The solicitor ran his practice from rented rooms above a newsagent's shop on the Springfield Road. His Jaguar was parked outside. It was seven o'clock and the sky made a grey blanket over the city.

A headache came in waves, punctuating the swells of nausea. The windows of an off-licence two doors down gleamed in the bruised evening. He ignored it. He knew Toner would come out soon. The lawyer would want to go drinking. Then Fegan would find out why the followers wanted that cop. When he knew who he was, he'd draw him out, get the cop to come to him.

Then he'd do it.

The RUC man would leave Fegan, just as the others had. Then Campbell and McGinty, tomorrow or the day after, and he would be free. He closed his eyes and pictured it: a dark, quiet room where he could lay his head down without fear of screaming.

Alone.

That word was bitter-sweet. He could close his eyes in peace, but he would be alone. He would have to run, leaving Marie and Ellen behind. At least they'd be safe and, really, that was all that mattered.

He opened his eyes as a chill crept to his center. Shadows gathered to him.

The light in Toner's window died.

"He's coming," Fegan said.

He made his way across the road, squeezing his hands into a pair of surgical gloves. The Jaguar's passenger side faced out, and Fegan hunkered down at its rear door and gripped the handle. A narrow staircase descended from Toner's office to the doorway below. Fegan heard the door wheeze open and closed, and the jangling of keys. Toner talked on his mobile phone.

"So, it's sorted?" he said. "Fucking glad to hear it. So long as they don't make a balls of it."

Fegan held his breath, readying himself.

"Let me know when it's done. I'll have a drink to celebrate."

He heard a beep as Toner disconnected, then a whir and clunk as he unlocked the Jaguar. *Wait*, Fegan told himself, *wait, wait* . . .

He pulled the handle the moment he heard Toner open the driver's door and slipped quietly onto the back seat as the solicitor lowered himself in. Fegan waited for Toner to pull the driver's door closed. When it thudded home, Fegan pulled his own door shut.

"Fucking Christ!" Toner twisted in the seat, his mouth open wide, his eyes gaping first at Fegan's face, and then at the pistol in his hand.

"Hello, Patsy," Fegan said.

He made Toner drive first east, then north. Horns blared on the Westlink as a rusted red van bullied its way through traffic ahead of them. The congestion eased as they climbed towards the M2's long sweeps. Fegan risked one glance across the river to the Odyssey complex, its lights coming to life for a busy Saturday night. Less than a week ago he had pulled the trigger and settled Michael McKenna's debt. He realised it had been no more than a hundred yards from this stretch of road.

"Hurry up," he said to Toner.

Twenty minutes took them to an industrial estate north-west of the city. As the sky darkened, Fegan instructed Toner to park up between the low buildings, out of sight of the rumbling motorway. He had been here before, nine years ago, when the two UFF boys died badly. Now those same UFF boys paced in the drizzle, hate and pain on their faces, touching themselves in the places where Fegan had opened them. He couldn't return their stares.

The estate lay derelict now, just rows of concrete and steel skeletons on waste ground, waiting to be demolished and replaced by a housing development. They looked like giant mourners at a graveside.

"Give me the keys," Fegan said.

Toner passed them back, his eyes flitting towards Fegan and away again. "What do you want, Gerry? You're scaring the shite out of me."

Fegan slipped the keys into his pocket. "Who's the cop?"

Toner blinked. "What cop?"

"The one you have inside. You told me about him the day I got lifted. The one who beat the shit out of me."

Toner held his hands up. "I don't know, Gerry. Just some peeler. I've never met him."

"You're lying. Davy Campbell told me he was your contact."

"No, that's not true. I swear to God, Gerry, I don't know who he is."

"Give me your hand."

Toner slowly shook his head. "No."

Fegan raised the pistol with his right hand, steady now, and extended his left.

"No," Toner said.

Fegan pressed the Walther against Toner's temple. The solicitor screwed his eyes shut and held out his left hand.

"I'll ask you one more time," Fegan said as he gripped Toner's little finger. "Who's the cop?"

"Aw, Christ, Gerry. Please, I don't know anything. I just run errands for McGinty when he needs me. I take his cases for him, that's all. I don't go near any of that other stuff."

Fegan placed the Walther on the seat beside him, well out of Toner's reach, and took the lawyer's wrist in his right hand. With his left, he twisted the finger back and up, first feeling the stiff elasticity of the joint, next the jolt of it giving way, then the looseness of the broken bone.

Toner screamed.

"You could've just told me, Patsy. That didn't have to happen."

"Ah, fuck!" Toner tried to pull his hand back, but Fegan squeezed and the solicitor screamed again.

Heat gathered around the break, the puffy swelling already filling Fegan's hand. He felt it pulse through the thin membrane of the surgical gloves. "Who's the cop?" he asked.

"Please, Gerry, oh God, please." Tears rolled down Toner's flushed cheeks. "I can't tell you. McGinty. Oh Christ, he'll kill me. Please, Gerry, don't."

Fegan gripped Toner's ring finger. "Who's the cop?"

"Gerry, please, I can't."

Toner screamed again, drowning out the sound of cracking bone.

Fegan sighed. He was surprised at Toner. He'd always taken him for weak; the solicitor was anything but. He ground the bones together.

"Who's the cop?" he asked. Toner's screams drowned out the question, so he asked again, louder. "Who's the cop?"

"Stop! Jesus, stop!"

Fegan released the fingers and moved his grip to Toner's wrist. The heat from the solicitor's hand seemed to fill the car, along with the thick smell of sweat and fresh urine. Nausea came rolling in, but Fegan pushed it back.

"Who's the cop?" he asked.

"Oh, Jesus . . . Jesus . . . Brian Anderson. He's a sergeant. We've had him for years. Since the Eighties."

"What does he do for you?"

Toner breathed deep through his nose, his face twisted in pain. "Not much these days. Tips us off sometimes, if there's a raid coming. McGinty pays him a few quid every week just to have him on side."

Fegan let his hand drift down so Toner's palm rested against his. "Not much these days, you said. Before that, what'd he do?"

"Information," Toner hissed. "Other cops. Their cars, where they lived, where they drank, where their kids went to school. He used to sell information to McGinty."

Fegan remembered. He remembered the RUC man's face when he saw the gun in Fegan's hand.

"He got hurt when he was a month on the job," Toner continued, panting between words. "A coffee-jar bomb when he was on patrol. Fucked up his hip. Crippled when he was twenty-three. He's been riding a desk ever since. Admin, records, answering phones, that sort of stuff. He's a bitter fucker. Started selling out his mates. I always handled the money. I paid him. Aw, Christ, Gerry. McGinty's going to kill me."

Toner's whimpering and pleading went on, but Fegan couldn't hear him. He had stopped listening and started remembering.

It was Fegan's first kill. Less than a week after his twentieth birthday he stood in the snow watching children emerge from a primary school. There was no sign of the RUC man's Ford Granada. McGinty said he always arrived five minutes early when he picked his son up on a Friday.

Fegan looked across the road. A boy stood apart from the others, looking up and down the street. Nine years old, McGinty said. He wouldn't see it. He wouldn't be out of school yet when his father arrived. That's what McGinty had said. McGinty was wrong. The RUC man was late, and the boy would see everything.

A bitter wind tore along the street, pulling snow with it. Fegan's nose tingled with the cocaine the lads had given him for courage. The buzzing in his head couldn't keep the cold or the urge to run out of his feet. Some of the parents looked at him, their faces lined with concern. They didn't recognise him. That's what they'd tell the police later. He was just some man, another parent they hadn't seen before. A little odd-looking, maybe, something about the way he wore his hat, or the strange lankness of his hair. Fegan had seen himself in the car's rear-view mirror and the wig looked convincing enough. They had dropped him at the corner and were parked up a street away, waiting for the sound of gunfire.

Fegan stopped breathing as the kid's eyes met his. The boy's brow creased as he stared back. Fegan couldn't look away. The kid's jaw slackened, parting his lips to let misted breath escape on the breeze.

He knew.

The sound of a car dragged the boy's gaze away. A Ford Granada slowing to a halt. The boy ran onto the road, screaming at his father, waving his arms at Fegan. The RUC man stood hard on his brake pedal, skidding on the snow. He stared at his son, confused. As Fegan approached, the gun already in his hand, the boy pointed at him.

The RUC man turned his head, slack-jawed, his face showing no understanding of his own death. That changed as Fegan raised the gun. He understood. His eyes saw his end and Fegan squeezed the trigger twice. The car lurched forward and stalled as the RUC man's feet left the pedals.

Quiet. A few seconds before, there had been the noise of children streaming from the school, the honking of car horns, the calls of parents. Now there was only the rushing in Fegan's ears.

The boy stood still, snowflakes glistening on his hair. He watched Fegan. His eyes were small dead things, black holes in a white face.

Then the screaming started and Fegan ran. The lads skidded to a stop at the end of the street and he dived into the back of the car. They cheered and whooped and slapped his back as the engine roared.

Fegan drank until he threw up all over the floor of the pub, then wept, then drank some more. Michael McKenna hugged him and Paul McGinty shook his hand. His back was sore from slapping, his throat and nose stinging from the vomit and cocaine. A black taxi carried him home to his mother's house and he struggled to let himself in.

One small suitcase and a bin liner lay in the darkened hallway. He looked inside the bag. It was stuffed full of his clothes. His mother stepped out of the shadows. He could see her eyes glint, fierce and bright.

"I saw the news," she said.

Fegan wiped his mouth.

Her voice cracked. "I saw what you did."

Fegan took a step towards her, but she held her hand up.

"Get out and never come back," she said, her voice soft and sad. She started climbing the stairs. She was almost gone from view when she turned and said, "I'm ashamed I carried the likes of you inside me. I'm ashamed I brought up a man who could kill someone in front of his child. May God forgive me for giving birth to you."

*

A gust of wind rocked the Jaguar on its suspension and dragged Fegan back to the present. The sky outside greyed and fat drops of rain splashed on the windscreen. The followers watched and waited.

"Phone him," Fegan said.

Toner stopped whimpering. "Phone who?"

"The cop. Tell him to come here."

"Why?"

Fegan squeezed Toner's hand and waited for the screams to die away. "Just do it. Tell him he has to come now. Tell him you have something for him."

Toner reached into his jacket pocket with his right hand and retrieved his mobile. He kept his watery eyes on Fegan as he dialled.

"Hello, Brian? . . . It's Patsy . . . Yeah, I know . . . I know . . . It's important. I wouldn't have called you otherwise, now would I? . . . Listen, I've got something for you . . . A bonus . . . But you have to come now . . . Now, Brian . . . In an hour . . . All right . . ."

Fegan listened to Toner give the cop directions as the rain pattered on the Jaguar's roof. The RUC man stared at him through the spattered window, a soft smile curving his mouth.

"Her car's not here," Coyle said.

"Well observed, Sherlock." Campbell opened the van door and stepped down, mindful of his injured thigh. A woman peered out at him from a cottage next to the hotel. He gave her a smile and a nod. She didn't return the gesture.

Coyle came around from the other side of the van. He pointed to the hotel. "This is the place, isn't it?"

"Looks like it."

"So, how do we do this?" Coyle looked nervous.

"Quietly, if we can. We'll find out if they're here first." Campbell limped out onto the road that ran across the front of the hotel. On the other side of the river mouth, past the old church, a long beach stretched into the distance where it met hills running down to the sea. On this side, the sun dipped towards the hill-top behind the hotel. It would be swallowed by the gathering clouds long before it reached the grass and rocks. Further along from the hotel and cottage, an ugly block of apartments scarred the cliff face. He couldn't be sure if they or the crude basalt block at the edge of the water, some sort of memorial, looked more out of place.

"Wait here," Campbell said. "I'll go in and have a sniff around. The state of your face, you'll scare the shit out of the customers."

"You don't look much better yourself." Coyle dabbed at his chin with his handkerchief.

"Fair point," Campbell said. "But still, wait here – all right?"

"What if Fegan's in there?"

Campbell shrugged. "If you hear shooting, come running. Otherwise, just fucking stay here. Clear enough?"

Coyle sighed and leaned against the van. He folded his arms and gave Campbell the hard eye.

Campbell entered the hotel to find a large room that might once have been a dining area. It was filled with tables and chairs that looked like they hadn't been used in years. A door led to another room from which Campbell could hear the crackling of a fire and the low throb of friendly conversation. He headed towards the sound, grimacing at the flames in his thigh and the sparks in his side.

It was a bar, with a grand fireplace at one end and a few drinkers perched on stools at the other. They all turned to look at him. Campbell walked towards them, and a bearded, white-haired man set aside his newspaper and stood up. Campbell beckoned him towards the far end of the bar, away from the handful of drinkers.

"Are you the owner?" he asked.

"Yes. Seamus Hopkirk. What can I do for you?"

Campbell lowered his voice and leaned in close. "You called us this morning." He glanced over the owner's shoulder. "About some guests of yours."

Hopkirk's eyes narrowed. "Are you the police?"

"That's right."

Hopkirk looked him up and down. "Can I see some identification?"

"Not just at the moment, sir. You see, this is a very delicate matter and we'd like to resolve it as quietly as possible. Now, if you could just tell me where I can find Miss McKenna and her friend, I'll be out of your way."

Hopkirk exhaled through his nose. "Listen, young man, don't mistake me for some yokel. I've sat on Larne Council for more than twenty years, and the District Policing Partnership for the last three. You're no more a policeman than I am. What I will tell you is they're not here. If you want to know any more than that you'll have to come back with some identification and a contact for the Duty Officer at your station. Now, if you'll excuse me, I have customers to attend to."

Campbell took hold of Hopkirk's wrist. "There's no need to get in a strop, sir. Just tell me what I need to know and I'll be no more trouble to you."

Hopkirk cleared his throat and looked down at Campbell's hand. "Young man," he said loud enough to draw the attention of the drinkers, 'please let go of my arm. They're not here, and that's all I can tell you."

Campbell held Hopkirk's gaze for a moment, then looked to the customers. The nearest of them, a large man, got to his feet.

"Everything all right, Hopkirk?"

"It's fine, Albert. This young man was just leaving."

Campbell weighed it up. He could either let him go and walk out, or . . . what? Tie them all up and beat it out of the old curmudgeon? He sighed and released Hopkirk's wrist.

"Thanks for your help." He smiled. Then he turned and limped out of the bar, through the old dining room, and into the thickening rain.

"Well?" Coyle asked. He had taken refuge in the van and wound the passenger window down when he saw Campbell emerge.

"He says they're not here."

A dog appeared at the window of the cottage next door and barked furiously at the strangers. Campbell climbed into the driver's seat.

"Do you believe him?"

"I don't know," Campbell said as he started the engine. "But we can't hang around. I think I put his back up."

Worry darkened Coyle's battered face. "McGinty's going to shit a brick if we don't get Fegan."

"Probably, but he's going to shit a fucking *house* if we get lifted by the peelers."

Something beyond the river caught Coyle's eye. "Here, who's that?"

Campbell followed the direction of his pointing finger to the far side of the bridge. "Jesus, it's her and the kid. No Fegan, though."

"He must be away in the car."

"Your powers of deduction are impressing the shite out of me today, Eddie."

"Go fuck yourself."

"Hang on," Campbell said. He put the van into reverse and backed out onto the road, twisting the wheel so they faced the bridge. He could hear the dog barking over the engine's clatter. The van roared as he swung it round the tight bend and onto the bridge where Marie McKenna walked with her daughter, oblivious to their approach.

Campbell veered to the other side of the road, ignoring the blaring of an oncoming car's horn. The woman's startled eyes found him as he stamped on the brake pedal. She looked in all directions for a place to run, but he was on the footpath before she could move. The little girl gaped up at him.

"Let's not have a fuss, Marie," Campbell said, clutching his side.

"What do you want?" Her eyes were everywhere.

"Don't run. It'll go bad if you run."

Tears sprang from Marie's eyes and her daughter hugged her thigh.

"It'll be all right," Campbell said. "Just get in the van. No fuss, no bother. Okay?"

"Please, let Ellen go. There's people in the cottage there. They'll look after her."

"Sorry, Marie." He stepped closer. "Both of you in the van. Now."

The shrouded sun had sunk well beneath the treetops of Glenariff Forest, a few miles south of Portcarrick, and a chill clung to the air. The only sounds were the gathering wind in the leaves above, the pattering of heavy raindrops and Marie McKenna's frightened sobbing. She sat in the middle of the van's cabin, holding her daughter close. Eddie Coyle leaned against a tree watching Campbell's lopsided pacing.

"Call me back, for Christ's sake," Campbell said to the mobile phone in his hand. The signal was poor and the thick spruce canopy didn't help, but they'd had to get off the road and decide what to do. It had been almost thirty minutes since McGinty had promised to call him back with a plan.

"I won't do the kid," Coyle said for the fifth time since they'd pulled into the gap in the tree line.

Campbell spun to face him. "Will you shut the fuck up about that?"

"I'm just saying, that's all."

Campbell crossed the clearing and stood toe to toe with Coyle. "Yeah, well you saying it isn't fucking helping. You're going to make her panic and then Christ knows what'll happen. So do me a favor and shut the fuck up, all right?"

"Shove it up your arse," Coyle said.

Campbell could smell his sour breath. "Just fucking try me, pal."

Coyle's bloodshot eyes flickered with anger and fear. Campbell was ready for him to move when the phone rang.

"Yeah?"

"All right," McGinty said, 'here's what we'll do. The Bull has an old farm just past Middletown, not far from the border. He was using it for fuel laundering until it got shut down, but it's kennels now. You know, for the dogs. He has a big pit with seating and everything in an old barn."

"Christ," Campbell said.

"You know what these old country bastards are like. Bloodthirsty fuckers. He wants them brought there. I'm heading down now. I'll try and make sure it doesn't go to shite, but his blood's up. He's seriously pissed off about Father Coulter. He's going to see to Fegan himself."

Campbell looked at Marie clutching her daughter to her breast. "What about the woman and the kid? After, when it's done?"

He could swear he felt McGinty's breath on his ear. "I don't know. We'll cross that bridge when we come to it."

"All right, it'll be a couple of hours till we get to Middletown. I'll call you for directions from there."

Campbell hung up.

"Well?" Coyle asked.

Campbell returned the phone to his pocket. "We've got a long drive ahead. I'm going for a piss and to get my head clear. Watch them."

Campbell turned and limped into the trees, into the shadows of the forest, pushing deeper among the branches. When he was sure Coyle couldn't hear him, he took the phone back out of his pocket. He hesitated for a moment before dialling the handler's number.

"Hello?"

"It's me," Campbell said.

"What are you doing calling from that phone?"

Campbell turned in circles, peering through the trees, making sure

Coyle hadn't followed him. "I've no choice. I need to talk to you now."

"What's happening?"

"We've got the woman and her kid. She says Fegan's in Belfast somewhere. She doesn't know where."

"So, what, you're holding her hostage?"

"McGinty's idea."

Campbell told his handler the politician's plan.

"Christ," the handler said. "All you can do is play along. So long as Fegan's taken care of, so long as they clear up their mess. Just don't let it get any worse."

"But the woman and the kid. McGinty isn't going to let them go when it's over. I know it. He has something against her, something other than her fucking a cop."

"They aren't our concern. Like I said, so long as McGinty clears up his own mess."

Campbell closed his eyes and breathed the damp air. "There's another option," he said.

"What's that?"

"Think about it. We'll have Paul McGinty and Bull O'Kane in one place, together, holding hostages. You time it right, raid the place just after Fegan's taken care of, you'll have them at the scene of a murder. Even if McGinty gets off the charge, he'll be destroyed. Think of all the people who've wanted to see him fucked, but he's always been too slippery, too sly. We can do it. We can have him."

The handler sighed. "Jesus, you really don't understand what's going on, do you?"

"What?"

"All right, say we give McGinty enough rope to hang himself and that old bastard O'Kane. What then? No matter how hard the leadership try to distance themselves from it, the Unionists will walk. Jesus, even the moderates will run a mile. Stormont will grind to a halt. We can't afford another two years of negotiations just to get back to where we are now. All the politics, all the money, all the work – all wasted. No. That's the word from on high, son. Stormont keeps running, whatever the cost. Yes, I and many others in my profession would dearly love to see McGinty swing, but it isn't going to happen. Now, do what you need to do, there's a good lad."

Campbell leaned his forehead against a tree trunk, feeling the bark scratch his skin.

"All right," he said and hung up.

He started limping back towards the clearing, his mind churning. He'd done worse things in his life. He could do this. The red paintwork of the van was just visible through the branches when he heard Eddie Coyle's thin cry.

"Davy! Davy!"

Campbell started a limping run, ignoring the fire in his side. He broke through to the clearing to find Coyle on the ground, clutching at his bruised face, and the van's passenger door open.

"The bitch clouted me," Coyle said as he scrambled to his feet.

Campbell scanned the trees, looking for a glimpse of ash-blonde hair. There, up ahead. She hadn't got far carrying the child. He pulled the pistol McGinty had given him from his waistband and dived into the trees after her. Coyle came panting and groaning behind.

Even with the stiff pain in his leg and the agony of breathing, Campbell was gaining on Marie. He could hear the panicked rasp of her breath. He aimed the pistol five feet above her head and pulled the trigger. She threw herself to the ground as the shot echoed through the forest.

Campbell slowed as he neared the woman. He cried out, his side screaming at the effort. He leaned against a tree, one hand clasped to his ribs, the other aiming the pistol at the woman's head. She lay on the ground, curled around her child. Her desperate eyes stared up at him.

"Please let Ellen go," Marie said. "Take me if you want, just let her go."

Campbell pushed himself off the tree and grimaced as he hunkered down beside them. Through the pain, he felt a cold leaden weight in his stomach. "Try that again and I'll kill her in front of you."

"Please—"

"Do you understand?" He placed the gun's muzzle against the girl's yellow hair. "I'll make you watch her die."

The child seemed to climb inside her mother, away from the pistol, into her arms.

Marie's voice was barely audible above the whispering of the trees, but her eyes screamed with hate. "Don't you touch her."

"Just get back in the van." Campbell looked up at Coyle's wide eyes. "Come on," he said.

All four walked back to the van in silence. When the woman and her child were safely in the vehicle's cabin, Coyle closed the passenger door and turned to Campbell.

"Would you have done it?" he asked.

Campbell started limping towards the driver's side.

Coyle came after him and tugged his sleeve. "Would you have done it?"

Campbell returned his stare. "We need to get moving," he said.

40

A sweep of headlights illuminated the inside of the Jaguar. Toner lifted his head from the misted glass, cradling his swollen hand. "That's him," he said.

Fegan could just make out a Volkswagen Passat through the condensation. A tall, broad man emerged from it and limped towards the Jaguar. Anderson. Fegan lowered himself in the seat behind Toner and listened to the solicitor's shallow breathing. The passenger door opened and a wash of cool air swept though the car, chilling Fegan's damp brow. The Jaguar rocked lazily on its suspension as the cop's weight settled in.

"Jesus, what's wrong with you?" Anderson asked.

Toner didn't answer, instead whining with terror.

"You look like shit. What happened to your hand? Have you pissed yourself?"

"I . . . I . . . I . . ."

"Listen, Patsy, what the fuck's going on? I left the wife at the restaurant. She's going to go through me for a short cut, so whatever's going on, you better—"

Fegan sat upright and raised the Walther.

"Fuck me!" Anderson grabbed for his pocket and pulled out a small revolver. Fegan was ready for it; all cops carried Personal Protection Weapons. The cop swung his arm around the passenger seat and Fegan grabbed his wrist, forcing Anderson's aim to the rear window.

"Oh, Jesus!" Toner curled into a ball, burying his head in his arms.

Beads of sweat broke on Anderson's brow as he struggled with Fegan, fighting to regain control of the pistol. The little gun boomed in the confined space and Fegan felt the bullet zip past his ear.

The noise set Toner moving and he opened his door, spilling out onto the ground. Fegan heard a scream as he landed, then the scrabbling of feet. He let his stare leave the cop's face for a moment to see Toner disappear between the derelict buildings.

Fegan raised the Walther to Anderson's forehead, but still the cop fought him. The revolver fired again and Fegan felt glass shower his back. He threw his weight against Anderson's arm, keeping the cop's wrist in his grip, and pushed with his feet against the Jaguar's door. The passenger seat made a fulcrum for leverage, and Fegan pushed with everything he had. He gritted his teeth, blood rushing to his head with the effort, until he felt the sudden jolt of Anderson's shoulder dislocating. The gun disappeared into the footwell behind the passenger seat and Anderson howled until his voice cracked.

"Sit still," Fegan said, a sudden clarity swelling in him.

Anderson squirmed, kicking at the Jaguar's dashboard.

"I said sit still."

The cop gave another hoarse cry before turning to face Fegan from the passenger seat. "Oh, Christ, what do you want?"

"You," Fegan said.

He screamed again when Fegan released his arm to flop uselessly between the seats. His legs writhed and his face turned from red to purple. At last, his screaming died and his breathing levelled. "I'm sorry . . . I'm sorry about the beating. Patsy told me to. McGinty's . . . McGinty's orders."

Fegan looked to the RUC man who leaned against the windscreen, peering in. His eyes blazed with savage joy. The car's interior lighting glared, picking out the sweat on Anderson's contorted face, glinting on his gritted teeth. The RUC man would see everything, just like his son had.

"You remember the RUC man you sold out?"

"Oh, Jesus . . ."

"Do you remember?"

Anderson shook his head. "I . . . I . . . Which one?"

"That's right." Fegan smiled. "You sold lots of them, didn't you? How much did you get for them?"

Anderson opened and closed his mouth, shaking his head. Sweat dripped into his eyes.

Fegan kicked the arm still hanging between the seats. When Anderson's screaming faded, Fegan asked, "How much?"

"It depended . . . who they were."

"How much for a constable? Just an ordinary peeler. How much for one of them?"

"Oh, God, I don't know . . . a few thousand . . . please, don't . . ."

"Think back. Do you remember one from 1982? It would have been the start of February. It had been snowing. I killed him in front of his kid."

Anderson's eyes darted back and forth, his breath was ragged. "At the school? I remember. Yeah, I remember. What was his name? Oh, Jesus, what was his name?"

"Doesn't matter," Fegan said. He placed the Walther back against the cop's forehead. "He wants you."

"Wh . . . what?"

"Look." Fegan indicated with his eyes. "Out there. He's watching. They're all watching."

"What are you talking about?"

"Look." Fegan pressed the Walther's muzzle against Anderson's cheek, turning his head to face out the window. "There he is. He's been waiting years for this."

Anderson began to weep. "There's no one there."

"It's time to pay for what you did."

The cop turned back to Fegan. Tears mixed with sweat on his cheeks. "But *you* killed him. Not me."

Fegan blinked. "I just pulled the trigger. He was dead as soon as you fingered him."

Anderson shook his head. "You're insane."

"I know. But I'm getting better all the time."

Fegan pulled the trigger.

FIVE

41

The smell of blood, sweat and alcohol rose up through the spectators to the top tier. The old man stood taller than anyone else in the barn, and he could see through all the raised fists waving euros and pounds. He always had the best seat in the house. After all, he owned the place.

The crowd's roar couldn't drown out the snarling and yelping from below. The dogs circled each other, snapping, growling and lunging. They were evenly matched, both of them with blocky jaws and thick necks. Both good, mature males, scarred and battle-hardened, with heavy balls hanging between their legs, filling them with fight. Choice pit bulls. Good animals. He loved good animals, as did any man worth a shite.

They'd been at it forty minutes now. Their snouts and barrel chests were caked in red, and fresh wounds glistened in the pitiless light. One had lost a piece of its cheek, and the other's shoulder was torn open, but neither tired of the struggle as their handlers goaded them to attack. Wooden boards lined the pit walls, wild arcs of blood, old and new, slashed across them.

The Brindle and the Red squared off, eyes locked together. The old man felt a surge in his loins, sensing this would be the final spar. The roaring of the crowd faded to a murmur, nearly sixty men waiting for the moment.

They didn't have to wait long.

Christ, they were fast. They looked stupid, just lumbering hunks of muscle and teeth, but think that and they'd have you. A good pit bull is quick; strong isn't good enough. They launched at the same instant, thick paws in the air, batting at each other, trying to get the other down. Their haunches bunched as they boxed, teeth snapping. Shouts began to rise from the crowd as the dogs danced and snarled, each trying to gain dominance, to push the other down and finish him. First it seemed the Red was gaining as its teeth pinched the folds at the back of the other's neck, but the Brindle forced its weight downward, throwing the Red off balance.

Then it was over. The Brindle's mighty jaws locked on the Red's neck, and a whimpering shriek echoed up through the old barn. A low, triumphant growl resonated in the Brindle's chest as it ground the Red's muzzle into the dirt. The Red's feet kicked out, but it was at the mercy of the other dog. The Brindle had no notion of mercy, and poured all its strength into its bulbous jaw muscles, breeding and instinct forcing its teeth together.

"All right, enough!" Bull O'Kane stepped downwards from tier to tier of the bleachers, his bulk making the scaffolded benches groan.

The handlers jumped into the pit to separate the dogs. "Release!" the Brindle's owner shouted. The pit bull was oblivious, blood trickling from between its jaws.

"Release!" He grabbed the dog's ear and yanked it.

The other dog's handler tried to pry the victor's jaws open with the metal rod he used to train his own animal. "For fuck's sake, he'll kill him."

The Brindle shook its head, reinforcing its grip.

"Jesus, get out of the way," O'Kane said.

He stepped down into the pit and pushed the handlers aside. The Brindle's scrotum dangled between its hind legs, tender and exposed. O'Kane's boot connected with a fleshy slap and the dog whimpered, but held on.

"Ignorant fucker," O'Kane said, wiping spit from his mouth. Once more, he drew his foot back; once more he buried his boot between the Brindle's legs. It staggered sideways, its hind quarters quivering, but still it kept its monstrous grip.

"This time, ya bastard." O'Kane was coming seventy, but he was still the Bull. He put all his weight behind his right foot, and now the dog opened its jaws and raised its snout to the corrugated roof. It howled, snarled, and turned to face its tormentor.

O'Kane locked stares with it. "Come on, then."

It lowered on its haunches, preparing.

O'Kane put his weight on both feet.

The Brindle didn't hesitate, coming at him with teeth bared, eyes rolling in its head, blood-tainted drool arcing from its black lips.

It didn't stand a chance.

O'Kane let it come at him, offering his callused hand. Just as it tried to clamp its teeth on his right fist, O'Kane forced his fingers to the back of its mouth and wrapped his left arm around its powerful neck. The Brindle opened and closed its jaws, struggling to gain purchase, but O'Kane pushed harder and seized its tongue with his thick fingers. He took his arm from around its neck as he twisted the slick pink flesh and pulled up until the dog's front paws scrabbled on the dirt floor. It coughed and gagged and whimpered as its eyes bulged.

O'Kane gave it a hard kick to the ribs as it hung there before lowering his arm, keeping the dog's head twisted to the side.

He turned his eyes to the handler. "If you can't control your animal, don't fucking bring him to my fights."

"Yes, Mr. O'Kane." The handler looked at the ground. "Sorry, Mr. O'Kane."

"Get this thing out of here." He released the whining dog's tongue as the handler slipped a chain around its neck.

O'Kane looked up to Sean the bookie and smiled, wiping his hand on his coat. Sean winked back and straightened his cap. Most of the crowd had put their money on the Red. It had been a good night so far.

A voice came from the barn's open doorway. "Da!"

O'Kane turned to see his son Pádraig, as tall as his father and twice as wide. "What?"

"Yer man's here."

O'Kane nodded and stepped up and out of the pit, past his son – who turned and followed him – and out to the farmyard. Dogs penned in the old stables barked and snarled as they passed, and he hissed at them to shut up. Wire cages on the opposite side housed the visiting animals. A diesel generator rattled by the side of the derelict house, giving it and the barn power. The place still had the acrid chemical smell from the fuel-laundering plant he'd housed here before Customs had raided it. The dogs didn't bring in as much money, but they brought him greater pleasure. As an old man, he took his pleasures where he could find them. Besides, he had plenty of other plants churning out stripped diesel along the border.

Languid rain drops slithered down the farmhouse windows. A soft light burned inside. O'Kane pushed open a door into what had once been a kitchen.

"Wait out here," he said to his son, and stepped inside, ducking his head beneath the top of the door frame.

There were three other men in the room. Tommy Downey from Crossmaglen, thin and wiry with slicked-back hair, leaned against one wall. Kevin Malloy from Monaghan, thickset like O'Kane but a full twelve inches shorter, leaned against the other.

Downey pointed to the third man, who was seated in the middle of the room. "Here he is, boss."

"Aye, so he is."

O'Kane walked over to the man. The pillowcase over his head puffed out and in again as he breathed. His well-cut suit had red blotches on it.

"What's this? Did he not come quietly?"

"Not really," Malloy said.

O'Kane tutted. "That's a shame."

He reached out and plucked the pillowcase from the man's head. The young man stared up at him. Blood congealed around his nose and mouth.

"Jesus, Martin, you're sweating like a pig."

Martin blinked.

"It's an awful pity you wouldn't listen to me, Martin. Now it's come to this, and there was no call for it."

Martin's eyes brimmed. "What do you want?"

"I want to give you money. But you won't take it from me. It's mad, isn't it? I want to give you two hundred grand and you're slapping my hand away."

"I told you to talk to my solicitor."

O'Kane waved the idea away. "Jesus, solicitors? Fucking crooks, the lot of them. Why pay one of them fuckers when you can just deal with me?"

Martin's voice shook with foolish defiance. "That land's worth half a million and you know it."

O'Kane leaned down, his hands on his knees. "Is it, now?"

"The estate agent told me."

O'Kane snorted and stood upright. "Estate agent? Sure, they're even bigger crooks than solicitors. You don't need an estate agent to deal with the Bull. No, no, no. Spit and a handshake, that's how I do it."

The young man held O'Kane's eyes steady. "All right, I'll sell you the land, but I need a fair price."

O'Kane smiled and patted his shoulder. "You're a brave lad, son. Not many men will stand up to me. But listen to me, now. You're pushing your luck. The only reason I haven't fed you to the dogs is 'cause your auld fella was a good friend of mine. That's why I let him keep that farm for so long. You pissed off to England to get your nice degree and your fancy job. Now he's gone and you come running back looking to cash in."

"He left the farm to me; I can do what I want with it. I can sell it to—"

"You can sell it to me, and that's all. No one buys or sells land in South Armagh without my say-so. The sooner you get that into your head the sooner we can get this done."

Martin stared straight ahead. "You can talk to my solicitor."

O'Kane sighed and placed his hand on the young man's shoulder. "Please, Martin. Your father was a friend of mine. Don't do this."

"These aren't the old days. It doesn't work like that any more. I can go to the police." Martin looked up at him. He looked just like his father.

O'Kane closed his eyes and shook his head for a moment. He turned towards the door. When he reached it he looked back and said, "All right, lads."

He stepped out into the night and raised the collar of his coat to keep the rain from the back of his neck. Pádraig passed him a cigarette, then cupped his hands around it. The match stayed lit just long enough to catch the tobacco. O'Kane pulled deep, feeling the gritty heat fill his chest. Sixty years he'd been smoking and all he had to show for it was a drop of phlegm in the mornings. *Fucking doctors know nothing,* he thought.

"You all right, Da?" Pádraig asked, his gormless face shiny and wet in the glow from the barn.

"Ah, grand, son. Just tired, that's all."

The walkie-talkie crackled in Pádraig's pocket. He pulled it out and thumbed the button on its side. "Yeah?"

A stream of static and hiss mixed with the sound of cheering and snarling from the barn. Dull thuds came from the house behind them, followed by small cries.

"Aye, we're expecting him. Let him through."

Pádraig returned the radio to his pocket. "It's McGinty."

O'Kane looked beyond the barn and saw headlights approaching from the lane. "Go and keep an eye on the fight. Make sure Sean isn't slipping his hand."

"Right, Da." Pádraig waddled across the yard, waving at the rusting Peugeot as it passed. Its wheels hissed on the wet concrete as it drew to a halt. The passenger door opened and Paul McGinty climbed out. He extended his hand.

"How're ya, Paul?" O'Kane squeezed the politician's fingers between his. Hard.

"I've been better," McGinty said.

"Where's your fancy limo tonight?"

"I was trying to be low-key." McGinty flashed his white teeth.

"Just right." O'Kane released his hand. "It's all arranged?"

McGinty's eyes darted to the farmhouse at the sound of a scream. "What's that?"

"Local problem. Nothing to worry about."

McGinty smoothed his jacket. "Yeah, it's taken care of. They should be here soon. Marie has a number for Fegan. We'll phone him then."

"The woman." O'Kane pointed a thick finger at McGinty's groin.

"Don't let your cock get in the way. You do what needs doing, never mind the past."

McGinty tilted his head.

"Didn't think I knew about that, did you?" O'Kane's belly shook as he laughed. "You boys in Belfast think I'm too deep in cow shit down here to know what's going on. I know everything."

"That's ancient history."

"Good, good. But, here. There's another wee thing I know about. Something you don't."

A crease appeared on McGinty's brow. "What's that?"

A long, loud shriek came from the house. O'Kane glanced over his shoulder, and then back to McGinty. "Your wee pal, Davy Campbell. He's got a surprise up his sleeve."

"What sort of surprise?"

"Well, we'll have to have a word with him when he gets this length."

The door to the farmhouse kitchen opened and Tommy Downey stepped out. O'Kane turned to face him.

"Martin accepts the offer," Downey said.

42

"For the love of Christ, what now?"

Edward Hargreaves saw the vein on his forehead pulse in the dressing-table mirror.

"It's urgent, Minister," the Chief Constable said. "I wouldn't have called you so late otherwise."

"Just a moment." Hargreaves pressed the phone's mouthpiece to his robed shoulder, covered his eyes, and breathed deep. The bedroom was strewn with the contents of the drawers, as well as the bedding – anything a wallet could hide under. That bitch. That sneaky, conniving whore. He brought the phone back to his ear.

"Go on."

"It's bad, sir."

"Oh, God." He steeled himself. "Tell me."

"One of my officers was found dead on an industrial estate just outside the city about thirty minutes ago. Shot once in the head, once in the heart."

"Fegan?"

"Most likely, Minister. But that's not the worst of it."

Hargreaves walked out of the bedroom to the large split-level lounge, rubbing the center of his forehead with his knuckles. The ornamental silver tea service was gone. "Christ."

"The car he was found in belongs to Patrick Columbus Toner," the Chief Constable said.

And the silver candlesticks from the fireplace. He'd only been in the bathtub for ten minutes. She'd said she'd join him in five, and he gave her another five to show he wasn't entirely desperate for her. But the wallet. Oh God, the wallet. "Who's Patrick . . . er . . . what was his name?"

"Patsy Toner to his friends. He's Paul McGinty's solicitor, and a prominent activist. Calls himself a human-rights lawyer. There's a team searching the area for him now."

Hargreaves couldn't bring his mind from one calamity to the other. The girl had his wallet. It wasn't just the cash, only a few hundred pounds after all, but the cards, his identification, his pass for the Commons, for Christ's sake. The tabloids would pay a fortune for them and he'd be demolished.

And now this. A bloody lawyer, a McGinty lackey, and something about his car. "I don't understand," he said.

Pilkington cleared his throat. "Well, Minister, I should have thought the ramifications were clear. I wanted to do you the courtesy of letting you know straight away so that you and the Secretary could prepare your strategy."

Hargreaves went to the powder-dusted coffee table where half a Monte Cristo No. 2 had rested in an antique crystal ashtray. Of course, the ashtray was gone, but the cigar remained. "Strategy?"

"Do I have to spell it out, Minister?"

"Please do." Hargreaves clenched the cigar between his teeth and scanned the room for his gold Cartier lighter. *Bitch*, he thought as he closed his eyes. She had good taste, there was no denying it.

Pilkington sounded perplexed. "Minister, the situation is very serious. I'm no politician, but even I can guess what's going to happen when the news breaks."

"Enlighten me." Hargreaves flopped onto the leather couch. At least she couldn't carry that.

"A police officer found executed in a car belonging to an associate of Paul McGinty? A party activist's nearly-new Jaguar with a cop's brains all over it? Things are delicate enough as they are, what with the trouble over the last few days. It doesn't matter if Fegan did it, or Patsy Toner, or bloody Santa Claus. The Unionists will have a field day. Even the moderates on the other side will be screaming for blood. Frankly, it'll be a miracle if you can hold Stormont together after this."

"A miracle," Hargreaves said. "Geoff, I am a government minister. I sign papers, I argue with civil servants, I bully backbenchers. I don't perform miracles."

"Perhaps it's time you started, Minister. You inherited a house of cards, and you'll need to move heaven and earth to stop it collapsing in the next few days."

Hargreaves pictured the cards scattering in the wind. He wondered if he cared enough to chase after them.

Pilkington continued. "It may not be my place to advise you on such matters, but I think you should start pulling your staff together to see what you can salvage before, if you'll pardon the expression, the shit hits the fan."

"No, it's not your place, Geoff." Hargreaves lay down flat on the couch. The leather was cool against his cheek. "The Secretary and I have a department full of overeducated, overpaid clock-watchers and pencil-pushers to advise us." He sighed. "I never wanted this job, you know."

"Well, I don't think that's—"

"I wanted a Cabinet spot. Foreign Secretary would have been nice. Lots of travel. Or Trade and Investment."

"We must do our—"

"Hard work, Trade and Investment, but the perks are good. Education, even. That's a fucking thankless task, but it's better than bloody Northern Ireland. And you volunteered to work there."

Several seconds of barely audible hiss at Hargreaves's ear passed before the Chief Constable gave a long, officious sniff.

"Some of us are cut out to meet a challenge, Minister, to face the demands of a difficult job. Some of us aren't."

Hargreaves raised his head from the leather cushion. "Pilkington?"

"Yes, Minister?"

"I don't like you."

"Likewise, Minister. Now, I'll leave you in peace. I think you have a long night ahead of you."

"Bastard."

The phone died. Hargreaves wondered first what time it was, then where he'd left his watch. Oh yes, he'd left it on the mantelpiece. He stood, crossed the room, and looked at the empty spot beneath the mirror.

"Bitch," he said.

43

Branches clanged and scraped along the side of the van as Campbell mounted the verge to let the oncoming cars pass. Old four-by-fours, muddied and dented. Farmers' cars, some towing trailers just the size for a large dog. Some of the men swigged from bottles as they drove. Some of them raised their forefingers from their steering wheels as they passed. The old country greeting, the one that said: *I belong here, I know this place. Do you?*

Campbell returned the gesture and drove on. The barn rose up at the top of the slope, light pouring from its innards. The child stirred in her mother's arms.

"How do you live with yourself?" Marie McKenna asked.

"Shut up," Eddie Coyle said.

"How can you bring us here? How can you do this to women and children and call yourselves men?"

"Be quiet," Campbell said. "There's worse people than us. You're about to meet one of them."

"I'm not afraid of you."

"Yes, you are."

"You tell yourself that. Make yourself feel like a big man. I won't—"

Campbell stood on the brake, pitching Marie forward. She jarred her forearm against the dashboard as she shielded her child. The girl squealed. Campbell reached out and grabbed a handful of Marie's hair.

"Listen, I've had enough, right? I've had enough of this shit. I want it over. It'll be over quick enough for you and your kid if you don't be quiet. Now, keep your mouth shut."

Coyle reached across and gripped Campbell's wrist. "Go easy, Davy."

Campbell looked hard at Coyle. Coyle dropped his eyes and released Campbell's wrist. Tears ran down Marie's cheeks as the little girl buried her face in her mother's bosom.

"Just be quiet," Campbell said. He let Marie's hair slip through his fingers. "You can get through this if you're quiet and do what you're told."

Her eyes reflected the headlights of one last oncoming car. She speared him with them and he hated her. His own eyes grew hot as he stared back. No, he didn't hate her, he didn't even know her. But hate was in his heart. Who for?

When the answer came, as hard and sure as any single thing he'd ever known, he could hold her gaze no longer. He looked straight ahead, put the van in gear, and began climbing the hill again.

The ground levelled onto a farmyard. The barn and house faced each other across potholed concrete, and a row of stables joined the two. Empty wire cages completed the square. Layered odors drifted on the night air; the low smell of dog feces coupled with the higher, acrid sting of chemicals. The copper stink of blood and fear mingled with both at the back of Campbell's throat.

Six men gathered in the shelter of the empty barn's doorway. McGinty was there, and his driver, Declan Quigley. Two more Campbell didn't know, but the two tall, stout ones – they could be no one else but Bull O'Kane and his son. Campbell's heart fluttered in his chest at the sight of O'Kane's bulk. Marie had become still and quiet. He wondered if she knew who stood in front of the van, shielding his eyes from the headlights. The engine rattled and shook as it died. Campbell opened the door and climbed down.

The group of men stepped out into the stuttering rain, O'Kane at the fore. "You're Davy Campbell?" he asked.

"That's right."

O'Kane stepped forward and extended his hand. "I've heard about you."

The fingers were coarse and thick. Campbell fought to keep from wincing at the old man's grip.

"Aye," O'Kane said, with a slanted smile. "I know all about you."

Campbell's stomach twitched. "It's good to meet you, Mr. O'Kane."

"Call me Bull. Now, how's our guests?" He released Campbell's hand and walked to the van's passenger side where Coyle waited. O'Kane ignored him and reached into the cabin. "C'mon out, love. You're all right."

Marie slid along the seat, the girl in her arms, and stepped down to the ground. She didn't pull away when O'Kane took her elbow. McGinty stepped forward and Campbell saw his and Marie's gazes meet, something cold passing between them.

O'Kane slipped his hands under the child's arms. "And who are you?"

Marie didn't let go of her daughter. "Don't."

"What's your name?"

The girl held on to her mother's sweater, but O'Kane pulled her free.

"Her name's Ellen." Marie's voice cracked as she spoke.

"You're a pretty wee girl, aren't you?" O'Kane took Ellen in his arms and pinched her cheek. She reached for her mother, but O'Kane stepped away.

"Do you like doggies?"

Ellen rubbed her eyes and pouted.

O'Kane walked towards the stables, holding her close. "Do you? Do you like doggies?"

Ellen nodded. Scraping and whining came from the stables. Campbell's mouth dried.

"Wait till you see this nice doggie." O'Kane unbolted the upper half of a stable door and let it swing open. A low whine came from inside.

Campbell looked to Marie. Her shaking hands covered her mouth. She was fighting hard to hold on to herself, hiding her fear from the child. Something that might have been respect rose in Campbell, and he had an inexplicable and desperate urge to touch her. He shook it away.

The other six men – Coyle, McGinty, the driver, O'Kane's son, the two Campbell didn't know – all watched the stable door.

McGinty took a step towards the old man. "Bull," he said.

O'Kane turned to face them. "It's all right. Sure, these boys are gentle as lambs with people. I train them right."

A murky scent drifted out of the stable. Heavy paws appeared above the lower door, followed by a square block of a head, dirt-caked and scarred. The dog's tongue lolled from its jaw, a viscous line of drool disappearing into the dark. O'Kane reached out with his free hand and scratched the back of the pit bull's thick neck. It squinted at the sensation of his callused fingers.

"There, see? He's a nice doggie. Do you want to pet him?"

Ellen shook her head and wiped her damp cheeks.

"Aw, go on. He's a nice doggie."

She looked down at the animal, rubbing her nose on her sleeve. She sniffed.

"He's a good doggie," O'Kane said. "He won't bite."

He lowered Ellen so she could reach its head with her small out-stretched hand. Her fingers created ripples on its brow. Marie squeezed her eyes shut when its tongue lapped at the girl's fingertips. Coyle placed a steadying hand on her shoulder.

"There, now. I told you he was a nice doggie, didn't I?" O'Kane hoisted the child up in his arms as she continued to reach out to scratch the dog's head. He looked at Marie, a fatherly smile on his lips. "You'll behave yourself, won't you, love?"

Marie stared back.

"Of course you will." O'Kane pushed the dog's head back down with his free hand and swung the upper stable door closed. He bounced Ellen in his arms as he walked back towards Marie. "You and your mummy will be good, won't you?"

Christ, let it be over, Campbell thought. The sudden trill of a mobile phone made his heart knock against the inside of his chest.

McGinty reached into his jacket pocket. "Hello?"

Campbell watched his face go slack. The politician walked away from the group, the phone against one ear, a finger in the other.

"Patsy, slow down. What happened?"

*

From a rickety chair in the corner Campbell watched McGinty and O'Kane pace the room. He chewed his lip as the balance shifted back and forth between them, O'Kane the old warhorse, McGinty the slick politico. Little more than a decade separated them, but they were generations apart.

"This changes everything," McGinty said.

"It changes nothing," O'Kane said.

A bare bulb driven by the generator outside picked out the patches where damp had peeled the wallpaper back. Downey leaned against the far wall of the living room, his thin arms folded across his chest. Quigley the driver sat cross-legged on the opposite end of a tattered couch from O'Kane's son while Coyle slouched against the wall, sparing Campbell the occasional dirty look. Malloy guarded Marie and Ellen in a room upstairs. Lazy waves of rain washed across the old sash windows and the sound of dripping water was everywhere. The smell of mold and mice lingered in Campbell's nose.

"Do you not understand, Bull?" McGinty stopped pacing and opened his arms. "Once this gets out, I'm fucked. A cop's dead body in my lawyer's car. I'll be forced out of the party. I won't have a political friend left. Even then, the Unionists will probably walk. They'll bring Stormont down and look like they're only doing what's right. Jesus, think of the party. Think of the pressure they'll be under. From London, from Dublin, from Washington."

He's right, Campbell thought. The world – especially America – didn't view terrorists with the same romantic tint these days, even if they called themselves freedom fighters.

O'Kane snorted. "We did all right for years without their help. They can fuck off."

"Christ, Bull, it's the twenty-first century. It's not the Seventies any more. It's not the Eighties. We need Stormont now. *I* need it. *You* need it. Think of the concessions the party will have to give the Unionists and the Brits just to keep Stormont together. You're a millstone around their necks as it stands. They'll cut you off as quick as me."

"Bollocks," O'Kane said, swiping the air with his shovel hand.

"Nobody pushes us around. The Brits couldn't break us after thirty years of trying. I'm not rolling over just 'cause you and your mates in the suits are scared of losing those salaries and allowances."

"It's not like that." McGinty put his hands on his hips. Campbell watched the politician's leg twitch.

"Aye, it is. You've gone soft, Paul. It's easy for you boys in Belfast, all those European funds you can dip your fingers into, all those community grants. Just stick your hand out, and the money lands in it. You're forgetting us boys out in the sticks. We still have to graft for it."

McGinty was fighting his temper, Campbell could see it. "We've achieved more in ten years of politics than you did in thirty years of war."

O'Kane nodded his head in mock respect. "Oh, aye. You achieved plenty." He picked imaginary lint from McGinty's lapel. "You lined your pockets and got yourself some nice suits. You got yourself a big limousine, a big fuck-off house with a sea view in Donegal. Aye, you did all right."

McGinty's face reddened. "So did you. We always kept you right. How many raids did my contacts tip you off on? How much property did the party's legal team let you buy without your name going near it? And the security posts. We did that for you. We negotiated the dismantling of every British army post in South Armagh so you could run your laundering plants. The party did that. Don't you forget it."

Campbell's hands tightened into fists as tension rippled in the air.

O'Kane stepped up to the politician. "So, you're the big man now, are you?"

McGinty was tall, but he had to lift his eyes to meet the Bull's stare. He swallowed and his tongue peeked out to wet his lips. "No. It's not like that. But Jesus, think, Bull. There's only one way out of this now."

"And what's that, then?"

"We give Fegan to the cops. Patsy Toner can testify he was there. We let the law take care of him. We'll be seen to cooperate with the police. The Unionists can't argue with that. They can't threaten to walk, and we get off the hook."

"He'll tell them he did McKenna and Caffola. All your bullshit's going to come back at you."

That's not all he'll tell them, Campbell thought. *He'll tell them about those two UFF boys and how they never posed a threat to McGinty.* His heart quickened.

"It's too late to stop that now. Besides, the press about the cop will bury that. We let it be known that Anderson was leaking information to us before the ceasefires. All the attention will be on him, not us."

The Bull stood still, holding his breath, and Campbell counted five seconds before he turned away. "No," O'Kane said.

McGinty glowered at him. "What do you mean, no?"

"We let Fegan away with this, we look weak. *I* look weak. He's a traitor, so we treat him like one. We make an example of him, just like we've always done." The Bull's voice rose to a roar as he stabbed the air with his finger. "He killed my cousin, for fuck's sake. If I don't take care of him, every fucker with a grudge will think I'm fair game."

McGinty crossed the room to O'Kane. "For God's sake, Bull, think it through. Think what it'll cost us."

"No."

"Listen to me. Think ahead. Say the Unionists walk; say Stormont breaks down. You won't have a friend in government to grease any wheels for you. You'll suffer as much as me."

"I said no, Paul. That's all."

McGinty gripped O'Kane's massive shoulder. "Get your head out of the past, for Christ's sake. Quit acting like a fucking street thug. We're past all that now. You're a dinosaur, Bull. You're going to cost me—"

McGinty sprawled on the floor, blood spilling from his lip, before Campbell could even wince at the sound of the slap. Coyle stared. Quigley began to get to his feet, but O'Kane pointed a thick finger at him.

"You sit the fuck down."

The driver did as he was told.

Campbell thought hard and fast. Quigley was too weak. Coyle was too stupid. He was McGinty's only ally in this shell of a house. But

Fegan couldn't live. Not with what he knew about Francie Delaney and the two UFF boys.

He stood up. "Mr. O'Kane's right," he said.

McGinty looked up from the red blotches on his handkerchief. "What?"

"Fegan's too dangerous. We need to finish him."

O'Kane slapped Campbell's shoulder. "Smart lad."

McGinty got to his feet, his eyes fixed on Campbell. "Whatever you say, Bull. You're the boss."

"Good." O'Kane slapped his hands together and grinned. "Now, get that woman and her kid down here."

44

Fegan saw Mrs. Taylor's sharp blue eyes in the window for just a moment before she closed the shutter, sealing out the darkness. His hand was half raised to wave, but she was gone. The dog barked somewhere inside the cottage. There were no lights from the hotel.

He walked from the parked car round to the hotel's entrance. The door didn't budge when he pressed it. Locked. Fegan turned in a circle, no idea what he was looking for. The moon was up there somewhere above the clouds, but below was darkness. Orange street lights formed a line along the bay and reflected off the river mouth, but the sea was lost in the black. Only the hard salt tang on the air and the sound of waves gave it away.

Sweat chilled Fegan's body and his legs quivered. He'd pulled over twice on the way here to let the shakes subside. His tongue rasped against the roof of his mouth as he swallowed.

The dog settled down and its barks faded away. Quiet now, just the whisper of water on sand. Fegan hammered on the door to break the stillness. He stepped back and looked up at the windows on the first floor.

Nothing. He slammed his fist against the door again, harder. A bead of worry settled in his chest. Why had Marie let Hopkirk lock the place up? Why wasn't she waiting for him?

His palm stung as he slapped the wooden panels again. He stood back and craned his neck. "Come on," he whispered.

A dim light appeared at the center window, followed by a passing shadow. Fegan clenched and unclenched his fists. The sound of doors opening and closing came from inside. A light in the glass above the entrance. Metal moved against metal, locks snapping open, bolts sliding. The door inched open and a bespectacled eye peeked out.

"What are you doing here? What do you want?"

"I want in," Fegan said. "I want Marie."

"Who?"

"I mean Mary. My wife."

Hopkirk's brow knotted. "I thought she was with you."

"What?"

"She and the little girl went out for a walk this evening. They didn't come back. I thought they'd left with you."

"Our bags. Where are they?"

"I don't know. I assumed—"

Fegan put his hand against the door. "Let me in."

"They might still be in the room. I'll go and look."

He pressed harder. "Let me in."

Hopkirk pushed back. "I won't be a moment."

Fegan shoved with his shoulder and the door gave way. Hopkirk staggered back against one of the dust-covered tables.

"Go on," he said, his eyes narrow behind his thick glasses. "Go and look. If your bags are there you can take them and get out of here. I don't want your money."

Fegan crossed the room. "Where'd she go?"

"I don't know. She took the little girl out for something to eat at about seven. She never came back."

"Was there anyone else around?"

Hopkirk's gaze dropped to the floor. "No."

"You're lying."

The hotelier breathed hard for a few seconds. "There was a man. He said he was a policeman, but I didn't believe him."

Fegan gripped his arm. "What'd he look like?"

Hopkirk tried to pry Fegan's fingers loose. "He was tall and thin, like you, but younger. He had reddish-brown hair and a scraggy beard. He looked like he'd been in a fight, and he had a limp."

"Campbell," Fegan said. "Campbell was here."

Hopkirk got free of Fegan's grip and sidled away. "He didn't tell me his name."

"What'd he say?"

"He just asked where you were." Hopkirk rounded the table, keeping it between him and Fegan.

"What'd you tell him?"

"The truth. I didn't know."

"Christ," Fegan said. He brought his palms to his temples to hold the fear in. "Christ."

Hopkirk continued to back away. "Look, why don't you get your things and go. I can't do any more for you."

Fegan walked to the stairway in the darkened corner, his stride slowing as he passed the door to the bar. He wiped his mouth and kept his head down, even as his throat tightened. The twisting steps brought him up to the first floor. The room was at the end of the corridor. When he got to the door he realised he had no key. It didn't matter. He kicked the door hard just beneath the handle.

"I've got the key!" Hopkirk cried from the stairwell. "Don't!"

Fegan ignored him and kicked again. The door burst inward with the sound of splintering wood. He pushed his way into the room and turned on the light. The bags were where they'd been that afternoon. His own was still at the foot of the bed, zipped closed. He went to check it anyway, but Hopkirk appeared at the door.

"Get out," Fegan said.

Hopkirk faded back into the shadows of the corridor. Fegan hoisted the bag onto the bed and opened it. The familiar greasy smell of money met his nose. He pushed rolls of banknotes and the few clothes aside to make sure what he needed was still there. Yes, the loose nine-millimeter rounds still rolled across the bottom. Campbell's Glock still clanked against them. Fegan took a quick glance over his shoulder before taking the Walther from his right pocket and dropping it into the bag.

The bag almost slipped from his fingers when his phone vibrated against his chest. Fegan took it from his breast pocket and looked at the display.

His heart leaped in his chest. He thumbed the green button and brought the phone to his ear. "Marie?"

There was nothing but a soft static hiss, the sound of weight shifting on floorboards, and grating sobs.

"Marie?"

A man's voice, hard and thin, whispering words Fegan couldn't make out. Something lodged in Fegan's throat, thicker than his aching thirst.

"Marie?"

"Gerry?"

Fegan closed his eyes.

"Gerry, they've got me and Ellen . . ."

45

"He's coming," Campbell said. He stood in the shelter of the barn, dark now, trying not to gag at the stench rising up from the pit.

"And?" the handler asked.

"And what? Fegan's a dead man. They'll take care of him as soon as he gets here."

"Don't they know what's happened?"

"The cop in Toner's car. Yeah, they know."

The handler was silent for a moment. "But surely that's changed the plan. If they don't offer up Fegan to the authorities, the Unionists will hold them responsible for the cop. They'll have McGinty by the balls. They could bring down Stormont with this."

"I told McGinty that," Campbell lied. "He wouldn't listen."

"But McGinty's smarter than that. He never took a stupid breath in his life."

"They want Fegan dead. That's all."

"Christ," the handler said. Campbell listened to him breathe. "Christ. There's no way to stop it?"

"None," Campbell said.

"You've got to try. This could set the political process back years. See if you can—"

Campbell saw a shaft of light break on the concrete beyond the barn door. "Got to go," he said, and hung up.

He heard footsteps, two people, one walking steadily, the other shuffling and faltering. Campbell eased back into the shadows of the barn.

"You should've gone when you had the chance," McGinty said. "You wouldn't be in this mess if you'd just gone."

"Let me go back inside," Marie said. "Please, let me go to Ellen."

"She's all right with Eddie. Why didn't you go? I couldn't have made it easier for you."

"Because I didn't want to go. I shouldn't have to go. Things are supposed to have changed. Jesus, Paul, it was so long ago."

"It doesn't feel like it. It still hurts me to think about it."

Marie laughed, the sound dry and hateful in the darkness. "Hurts you? Nothing hurts you."

"You're wrong. People think I'm a hard man, but I've got feelings. Seeing you with Lennon – a cop, for Christ's sake – what do you think that did to me?"

"I couldn't live like that any more. Can't you see that? Pretending to myself you weren't married. Pretending all that . . . that . . . other stuff didn't matter. The things you did."

"I never did anything to—"

"You pulled the strings. Stop passing the blame, Paul."

McGinty's voice hardened. "There were people wanted you dead back then."

"You think I didn't know that? Have you any idea how scared I was?"

Campbell edged to the barn door until he could just make out their shapes in the poor light from the farmhouse.

"Maybe I should have let them kill you and that cop," McGinty said.

Campbell flinched as Marie lashed out, and the sound of her palm on McGinty's cheek reverberated around the yard. He flinched again when McGinty returned the blow, sending her sprawling on the wet concrete. She stared back up at him.

"And what are you doing with Fegan?" McGinty asked.

"Go to hell."

"Answer me."

Marie spat at him.

McGinty crouched down. "For Christ's sake, Marie, he's insane. He's sick in the head."

"Sick? Is he any more sick than you, or that thug O'Kane?" She pointed to the farmhouse.

"Don't you know what he's done? He killed a cop in Belfast just a couple of hours ago. He killed Vincie Caffola and Father Coulter." He rested his hand on her shoulder as she shook her head. "He killed your uncle Michael."

"No," she said. "You're lying. You said the police killed Vincie Caffola. You're twisting things the way you always do."

McGinty brushed hair away from her forehead. "It's the truth, Marie. You can put your act on for everyone else, but I know you. You're more like your uncle than you let on. You've got that same cold streak in you, like stone. And now you've latched onto Gerry Fegan. What are you using him for? It's the same as the cop, isn't it? Just a way to get back at me." He sighed. "You always went for the wrong type, didn't you?"

Her gaze dropped. "Let me go back inside."

"All right," McGinty said. He stood upright and helped her to her feet. "Away you go."

Marie wiped her eyes as she went back to the farmhouse. She was silhouetted in the doorway for just a second. A second was long enough for the light to find Campbell. He ducked his head back inside the barn.

"Davy?" McGinty called. "Davy, is that you?"

Campbell screwed his eyes shut and cursed under his breath. He stepped out into the yard. "Yeah, it's me, Mr. McGinty."

McGinty took a slow step closer. "What are you doing there?"

"It stinks in that house. I was just out getting some air."

"In the barn?"

"I heard talking. I thought you'd want some privacy."

A step closer. "What'd you hear?"

"Nothing," Campbell said. "Just voices. Nothing I could make out."

Light cut across the yard once more, only to be blocked by the hulking form of Bull O'Kane. He came trudging across the concrete, his heavy feet slapping on the ground.

"Come on back inside now, lads."

McGinty stood still for a few seconds, then gave a slow nod. "We're coming. I think you wanted a word with Davy, here, didn't you?"

"That's right." A smile split O'Kane's ruddy farmer's face.

Campbell took a sideways step. "What about?"

O'Kane, impossibly quick for his size, had Campbell's upper arm in his grip before he could move. "Just a word, son."

McGinty came to his other side. "Just come inside, Davy."

Campbell made one desperate grab for the gun tucked into the small of his back, but McGinty got his wrist first.

"Don't, Davy." McGinty's voice was as soft and warm as the rain. "You'll only make it worse."

46

Bull O'Kane walked a slow and steady circle around the room, eyeing each of the other occupants in turn. He drew on his cigarette and hot fingers of smoke probed his throat. Pádraig took up almost half of the old couch while that idiot Coyle sat at the other end, grinning a lopsided grin. McGinty stood opposite, resting against the window-sill, smoking a cigarette. His driver had taken over from Coyle, keeping an eye on the woman and her child. O'Kane couldn't read the politician's face. He was a slippery bastard, that one. Always thinking, always finding the angles. O'Kane wouldn't trust him for a second, but he was smart, there was no getting away from it. Lately, he'd been getting too smart. The balls of him, arguing with the Bull in front of the others.

Downey and Malloy were down the lane, waiting for Fegan. The regular boys had been sent home. This was secret business, only for those who needed to know.

And there was Davy Campbell, standing alone at the center of the room, the Black Watch turncoat, the Scotsman fighting for Ireland. O'Kane wondered how he'd gotten away with it for so long. He stank of tout. You could smell it on his sweat. Any fucker could see it.

"You want to tell us something, Davy?" O'Kane ground the cigarette into the floorboards with his heel.

Campbell's voice was steady, but his eyes flickered. "What do you mean?"

O'Kane continued to circle, keeping Campbell fixed in his gaze. "Just what I said. Do you have something to tell us? Anything on your mind?"

"I don't know what you're talking about."

O'Kane kicked the back of his knee. Campbell went down hard, his kneecap cracking off the wooden floor. He cried out, then grabbed for his side, his face reddening.

"We're not fucking about here, Davy. No games."

O'Kane could have told him he'd live if he spoke the truth, but Campbell wasn't stupid. The Scot would know he was dead if he let the lie slip. He would string it out, hoping they'd eventually believe him. But O'Kane was certain of his facts. That stuck-up English ponce from the Northern Ireland Office was getting a holiday home in the Algarve for this information, along with a significant contribution to his retirement fund. Anyone in the NIO knew Bull O'Kane was not to be lied to, not for any price. The information was solid. Now he wanted more.

"You tell me the truth," the Bull said. "Stop your shite-talking and you'll go easy. Tell me who else is touting for your handler and I might make it even easier. I can't be fairer than that."

Campbell looked up from the floor. "I don't know what you're—"

O'Kane drove his boot into Campbell's ribcage with a solid thud. The Scot writhed in tortured spasms, his mouth wide in a soundless scream. Silent tears sprang from his eyes, giving O'Kane a sweet satisfaction. It took something to make a hard man cry, but he'd never found it difficult.

He looked at Coyle. "You want a go?"

"Too fucking right." Coyle stepped forward, his battered face twisted in a pained sneer.

O'Kane moved back. "Work away, but stop when I tell you, right?"

Coyle reached down and grabbed a handful of hair. He pulled Campbell's head upwards. "I'm going to enjoy this, you cunt."

Campbell got his knees under him. "Fuck you," he hissed.

Coyle swung his foot into Campbell's crotch. The Scot gave a low groan and started to slip towards the floor, but Coyle held his hair firm. "Fuck me?" Coyle's laugh was raw and savage. He leaned over and spoke into Campbell's ear. "Fuck me? It looks like you're the one getting fucked, Davy."

Coyle drew his right arm back, made a fist, and punched Campbell's jaw. The hard smacking sound made McGinty wince.

O'Kane had to suppress a laugh when he saw Coyle grimace at the pain in his knuckles.

Campbell went limp, but still Coyle held him by his hair, keeping him from collapsing to the floor. He slapped the Scot hard across the cheek. "Come on, you fucker. Look at me."

A small whisper came from Campbell's lips. Unease pricked at O'Kane's gut, but he held his tongue.

Coyle slapped him again. "What?"

Campbell lifted his eyes. His mouth moved as he mumbled softly.

Coyle leaned down, his ear close to Campbell's mouth. "What?"

"Stupid bastard," O'Kane said as Campbell's teeth locked on Coyle's ear. He sighed and shook his head at the scream. "All right, that's enough, for Christ's sake."

Another kick to Campbell's injured rib took the fight out of him and he sprawled on the floor, twisting his arms and legs, blood dribbling from his mouth. Coyle's blood. Coyle fell to the floor beside him, crying and pressing his hands to his ear.

"Holy Mother of Christ," O'Kane said to McGinty, 'where'd you get this stupid shite? He's as much use as tits on a boar."

McGinty just shook his head as he ground his cigarette butt into the windowsill.

"Here." O'Kane took a handkerchief from his pocket and tossed it to the floor. "It's clean. Hold it against your ear. Pádraig, help the silly cunt up, will you?"

"Right, Da." Pádraig heaved himself out of the couch and huffed over to Coyle. He picked up the handkerchief, wadded it into a ball, and held it to Coyle's ear. "Come on, now. You're all right."

Coyle struggled to his feet and went to kick Campbell's exposed cheek. Pádraig held him back.

"I want to do him." Coyle's voice was choked by tears. "When you're finished, you let me do him."

"Get him out of here," O'Kane said. "There's bandages and stuff for the dogs over in the barn. There's a bottle of chloroform in there, too. Bring it and some cotton wool over, there's a good lad."

"Right, Da." Pádraig led the weeping Coyle out of the room, into the kitchen. The sound of barking drifted in as the outer door opened to the night, and then disappeared as it closed again.

O'Kane stood over Campbell's wretched form. "You know the score, Davy. You know there's no getting out of this. You're going to die tonight."

He looked at his watch as he crouched down, his knees creaking. "Well, morning, actually. You're going to die, and that's all there is to it. The only thing you've got to worry about is how much you suffer. Can you hear me, Davy?"

He stroked Campbell's sweat- and rain-soaked hair.

"Answer me, Davy."

Campbell's voice was a hoarse whisper. "I don't know what you want."

"The truth, that's all."

The Scot turned his head, a bloodshot eye fixing on O'Kane. "But I don't know what you think I've done. Please tell me."

O'Kane sighed. "You're a tout, Davy."

"No."

"Don't lie to me, there's no point. It's not a question; I know it for a fact. You've been sold out by the same cunts you've worked for all these years."

Campbell pressed his forehead into the floor.

"I've got it straight from the NIO. A stuck-up gobshite, talks like he's the fucking Queen's second cousin. He says him and you sat in a car in Armagh just a few days ago, talking about what our friend Gerry Fegan was up to."

Campbell made fists with his hands.

"He says you've been working for Fourteen Intelligence Company since the Nineties. He says you're the best they've got. But you're not that good, are you, Davy?"

"Christ," Campbell said.

"Now, listen to me, Davy. You can go easy or you can go hard." O'Kane leaned down, watchful of Campbell's teeth. "And I mean harder than anything you ever heard of, anything you were ever trained for, anything you ever had nightmares about."

"No," Campbell said.

"I'm going to hurt you. I'm going to hurt you worse than you ever thought you could live through."

Campbell closed his eyes. He wasn't stupid. He'd heard of the things O'Kane had done to men like him.

"And if you don't talk to me, I'm going to take you out to the stables. Those dogs don't normally go for people, but if they get the smell of blood . . ."

O'Kane patted Campbell's back and laughed. "Jesus, Davy, you'll be watching them eat your guts. But you never know; one of them might go for your throat first. If you're lucky, that is."

"Please," Campbell said.

O'Kane stood upright. "So, let's get started."

He reached down, gripped Campbell's left wrist, and lifted his hand. He placed his foot on the tout's injured side and put his weight on it while he pulled upwards.

Campbell screamed, then gasped, then screamed, then gasped. O'Kane took his foot away and lowered the arm slightly. He kicked Campbell's ribcage once then waited for the writhing and ragged sobs to die away.

"Tell me the truth. Tell me who else is touting for your handlers."

A line of bloody drool connected Campbell's mouth to the floor. "I swear to God, I don't know what—"

"Fuck's sake." O'Kane put his weight on Campbell's side again and heaved on his arm. The ribcage flexed beneath his foot. Campbell's scream became a high whine. O'Kane released the pressure before swinging his boot hard into Campbell's flank once more. This time he felt a shift, a grinding, something giving way.

Campbell seemed to have lost the power to scream. He just opened his mouth wide, screwed his eyes shut, and leaked air. His cheeks glistened with tears.

"Christ, just tell me, Davy."

"I don't . . . I don't . . ."

O'Kane brought his heel down on Campbell's side, felt the spongy grinding, saw the coughed-up blood spill from his mouth.

"Tell me."

"Toner . . . Patsy . . . Toner . . ."

"Jesus," McGinty said.

O'Kane raised a hand to silence him. "What about Patsy Toner?"

Campbell hung from O'Kane's grip like a bag of sticks. "He's . . . their contact . . . he's . . . he's the . . . one who . . . who got me in."

O'Kane lowered Campbell's arm to the floor and squatted next to him. "Breathe easy, son. Small breaths. What else?"

"He tells them . . . everything . . . all the press . . . he tells them . . . before McGinty even gets it out. They know . . . every move . . . McGinty makes . . . before he makes it."

O'Kane brushed Campbell's cheek. "Good boy. Who else?"

Campbell shook his head.

"Now, son, don't be stupid."

"Toner . . . just Toner."

Pádraig waddled into the room, a large brown bottle in one hand, a bag of cotton wool in the other. "I've got the chloroform, Da."

"Good lad," O'Kane said.

He stood and took the bag of cotton wool from his son. His thick fingers grabbed a ball of the white material and tore it from the bag. "Open that."

Pádraig twisted the cap off the brown bottle and handed the chloroform to his father. O'Kane tipped the bottle up, soaking the cotton wool while he held it out at arm's length. The cloying smell made his head tingle. He turned to McGinty. "We use this to put the dogs down when they're hurt too bad to fix. We'll knock him out till we see what Fegan has to say. We might have some more questions after that."

O'Kane crouched down and pressed the soaked wad against Campbell's mouth and nose. "That's it, son, just breathe nice and easy."

Campbell pulled away, batting weakly at the cotton wool. "McGinty," he said.

"What's that?"

His eyes held O'Kane's, a sickly smile on his lips. "McGinty . . . he did it . . . he set them up . . . Fegan isn't . . . working alone . . . it's McGinty."

McGinty stepped away from the wall. "He's lying."

O'Kane gripped Campbell's hair and forced his face into the cotton wool.

"Jesus, Bull, he's lying."

Campbell fought against O'Kane's grip. His eyes bulged and the Bull ignored the sting of fingernails tearing at his wrists. Soon, Campbell's eyelids began to droop, his body grew limp, and the struggling died away.

O'Kane lowered Campbell's head to the floor. A string of red-streaked saliva stretched from the cotton wool as he took it away from the Scot's mouth. He stood and turned to face McGinty.

"He was lying, Bull." McGinty's face paled beneath the bare light bulb. "He was just trying to get back at us, to turn us against each other. You can see that, can't you?"

O'Kane watched the politician's veins bulge, his Adam's apple bob above his shirt collar. "We'll talk about it later. After Fegan."

"Come on, Bull, you know he was—"

A burst of static made McGinty jump. O'Kane turned to see his son raise the walkie-talkie to his ear. A distorted crackle that might have been a voice came in a short burst of chatter.

Pádraig thumbed the button. "Right," he said. He lowered the radio to his side. "It's him. He's coming."

47

A flashlight waved from side to side twenty yards ahead. Fegan slowed the Clio as he approached the undulating light. The country lane was narrow, barely room for two cars to pass, and lined with hedges. Fields sloped up into the night on either side. A short, stocky man in a woollen hat and green combat jacket stepped into the road and raised his hand. Fegan brought the car to a halt. The man walked around to the driver's side window and made a winding motion with the flashlight. Fegan did as he was told.

"You Fegan?" the man asked.

Fegan squinted against the torchlight. "Yeah."

Another man, tall, thin and armed with a double-barrelled shotgun, emerged from the hedgerow. He aimed the gun at Fegan through the windscreen.

The stocky man shone the light into the dark corners of the car, into the footwells at the front, and then the back. "Get out," he said. He stepped back to let Fegan climb out.

"Put your hands on top of your head," the one with the shotgun said.

Fegan obeyed as the stocky one began searching his pockets. "I'm not armed," Fegan said.

The stocky man spared him one glance. "If it's all the same to you, mate, I think I'll see for myself."

Fegan stood still as warm rain licked at his closed eyelids. He sensed the shadows watching. His temples pulsed and a chill crept towards his center.

"You won't find anything," Fegan said, opening his eyes.

The stocky man looked up from his search. "Shut up." When he was satisfied he said, "Open the boot."

They walked to the rear of the car. Fegan opened the boot and the hatch rose with a hydraulic whine. The stocky man shone the torch into the far corners. He pointed to the canvas bag.

"Lift that out."

Fegan reached in and lifted the bag. He rested it on the sill and unzipped it. The stocky man kept his distance as he peered inside. His brow creased and he leaned forward. He lowered his hand down into it, pushing clothes aside to see the greasy paper.

"Fuck me," he said. "How much is it?"

Fegan shrugged. "I don't know."

The man with the shotgun came forward. "What is it?"

"Look," the stocky man said, pointing.

"Jesus."

The two men looked at each other. A dozen possibilities passed between them, but finally they shook their heads.

"Come on," the stocky man said, taking the bag. "The Bull's waiting."

Fegan drove the last few hundred yards with the shotgun's twin muzzles at the back of his head and the stocky man beside him, cradling the bag of money in his lap. The Clio's headlights caught the narrowing of the lane as it rose to meet an old farmyard. A barn stood open, bright light flowing out. Eddie Coyle stood just inside, tying a blood-drenched bandage around his head. He glared back at Fegan.

The car shuddered around them as its engine died. Fegan heard dogs bark and scratch at the stable doors over the sound of a generator. This place smelled of death: painful, frightened death. Its stink crept in through the open window. Shadows moved across the yard, turning, searching.

Bull O'Kane and Paul McGinty stepped out into the rain. The Bull crossed to the car and leaned down so he could see inside.

"Come into the house, Gerry."

Fegan opened his door and climbed out. The other men got out too. O'Kane waved a hand at them.

"You know these boys?"

"No," Fegan said.

"Tommy Downey and Kevin Malloy. They'll rip you to pieces if you so much as look like you're going to make a wrong move. If you fuck about with me, I'll let these boys loose on that woman of yours. You understand?"

"I understand," Fegan said.

O'Kane smiled. "Good. It's been a long time, Gerry."

"Twenty-seven years."

"Jesus, is it?" O'Kane laughed. "I wish I could say it was good to see you. But you've let me down. Me and Paul. Ah, well. Come on inside, now."

"Where's Marie?"

"Don't worry, you'll see her soon enough. Come on."

O'Kane turned and walked towards the house. Fegan felt a shove at the small of his back. McGinty stared at him hard as he walked to the door, but said nothing.

A damp chill filled the derelict farmhouse. Fegan let it soak into him as he followed O'Kane through the kitchen. Downey came behind, the shotgun pressed between Fegan's shoulder blades, followed by McGinty and Coyle.

They entered the next room where Campbell's unconscious body lay on an ancient couch. A sweet chemical odor pushed aside the smell of damp and mildew.

A younger man, as tall as O'Kane, but heavier, placed a wooden chair at the center of the room. Fegan guessed him to be Pádraig, the Bull's son.

"Sit down," O'Kane said.

Fegan obeyed as McGinty and Downey made their way into the room. McGinty's face was impassive as he lit a cigarette. The others waited in the kitchen.

"I want to see Marie and Ellen," Fegan said. His hands didn't shake, but his mouth was dry.

"All right," O'Kane said. He looked at Pádraig and tilted his head towards another doorway. His son disappeared through it without a word.

O'Kane stared at Fegan for what seemed like hours before he spoke again. "So, what happens now, Gerry?"

"You let Marie and Ellen go," Fegan said. "Then you kill me."

O'Kane smiled. "Not so fast. There's something I want to get straight first."

"What?"

"I want to know why, Gerry."

Fegan looked to the doorway as Marie entered, cradling Ellen, escorted by Quigley. Pádraig followed and closed the door behind him. He guided Marie to the corner. Ellen wriggled in her mother's arms.

"It's Gerry," she said.

"I know," Marie said, her voice calm and even. "Be still, sweetheart."

Ellen kept squirming until she slipped from her mother's grip and dropped lightly to the floor. She ran to Fegan. "Have you come for us?" she asked as she climbed into his lap. She weighed nothing at all.

"Yeah," Fegan said.

"Mummy's scared."

"I know. But she shouldn't be. Neither should you. It's going to be all right. I promise."

"When can we go home?"

Fegan cupped her face in his hands. "Soon. Go back to your Mummy."

Ellen dismounted from Fegan's knee and went to her mother. Marie crouched down and wrapped her arms around her daughter. Fegan smiled at her and she nodded in return before lowering her eyes.

O'Kane moved between them, blocking Fegan's view. "You didn't answer me, Gerry. I want to know why you did all this. Tell me."

Fegan looked up at his red face. "Because I had to."

"You had to. What does that mean?"

"I had to do it. It was the only way."

"The only way to what?"

"To get them to leave me alone."

"Who?"

Fegan looked to the floor.

"To get who to leave you alone?" O'Kane crouched down and placed his finger under Fegan's chin. He turned his head so their eyes met. "Who made you do it, Gerry? The Brits? Someone else? Maybe someone we know? It's all right. It's all over now. You can tell me."

"No," Fegan said as the chill reached his center. The shadows drew in from the periphery of his vision, and moved between McGinty and Campbell. Their shapes came into focus, solidified. Fegan tried to push them back, but he couldn't. Their eyes burned into him.

"Tell me," O'Kane said. He gripped Fegan's face in one massive hand. "Tell me."

"Them." Fegan pointed to the woman, her baby, and the butcher as they executed McGinty over and over. He pointed to the UFF boys standing over Campbell. "And them."

McGinty's eyes darted from O'Kane to Fegan, his cigarette held two inches from his mouth.

O'Kane stared back at McGinty. "You mean Paul? Did Paul make you do it?"

McGinty dropped the cigarette. "Jesus, Bull, he's mad. He doesn't know what he's saying."

O'Kane turned back to Fegan. "Did Paul McGinty and Davy Campbell make you do this?"

"No, not them," Fegan said.

"Then who the fuck were you pointing at?"

"Them." Fegan aimed his finger at each of the followers in turn. "The people I killed."

Campbell floated above them, watching from the ceiling, seeing them as shadows and light, hearing their voices as echoes and memories. He could see his own body down there. That was where the pain lay. It had almost broken him, almost eaten him up, but now it was away from him, bound up in that body on the couch.

A strange, cold sweetness flooded him, like he had drowned in sugary water. He tried to find order in his mind, but it was so hard to hold onto his consciousness when it drifted free like this. There had been the pain, thunderous and boiling hot. Then there had been a great tidal wave of joy, euphoria sweeping through him as someone poured the sweet, cool liquid into his nose and mouth.

And then there was this.

But there had been something else. Some thought that had pierced his mind just before it was cut adrift from his body. He tried hard to sort through the misted fragments of himself. What had it been?

A voice rose up from below in anger. The sound of one man striking another, the wailing of a child.

Oh, yes.

Now he remembered: a secret thing, only for him to know. It was cold and hard and jagged. It clung to his ankle, waiting.

O'Kane rubbed his stinging palm, and turned to the wailing child and her mother. "You shut that kid up or I will."

Marie pulled the girl close and rocked her as she stroked her hair. The child squealed into her mother's bosom and O'Kane grimaced at her piercing cries. He liked children well enough, but he couldn't be doing with their tears. If any of his seven sons and daughters had ever wailed like that, they'd have got a slap to shut them up. He looked down at Fegan, sprawled on the floor.

"Pick yourself up."

Fegan climbed back into the chair.

"Are you saying you did all this because the people in your head told you to?"

Fegan kept his gaze on the floor. O'Kane reached out and grabbed his hair. He pulled Fegan's head up so he could see the madman's eyes. Anger churned in his belly, anger at the stupidity and the waste of it. He looked to Marie and her child, and then back to Fegan.

"Answer me or I'll cut their throats."

"Yes," Fegan said.

"Jesus fucking Christ." O'Kane released his hair and took two steps away. He turned it over in his mind, trying to find some kind of reason in it. Of course, there was none. He regarded Fegan's blank face. "And why now, after all these years? What set you off?"

"His mother," Fegan said.

"Whose mother?"

"The boy's. The boy I killed for McKenna. She came up to me in the graveyard. She knew who I was, what I'd done. She asked me where he was buried."

O'Kane shared a glance with McGinty. "And you told her?"

Fegan nodded.

"That's why there's cops digging up the bogs round Dungannon," O'Kane said. "What good did you think that would do?"

"I thought he'd leave me alone," Fegan said. "He didn't. He wanted more. He wanted Michael."

"Christ." O'Kane struggled to grasp the madness of it.

"His mother told me something else," Fegan said.

"What?"

Fegan looked up at O'Kane, and a sudden fear brightened his eyes. Not fear of the Bull, or of anyone here. The fear was of something else, something far away.

"Everybody pays," Fegan said. "She said sooner or later, everybody pays."

O'Kane shook his head. "So you did all this, caused all this damage, because some woman tackled you in a graveyard?" He turned to Marie. "And you helped him."

She looked up from her daughter. "What?"

"You helped him after he killed my cousin."

Marie shook her head. "He said he didn't do it."

"He killed your uncle, for Christ's sake."

She stared at Fegan. "He swore he didn't. He swore on my daughter's life."

O'Kane looked from her to Fegan, seeing something break between them.

"Gerry, you swore on my daughter's soul."

Fegan closed his eyes. "I'm sorry."

She buried her face in the child's hair and began to weep. O'Kane felt a smirk creep across his lips. He went back to Fegan and leaned over, his hands on his knees.

"I don't think either of you has been honest with each other. I bet she didn't tell you the whole story, did she?" He gave Marie a sideways glance. "Eh? Did she tell you about her and our friend, the politician?"

"Don't," Marie said.

O'Kane ignored her. He watched Fegan's lined face as he spoke. "Not many know about it. You see, your friend Marie McKenna used to be very close to Paul McGinty. Very close. If it hadn't been for him being married already, they wouldn't have had to keep it a secret."

He turned to Marie. "How long was it?"

"Stop it," she said.

"Two or three years, wasn't it? But she got fed up waiting for him to leave his wife for her, so she finished it. And then she goes and takes up with a cop, just to rub it in. What do you think of that, Gerry?"

Fegan's face gave nothing away, save for the faintest twitch in his right cheek. "She's got nothing to do with this. Let her go."

O'Kane straightened, wincing at the ache in his lower back. "Well, that depends on you, doesn't it? Do as you're told, don't give us any trouble, and she can take her wee girl home. Fair enough?"

Fegan looked from Marie to O'Kane. He nodded. "Fair enough."

"Right, then." O'Kane looked at his watch. "I think it's time we got things sorted."

He went to the kitchen door and beckoned Coyle inside. He pointed to Campbell. "Take him out to the barn. Pádraig, you help him."

He turned to Downey. "Bring Gerry out, too. If he tries anything, you know what to do."

Downey aimed the shotgun at Fegan's head. Fegan stood up. He was tall, but not as tall as O'Kane.

"Remember, Gerry. Do as you're told and she can go home. Don't, and . . . well . . . you know."

Fegan nodded, walked to the doorway, and waited as Coyle and Pádraig wrestled Campbell's limp body through it. He turned to Marie.

"I'm sorry," he said. "For everything."

Downey pressed the shotgun against Fegan's back and followed him out of sight.

"Wait," Marie called. She went to go after him, but Quigley gripped her elbow.

"There's nothing you can do for him," O'Kane said.

Her eyes welled. "Please don't hurt him."

"What do you care?" O'Kane crossed to her. "He's a lunatic. He's dangerous. He killed your uncle."

Tears ran freely from her eyes as she clung to her daughter. "But he doesn't deserve to die."

O'Kane sighed. "Jesus, who does?"

He reached down and gripped Marie's forearms. She was strong, but not strong enough. It was easy to take the child from her, even though she fought hard. He put the little girl in Quigley's arms. She stared back at her mother, red-faced from the tears.

The ball of bloodstained cotton wool still lay on the floor next to the couch. O'Kane picked it up. He took the brown bottle from the windowsill, opened it, and poured the sweet-smelling liquid onto it.

Marie backed into the corner. "No."

"Don't worry, love." O'Kane walked slowly towards her. "It won't hurt."

She only fought it for a few seconds, scratching at his face, kicking at his shins. By the time she thought to raise a knee to his groin she was too weak to put anything behind it. O'Kane lowered her to the floor as she went limp. He looked to the screaming child.

"She's all right, sweetheart. Look, she's only sleeping."

The little girl's cries continued to stab at him. He showed her the cotton wool. "Do you want to take a wee sleep, too? When you wake up you can go home."

McGinty took the trembling child, quiet now, from Quigley. "No. That's enough."

O'Kane stood up so he could look down on McGinty. The politician stared back, defiant. O'Kane nodded. "All right. Take them back upstairs. You can keep an eye on them."

He stroked the child's blonde hair, soft against his rough skin. "You'll be a good girl, won't you? Uncle Paul's going to look after you for a wee while."

McGinty took a step back, bringing the girl with him. "What about Fegan?"

"Don't worry about him. I'll take care of it. Just you wait here. We need to have a talk when this is done."

O'Kane turned his eyes to the kitchen door. "Kevin?"

Malloy entered the room, his pistol drawn.

"Make sure our guests don't go anywhere." O'Kane walked towards the kitchen. "I won't be long."

50

For just a moment, Campbell was dragged back to his body where the pain waited for him. He screamed inside his own mind, unable to draw the breath to make the sound real. And then he was free of it again. From above he could see the vague forms carrying his body out into the gloom and the rain. Even up here the stench of the place was inescapable.

The procession marched across a sea of grey to a burning sun. The barn, lit up for their arrival. Campbell knew that much. This was the place where the dogs fought for their lives.

The dogs.

In Campbell's swirling consciousness, he imagined them, the dogs, slavering over his body. He was going to die soon, he knew, and the dogs would have him.

No. Not like this. Not here.

Wake up. No matter how much pain lies below, no matter how much it hurts, wake up.

51

Fegan saw the first hint of dawn beyond the stable roofs as he crossed the yard. Coyle and Pádraig heaved Campbell's limp form into the mouth of the barn. The Scot gasped and moaned as they lowered him to the ground at the edge of the pit. Downey kept the shotgun's muzzles at the small of Fegan's back all the time.

Five shapes followed in the emerging light, shadows no longer.

O'Kane fetched a roll of plastic sheeting from a dark corner. He brought it with him to the pit and unrolled it on the blood- and feces-stained earth. Pádraig helped him. The smell rising up clung to the back of Fegan's throat, and he forced himself not to gag. He didn't want to die here.

"I'm sorry," he said to the followers. The UFF boys looked up from Campbell's unconscious body. The woman and the butcher stood by his side. "I couldn't do it. I tried, but I couldn't. I'm sorry."

O'Kane looked up from the pit. "Are you talking to your friends, Gerry? The ones in your head?"

Fegan nodded. "Yes."

O'Kane beckoned. "Come on, son."

Fegan stepped down into the pit. Downey followed, pressing him forward. "You'll let Marie and Ellen go?" Fegan asked.

"I told you, didn't I?" O'Kane said. "Jesus, whatever happened to you? The great Gerry Fegan. You remember the last time we met? How long did you say, twenty-five years ago?"

"Twenty-seven," Fegan said. "I was eighteen."

O'Kane addressed the others. "He was just a kid, but he had a reputation already. The only fella ever raised a hand to me and lived to tell the tale. That was the first time we met. The next time would've been, oh, 1980. Those were fierce times. We had a tout to deal with. This girl from Middletown was fucking a Brit. She'd tried to run, tried to get a boat from Belfast, but McGinty's boys caught her at the docks. McGinty and Gerry here brought her down to me. Isn't that right, Gerry?"

Fegan remembered. "That's right."

"McGinty puts the gun in his hand, says, 'Here you go, Gerry. Now you can break your duck.'' O'Kane pointed to Campbell. "Bring him down here."

Pádraig walked over and helped Coyle to lower Campbell into the pit. The Scot's face contorted as they laid him on the plastic and he cried out in his stupor. Coyle drew the pistol from his waistband and put it to Campbell's head.

"What are you at?" O'Kane asked.

"I want to do him," Coyle said.

"All right, but you'll do it when I tell you, not before."

Coyle gave an impatient sigh and tucked the gun back into his waistband. Pádraig went to his father's side.

O'Kane continued. "Anyway, Gerry here takes the gun and just looks at us. McGinty asks him what's wrong, and Gerry goes 'No, I can't, I can't.''

"She was just a girl," Fegan said, 'no older than me. She was scared. And she was pregnant."

O'Kane stepped closer. "Aye, she was pregnant. She had a Brit's bastard inside her. So what? She was a tout. That's all there was to it. And you didn't have the guts. I had to do it for you."

Fegan remembered her eyes, pleading, terrified. Tears burned his cheeks. "I couldn't help her. I couldn't stop it."

"No, you didn't even have the guts to watch. You ran away. You were weak. She was a tout, the lowest kind of shite that walks the earth. The kind that turn on their own people. Like you, Gerry. And touts get no mercy."

He reached out and wiped the tears from Fegan's cheeks. "No mercy, Gerry. Not then. Not now."

The woman took Fegan's hand, her fingers cool and soft. He

turned to see her smile up at him, her eyes sad, the baby calm in the crook of her arm.

"I'm sorry," he said.

She nodded.

O'Kane took a step back. "It's time, Gerry."

Fegan felt the twin muzzles at the back of his head.

He closed his eyes and the woman's fingers slipped away from his.

52

Stay awake.

Every shred of Campbell's will focused on this one thing, this one task. To grab the knife taped to his ankle, open the blade, and get to his feet. If he could do those simple things, he might live.

But there was the pain.

The last jolt had pulled him back to some form of consciousness when they lowered him to the plastic. Now his mind teetered on the cusp of aware and unaware, and only the pain kept him from slipping back into the fog. He knew the movement would waken the smoldering in his side and the pain would be unbearable. But he would have to bear it. If he screamed before the thing was done, he would not survive.

His brain thundered inside his skull as his eyes tried to make sense of the hazy shapes before him. How many were there? He couldn't be sure. His vision didn't stretch that far. The one in front of him, though, the one whose feet shuffled in front of his face: Coyle.

Campbell kept his head still but let his eyes work upwards, along the backs of Coyle's calves, over his thighs, up to his waistband. A pistol, small, but it would do.

And what would he do with it?

Think.

Think.

Falling.

Who were these men standing over him, their fingers pointed to his head?

Falling into the dark again. No, come back.

He inhaled, letting the explosion of pain wipe away the mist, and held the air there. It had to be now. Fuck the pain. He ground his teeth together.

Now.

53

The desperate scream rose up to the barn's rafters and Fegan felt the shotgun muzzles move away from the back of his head. He opened his eyes. Campbell had a knife to Coyle's throat with one hand, and a small pistol in the other. Both men staggered in a lazy, lopsided dance as Campbell seemed to fight gravity. His eyes rolled, unfocused, like a drunk's. Coyle's mouth hung open. The scream hadn't been his.

Campbell aimed the gun at random targets, sometimes air, sometimes shadow, sometimes flesh. "Stay back."

Downey stepped around Fegan, the shotgun trained on the two shambling men.

O'Kane held his hands up. "Now don't be silly, Davy."

Campbell pointed the gun at the voice but his eyes seemed to focus on a place far beyond. "Stay back or I'll cut his throat."

Pádraig moved to flank Campbell, but the Scot turned to the side. "Get back."

O'Kane took a step closer. "Come on, now, Davy. You're in no fit state for this. It'll only make things worse."

Campbell moved his aim back and forth between O'Kane and his son. "I'll fucking shoot you if you don't get back."

"No, you won't, Davy. Jesus, you can barely stand."

"Get back."

Pádraig took one more step to Campbell's left and the Scot pulled the trigger once, twice, three times. The first shot cut nothing but air, but the second punched Pádraig's shoulder, and the third his throat. He stood there for a moment, mouth open in surprise, blood flowing down his barrel chest and pattering on the plastic.

"Da?" he said, his voice a throaty gargle. He took two steps backwards and sat down heavily on the edge of the pit.

Fegan looked to O'Kane. The old man's face was a slab of stone, his eyes red. "The dogs will have you, Davy. I'll watch them eat you alive."

"Don't move," Campbell said.

Pádraig lay back on the dirt floor, his breath coming in shallow bubbling gasps. He tried to say something, but the words drowned in his throat.

"Give me the shotgun, Tommy," O'Kane said, inching his way towards Downey. Downey passed it over. O'Kane raised it up to his shoulder and aimed at Campbell.

Coyle squirmed in Campbell's grip. "Jesus, don't shoot! Don't!"

Campbell blinked hard and shook his head. He brought the pistol to Coyle's temple. "I'll kill him, I swear."

O'Kane cocked the shotgun. "You think I give a shite?"

The boom filled the barn like a thunderclap, and time stood still for Fegan. He saw Coyle's chest explode, throwing him and Campbell backwards against the low pit wall. The muzzle of Campbell's pistol flashed as he and Coyle fell onto the lip of the pit, and something sliced the air beside Fegan.

He saw Downey reach inside his jacket. He heard Campbell's pistol fire once more as Coyle's body rolled away from him. O'Kane took a step back before letting the shotgun's second barrel go with another booming discharge. Fegan flinched as a red sun burst from Campbell's stomach. He dropped to the plastic-covered earth as Campbell writhed, pulling the trigger over and over.

Fegan covered his head with his hands and listened as the pistol's angry barks turned to dry clicks. He felt two bodies hit the ground, one heavier than the other.

Breathing and crying. Then a tattered howl that seemed to come from somewhere deep inside the earth. That howl was answered by the dogs across the yard. He heard their panicked yelps cut through the dawn, their frantic scratching at the stable doors. Fegan let his eyes rise up from the plastic, over its sleek surface, until they found Downey's twitching body, a revolver by his quivering hand. A pool of deep red spread from beneath him.

Fegan turned his head to the right. O'Kane lay on his side, alive, breathing hard. His face was burning pink and shining with sweat. A bloody hole had been torn just above his kneecap, and another in his belly, above his groin. His eyes found Fegan.

"Jesus, Gerry, he got me."

Fegan pushed up with his hands and got his shaking legs under him. He coughed as acrid smoke scratched at his throat, and went to Downey's body. He took the revolver from his side.

O'Kane's laugh had a shrill edge. "The fucker got me."

Fegan looked to Campbell. The Scot's chest hitched with tiny gasps. His belly had been torn open and Fegan tried not to see the mash of blood and flesh. The UFF boys lingered over him, savage grins on their faces.

"You got him too," Fegan said.

He walked over to O'Kane. The old man craned his neck to meet Fegan's eyes. His breath came in hissing stabs through gritted teeth. He looked at the gun in Fegan's hand.

"I'll give you anything you want," O'Kane said. "Anything. Any price. Just tell me."

"No," Fegan said.

"Get me out of here. Get me to a hospital. A million. I'll give you a million." He reached out and gripped Fegan's ankle. "You can take the woman and the child and go anywhere. Two million. I'll give you two million. Think of it, Gerry. Two million pounds."

"I don't want your money," Fegan said, pulling his leg away from O'Kane's grasp. He aimed the revolver at O'Kane's forehead.

Tears sprang from O'Kane's eyes and dropped to the plastic. "Then what? Just tell me what you want. I'll give it to you."

Fegan hunkered down. He could smell O'Kane's sweat. "I won't kill you. If you can get out of here, I won't come after you. But you have to promise me something."

"Oh, Jesus, anything."

"When it's over, you won't come after me. Or Marie. You leave us alone. I'm going to kill Campbell now, and when I've done that, I'm going to the house to kill McGinty. Then I'm gone and you won't ever hear of me again. You won't look for me; you won't put a price on me. Promise me that, and you'll live."

"Pádraig . . ."

"It's too late for him. Swear you'll leave me and Marie alone."

O'Kane nodded. "I promise. I swear to God."

"Swear on your children's souls."

"I swear."

"All right," Fegan said.

He stood upright and crossed the pit to where Campbell sprawled on its edge, clinging to the last threads of life. His eyes were focused on something above and his lips moved silently. The UFF boys stood back, their faces glowing with animal pleasure.

54

"Davy."

Campbell searched for his name among the bloodied faces. All these people reaching for him, clutching at him, pulling him down with them.

Who had spoken his name? Those men with the shaven heads and tattoos? No, they were dead years ago, broken into pieces in a cold concrete room. What did they want with him now? Their faces blazed in ecstasy.

What do you want? His lips moved, he felt them, but no sound came.

Something nudged his foot.

"Here, Davy."

Campbell tried to raise himself, but his body split in two. His core spilled out from him as he moved. Oh yes, the shotgun. It had torn him open. Cool air seeped into the place where his stomach had been.

He forced everything into his neck, lifting his head to see the voice. Hurricanes roared in his ears and his skin burned. A shape emerged from the fire, tall and thin.

Gerry Fegan.

He had something shiny and beautiful in his hand.

"They want you, Davy," he said.

"Who?" Campbell asked, his voice a thin hiss.

Fegan pointed to the tattooed men. They grinned at Campbell and he wanted to scream, but there was no air.

"The UFF boys you set up," Fegan said. "The ones you had me kill to cover your own tracks. It's time to pay, Davy."

Fire turned to ice and tremors spread out from Campbell's center.

He recognised the shining thing in Fegan's hand and heard its hammer click into place.

"Fuck you," he said.

"Everybody pays," Fegan said as the revolver's muzzle stared Campbell in the eye. "Sooner or later, everybody pays."

Fury tore at Campbell's heart. He wanted to taste Fegan's blood, feel his flesh burst and split beneath his fingers, but the blackness flooded in.

The UFF boys leaned close, grinning and hateful. The other faces, the bodies, the limbs, all dead and rotting, swarmed on him. One form moved closest, a tattered hole in his forehead, the sergeant's insignia still on his epaulettes.

Sergeant Hendry?

The long-dead soldier sank his teeth into Campbell's skin, tearing at the remains of his body.

Fegan towered above them all.

"Fuck you!" Campbell screamed. "Fucking do it! Do it now. Pull the fucking trigger. Come on, pull it. Shoot me. Pull the—"

THREE

55

The revolver's crack silenced the dogs for just a second. Fegan turned to the butcher, the black-haired woman and her baby. The woman gave him her small, sad smile.

Fegan nodded and walked past Bull O'Kane, who kept his gaze on the ground. He walked towards the yard, where the farmhouse waited. He stopped just inside the barn, leaning out to see it. The world had taken on the strange blue light of early morning as the rain thinned to leave a dull sheen on the farmyard. Low growls and whines came from the stables.

He breathed the tainted air for a moment, savoring the vivid clarity in his mind and the steadiness in his hands. His senses rang with life amid the smell of death. The chill at his center had become a bright flame, incandescent in his chest. Fegan studied the windows, looking for any sign of activity.

McGinty and the others would have expected shots, but not a firefight. They would be watching.

The Clio remained where he'd parked it, in the middle of the yard, between Fegan and the house. He had to get to it and the plastic bag taped under the passenger seat. He gave the windows and door another scan and set off at a crouching run.

The kitchen door opened inward and Fegan dropped to his knees, just feet from the car. A shot came from the doorway and something cut the air above his head. The dogs started howling and barking and scratching again.

It was Malloy. Fegan had just caught his stocky frame through the Clio's windows. He listened for footsteps on the concrete. The noise of the dogs made it hard to be sure. He crawled towards the car, the wet concrete cold on his hands and knees.

Another shot rang out. Fegan heard the bullet pierce the barn's corrugated metal shell. It sounded like it came from the doorway. Malloy was still inside. Fegan reached the Clio's rear driver's-side door and edged up to the glass. The kitchen door was cracked open and he could see a disruption in the shadow beyond.

He ducked down, his mind running in all directions. He didn't want to kill Malloy, but he had to get past him.

Fegan inched back up to the glass and peered through. He saw a hand appear from the shadows. It held a pistol. A shot blew glass around him as he covered his head.

"I don't want to kill you," he called.

He waited. No reply.

"I only want McGinty. You can go if you want. I won't hurt you."

"You're a dead man, Fegan." Malloy's voice had the glassy edge of fear as it echoed round the yard.

Fegan chanced another quick glance through the Clio's windows, and ducked down again when he saw Malloy peering back through the narrow opening of the doorway. "You don't have to die with McGinty. Not if you go now."

A bullet struck the Clio's bodywork, somewhere on the other side of the car.

"Please," Fegan called. "I don't want to kill you."

"Go fuck yourself!"

Fegan sighed and closed his eyes. "I have to," he whispered.

He crawled along the Clio's flank, from the rear to the front, keeping his head low as he approached its nose. He edged around the front, still hidden from the doorway. Looking up, he realised he would be visible from the upper floor on that side of the house. He watched the damp-stained net curtains for any sign of movement.

Just a few more inches and the doorway would come into view. If Malloy still had the door only slightly open, Fegan would be obscured by the wood. He crept forward until he could see its flaking green paint. Malloy's pistol appeared and a bullet struck the Clio's rear quarter.

He thinks I'm still there, Fegan thought.

He came up over the Clio's hood, steadying his arms on it, and put four shots through the wooden door. He listened, keeping the revolver's smoking muzzle trained on the doorway.

After a second or two he heard a weak cry and the sound of a body sliding down a damp wall and hitting the floor.

Fegan cursed, bitter anger at the waste rising in him.

He moved back behind the shelter of the car and edged his way round to the driver's door. He hadn't locked it. It creaked open and shattered glass spilled out. Fegan lay flat across the driver's seat, dropped the revolver into the footwell, and reached down under the passenger seat. His eyes stayed on the house, at least what he could see of it through the cracked window. He found the plastic bag with its cold, hard contents, and pulled the tape away. It tore and he felt nine-millimeter rounds spill through his fingers onto the floor. There was a heavy clunk as the weapons fell away.

Somewhere beneath the frantic barking and scratching of the dogs, Fegan caught the hint of voices from inside the house. He studied the windows as he drew his Walther from under the seat, followed by Campbell's Glock. A net curtain in a window above the doorway swayed, disturbed by some passing shape. He threw himself backwards, a gun in each hand, just as a hole was blown through the car's roof and a bullet gouged the upholstery where his head had been.

The dogs' whining and howling rose to a new pitch and blood thundered in his ears. But through that clamor came a sharper, more frightening sound. A high, terrified crying.

"Ellen," he said.

"Stay away, Fegan!"

McGinty's voice, shrill and jagged.

"Stay away or I'll kill them!"

Fegan clung to the side of the car, listening to the girl's cries. His heart threw itself against the walls of his chest; his stomach sank low inside him.

"Ellen."

56

Fegan looked to the followers standing over him, watching. The woman held her baby in one arm and raised the other towards the house. Her eyes told him, ordered him, to do it. Run, they said.

Run, now.

"Christ."

He tucked Campbell's Glock into his waistband and scrambled along the side of the car towards its front. The stable doors rattled in their frames as the dogs flailed against them. He gave the upper windows one more glance before hurling himself at the house. A shot rang out and something tugged at his left shoulder.

Fegan hit the door hard and stumbled over Malloy's outstretched legs. He slammed against the far wall, dislodging loose tiles where the grout had rotted away. They shattered on the floor and he saw red spots appear among the fragments. His left arm felt heavy, like a stone had been tied to his wrist. He craned his neck round to see his shoulder. Nothing, just a nick.

He looked back at Malloy's prone form. The stocky man's chest rose and fell in a skewed rhythm. His glassy eyes stared at something far away. The followers entered and lingered over him, tilting their heads as they studied him.

Quick footsteps moved across the ceiling above.

"Gerry?" McGinty, his voice muffled by the wood and plaster between them. "Gerry, don't come up here, I'm warning you. Don't. I'll . . . I'll . . . you know I'll do it."

Ellen, crying.

The woman stood beside Fegan, pointing to the doorway to the next room. The room where he'd last seen Marie and Ellen. The butcher joined her.

"All right," Fegan said.

He headed for the door, the Walther leading the way. The old tattered couch still sat against the wall, sodden with damp and blood. Weak fingers of early light clawed through the grimy window. Fegan could see trees beyond what had once been a garden but was now lost under years of neglect.

What was that?

He stopped and listened. Hard, fast breathing. The sound of panic. It came from beyond the far door. The same door Marie and Ellen had come through not so long ago. How long had it been? Fifteen minutes? Thirty? An hour?

The woman and the butcher took their places by Fegan's side. They cocked their heads, listening. The baby was quite still in its mother's arms.

She turned to Fegan and smiled. She reached up and brushed his cheek. She nodded.

Fegan looked back to the doorway and the darkness beyond. The breathing drew closer, its urgency growing. He stepped quietly towards the sound, the Walther between him and the shadows.

A stair creaked. The breathing faltered, then came back, quicker than before. Fegan heard the hiss of fabric against wallpaper, someone sliding along the wall.

Steady.

A man's high, nasal whine. Terror.

Fegan stepped closer, shifting his weight slowly on the ancient floorboards. He kept the Walther drawn at waist level, in case they came in low. Closer. He could almost reach out and touch the door frame now. The breathing grew faster and faster, harder and harder.

Then it stopped.

Quigley burst from the shadow, a small pistol locked in both hands, his eyes bulging, his face burning, his knuckles white. He cried out when he saw Fegan's Walther aimed at his heart, but he didn't shoot. He stood frozen, staring, his breath held in his chest. Fegan saw the fear on him; he smelled the panic. This man was no killer.

"Breathe," Fegan said.

Quigley stared back, veins standing out on his forehead and temples. His hands quaked. They held a .22 target pistol, little more than a toy.

"Breathe or you'll faint."

Air exploded from him in a long, desperate hiss. He inhaled with a tremulous gasp, and let it out again in a low moan.

McGinty's voice came from above. "Shoot him, Quigley!"

Ellen cried.

"You don't want to die," Fegan said.

"Just shoot him!"

"You don't have to die," Fegan said.

Quigley couldn't keep the gun aimed in one direction. It danced in his hands.

McGinty's voice was high and fractured. "For fuck's sake shoot him!"

"It's your choice," Fegan said. "You can live if you want to."

Despite its leaden weight, he raised his left hand, open. Quigley stared back, his eyes searching Fegan's face.

"You can live if you want to. Malloy and the Bull are hurt bad. The rest are dead. McGinty's going to die soon. You don't have to die with him. Choose."

Quigley's eyes fell away and his shoulders slumped.

"Quigley?" McGinty's voice had lost its anger. "Quigley, what's happening?"

Quigley placed the gun in Fegan's outstretched hand, his stare fixed on the floor.

"Go," Fegan said, slipping the gun into his jacket pocket.

"Thank you," Quigley said. He hurried to the kitchen door without raising his eyes.

Fegan turned back to the shadows Quigley had emerged from. A door stood slightly ajar on the other side of a hallway. Morning light crept in from somewhere. Fegan pictured the rear of the house. There was a window at the center of the upper floor.

"It must be at the top of the stairs," Fegan said.

The woman stepped closer to the darkness. With her free arm she signalled in and upwards. Fegan edged up to the door frame.

"Quigley?"

"He's gone," Fegan said.

"Bastard! Fuck!"

The voice wasn't far away. Just at the top of the stairs, it sounded like. It resonated in the narrow hallway. Fegan eyed the door on the other side.

"Don't come up here, Gerry. I'm warning you."

Fegan took one breath before diving sideways, his left shoulder aimed at the door across the hallway. He caught a glimpse of McGinty's silhouette against the window, Ellen writhing in his left arm, a revolver in his right hand. The gun boomed in the narrow passageway just as Fegan's wounded shoulder connected with the door. The bullet scorched the air above Fegan's head. The door burst inward, and he cried out in pain as he tumbled into the room. He fell against a stack of wooden chairs, sending them crashing to the floor.

"Stay away, Gerry. Don't make me hurt them."

Ellen screamed and cried.

Fegan scrambled to his feet, his mind working fast. A revolver, six shots. He counted.

"He's fired three," he said.

The woman turned to him and nodded. Fegan held her burning gaze.

"He's got three left."

She stepped back out into the hallway, the baby wriggling in one arm, and pointed upwards with the other. Her fingers formed a pistol. The butcher stood alongside her and did the same.

Together, they took aim at Paul McGinty, firing again and again, their mouths twisted and their teeth bared.

"I know," Fegan said, feeling a warm trickle down his left arm. Weariness gnawed at the edges of his clarity. "I know."

57

Fegan listened to the sounds of McGinty's hard breathing and Ellen's soft cries. Three shots left. If he didn't have more ammunition, that was. Fegan had to gamble on that. He had to make McGinty waste them.

It was dark at the foot of the stairs. The only light came from the window behind McGinty and, even then, it was the thin glow of early morning. McGinty knew Fegan was a poor shot and he couldn't risk hitting Ellen while trying to wing the politician. But McGinty also thought Fegan was crazy enough to try.

Fegan looked around the room. The chairs lay scattered across the floor, and beyond them was a pile of old curtain material. He righted one of the chairs and draped a thick sheet of dark velvet over it. It was heavy, but he could manage with his good arm. He took quiet steps towards the door and raised the chair so it was level with his own shoulders. The woman and the butcher stepped back to give him room.

He extended his arm, letting the curtain-draped chair's shoulder creep out into the shadows of the hallway. Inch by inch, centimeter by centimeter, he let the oblique shape reveal itself to McGinty, hoping the folds of darkness might make it seem—

A boom filled the hallway, and the chair jerked from Fegan's grip to fall to the floor with a wooden clatter, the torn curtain fabric fluttering after it.

Ellen's scream was followed by seconds of silence, and then McGinty hissed and cursed. One more shot wasted.

"You've only two left, Paul," Fegan said.

"That's one for each of them, Gerry. You don't want that to happen. Don't make me do it. Don't come up here."

"I have to, Paul."

"Don't! Don't, or I'll . . . I'll . . ."

"You'll what?"

"Christ," McGinty said.

"Killing isn't easy, Paul. Not when it's your own finger on the trigger."

"I'll do it. Believe me, I'll do it."

Fegan stood back from the doorway. He saw McGinty's shadow against the wall as early light made its way down the stairs. "You've never had the guts to do it yourself, Paul. It was always people like me. The ones you filled full of hate. You never got blood on your own hands."

McGinty's shadow moved back and forth as he paced above, Ellen locked in his grip. "Don't push me, Gerry."

"You used people like me. You told us we didn't have a future. You said we had to fight for it. You put the guns in our hands and sent us off to do your killing for you."

"You volunteered, Gerry. Just like the rest of us. Nobody made you do anything."

"You lied to us."

"Nobody made you pull the trigger, Gerry. Nobody made you plant that—"

"You lied to me." Fegan rested his forehead against the wall, feeling the cold dampness against his skin. "You said there was a Loyalist meeting above that butcher's shop. You told me there was UVF and UDA, all sitting together. You said the timer was set for five minutes. Time to get the people out."

"It was a war. Sometimes innocent people get hurt."

Fegan laughed. "Sometimes. It's never the guilty, is it? But everybody pays. What day's today?"

"What?"

"It's Sunday, isn't it? Is it a week ago? Jesus. This day last week an old woman told me everybody pays, sooner or later. A woman whose son I killed. Michael McKenna paid for him. Now you have to pay. Three of them died. A butcher. A baby, for Christ's sake. A mother and her baby."

Fegan lifted his forehead from the wall and looked back out to the hall. McGinty's shadow was still now.

"Just go, Gerry. Just get out of here. No one else has to get hurt."

"She's here, Paul."

"Who?"

"The woman. And her baby. Christ, I don't know her name. She's here and she wants you. Her and the butcher. You remember how it happened? It was on the news at the time. He went to pick it up, probably thought someone had forgotten their shopping. Him and the woman were closest."

"Don't, Gerry."

"And what was it for?"

"I was told the same as you. The Loyalists were meeting above the shop."

"You're lying. You knew it was just storerooms above that shop. What was it for? Tell her what she died for."

McGinty's shadow struggled with a writhing shape. Ellen jerked in his arms, still trying to break free.

"Tell that woman and her baby what she died for, Paul. She deserves to know."

"There's nobody there, Gerry. Don't you understand that? She's in your head."

"Tell her, Paul."

McGinty's sigh slithered down the walls of the stairwell. "To make my mark."

Fegan brought his right hand to his left shoulder, feeling the heat there. Blood trickled down to his fingertips. "Make your mark."

"Yes. To make the leadership notice me. I'd been on the sidelines too long – I needed something big to get the headlines they wanted."

"You had me plant that bomb, kill those people, for headlines? To make a name for yourself?"

"I had to, Gerry. And it worked. I saw the way things were going, even then. The politics, the elections. I had to get a leg up then, or I never would. I'd just be another foot soldier like you or Eddie Coyle."

Fegan looked to the woman and her baby. And the butcher with his round, red face. "To make a name for yourself. They died to make your name."

"But I did good, Gerry. Think about it. I helped build the peace. I kept the boys on the streets in line. Me, Gerry. It would've fallen apart if it wasn't for me. But you've risked it all. Do you hear me? All those lives for nothing, all that labor, the heartbreak, the years – you might have wasted them all. And what for? For some figments of your imagination?"

McGinty's voice had taken on that familiar color: the politician's sheen, the twisted rhetoric.

Fegan rubbed his eyes with his knuckles, the Walther still in his grip. "What was her life worth?"

"Enough, Gerry."

"And her baby's?"

"Come on, you know the—"

"And the butcher. What was his life worth? Or any of them? What were they worth to you, Paul?"

"It was you, Gerry. You killed them. Nobody else."

Fegan brought his bloodied hands to his temples, the Walther cold against his scalp. "I know."

McGinty's voice hardened. "Don't tell me you didn't like it. Don't tell me you didn't love the power of it."

"Shut up."

"All that respect you got. Everywhere you went, people looked up to you. The great Gerry Fegan. And you pissed it all away. What are you now, eh?"

"Shut up."

McGinty laughed. "You're just a drunk who's gone soft in the head. So you turn against your own just so you can make yourself feel like a big man again. Is that it, Gerry? Is that what this is about? You're just a lonely, drunk has-been who's nothing without a gun and someone to point it at."

Fegan screwed his eyes closed. "Shut your mouth!"

"And what about when it's over, eh? What then? What'll you be, Gerry?"

Fegan dropped low and ducked his head out into the hallway, the Walther aimed upwards. McGinty's revolver flashed and a bullet threw splinters and plaster dust into Fegan's face. He fell back into the room, coughing as dust hitched in his throat. He wiped his sleeve across his eyes.

One left.

He looked up to see the woman and her baby, the butcher at their side. The infant squirmed as the woman and the butcher pointed up at McGinty. Fegan watched the shadow move along the wall as the politician paced. Ellen whimpered and moaned, seemingly too exhausted to wail as she had before.

"You didn't answer the question, Gerry."

Fegan got to his feet, wincing at the throbbing from his left shoulder. His arm grew heavier by the moment and his legs quivered as fatigue dissolved his strength. He had to end it soon.

"You've only one bullet left," he said.

"One's enough," McGinty said.

"Not if it doesn't put me down."

"It's not for you. It's for her."

Fegan looked to the shadow. The shape was becoming clearer, harder in the growing light. He could make out McGinty's form, crouched, Ellen held close. Where was the gun?

He looked to the woman. "Jesus, where's the gun?"

She had no answer; she just kept her fingers trained on McGinty. The politician's shadow shifted on the wall.

"Come and see, Gerry."

58

Fegan edged to the doorway and slowly leaned out to see the window at the top of the stairs. McGinty hunkered down beneath it, Ellen held in front of him, the revolver behind her head where she couldn't see it.

"Gerry," she said, "I want to go home."

"Soon, sweetheart. You and your Mummy and me. We'll all go home together. I promise."

McGinty gave a high, watery laugh. "You didn't answer me, Gerry. What happens next?"

Fegan stepped out into the hallway, the Walther lowered to his side. He moved it behind his body so Ellen couldn't see it.

"I don't know," he said.

"Do you think you'll go home and play happy families with Marie McKenna? Do you think you'll be a father to this wee girl? You think Marie's going to want anything to do with you, now she knows what you've done?"

The woman and the butcher made way as Fegan moved towards the bottom step. "I don't know."

McGinty's hand trembled. Pale slivers of early light reflected on the revolver's barrel. "You don't know. There's a lot you don't know." He smiled, sweat shining on his upper lip. "You don't know about Marie calling me when she found out that cop was cheating on her. Or how I went round to see her that night, and how she pulled me into her bed. She did it just to spite him, to get back at him, same way she's used you to spite me."

Fegan climbed up two steps.

McGinty pressed his lips against Ellen's hair. "She never told me if the child was mine. Stop there."

Fegan froze with his bloody hand on the rail, his right foot two steps above his left, the Walther pressed against his thigh.

McGinty's eyes went far away. "I asked her, but she wouldn't tell me."

Fegan brought his left foot up to join his right. The smooth rail slipped through his blood-slicked fingers. "I don't want her to see this," he said. "Neither do you."

"Just let me go, Gerry."

"I can't do that. Where's Marie?"

McGinty nodded to the side, somewhere beyond Fegan's vision. "She's in there. Bull knocked her out. Let me go, Gerry."

Fegan climbed another step. "Is she all right?"

"She's fine. She's just sleeping. Let me go. Please."

And another step. "No, Paul, I can't. Let Ellen go to her mother."

"I'm taking her with me."

And another. "No, you're not."

McGinty's shoulders shook as he exhaled. "Christ, please, Gerry. Let me go. I'm begging you. Don't make me do . . . this."

One more step. "You won't hurt her," Fegan said. "Let her go to Marie."

McGinty's eyes were blue and glittering. Fegan's own stare fixed on them as he took another step. McGinty's breath came in thin, keening whines. He blinked sweat away from his eyes. His lip trembled.

He pushed.

59

Ellen slammed into Fegan's chest, sending him reeling backwards. He grabbed at the rail with his left hand to save them both from tumbling down the stairs, and pain flared as he wrenched his injured shoulder. His good arm snaked around the girl as McGinty disappeared into the shadows above.

Ellen scrambled up Fegan's torso as he found his balance, wrapped her arms around his neck and legs around his middle. "Gerry," she cried, 'take me home."

"It's all right," he said. "I've got you."

She buried her face between his neck and shoulder. The sweet smell of her hair filled his head and his heart.

"You're cut," she said.

"I'm all right. Where's your Mummy?"

"Does it hurt?"

"No, sweetheart." Fegan climbed the last few steps to the top, keeping his eyes on the shadows that had swallowed McGinty. "Where's your Mummy?"

She looked to the door to Fegan's left, the opposite direction to McGinty's flight. He opened it and took one glance back at the shadows before slipping inside and closing it behind him.

A single stained mattress lay on the floor at the center of the room. Marie McKenna sprawled across it, her mouth open, her eyes moving behind closed lids.

Fegan carried Ellen to the mattress and lowered her to rest beside her mother. Marie's eyes fluttered open, her pupils dilated, unfocused.

"Gerry?"

Fegan kneeled over her. "It's all right. You're safe."

"Safe," she said. She smiled once, and then her eyelids flickered and closed. Fegan smoothed Ellen's hair, tainting the strands red.

"You wait here with your Mummy till I come and get you, all right?"

Ellen grabbed his lapels. "Don't go!"

"I'll be back soon. I promise. Stay here with your Mummy. Don't come out, no matter what you hear. All right?"

She nodded and released his jacket.

"Good girl," Fegan said. He touched her cheek as she lay down and rested her head against her mother's bosom. Then he stood and went to the door. Turning back to her, he said, "Remember, stay with your Mummy, no matter what you hear."

Fegan put his eye to the crack of the door and eased it open. The corridor was empty. He opened the door fully, slipped out, and closed it again. There were two more doors: one just beyond the stairway, facing back to the rear of the house, and the other at the end of the corridor, facing him. Both were closed.

He raised the Walther and inched forward, his breathing slow, listening, as the followers stayed close behind him. Two steps took him to the top of the stairway, another three to the door beyond. He pressed his ear against it. Nothing but dripping water. The doorknob was slippery in the bloody fingers of his left hand. Weakened and clumsy, they struggled to grip the brass. He turned it, pushed hard, and raised the Walther.

The door swung back on its hinges to collide with the wall. Dislodged tiles splintered on the floor. Fegan winced at the noise. The room held an old scroll-top bathtub, a toilet and a washbasin. Water pooled on the linoleum-covered floor, and a deep, dank smell climbed into Fegan's nose and mouth.

No McGinty.

He looked to the other door. A noise, the faintest of rustlings, came from beyond it. Fegan took slow, soft steps towards the room. The rustling stopped. He reached out to the doorknob, his pistol ready, his breath held firm in his chest.

Fegan moved fast, turning the handle, pushing, dropping to his knees, aiming. The door frame exploded in a shower of rotting wood and he fell back, landing on his wounded shoulder. He pushed the pain away, and scrambled to a crouch. The room was in darkness. He'd barely seen the muzzle flash from inside.

The woman and the butcher stepped forward. They both looked at Fegan and stabbed their fingers towards the room. McGinty was in there, hiding in the thick shadows.

"He's got no ammunition left," Fegan said.

The woman smiled and nodded as she rocked her baby.

Fegan stood upright and advanced slowly to the door. His eyes searched the darkness but he found only shades of grey and black. He raised the Walther in his right hand, and tried to bring his left up to steady it, but it was too heavy. His left shoulder throbbed with a spiteful heat, and he felt warmth spread down his side.

The dark shapes solidified as Fegan's eyes attuned to the shadows. Old furniture was piled in here, tables, chairs, cupboards, dressing tables. McGinty could be hiding in or under anything. Fegan eased over the threshold, floorboards creaking under his feet. Dust crept into his nostrils and he fought the urge to sneeze. It snagged the back of his throat and he wanted to—

A thunderbolt struck Fegan's head and the room spun away from him. He careened into the wall, the Walther slipping from his fingers to skitter across the floorboards into the shadows. McGinty screamed as he brought the revolver down again, but Fegan got his forearm up in time to deflect the blow. He pushed back and McGinty stumbled away, crashing into an upturned table. Fegan dived at him, but McGinty threw himself to the side, leaving Fegan to fall against the upended table legs. He cried out as the wooden feet gouged his stomach and ribs.

McGinty tried again to slam the side of the pistol into Fegan's temple, and he came close, but Fegan pulled his head back, leaving McGinty punching uselessly at empty air. Fegan turned as McGinty's balance deserted him and he drove his fist into the politician's temple.

McGinty went down hard, his chin cracking on the floorboards, and Fegan was on his back before he could recover. Fegan wrapped his right arm around McGinty's neck, the crook of his elbow beneath the other's jaw, and squeezed. McGinty bucked and writhed, and Fegan put his weight on the other's back, but still he struggled. He clawed at Fegan's hand, scratching, but Fegan only increased the pressure on his neck.

Fegan tried to find his pocket with his left hand, to get Quigley's .22, but his dull, stupid fingers only fumbled at the fabric while McGinty threw his weight from side to side. Fegan put the last of his strength into his good arm and squeezed harder.

McGinty's thrashing became more desperate and he reached up, searching for Fegan's face. Fegan ignored the scratching and grabbing, feeling McGinty's body slowly soften.

"Everybody pays, Paul," he said through gritted teeth. "Sooner or later. That's what she said to me."

McGinty's thrashing began to fade, and his hands fell away. Fegan kept the pressure on the man's neck as his body twitched, fighting to live.

"Everybody pays," Fegan said again. "Everybody. Even you."

McGinty shuddered once as his life slipped away. Fegan lay there, across his back, for what seemed like centuries, feeling the stillness of McGinty's body as his own screamed with adrenalin and pain. When his heart came under control, Fegan looked up to the shadows of the room. He released McGinty's neck and gently lowered the dead man's head to rest on the floor.

Fegan climbed to his feet, feeling the steady throb from his shoulder joined by new shades of pain. He turned in a circle, alone, all alone, nobody here but—

The woman stepped out of the shadows, her face slack, her hands outstretched. She looked down at her fingers, her arms, so empty now with no infant to carry. Her mouth was open and her eyes were bright circles. She held her hands out for Fegan to see how empty they were.

Empty.

So empty.

Fegan shook his head. "I don't understand."

Her face hardened. She stepped closer, forming her right hand into the shape of a gun. Her fierce eyes on Fegan's, she reached up and placed her fingertips against his forehead. They were cold on his skin as she executed him.

ONE

60

"No," Fegan said.

She pressed her fingertips against his forehead, harder. Her lips made a silent plosive as she pulled the trigger, and her eyes burned into his.

Fegan took a step back. "No, I did what you wanted."

She followed, her finger-pistol trained on his head.

"I did it," he said. "I killed them all. I did them all for you, so you could go. I did what you wanted. Please. Let me go."

His legs rippled with spent energy and he had to steady himself against the wall. He turned and walked to the door. She came behind him. He could almost feel the bullets strike the back of his head.

"Please," he said.

The woman walked in step with him, her fingertips against his temple now. He staggered to the bathroom, his feet splashing in the water pooling on the floor. A fractured mirror hung above the washbasin. He looked at the hollows of his face, the darkness under his eyes.

"All I wanted was some peace," he said. "I just wanted to sleep. That's all."

Fegan saw her in the mirror, the finger-pistol locked on him, her eyes clinging to the reflection of his own. "Why didn't you just take me? Why all this?"

The sound of groaning pipes roamed through the old house as he turned a tap. Spurts of brown water soaked his hands and he rinsed the blood away. When the water cleared he splashed a handful of it on his face, feeling the coarse stubble. He took another handful and brought it to his mouth, swallowing the copper taste.

"Oh, God." He shut off the tap and wiped his eyes.

He shuffled over to the bathtub and lowered himself to its edge. His body felt so heavy he couldn't hold it any more. There was a pressure at the small of his back: Campbell's Glock.

"Please." He looked up to the woman. "I can have a life."

She stepped forward and returned her fingers to his forehead. Fegan reached up and took her hand in his. A thought flashed in his mind: he had never reached out and touched her before. She had touched him, but he had never touched her. He wrapped his fingers around hers. He looked up into her hard eyes.

"I can have a life. I can be a real person, a whole person. I know I can't be with Marie and Ellen, but I can be clean. Please let me have a life."

Her eyes wavered, something soft moving behind them.

"Mercy," Fegan said, the word catching in his throat. He squeezed her hand in his, feeling her slender bones. "Have mercy."

Something flickered across her face, just for a moment, and then it went slack. She pulled her hand away, formed the shape of a gun once more, and placed her fingers at the center of his forehead. There was no anger or hate in the lines of her face now, only sadness.

Fegan closed his eyes. He reached around to the small of his back and found the Glock's grip. It fitted snugly in his hand, and the pistol came free with the sound of metal on fabric, leaving a cold place where it had been. It was heavy and it clanked against the side of the bath. He opened his eyes.

"Can we go now?" Ellen asked from the doorway. The gold in her hair blazed in the morning light. Water rippled around her feet as she walked to him.

"Soon," he said. He let the gun hang inside the bath, away from her pretty eyes.

"Why are you crying?"

"I don't know," he said.

She slipped between his knees and propped herself on his quivering thigh. Her fingers were soft and warm as she touched his tears and felt the stubble on his chin. She leaned in close and whispered.

"Where's her baby?"

Fegan blinked. "What?"

"The secret lady. Where'd her baby go?"

Fegan swallowed. "To Heaven."

Ellen smiled and rested her head on his chest. Fegan's left arm felt so heavy he could barely lift it and wrap it around her.

The woman's eyes sparked and danced. She lowered herself to her knees as her lip trembled. Her fingertips brushed the loose strands of Ellen's hair, smoothing them. She looked into Fegan's eyes and gave him the softest, faintest, saddest of smiles. She stood and walked slowly, gracefully to the doorway.

As she disappeared into the morning light beyond, she turned to look at Fegan once more.

"Mercy," she said.

61

The two Chinese sailors argued between themselves as they counted out hundred-pound notes on the Clio's hood. Huge containers of coiled sheet steel, fresh off their cargo ship, surrounded them. The warehouse at Dundalk Port was cold and damp on this early morning, but the sailors were clearly in good spirits. Getting three thousand pounds sterling apiece just for letting a thin man stow away would give anyone cause to smile. They weren't concerned about the car's broken windows or the holes in its bodywork. They had rough hands and knowing eyes; they had no fear of someone like Fegan.

Fegan grimaced as he adjusted the wadded-up material stuffed into the shoulder of his jacket. His left arm hung leaden and useless at his side. In broken English, the sailors had promised him their ship's medical officer would take care of the wound for another thousand pounds. They didn't ask how he'd gotten it; they simply grinned and took the money.

Ellen slept in the back of the car, safely strapped into her child seat. Marie cradled her head in her hands as she leaned her back against the passenger door. The chloroform had left her aching and foggy.

"Sleep for a while," Fegan said. "Nobody will bother you here. When you wake up I'll be gone. Then you can go to the cops."

She raised her head. "What'll I tell them?"

"The truth," Fegan said. "Not that it'll matter."

By the time Fegan had carried Marie down to the car, Ellen clinging to his jacket, the Bull and Malloy were gone. Quigley must have taken them. Like Fegan, he would have headed south across the border. It had taken only thirty or forty minutes to drive to Dundalk Port, but it took another hour to find these two sailors and persuade them to smuggle Fegan on board their boat. Officers of the *Garda*

Síochána, the Republic of Ireland's police force, might already be questioning Quigley at some hospital or other. Fegan didn't know if he'd talk, but it was only a matter of time before the bodies were found at O'Kane's farm.

And what then?

The politicians and the media would convulse, accusations would be hurled, recriminations threatened. Stormont might collapse again, or perhaps more concessions would be given by the British and Irish governments to keep the Assembly afloat. The European Union might throw more money into community grants to quiet the streets of Belfast. Maybe the British would blame it on the dissidents; they were friendless anyway.

Fegan didn't know. All he knew was this place had no more thirst for war. That had been quenched long ago. Men like him no longer belonged here. Exhaustion washed over him in a heavy grey wave.

Marie's face was a stone mask, her eyes unfeeling. "Where'll you go?" she asked.

"I don't know," he said. He wouldn't have told her even if he did. "Far away from here. I can't come back. Ever."

Marie nodded and the mask slipped just a little. She leaned forward and placed a kiss on Fegan's lips. Its warmth lingered for a few moments before turning cold. She walked around the car and opened the driver's door.

"If I ever see you again," she said, "I'll turn you in. I won't hesitate. Not for a second."

Fegan looked at Ellen's sleeping form. He knew the danger he could put her and her mother in.

"I understand," he said. "But one thing."

"What?"

He took the phone from his breast pocket. It was sticky with blood. He held it out for her to see. "If anyone comes at you, threatens you, if you're afraid. You know how to find me."

Marie nodded, a possibility of a smile on her lips. It was gone before he could be sure.

The Chinese men gathered their money and walked away from the

Clio, gesturing for Fegan to follow. He slipped the phone into his pocket and looked back to Marie. She didn't meet his eyes as she lowered herself into the car.

"Come! Come!" one of the sailors called. "Go now. Is time."

Ellen woke at the noise of the car's door closing. She rubbed her eyes and squinted at Fegan. He raised his right hand and waved. She waved back. He stooped, picked up his bag, and turned to walk towards the boat. As he left the warehouse, gulls quarrelled and rolled in the sky. Rain washed and cooled his skin.

No shadow followed but his own.

ACKNOWLEDGMENTS

Many people have helped me on the road to publication, but I must express my deepest gratitude to a few of them:

My agent, Nat Sobel, and all at Sobel Weber Associates, Inc, for giving me the opportunity of a lifetime. Nat, I owe you more than I can say.

Caspian Dennis and all at Abner Stein Ltd for such excellent work.

Geoff Mulligan, Briony Everroad and all at Harvill Secker for their skill, professionalism and tolerance of my daft questions.

Laura Hruska at Soho Press for taking a chance in uncertain times.

Betsy Dornbusch, without whose belief, encouragement and friendship this book would never have been written.

Shona Snowden for her sharp eye and excellent critiques.

Josephine Damian for her enthusiasm and support.

Juliet Grames for her wisdom and advice.

My PR, Hilary Knight, for spreading the word.

Declan Burke and Gerard Brennan for championing the cause.

The online writing community for, in varying proportions, its friendship, support and advice. There are far too many people to list here, but just a few are: Adrian McKinty, Chris F Holm, Cindy Pon, Ellen Oh, Jeremy Duns, JJ De Benedictis, Moonrat and Nathan Bransford. A special mention must go to the redoubtable Miss Snark, wherever she may be, for beating us writers with the clue-stick so many times that some of us took heed and actually made it over the transom.

My friends and family for . . . well, you know.

Turn the page for a sneak preview of

COLLUSION

the exciting sequel to *The Ghosts of Belfast*

I

"We're being followed," Eugene McSorley said. The Ford Focus crested the rise, weightless for a moment, and thudded hard back onto the tarmac. Its eight-year-old suspension did little to cushion the impact. McSorley kept his eyes on the rear-view mirror, the silver Skoda Octavia lost behind the hill he'd just sped over. It had been tailing them along the narrow country road since they crossed the border into the North.

Comiskey twisted in the passenger seat. "I don't see anyone," he said. "No, wait. Fuck. Is that the peelers?"

"Aye," McSorley said. The Skoda reappeared in his mirror, its windows tinted dark green. He couldn't make out the occupants, but they were cops all right. The tarmac darkened under the growing drizzle, the sky a blank, heavy sheet of gray above the green fields.

"Jesus," Hughes moaned from the back seat. "Are we going to get pulled?"

"Looks like it," Comiskey said. "Fuck."

Hedgerows streaked past the Focus. McSorley checked his speed, staying just below sixty. "Doesn't matter," he said. "We've nothing on us. Not unless you boys have any blow in your pockets."

"Shit," Hughes said.

"What?"

"I've an eighth on me."

McSorley shot a look back over his shoulder. "Arsehole. Chuck it."

McSorley hit the switch to roll down the rear window and pulled close to the hedgerow so the cops wouldn't see. He watched his side mirror as Hughes's hand flicked a small brown cube into the greenery. "Arsehole," he repeated.

Comiskey peered between the seats. "They're not getting any closer," he said. "Maybe they won't pull us."

McSorley said nothing. He raised the rear window again. The car rounded a bend onto a long straight, the road falling away in a shallow descent before rising to meet the skyline half a mile ahead. He flicked the wipers on. They left wet smears across the windscreen, barely shifting the water. He'd meant to replace them a year ago. McSorley cursed and squinted through the raindrops.

A white van sat idling at a side road. It had all the time in the world to ease out and be on its way. It didn't. Instead it inched forward to the junction, the driver holding it on the clutch. McSorley wet his lips. He felt the accelerator beneath the sole of his shoe. The Focus had a decent engine, but the suspension was shot. Once the road started to twist, he wouldn't have a chance. He eased off the pedal. The van drew closer. Two men in the cabin, watching.

McSorley's stomach flipped between light and heavy, heavy and light, while adrenalin rippled out to his fingers and toes. He fought the heaving in his chest.

"Christ," he said out loud, without meaning to. "Nothing to worry about. They're only cops. They're going to pull us, that's all."

The Focus neared the white van, and McSorley saw the men's faces. They stared back as he passed. His eyes went to the mirror. The Skoda's reflection swelled. Blue lights flickered behind the grille, and its siren whooped. The van edged a foot or two out of the junction.

The Skoda accelerated, disappeared from the mirror, and reappeared alongside the Focus. McSorley saw white shirts and dark epaulets. The woman cop in the passenger seat signaled to the side of the road.

"Fuck," McSorley said. He gently squeezed the brake and shifted down. The Skoda slipped past as he let the Focus mount the grass verge. It skidded on the wet grass and mud. The Skoda stopped a few yards ahead. Its reversing lights glared, and it rolled back to stop just feet from the Focus's bonnet.

"Keep your mouths shut, boys," McSorley said. "Answer them when they talk to you, but don't give them any lip. Don't give them any excuses. Right?"

"Right," Hughes said from the back.

"Right?" McSorley said to Comiskey.

Comiskey gave him a quivering smile. "Aye, no worries."

Two cops got out of the car, donning hats and bright reflective jackets. The woman wasn't bad looking, light brown hair swept up under her cap. The man was tall and in good shape. His rich tan looked alien beneath the gray sky. They approached the Focus, the man leading.

The wipers scraped across the windscreen, the rubber-on-glass creak in counterpoint to McSorley's heartbeat. He put his finger on the button, ready to lower the window when the cop asked. Instead, the cop grabbed the handle and opened the door. Rain leaked in. It had been raining for nearly three months solid. All day, every day, no let-up. McSorley blinked as a heavy drop splashed on his cheek.

"Afternoon," the cop said. He had an English accent, hard and clipped. "Shut your engine off, please, sir."

McSorley turned the key. The engine died, freezing the wipers in mid-sweep.

"Just keep your hands where I can see them, there's a good chap," the cop said.

That accent, McSorley thought. Officer class. It spoke of parade grounds and stiff salutes, not traffic patrols and police checkpoints.

The cop ducked his head down. "You too, gentlemen."

Comiskey put his hands on the dashboard; Hughes placed his on the back of the passenger seat. McSorley gripped the steering wheel and studied the cop's face. His skin was a deep brown, not the shallow tan of a week at the beach. His lips were shiny from balm applied to the cracks, as if they'd been baked in some arid place. A vision of this cop crawling across a desert flashed in McSorley's mind. The image terrified him, and he couldn't think why.

The cop's hands stayed out of view until he reached in and took the key from the ignition. A black leather glove, expensive looking.

"What do you want?" McSorley asked. His voice bubbled in his throat.

The cop straightened and looked back down the road. "You're not wearing your seat belt. Any reason?"

"I forgot," McSorley said. He looked to the rear-view mirror, knowing what he'd see. The van pulled out of the junction, turning toward them.

The woman cop walked to the passenger side. She leaned down and peered in, first at Comiskey, then at Hughes. Comiskey gave her a weak smile. She did not return it.

"Well, that won't do," the tanned cop said. "You don't want points on your license, do you?"

The van filled the rear-view mirror. The woman cop waved, and it pulled alongside the Focus. The tanned cop reached in and hit the button to open the boot. It would have sprung up a good six inches when the car was new, but now it just loosened itself from the seal. The woman cop went to the back of the Focus, and the boot lid whined as she opened it fully. Cold, damp air kissed the back of McSorley's neck. The smell of manure from the fields around them mixed with the bitter sting of his own sweat.

The two men stayed in the van's cabin, but McSorley heard heavy feet moving inside, and then its rear doors opening. He went to crane his head around, but the tanned cop hunkered down beside him, smiling.

McSorley studied the peeler's face and all at once knew every tale the lines and cracks told. He had been in a dry and barren place, crawling in the dirt, hunting his prey. Iraq, maybe Afghanistan. Maybe somewhere the Yanks and the Brits would never admit to. And now he was here, not far from the Irish border, his sun-scorched face blank and unyielding. Just another job.

"You're not a peeler," McSorley said.

The cop's hard smile didn't even flicker. "Where are you headed today, sir?"

"I said, you're no peeler. What do you want?"

Footsteps scuffled behind the two vehicles. Something screeched and groaned as it was dragged along the floor of the van. Voices issued orders, hissed and strained. The cop's eyes never left McSorley's.

A voice said, "On three. One, two, three—hup!"

The Focus lurched and leaned back on its rear axle as something monstrously heavy was dumped in the boot.

"What the fuck was that?" Comiskey asked.

Hughes turned in the seat, but the parcel shelf blocked his vision. McSorley watched shifts in the light in his rear-view mirror. He wanted to weep, but smothered the urge. He heard more scuffling, then the thudding of feet clambering back into the van. The car's boot lid slammed down, and McSorley saw the woman cop through the back window, along with a heavy-set man. The parcel shelf didn't quite find home; something pushed it up from beneath.

The woman cop carried a long sports bag. The heavy-set man raised an automatic rifle. It looked like the Heckler & Koch G3 McSorley had fired behind a Newry pub years before. The man approached from the driver's side, keeping the rifle on McSorley.

McSorley felt the heat of tears rising behind his eyes. Fuck if he'd cry. He swallowed them. The rear passenger side door opened. He looked back over his shoulder.

The woman cop reached in and dropped something metallic. Its weight thudded on the carpet between Hughes's feet.

"Oh, fuck," Hughes said. He scuttled sideways, behind McSorley, away from whatever lay there.

She tossed something else in. It clanked against the first object.

"Oh, Jesus," Hughes said, his voice rising into a breathy whine.

The woman drew a pair of long cylinders from the bag. McSorley stared at them for a moment, his brain struggling to catch up with what he saw, before he recognized the twin barrels of a shotgun. She placed it butt-first into the footwell, letting the long barrels fall across Hughes's thigh.

"Fuck me, they're guns," Hughes said as the door swung shut. "What's going on, Eugene?"

McSorley looked back to the tanned cop. The cop smiled, winked, and closed the driver's door. He held up the car key, showed it to McSorley, and thumbed it twice. The locks whirred and clunked. The cop placed the key on the bonnet, just beneath the glass.

"Christ," McSorley said.

"What are they doing, Eugene?" Comiskey asked.

"Oh, sweet Jesus." McSorley crossed himself. His bladder screamed for release. He fought it.

The two cops, who McSorley knew were not cops at all, got back into the Skoda and pulled away. The van eased in front of the Focus. The man with the rifle grinned at McSorley. He kept the gun trained on him as he climbed into the open back.

Comiskey tried the handle. "Open the locks," he said.

"Can't," McSorley said. Tears warmed his cheeks. "The bastard double-locked it. You need the key to open it."

The van moved off, picking up speed. The man with the rifle waved. McSorley's bladder gave out.

"Oh, God," McSorley said. "Jesus, boys."

Comiskey slammed the window with his elbow. He tried it again. Hughes lifted the shotgun and rammed the butt against the rear window.

McSorley knew it was pointless. "Oh, Christ, boys."

Hughes hit the window once more, and it shattered. He lurched to the opening. Comiskey scrambled to climb back and follow.

Waves of rainwater smeared the windscreen as the van grew smaller in the distance. Hughes roared as he forced his shoulders through the gap.

"Jesus," McSorley whispered. "Jesus, boys, they killed us."

He barely registered the detonator's POP! before God's fist slammed him into nothing.